Fly Away Home

Fly Away Home

JUDITH KELMAN

HEINEMANN : LONDON

First published in Great Britain 1996
by William Heinemann Ltd
an imprint of Reed International Books Ltd
Michelin House, 81 Fulham Road, London SW3 6RB
and Auckland, Melbourne, Singapore and Toronto

A CIP catalogue record for this title
is available from the British Library

ISBN 0 434 38655 3

Phototypeset by Intype London Ltd
Printed and bound by Clays Ltd, St Ives plc

To Mom

Acknowledgements

For their generous assistance, the author wishes to thank: Bambi and Dave Arnold of the Manor on Golden Pond, John Atkin of the Long Island Sound Task Force, Hillard Bloom and Jim Reilly of Tallmadge Brothers Oyster Company, Laurel Martin, Diane Allen, Ralph Bloom of the Norwalk Historical Society, and Lillian Gould.

Special thanks to my extraordinary agent, Peter Lampack, and my talented editor, Kate Miciak.

1 Something was wrong in the baby's room. Eva Haskel awoke to an angry crackling noise. Silence followed, thick and expectant. A noose of terror cinched around her neck.

Listening hard, she caught the first of a threatened storm. Rain prattling. Clack of whipped branches. Whine of a mournful wind.

No repeat of the crackling sound. Maybe she'd imagined it. The horror eased its grip and edged away.

Beside her, Cal muttered in his sleep. Eva studied his square chin and the scaffolding of his cheekbones. She memorized the furrows in his brow, etched by long habit of serious thought. Slim nose. Lips like a child's sketch, full and sure. Lightly, Eva traced their contours with her tongue.

Cal's eyes darted beneath his lids, tracking a dream. Leaning back, Eva took in his lanky form. She ran a finger across his chest, spanned the bumpy road of ribs, ran a teasing circle around his groin.

Cal moaned.

With a feathery touch, Eva stroked him. Watched him stir.

She felt a quickening in her womb. A hard pinch of sorrow. Tomorrow Cal would leave her. When she needed him most, he always did.

Again, she heard the noise. Electric snake. Sizzling menace.

This time, she acted before the fear took hold. She had to check the nursery.

Cinching the belt on her terry robe, Eva nudged her feet into plush slippers. The woodstove must have burned itself out. Late summer still proclaimed itself in daylight, but the sunset brought a bite of autumn chill.

Her stomach churned. Cold was bad for an infant. Dangerous. Cold could seep through fragile skin. Topple spare defences. Lead to who knew what.

Shadow webs swagged the hallway. In their midst Eva paused to compose herself. Worry charged the air and turned it sour. Like feeding a child curdled milk, she thought, battling a swell of revulsion.

Her mood lifted as she entered the baby's room. Bright boats sailed the walls and curtains. Miniature lighthouses, modelled on the ones marking the perilous shoals of the Norwalk Archipelago, served as lamps. There were sailor dolls and pirate bears and a fleet of bright toy vessels. The shelves were crammed with story books featuring naval heroes, brave fishermen, and mighty denizens of the sea. The burnished maple furnishings had rocked and coddled Haskel family infants for six generations.

Nothing's the matter, Eva. Nothing but your fool nerves acting up again.

Maybe that's why people on the mainland called her crazy. Just last week, she'd overheard a pair of them talking when she ferried to South Norwalk for supplies.

Eva had stopped at the Water Street Café for an iced tea. They served it the way she liked, with a sprig of fresh mint and raw sugar.

Sitting at the dockside rail, she'd caught scraps of conversation from the pair across the aisle.

'Isn't that the Haskel woman?'

'The mother, you mean?'

'Ssh. She'll hear you.'

They were strangers, but Eva knew them all too well. As a child, she'd often tagged along when her father made deliveries to the finest dining establishments in Southern Connecticut. While Daddy and the staff hauled bushel sacks into the kitchens, Eva waited in the cab of the truck marked HASKEL AND SONS, THE BEST IN BLUEPOINTS SINCE 1863.

To pass the time, Eva studied the women as they pulled up in their fancy cars for lunch or tea. She watched them

2

pivot in their glove-leather seats. Glide forth as if they were mounted on castors. Eva learned their dance: toss the hair, strut – strut, heft the nose – frown.

There were hundreds of them, all identical twins. Every one of them belonged to the country club and the yacht club and the health club and the Junior League. They'd all been primped and pampered to within an inch of their lives.

Eva came to understand that those women were strictly ornamental. No serious purpose to them. They were like cars in a print ad. Blindingly perfect outsides, nothing to speak of under the hood.

Still, their words stung. Eva hated to be talked about, even when the talk was complimentary. Her cheeks flamed as she pretended to watch the harbour.

That's her all right, one breathed. *Saw her on the news.*

A coiffed head bowed in mock concern. Red lips spat poison whispers. *Terrible thing. Heard it drove her right around the bend.*

Sure looks that way. My Lord, that hair.

Eva stirred her tea angrily, raising a sugary haze. Dumb twits didn't have the first idea.

All the Haskel women stopped cutting their hair once they gave birth. Eva was unclear about the reason, but the custom dated back centuries. It had been handed down to her along with the leaf-pattern china and the hand-embroidered christening gown and the gold watch with the shattered crystal. Family traditions were as deep and inexorable as the tides, Eva knew. Impossible to defy them. Foolish to try.

Eva's dark headstrong mane now drooped below her waist. She favoured shapeless shifts that barely grazed her wisp-thin body. She hated shoes and had no use at all for jewellery. But none of that meant she'd rounded any bends.

Or did it?

Standing in the nursery now, she had to wonder.

Open your eyes and look, Eva. Everything's fine. That noise must have been the storm's mischief.

But as she crossed to check the crib, she heard the sound again. It sizzled behind her. Wheeling quickly, she spotted the flickering bulb. The lamp was a model of the Green's Ledge lighthouse. It had a stone base. White tower haloed by metal railing. When the flashing stopped, the light was dimmer. Nearly spent.

Eva's temper flared. She'd bought that bulb from one of those charities forever nagging at her for contributions. Every mooring of Jackson Quint's mailboat brought a fistful of slick pleas for some group or the other.

She remembered this one well. 'Help bring light into the lives of blind and partially-sighted children,' read the sales pitch. The pamphlet featured a cherubic little boy. The child was achingly beautiful. Perfect except for his eyes. They were dull moons, drowned in heavy fog. Those sorry eyes had reached right up from that brochure and ripped Eva's heart out.

She'd sent off her twelve dollars plus two ninety-eight for postage and handling on the very next mailboat. Two months later, Jackson Quint dropped off a box containing two measly sixty-watters. According to the fancy certificate inside, they were guaranteed to last a hundred years.

Naturally, Eva had scoffed at that. Who'd be around to take complaints in a century? And who'd be here to make them? Still, she liked the idea of sturdy lights in a nursery. Babies had a rightful terror of the dark. Dark was a thief and a liar. Dark was evil's mask. Death's playground. Nothing good had ever come of the dark but morning.

The lamplight sputtered again.

'Don't be scared, darling,' Eva crooned. 'Momma's here.'

She lowered the crib rail and slipped her hands beneath the bundled blankets.

Settling in the rocker, she hummed softly. She was lulled by the rhythmic creaking of the chair and the solid press against her bosom. Suffused with warmth. Light and easy. The raging storm outside felt miles away.

4

'Momma's little love.'

Suddenly, a spike of lightning split the night sky. A fierce concussion shook the house. Eva heard the jetty creak. Roiling surf challenged the breakwater.

She snuggled her bundle closer. Patted and soothed. 'There, there, precious. It's all right.'

Little ones were so frightened by a storm. Best to seek a distraction. Eva chanted the first rhyme that occurred to her: '*Ladybug, ladybug, fly away home –* '

Melting calm seeped through her. She felt so right.

'*Your house is on fire, and your children will –* '

She swallowed back the final word. Horrid notion. Why did so many nursery rhymes have violent, disturbing themes? She would not allow a child of hers to hear such things. Mothers were meant to keep the ugliness away from their precious babies.

'Momma will always protect you, darling. Always.'

Eva shut her eyes and locked her mind away from the unthinkable truth.

The blankets she held were empty. The crib held nothing but a matted ring of dust.

2

'Who saw him die?'
'I,' said the fly.
'With my little eye,
I saw him die.'
           'Who Killed Cock Robin?'

I hold my breath. No blinking. In a blink, the kid could drown.

'You got me, Ms Logan?'

'Yes, Billy.'

'Stay right there. Don't move!'

'I won't. I promise. Now try to relax.'

I wait out a silent ten-count. Slowly, I ease away the hand supporting his back. For a beat, the boy stays afloat. Then he realizes I've let go.

'*Help!*' His body jerks like a hooked fish. His arms flail, and he goes under. I hoist him up at once, but he's livid and spluttering.

Metal terror grips my throat. I swallow hard to clear it. 'How many times do I have to tell you, Billy Brodsky? No diving in the shallow end.'

Billy catches his breath and slays me with a look. 'You *said* you'd hold on to me.'

'I said I'd be right here, and I am.'

Wheeling in a rage, he trudges through the waist-high water towards the pool stairs.

'Come on, Billy. Let's give it one more try.'

'I can't do it. I'm a stupid, dopey jerk.' His sopping head hangs in defeat.

I throw up my hands. 'That's it. I'm not supposed to reveal the Pasha's Magic Floating Secret, but I guess I have no choice.'

He slows. Stops to nibble the bait. 'The *who's* what?'

'Forget it, Billy. We're talking very, *very* powerful magic. I don't think you're old enough.'

'Am too. I'm seven and a *half*.'

'Pasha secrets are serious business, my friend. I'm not supposed to reveal this to anyone, *ever*.'

He's hooked. 'Come on,' he pleads. 'I promise I won't tell.'

'Sure you can be trusted?'

'I swear it.'

'You're not with any subversive agency? CIA, ABCD? You promise?'

'Cross my heart.'

I beckon him closer. Dipping into the water, I lift the string snaking from the waistband of his Tweety and Sylvester bathing trunks. In a solemn hush, I spill the Pasha's beans: 'This string is the secret,' I tell him. 'As long as you hold on to it, you will never, ever sink.'

Billy scowls. 'Yeah, sure.'

I raise two fingers in an oath. 'Since the dawn of time, it has never been known to fail.'

He studies my face. Finds no incriminating evidence. With a shrug, he arches back until his head skims the water. His feet rise. So does the small hand clutching the string.

'Hey look! It works,' he exults.

'That's great!'

Great is a major understatement. This is a bona fide four-foot, fifty-two-pound miracle. Even the setting is sublime. Sun jewels fleck the pool's rumpled surface. Floating in their midst the boy looks luminous. I watch his heart thump and the breathy flutter of his ribs. His hair fans in a crown of liquid gold.

'Hey, watch me, Ms Logan. Look!'

The moment swallows me whole. Everything else dims to backdrop. At a fuzzy remove, I hear cars whizzing past on the access road. The strike of a bat. Boisterous voices flare and settle on the green.

'Keep watching,' Billy orders.

'Don't worry.'

'Don't move.'

'I'm not.' I can't. I wouldn't budge on a substantial bet. This child's distrust of the water is a speck compared to mine.

Years ago, I witnessed a drowning. I watched the victim's struggles. I heard her cries fade as they surrendered their power to the sea.

For a long time after her head sank beneath the surf, the bubbles continued to rise. They came in ragged bunches, like a jeering code: *You're to blame, Bethany Logan. You should have done something. You should have stopped it. My death is all your fault.*

If I try, I can still see those bubbles.

I try not to try.

The incident left me devoted to dry land. I can tolerate water in containers, but the larger they get, the less secure I feel. I'm happiest far removed from any significant coastline. I shrink in the face of an ocean's obscene vastness. I'm a mite. Less.

That's part of the reason I came to work at the Hinsdale School in Grangeville. Here, the rest of New Hampshire and all of Maine shield me from the monstrous Atlantic.

Of course, this place has more important virtues. I adore the moss-covered stone halls and sprawling property. I love the towering oaks that hover overhead like protective parents. The air has the nourishing feel of homemade broth.

The school and the town share a timeless quality. Both were founded in the 1860s. Both combine the dignity of age with youth's clear-eyed wonder. Both Grangeville and Hinsdale are open and welcoming, except when it comes to unnecessary change.

In many ways, the Hinsdale School looks and functions exactly as it did during the Civil War. Every day begins and ends with a general assembly in the meeting house adjoining the chapel. Students still wear hunter green blazers emblazoned with brass buttons and the Hinsdale crest:

a silver sword of knowledge piercing a squat embroidered 'H'. Ancient rituals and rivalries have been carefully preserved. Girls who enquire are still referred to the Towne School up the road.

Grangeville, too, retains the pace and tenor of an earlier era. So far, the town has escaped golden arches, factory outlet stores, and coffee boutiques. There's no place in Grangeville to get nail wraps, signature lettuce, or tofu masquerading as genuine food. No merchant would ever dream of stocking hundred-dollar baby shoes or anything by Chanel. The choice in coiffeurs is a straight-across or a buzz cut at Lester Parrish's Unisex on High Street. After sizing me up on my first visit, Lester recommended the straight-across for my auburn hair. It suits me fine.

Most everything here does. Above all, I embrace Hinsdale's philosophy. The school subscribes to the radical notion that diversity is a virtue and success a matter of definition. Hinsdale has its share of stars and distinguished alumni, true. But it refuses to be just another slavish link in the Ivy League food chain. In addition to the boarding students with their designer genes and monstrous advantages, this school educates as many local applicants as space and the scholarship fund permit.

I run the support programme for kids in need of extra, individual help. Many of them have been battling academic demons for years. Many have deep psychic wounds or seriously flawed wiring. For some, Hinsdale's signature 'H' has come perilously close to signifying 'hopeless'. But since starting here almost a year ago, my success rate has been extraordinary.

Parents and colleagues presume I have a talent for teaching. My real secret is a monumental stubborn streak. I batter my students with encouragement. I wear them to a pulp with praise. Whatever works, is my motto. When all else fails – try *something*. Eventually, even the most down and defeated kid gives in to my incessant positivity and learns.

Which is how I come to be teaching Billy Brodsky to

swim this summer term. Billy trusts me. We've survived first grade together. Swimming is one of Hinsdale's few unbendable requirements. Matter of safety, says the Board. Less than a week remains in this session, which combines traditional summer camping with remedial and advanced academics. Before that time expires, Billy must be able to float on his back and tread water. Having memorized Dick and Jane's life stories and counted a mountain of popsicle sticks to get this far, I am not about to let young Master Brodsky sink in a couple of feet of filtered, heated, chlorinated water.

Somehow, he drops the string. His eyes snap open. A desperate hand clamps my wrist. '*Help!*'

'Easy, champ,' I soothe. 'Once you've held the string, the magic lasts a long, long time.'

'Unh-unh. Not for me.'

'It will' – noting the set of his face, I back off. '– by tomorrow.'

I pry him loose and rub my wrist to restore the circulation. This time I attach the string to his index finger with a double knot. 'There you go, pal. Now you can't lose it.'

Reluctantly, he leans back. The water rocks him gently. His muscles ease.

'Look at you,' I say. I want to shriek with joy, but the moment is far too fragile.

'I'm doing it.' He's trying on the notion, relishing the feel of it. 'I'm really floating.'

'That you are, buddy.'

He risks a tiny smile. 'Like a pasha?'

'Better than any pasha I've ever seen.'

Loose as kelp he drifts. The sun is sinking. Shadows mass and stretch across the deep end of the pool. When they reach us, the temperature will plummet. Late August in New Hampshire means that winter is on deck.

I decide to let Billy keep floating as long as possible. I want his confidence fully inflated. First thing tomorrow,

I'll get Richard Bruce, the Physical Education Director, to administer the swim test.

The child is totally relaxed. I catch his contentment. What could compare to this?

I think of a game that's popular with the youngest kids: 'I spy, with my little eye, someone who floats like a cloud in the sky.'

Billy smiles. It's baby stuff, but he'll condescend for my sake. His lids stay closed, but he makes his contribution: 'I spy, with my little eye, a teacher as round as a blueberry pie.'

So much for his lousy visual perception skills. But I'll forgive this kid anything right now, even the sin of honesty. Fresh air and cookouts have added a few extra pounds to my collection. I'd like to take them off, and I intend to. I also aspire to go on a world cruise and win a Nobel Prize. But not today.

The shadows are closing in. Time to go. 'I spy, with my little eye, that it will be dinnertime, by and by.' I want to usher him out of the pool in a blaze of glory. 'Kick your feet, champ. Bet you can make it all the way to the side.'

He's game. I back up beside him as he putters towards the stairs.

'I'm doing it, Ms Logan. Look!'

'You sure are.'

His smile spreads. Over my shoulders, I check the distance to the edge. Five more feet, and the kid can take his victory home.

'Almost there, Billy,' I report.

'How much further?'

Before I can answer, there's a banshee shriek. Something streaks up behind me and hurtles headlong into the pool. It lands with a giant splat, nearly on top of Billy.

Dizzy confusion follows. Desperately, I try to sort out the thrashing appendages. Before I can, I lose my footing. Churning water pummels my face. I slip to the bottom of the pool.

Quickly, I wrestle to the surface. The sight of what's

below hits hard as I gulp the air. Billy is down there, bug-eyed and unmoving. I duck under again, grip the boy across the chest, and heft him towards the light. He's a stone, inert and heavy.

'Billy?'

No response.

'Billy, speak to me! Are you okay?'

I drag him to the side, carry him up the ladder, and lay him on the grass. I check him out: colour, pulse, pupils, limbs.

Nothing damaged but his pride. The kid is still frozen but otherwise unhurt.

'It's okay, champ. You're going to be fine.'

When the shock cuts him loose a moment later, he starts wailing like a car alarm. Helping him to sit, I untie the string from his finger and wrap a towel around his shoulders.

Meanwhile, the cause of his misery takes a victory lap to the deep end. With a flip turn, the other child heads back our way. Before he can reach us, Billy squirms loose. Snivelling, he slips on a sweatshirt.

'You did beautifully, kiddo. Fantastic,' I say, though I know the words are useless. Broken miracles are like a ruined cake. You have to trash the sorry remains and start over.

I direct my fury at the interloper. His gap-toothed grin reeks of nasty satisfaction. I know he's staged this assault for my benefit. Most kids like, or at least tolerate, me but this one lives to make me nuts.

Last week, he purposely dropped and trampled another kid's prized paper. The week before, he knocked over the cupcakes I had baked for a classmate's birthday. Since we started working together four months ago, this child hasn't missed one rotten opportunity.

I've tried to reason with him. I've offered sympathy and understanding. I've sunk to bribery and seriously intimidating threats. But nothing has put a dent in his defiance.

'That was rotten,' I snarl.

12

'What'd I do?'

He's a scrawny kid. Limbs and angles. Copper-flecked green eyes light a doll-sized dimpled face. Cover the horns, and the little beast could pass for an angel. Though not for long.

It's tough to stay angry at him, but I manage. 'You know very well what you did. Apologize to Billy.'

Billy's anguish has dimmed to a whimper. His puffy eyes glance my way. An apology would help.

'Why should I?' the boy challenges.

Several highly inappropriate responses leap to mind. But I control myself. I'm not going to win with this kid, especially if I let him make the rules.

'Get changed and march yourself over to the head-master's office. I'll meet you there at five.'

With a smirk, he darts across the green. Watching him go, my heart sinks. The boy is eight, far too young to wear such thick, protective armour.

My shattered pasha struggles into his sneakers. I set a hand on his scrawny shoulder and walk Billy towards his dorm.

3

Tell tale tit,
Your tongue shall be slit,
And all the dogs in our town
Shall have a little bit.
                    'Tell Tale Tit'

Hinsdale's youngest boarders bunk in Weldon House, a rambling white Victorian building at the head of the primary green. I turn Billy over to the effusive ministrations of his dorm mother, Patsy Culvert. Ms Culvert also runs the Dramatic Arts programme, and it shows. She's a human Wonderbra: stiff, phoney, and irresistible to men.

On the dorm job, Ms Culvert's thespian skills come in handy. She's equally adept at playing Florence Nightingale, Mary Poppins and Mommie Dearest. Noting Billy's distress, she emotes a heartrending 'Poor baby.' She envelops the soggy kid in a hug, taking care to protect her daisy-blonde hair. His face, mashed against her cleavage, looks happy enough. I can go.

My route to the headmaster's office takes me past staff housing on East Campus. My apartment is a charming three-room on the top floor of Hammond Hall. I've left just enough time to run up and change into something more professional than my oversized T-shirt and fetching flip-flops.

My Aunt Sadie awaits me at the door. She has nothing to say, but her face drips disapproval. As usual, she has tidied the place in my absence. Aunt Sadie hates the clutter I invariably leave behind. As soon as I depart, she shoves the mess out of sight. Unfortunately, the best she can do is hide my things behind the drapes or under the furniture. Her intentions are flawless, but even the most fastidious

14

dogs are ill-equipped for housework. Nevertheless, she persists. I suppose she clings to the empty hope that someday I'll be housebroken.

Aunt Sadie is a native of Grangeville, born here years before I arrived. I'm told she's the love child of a champion Irish Setter and a randy mutt from neighbouring Independence Center. Whelped in disgrace, the story goes, Sadie was given to Mary-Beth Campbell, who manages the IGA. Mary-Beth's oldest, Daryl, turned out to be allergic, so Sadie became a store dog. I suspect that's where she learned to sniff out impending mischief and ward it off.

Years later, Mary-Beth developed a Sadie allergy worse than her son's. She posted a sign in the bakery section offering the dog for adoption. That same day, fate nudged me into the IGA against my will to buy a brownie. Sadie bounded out from the back room to dissuade me. Despite her bossiness, I was charmed by her fluffy beige coat, proud carriage, and sparkling black eyes. Ever since, most of the mischief Sadie wards off has been mine.

She monitors my diet, approves my wardrobe, and argues against my reckless tendencies. She's pushy and opinionated and far too often right. I call her 'Aunt' Sadie because she refuses to answer to 'Attila'. With four legs to dig in, the dog is even more pigheaded than I am.

She snarls when I drop my wet shirt and bathing suit on the living-room floor. Chastened, I pick them up. I'm a slob by nature, not by design. The apartment is wonderful, and I share the mutt's view that it deserves to be treated with respect.

The school's property was once the summer retreat of a New York financier, and Hammond Hall was the guesthouse. My place, formerly known as the Garden Suite, has large airy rooms, leaded glass windows, plump antique furnishings, and a broad stone hearth. The ceilings are vaulted. The carved mouldings have been mercifully spared from paint. Hand-tiled floral mosaics grace the bathroom walls. There's a huge clawfoot tub, an ancient stall shower, and a ceramic sink painted with pond lilies.

15

I take a quick shower and toss on my most flattering outfit: black slacks and an emerald green tunic top that sets off my eyes and deftly lies about my waistline. I decide my little nemesis can wait for the extra few minutes it takes me to brush on mascara and a set of cheekbones.

Aunt Sadie lopes into my bedroom, a vision in shaggy beige. Angling beside me, she cocks her head.

'What's the verdict? I look okay?'

Her response is a noncommittal sneeze. She flops down, muzzle on paws, and falls asleep.

When I'm ready to leave, I circle her snoring form and tiptoe out of the room. But before I get to the door, the dog is up and barking. She streaks into the foyer after me. Herding me toward the closet, she makes sharp warning noises. It's obvious she wants me to take a jacket, but I play dumb. Give the mutt an inch, she'll have me trained in no time.

'See you later, girl.'

Irritation rumbles deep in her chest. She circles the closet like a fretful beige bear, determined to win her point.

''Bye, honey.' I push past her and slip out. After a beat, she works her Houdini trick on the door and follows. I try to ignore her as she pants and darts around me, her breath hot on my shins.

The dog gives up at the edge of Central Green, where she knows she's not allowed. Her exasperated yapping follows me for ages.

Approaching Campus Center, home to Administration and Special Services, I spot the lights from the headmaster's ground-floor office.

The secretary has gone. My knock draws Adam Stafford's ripe baritone. When I enter, he is on the phone. He motions me to sit in one of the burgundy leather chairs facing his desk.

Stafford is a suave and sexy six-foot two. Thick greying hair caps a strong-boned face. His dark eyes beam intelligence. His body language is fluently self-assured. A few wiry chest hairs poke through the open collar of his blue

16

shirt. His rolled sleeves showcase muscled forearms. His hands are large with long, tapered fingers. I've often thought they'd be perfect for playing an instrument, like my skin.

From this side of the conversation, I gather he's wooing a contributor. 'Wonderful, Sean,' he says. 'I'm sure you know how much Hinsdale values your friendship.'

Thanks to Stafford's persuasive charm, the school's endowment is at a record high. Buildings and grounds are in peak condition. Ditto the scholarship fund. I suffer a sudden attack of nerves. The headmaster knows how to make things happen. I do not want certain of those things happening to me.

As he hangs up, the sales smile fades. 'What can I do for you, Bethany?'

'I asked Pip to come to see you. Has he been here?'

'No. What's the problem?'

'I'm worried about him. He's been acting up.'

'How so?'

His unwavering gaze made me squirm. 'Different things.' I report what happened with Billy Brodsky in the pool.

Stafford frowns. 'Are you suggesting Pip was purposely trying to hurt Billy?'

'He's the best one to answer that.'

His frown deepens into a scowl. 'You said you asked him to meet you here?'

'Ten minutes ago.'

The headmaster dials a campus extension. Waiting for an answer, he tips back in his chair and presses the bridge of his nose. His tone softens when Patsy Culvert comes on the line.

'Patsy, hello. It's Adam Stafford. Is Pip with you? Right – thanks.' As he hangs up, the edge in his voice returns. 'He's on his way.'

While we wait, Stafford busies himself with paperwork. He proofreads and signs a stack of memos. Flipping a page in his datebook, he reviews his crowded schedule for tomorrow. Reading upside down, I note that he has lunch

17

with the Governor and an afternoon meeting with the president of the local bank. Before and after are sessions with department heads, a major contributor, a radio interviewer, and an official from the State Education Department. Dinner is a fundraiser for the Grangeville Public Library. Afterwards, he's pencilled in coffee with a group of upper-school parents.

The office door swings open and Pip saunters in. Ignoring me, the child crosses to Stafford's desk and offers his scrawny hand for a high-five.

'What's up?' Pip asks. 'Jonah's waiting outside.'

'He can wait. Sit, please.'

The boy takes the chair beside mine. 'Okay. What?'

'Ms Logan tells me you've been misbehaving.'

'Have not.'

Stafford persists. 'What about jumping into the pool today when Billy was having a lesson?'

'*She* was in the way. I didn't even *see* Billy. All I wanted to do was cool off after softball.'

'You're *sure* of that?' Stafford asks.

''Course I am.' He aims a poison puss my way. 'She just wants to get me in trouble.'

Stafford waits for me to answer the charge.

'No, I don't, Pip. But I *am* concerned about you.'

'Yeah, sure. All she cares about is *Billy*. He's her little *pet*,' he mocks.

'That's ridiculous!' I wince at my own defensive shrill.

'Ask anyone. Ask Jonah. She's the *worst* teacher in the *whole* school. Everyone *hates* her!'

Stafford's fists clench. 'That's enough, Pip. Go on to dinner now. We'll talk more about this later.'

After the child has gone, the headmaster eyes me squarely. 'Sounds to me like a simple personality conflict, Bethany. I'll assign someone else to work with Pip in the fall.'

'That's not going to solve the problem. Pip's angry with me because he's frustrated about his reading problem. I represent everything he wants to forget.'

18

'Calling it a *problem* seems a bit extreme. Plenty of boys his age find reading difficult.'

'As I've told you before, this is different. Pip's dyslexic.'

'You *know* how I feel about labels.'

'I'm not labelling him. I'm just trying to explain why he's having such a hard time. Pip's way of seeing and hearing things is atypical. He has trouble with letter reversals and discriminating sounds.'

Stafford's lips narrow. 'I will *not* allow any Hinsdale student to be damned by test scores.'

'That's not what I'm suggesting at all. He'll learn to compensate, but it's going to take time and hard work.'

'Frankly, I disagree. I believe I know Pip better than you do.'

'Of course you do. You're his *father.*'

The boy's full name is Adam Phillip Stafford, the Third, but 'Pip' says it better. Reading demons aside, he's one of the smartest kids in his class and its fearless leader. The kid is a top athlete too, quick and outwardly sure of himself. Most of my colleagues have the good political sense to voice only kind thoughts about the boss's son. But in my heart, I know this child's sassy tongue and swagger are trouble signs. The boy is hurting. And his nasty mischief is a cry for help.

'The longer he's able to avoid the issue, the harder it's going to be to fix,' I persist.

Stafford's jaw twitches. 'Don't patronize me, Bethany. I know what's best for my son!'

'Sure you do, but – '

'But *nothing*! Pip *will* be reassigned, and *that's* the *end* of it!'

I'm shocked mute. I've seen Stafford use his temper many times, but he's never been known to lose it. The man is a rock. Rocks don't burn.

His chest expands. When it settles again, so does he.

'I know you mean well, Bethany. But your worry is misplaced here. Pip has experienced certain difficulties that affect his pattern of development. I've seen it before. He comes around.'

Stafford is notoriously guarded about his personal history and his son's. I know that Pip's mother is out of the picture, but not where. Rumour has it she ran off with a close friend of the headmaster's, though I find it hard to imagine anyone being wooed away from this powerful magnet of a man.

The ice is razor thin, but I charge out anyway. 'What kind of difficulties?'

'Those are private matters.'

'I understand. But it's helpful to know a child's history. It can explain – '

'Anything relevant to Pip's education is in his file.'

'But – '

'I *said*, Pip will be fine. Anyway, he's no longer your concern.' He takes a pointed look at his watch. 'Now, if you'll excuse me . . .'

I resist the urge to press him further. The man is not about to bend on this one. Anyway, he's given me a better idea.

Venturing out, I feel a sudden chill.

4

There was a man in our town,
And he was wondrous wise.
He jumped into a bramble bush
And scratched out both his eyes.
                    'There Was a Man in Our Town'

Except for Stafford's office, Central Green is deserted. Crossing Schoolhouse Lane, a narrow footpath that connects the main campus quadrangles, my feet crunch through dried twigs and the first of Fall's fallen leaves. Pine and woodsmoke weight the air. The sun slumps toward a dark horizon.

It's freezing. I hug myself, but it doesn't help. I should have listened to Aunt Sadie and taken a jacket.

Meals are served in Grantham Hall, adjoining the soccer field. The squat cut-stone building boasts marble tile floors, stained-glass windows, and ponderous iron chandeliers. I pause to thaw at the sighing radiator in the foyer. When my blood is free again of major icejams, I head for the cafeteria.

For me, teaching in a boarding-school offers a special advantage. The food here is tuned to a child's palate. By happy coincidence, my taste buds never matured past prepubescence. I can't imagine ever tiring of meatballs and spaghetti or macaroni and cheese. Sugar and ketchup are my condiments of choice. I staunchly defend dessert as a basic civil liberty. If I were limited to packing two compact items for a solitary stint in the wilds, I'd choose peanut butter and Mel Gibson. Hands down.

At the entrance to the grub line, I inhale the heady bouquet of franks, beans, lime Jello mould, and raspberry bug juice. I heap a bit of everything on my plate. Hinsdale's

21

cook has been known to hide essential nutrients in the oddest places.

The student dining hall holds a grid of oblong tables. Kids are seated by class, which puts the youngest, messiest eaters in front. I greet familiar faces capped by mustard moustaches and purple-tongued smiles. 'Hey, Michael. How's it going, Jason?'

The affection I feel dissolves at the sight of Pip Stafford. His arms are crossed in defiance, raw hatred warps his face. Keeping a hard eye on me, he leans toward his friend Jonah and speaks in a stage whisper.

'Watch out! Here comes that *big, fat, giant* witch!'

'Hello, Pip. Hi, Jonah,' I say pleasantly. 'Lovely evening. Bit of a nip in the air.'

The boys dissolve in cruel giggles. I pass them with a resolute stride, refusing to be touched by such foolishness. I'm a grown woman after all. No *scrawny, little, midget* monster is going to get me down.

I'm instantly ashamed of myself. Imitating a spiteful eight-year-old may feel good, but it's clearly not the answer.

If only I knew what was.

Many of the teachers live off campus and normally eat dinner at home, but tonight the staff dining room is packed. Summer term awards for academics, athletics, and citizenship will be presented in an evening ceremony, which everyone is expected to attend.

I claim the vacant seat at my regular table. Like kids, teachers tend to cluster with their own kind. The coaches sit with Health and Physical Education. Chemistry and Physics sit with Math. English claims two tables, one for the writing people, one for Literature. Foreign languages sit together with French at *la tête* and Italian *a piedi*. Administration sits apart. The prime table under the bow window is saved for the clerical staff. It's common knowledge that secretaries are the blood and backbone of any school. Everyone else, save the janitors, is expendable.

My group consists of the miscellaneous others. There's Norma Molina in Speech, Hal Kreidman in Computer

Science, Francine Effren in Life Sciences, Media specialist Denny D'Amato, and Patsy Culvert in Hysterics.

'My Lord, Bethany! Have you lost your mind?' Patsy rants as I transfer my dishes to the table from the tray. She's almost dressed in a low-cut sweater, a minuscule skirt, high black boots, and giant hoop earrings.

'Not that I've noticed.' Why? I'm aching to ask. Have you finally *found* one?

'You don't complain about the headmaster's son, sweetie. *Bad* idea. *Very* bad.'

'Really? Gee, that never occurred to me.' A pimple is rising on Patsy's plastic nose. I hope it hurts.

'You needn't be *sarcastic*, Bethany. I'm just trying to save you from yourself.'

I wash down a bite of hot dog with a long, cool slug of juice. Patsy nibbles naked greens and sips an Evian.

'Thanks anyway,' I tell her.

'Stafford's a bear when it comes to Pip, Bethany. I'd back off if I were you. Honestly.'

'Thanks anyway, Patsy. *Honestly.*'

I turn to talk to Hal Kreidman. Hal's the man of my dreams, and he knows it. He's smart, sweet, cute, and lovable. He has exceptional common sense and a terrific sense of humour. Our friendship dates to my arrival at Hinsdale a year ago, when Hal instantly took me under his wing.

More than once, I've tried to push for something closer, but Hal resists. From his lame excuses, I can tell he's simply not interested. He keeps harping on insignificant little things like the forty-year age difference. Youth is one malady from which all of us recover in time, I argue. Hal's reply is to smile and note that I remind him of his grand-daughter, Ellen: the one with the big mouth.

'How's it going, Hal?'

'Just dandy, Beth. How are you?'

'She's suicidal. That's how she is,' Patsy says.

'How so?' Hal's pale eyes narrow under puffy brows. His

sparse hair is milk-white. A blue shirt and a navy V-neck set it off.

'Reporting Pip Stafford for disciplinary action. That's how so.' Patsy seals the charge with a hitch of her blemished nose.

'Good for you, Beth.' Then, to Patsy, 'That's not suicidal, my dear. It's called integrity.'

'Integrity, unemployed. Whatever.' Patsy's hand flutters in dismissal. Angry colour scales Hal's neck.

'Bethany is too honest and dedicated to ignore a child's welfare. Any child's.'

Pointing to herself, Patsy drawls: 'Momma always taught me to put *this* child's welfare first.'

'You should eat that salad, Patsy. Before it gets cold,' says Hal.

For the remainder of the meal, I chat with Hal, Fran Effren, and Denny D'Amato. Ms Culvert and Norma Molina trade studied monologues. I down two hot dogs, a heap of chips, and a bowl of Jello. I suspect I'm going to need my strength.

At seven, the last of the students straggle into Saxton Hall, the meeting room adjoining the chapel. Soaring Palladian windows frame massive oils of Ardus and Sylvan Hinsdale, the school's founding brothers. Rows of connected seats face the stage, where our nation's flag is dwarfed by a mammoth green and white Hinsdale banner.

The plank floors have been dulled by a century of enthusiastic trampling. Ancient fixtures leak ragged pools of light. Bronze plaques recall alumni who gave their lives in various battles. Larger, brighter ones acknowledge those true heroes who donated money to the endowment fund. The honour board, a broad panel locked behind glass doors, holds lists of top student achievers in various categories for the last five years. Their ranks will be swelled by those boys named tonight.

After all of the students are seated, Grace Amundsen, head of Music, takes her place at the organ. Grace and the organ are two of a kind. Both are broad, burnished types with wooden bearing and large, impressive pipes.

Soon, Hinsdale's school song fills the hall. Everyone stands and sings along to the sombre strains of 'Oh Tannenbaum'.

> *On fields of green*
> *the heart and mind*
> *reflects for all eternity.*
> *The sword is raised,*
> *our banner waves.*
> *The Hinsdale name lives on in me.*

It's sappy nonsense, but my eyes fill. I grew up on Long Island in a prefab bedroom community with no personality and precious little soul. After my mother died, Dad moved us from place to place to place as if he and Atlas Van Lines could somehow outdistance the ugly truth.

My education was a hodgepodge. I went to country schools, where all the kids were tossed together like a stew hastily concocted after the freezer fails. I went to city schools, where the average class had forty kids and the teacher's sole objective was survival. I was never in one place long enough to feel settled. I never enjoyed the smug self-importance that comes with being a seasoned insider. Bethany, the new kid, that was me. A plump, green-eyed curiosity.

I've often dreamed of being a permanent part of things. Setting roots. But running is a hard habit to break. At thirty-two, I've worn down the treads on dozens of bright ideas and high expectations. I've changed careers, towns, men, and destinations so often, it's hard for me to remember who and what happened where.

At Hinsdale, for the first time, I've stopped fighting the ceaseless press of wind at my back. I feel free of irksome restlessness. Hinsdale's warm hug gets me every time. From the gleaming eyes around me, tonight, I am not alone.

The song ends; Grace segues into a spirited march. Everyone stands as flagbearers from the primary, middle, and secondary divisions carry in their colours. Deans Halloway, Perkins, and Rawson trail behind. Adam Stafford brings up the rear. Even in academic robes, which the top brass don for such occasions, the headmaster looks sexy as hell. I imagine sliding my hands under the gown. Then the rest of me. Stafford fills me with an odd mix of lust and terror. I suppose nothing spices a hormone stew like a dash of TNT.

I choose an aisle seat near the rear of the auditorium. I've nominated Billy Brodsky for an outstanding achievement award, and I don't want to miss the look on his face when he's called. Fortunately, his moment comes early. As soon as he's back in his seat, clutching his ribboned scroll and gleaming like a full moon, I duck out.

Passing the chapel, I cling to the shadows. Beyond, I can no longer be seen from the meeting house. I hurry anyway, eager to put this craziness behind me.

The cold has intensified. Harsh wind nips my fingers. Arrowhead Trail is a narrow footpath that marks the border of the Administrative Green. Shivering, I race across the lawn toward Campus Center. Blacked out, the building hulks at the green's edge like a predatory beast.

My breath is sharp. Circling to the rear, I unlock the door beside the dumpster and slip inside. My office is halfway down the hall, at the side of the building. For insurance, I open the door and flip on my desk lamp. If I'm caught, I can claim I stopped by to retrieve something I forgot.

Like my brains.

I don't have a key to the main office, but there's a back way in through the copy room. In the dark I manoeuvre past reams of paper and stacks of documents awaiting their turn to be cloned.

Student records occupy three tall file banks behind a quartet of clerical desks. Initials M through Z are in the cabinet on the right. STA–TRU occupies the third drawer from the top. I tug the handle. It's locked.

I lose precious minutes rummaging through the secretaries' desks for a key. Only after I've been through every drawer do I stop to remember the last time I came here to requisition a student's permanent file. I recall Arnel Witte, assistant to the Dean of Students, fishing the key from the top of the cabinet.

At five-ten, Arnel has a good six inches on me. No way I can reach the top of the cabinet. I pull over a desk chair and nearly kill myself trying to mount the thing, which is mounted itself, on wheels. Balanced on several phone books instead, I find the key.

Turning on a light is far too risky. This office fronts Central Green. Anyone who happened to pass would surely wonder what someone was doing here at this hour. In the gloom, I flip through tight-packed files, seeking Pip Stafford's.

As the headmaster mentioned, I have a copy of Pip's so-called file in my office. Student records are sent to me along with the referral form for special services. But plenty of information is left out. I'm not privy to confidential medical records or financial data. I don't get to see the 'green' slips, special flags designed to cue administrators about custody arrangements, parents temporarily incarcerated or enrolled in substance abuse programmes, or other matters of a 'delicate' nature.

What I've received on Pip is especially sparse. I've had to flesh out that skeletal information with standardized tests and the little I've been able to learn first hand. Most kids are delighted to reveal themselves, but not Pip Stafford. He snaps shut like a clam when the subject is himself or family. The mental picture I have of him is woefully incomplete.

It's too dark for me to decipher the names on the folder tabs. I pluck an armful from the drawer and cross to the window. There, I'm able to make out the names by moonlight. Pip's is not among them.

Repeating the process several times, I finally winnow out the file marked: 'Stafford, Adam Phillip III'. The typed sheets inside are too faint to read. I round the corner to the copy machine and grope for the switch.

The copier surges on. Holding my breath, I listen for angry footsteps. Challenging words. Shouts of outrage.

Nothing.

Appalled at the light and noise the machine gives off, I feed in the pages as fast as I can. Still, it seems for ever before I'm able to flip off the power switch.

I return Pip's file and head for my office. I don't intend to stay and study the contents here, but I want to make sure I've gotten what I need.

At a glance, I see that even his permanent record is sorely lacking. There's no birth certificate. No immunization chart. No record of blood type, allergies, or early illnesses. The section on birth and early developmental history is blank.

The educational summary indicates that Pip attended a pre-school and kindergarten, but there's no mention of the school's name or address. There's no transfer slip. None of the standard anecdotal or progress reports meant to ease a child's adjustment to a new setting. From this file, you'd think Pip popped into existence the day his father signed on to run Hinsdale two years ago.

Sloppy, I think. Worse than sloppy. Student records are subject to random audit by the state. Some of the data missing from Pip's file is required by New Hampshire law. A file like this could threaten Hinsdale's accreditation.

Adam Stafford knows better than anyone how serious these omissions could prove to be. The headmaster's a stickler for meticulous record-keeping. It's a stuck-needle theme in faculty memos and meetings.

So what's going on here?

The sensible thing would be to forget it, but curiosity wrestles my sense to the ground. Once Stafford cools off, I'm sure I can convince him to let me keep Pip on my rolls. But turning this child around will take more than time and gentle prodding. To solve the puzzle that is Pip, I'm going to need all the pieces.

Once again, I make my way along the darkened corridor to the front of the building. I slip through the copy room to the main office and pass beyond. Personnel records are kept in the file banks in the anteway. Mine is extracted from there ceremoniously every few months when I'm summoned for a performance review.

The key is locked in the headmaster's desk. Delving into Stafford's private space takes serious nerve, and mine is fast expiring. I keep feeling eyes on me. Hearing noises. Fortunately, the drawer yields after a few insistent pokes with Stafford's letter opener.

Better yet, I find a penlight in the drawer beside the file key. Tracking its beam, I'm able to locate the folder I need in seconds. Starched with fear, I slip out the file.

It's empty except for a single sheet of stationery. The note is a requisition from the chairman of Hinsdale's Board of Directors. Stafford's contract period will soon expire. The Board requires his full record for review.

I have no idea how long they'll keep Stafford's file or where it might be stored in the meantime. The Board's chairman, Joe Whatley, owns the First Fidelity Bank. Board meetings are held there in the conference room. Chances are the minutes and other important papers are somewhere in the bank.

I'm as reckless as the next person, but I draw the line at breaking and entering a bank. I have no special contacts on the Board any more. No one I can count on to sneak me a look at Stafford's file.

Facing a dead end, I fold the copies from Pip's record and tuck them into the waistband of my pants. The tunic covers the pages, but odd movements make me rustle. I replace Stafford's empty folder and return his key and penlight. I can't get his desk lock to engage, but I tell myself it's not a major worry. When he finds nothing missing, the headmaster will likely dismiss the open lock as an oversight.

All that remains is to slip out unnoticed and return to the awards ceremony. If I've been missed, I'll plead a sudden bout of indigestion. Given the way I stuffed my face at dinner, it's a perfectly plausible excuse. Besides, it's true. Iced acid fills my gut.

I retrace my steps toward the rear of the building. I strain to listen for trouble past the raging blood in my ears.

I walk faster; break into a run. I'm dying to get out. The air has thickened so I can barely breathe.

At my office, I pause to turn out the lights and lock up. I'm about to start down the hall again when I hear a noise.

There's a harsh strike of footsteps. A scurry of motion. More steps, closer this time.

God, no!

Someone's coming. I turn to run, but I can't. My legs refuse to heed the frantic signals.

I cast around for a convincing excuse. But my mind is running in useless circles. Leaning against the wall, I close my eyes and try to calm down. I beg my throat to open so I can squeeze out some plausible explanation.

The footsteps are nearly upon me. Straightening, I prepare to face whoever it is.

In a rush, something charges at me. There's a weight on my chest. Gritty wetness slops across my face.

'Goddamnit, Aunt Sadie! Get down!'

Settling on all fours, the dog yaps playfully.

'You scared the hell out of me!'

She licks my hand, trying to make nice. But my fury has a few lashes left.

'You are *not* supposed to be on central campus! You are *not* supposed to sneak up on me! And you are *not* supposed to give me a stroke and a heart attack! You got that?'

She sloughs off the rebuke with a shudder. Edging closer, she grabs my tunic in her teeth and tugs.

'Let go!'

Insistently, she urges me toward the rear door.

'Cut it out, Sadie. I'm leaving on my own.'

30

She releases the fabric but keeps her nose pressed against my kidney like a gun butt until we're out the door.

I fill myself with clear, frosty air. The fear subsides. My anger evaporates.

'Thanks for caring, sweetheart.'

The dog eyes me balefully as I scratch between her ears. 'Sorry I yelled, but you scared me.'

My apology is not accepted. In a huff, Aunt Sadie turns and trots across the green. Her posh beige coat shimmies tartly as she goes. She's strutting like a short fat stripper.

'All right. Be that way,' I call after her.

Back at the awards ceremony, I'm a nervous wreck. Pip Stafford is called to the podium for an outstanding athlete award. The room explodes in thunderous applause.

5

Here comes a candle to light you to bed,
Here comes a chopper to chop off your head.
'Oranges and Lemons'

As soon as the last scroll is awarded, I head out. Hal
Kreidman stands cross-armed, blocking the door.

'Excuse me, Hal. See you tomorrow.'

'Not staying for refreshments, dear?'

I clutch my stomach. An unexpected rustling noise
makes me wince, but Hal doesn't seem to notice. 'My
insides haven't forgiven me for dinner yet. I'd better pass.'

'Maybe you should stop at the clinic, Bethany. There's
that bug going around.'

'It's nothing like that. I just need to start treating my
body more like a temple and less like an amusement park.'

'You sure? I'll gladly walk you over.'

'For that, I'll gladly go.' My wink makes him flush. Flirt-
ing is the surest, quickest way to make Hal disappear.

He clears his throat. 'Actually, a few of the boys are
waiting for me to join them inside. So if you're sure you're
not ill . . .'

'I'm fine, Hal. And you're a sweetheart.'

He ambles away, flapping off the pesky gnat of praise.

I watch him fondly. I've done enough sampling to know
what I want in a man. Perfection would be Hal's insides
poured into Adam Stafford's outsides. My head fills with
the headmaster's sultry gaze and full-lipped mouth. I
imagine his kiss, his touch. I picture his strong, deliberate
hands. That man has incredible hands:

All the better to wring your fool neck with, my dear.

Entering my apartment, I'm struck by the emptiness. No
cool nose greets me at the door. I call Aunt Sadie's name,

but I know it's useless. The dog goes off to sulk, sometimes for days, when she feels slighted. I've yelled at her, which is more than sufficient grounds for an extended huff.

There are plenty of places on campus where she can enjoy a nice, long mope with all the trimmings. The kids treat her to an orgy of junk food. They pet and play with her endlessly. I suspect she only comes back after a while because she doesn't trust me left to my own devices.

Tonight, I suffer her absence. My next-door neighbours, Brett and Shelly Kolar, are newlyweds from the Art department. They devote every spare moment to Olympic-calibre sex, which sets off a tremor in my living-room chandelier. They're quite an act, those two. Little lovebirds even provide their own colour commentary.

'No, don't stop!'

'Oh, baby. Oh yes!'

'Right there. Mmmmmm!'

I've thought of mentioning the little acoustical problem, but they're too cute and I'm too tongue-tied. Not to mention jealous. Loneliness settles on me like a fog.

I cast around for someone to call. My father is still running, but these days he does so by jet. Dad's third wife, Lillian, is a wealthy young widow. They're off seeing the world together, a project expected to take years. I get glamorous postcards and calls at odd hours because Lillian is time-zone disabled. She's still searching for the day she lost crossing the International Date Line last spring.

'How could it disappear like that?' she asks in awed sincerity. 'I mean, a whole, entire *day*.'

When Dad married Sylvie, his second wife, I imagined gaining a real mother-substitute. But Sylvie was a birdlike creature, brittle and shrill. Lillian has a better heart, but she's no one's idea of maternal. She's a garish package of strong scents and screaming colours and bangly jewels that compete for misguided attention with her mouth. She says priceless, ridiculous things. They would be funny if they came from a stranger. But from my father's wife, they make me want to stop snickering inside and cry out loud.

I don't understand how my father can bear Lillian's stunning lack of intelligence, but who am I to judge? My last mock-serious romance was three years ago. I was working days in the management office of a posh East Side apartment building in Manhattan to pay for my Master's in Education at NYU. I met Jonathan when he came to speak at the film school. He was a sportscaster for NBC and seemed like the perfect catch. Big fish. Very appealing. Unfortunately, he failed to mention the wife and guppies in Scarsdale. Must have slipped his slippery mind.

Ever since, I've been more than a little guarded around the unfairer sex. I sleep alone, except for stormy nights when Aunt Sadie bounds into bed to join me.

At last, I've found a place I love in Hinsdale, but my life still feels like a furnished sublet. Some day, I hope to fill it with permanent things of my own, but the choices are so daunting. A spouse? Children? I get stumped when someone asks whether I prefer my rye bread with seeds or without.

Sometimes I wish I could trade with my sister, Ruthann. She has it all in mammoth quantities: two darling kids, a house for every season, a pile of civic concerns, and a booming career as a realtor.

Unfortunately, she also has Lee Atkinson, wunderkind bond trader, for a husband. Lee is a florid, arrogant little person. He's a vocal snob and an unabashed bigot. His only true redeeming virtue is frequent absence. He golfs, plays bridge, dallies with cronies at the club, and devoutly neglects my sister and their kids. Considering his narrow footpath of a mind, I'm inclined to think he's doing them a favour.

I flop on the bed. The pages I pull from my waistband are wrinkled, but the print is clear enough. I read through Pip's file again, word for word as if the missing data might surface by magic.

Nothing does.

My stomach grumbles. It's probably a protest, but I choose to deem it hunger. Rummaging in the kitchen, the

34

most promising snack I find is a bag of unpopped corn. While it nukes in the microwave, I yield to the impulse to dial my sister's number in Stamford, Connecticut.

The voice that answers turns my heart to mush.

'H'lo?'

'Hello. I'm calling for the most gorgeous, brilliant five-year-old girl in the universe. Is she in?'

'Aunt Beffney?'

'That's right. How's my delicious girl?'

'Good. When are you coming to see me?'

'As soon as I can, honey.'

It's been far too long. Almost six months since I've seen Amelia and her ten-year-old brother, Greg. I long to spend more time with them and my sister, but there's always a ghost along when I do.

I see the victim walking in the surf. Sinking. A boulder of guilt fills my chest.

Your fault, Bethany. You did nothing to stop it. Nothing.

'Come tomorrow,' Amelia orders.

'I can't, sweetie. But soon.'

'You promise?'

'If you promise to stop growing and changing until I get there.'

My foolishness makes her sigh. 'I *have* to grow, Aunt Beffney. I'm *little*.'

'Okay, but no big changes. Don't marry a frog or dye your hair purple. Nothing like that.'

'I hate purple. Mommy took Greg to practice. Want to talk to the sitter?'

'No thanks, sweetie. Just tell Mommy I called.'

'I will. And when you come, bring me a *big* surprise. Okay?'

'Okay.'

'I'd be really, *really* surprised by a teddy bear backpack.'

Toting a bowlful of popcorn, I return to the bedroom. The mystery of Pip's file keeps nagging at me. There has to be a simple, logical reason why so much has been left out.

I try to dismiss the whole foolish business. The gaps in

Pip's records could stem from simple sloppiness. Or they might represent someone's understandable reluctance to question the boss.

Forget about it, Bethany.

I do my best. I struggle to lose myself in mindless TV, but it doesn't work. I try to concentrate on my lesson plans for tomorrow, but the vexing questions keep returning. Why is Adam Stafford so secretive? How come Pip never mentions his mother or his past? Isn't there some other way to unearth the child's elusive history?

Faced with a dangerous hole, the sensible move is to step gingerly around it. But jumping in has always been more my style. I can't help Pip unless I understand who he is. I can't turn my back on a kid who needs me.

Inaction had brought me the deepest, largest sorrow of my life.

You're to blame, Bethany. Why didn't you stop her?

Never again.

Suddenly exhausted, I settle down in bed. Turning off the lights, I think of a fresh possibility. Satisfied, I shut my eyes and drift toward sleep. Halfway there, I'm dragged back by melodious tinkling.

It's my amorous neighbours performing the Symphony for Bedpost and Chandelier. Thinking of Adam Stafford, I close my eyes again and hum along.

6 In her dream, Cal was leaving. Eva strained to stop him, coiling him tightly in her arms, but he always wriggled free and plunged headlong into the Sound.

Standing on the jetty, Eva watched him swim away. Pieces of her broke away and trailed him. Bits of her soul tossed like bait to the hungry surf.

The tides were brisk. Cal sliced through them, knifelike. His arms arched in easy rhythm. His legs raised a churning plume.

With horrifying speed, he spanned the distance to the shore. Eva squinted as he faded to a sliver, a speck. He was vanishing. Shrinking to memory. Her heart squeezed with the bitter pain of loss.

'*No*, Cal,' she groaned. '*Come back!*'

A thick arm circled Eva's ribs. Warm fingers pressed her. For a moment, Cal went still. From the depth of his breathing, Eva thought he'd fallen back to sleep.

Then, as she lay unmoving, his fingers came alive again. Cal stroked upward, seeking her breast. He worked her knowingly. Teasing tickles followed by a hard, seductive squeeze. Eva's body responded by rote. She tensed, straining towards him.

'Please don't go, Cal,' she breathed. 'I need you here, especially now.'

He silenced her with a deep kiss. His probing tongue turned her liquid.

Eva ordered herself to stay in control. Maybe this time, she could use his building urges. Maybe this once, she could have her way.

She closed her eyes. A naughty fantasy filled her mind. There was Cal, stark naked. There was Eva the temptress, dressed in lacy black. Her lips were parted coyly. Eyes veiled. She was in perfect control. In charge.

Ready to explode.

The temptress dissolved. Eva's will evaporated. She was assailed by a rush of raw sensations. Rising, almost there.

Cal sensed what she was feeling. He drew back. Pulled away from her.

Eva's body ached with wanting him. *Don't beg, Eva. Don't let him know.*

But the need inside her built like trapped steam.

'Now,' she breathed. 'Please, Cal.'

A devilish smile played on his lips. He moved on her again. Deftly, he edged her towards release.

Eva bit back the cries. She grabbed the reins on her runaway passions. Somehow, she held her body still.

Cal kept at her, confused. 'Soon?' he asked.

She shook her head, no. Not yet.

Keep it up, Cal. Forget this time. Lose yourself in the moment.

Eva couldn't help but get lost in it. It was happening now. She clenched her teeth against the exquisite rush. Her pulse raced. Body clenched. Despite herself, she rose, rode the breathless crest, then lapsed to nothingness.

Her face blazed with shame. She'd let her body betray her again. As always, she was powerless against Cal.

But wait. He was still there, still moving. Maybe she'd fooled him after all.

She stifled a cry of triumph. *That's it, darling. Keep going.*

Cal's breath quickened. Eva sensed his urgency. *Good*, she thought. *Almost there.*

Eva's hopes rose. She moved with him. Slowly, she slid her legs around him and locked her heels.

Closer. Faster. *Don't stop. Don't!*

But Cal went rigid. With a hard breath, he wrenched free of her. Rolling away, he flopped down on his side of the bed.

Tears stung Eva's eyes. Her chest heaved. Cal reached out and brushed the hair back from her forehead.

'You know we can't, honey,' he soothed.

'Why not?' Eva whimpered.

'You *know* why.'

'It'll be different this time, Cal. You'll see.'

'Stop it, Eva. There's no use.'

Wiping her eyes, she tried a different tack. 'We could leave here. Start over.'

'Forget it, Eva. I *mean* it.'

His anger stung. 'All right, Cal. I'm sorry.'

'I just don't want to talk about it any more.'

'Don't be mad.'

'I'm not.' He reached over her and brushed his lips on hers.

Eva snaked her arms around him, drawing him closer. She could feel him responding, his hardening press against her thigh. There was still a chance. Reaching down, she rubbed the way he liked.

Cal wrenched her hand away. 'Damnit, Eva. I said *no!*'

In a huff he rose and crossed to the closet. He pulled on a T-shirt and jeans and slid his bare feet into loafers. Then he retrieved a suitcase from the shelf. Tossed in more than enough supplies to last the week.

Finished, he shut the latches. The finality of the sound pierced Eva's heart. 'Please, Cal. I didn't mean anything by that. It wasn't what you think.'

Head bowed, he rifled through the architectural renderings on his desk. He selected several and slipped them into a presentation case. Frowning, he eyed his watch. 'Have to run. Ferry's due in five minutes.'

'They're always late. Let me fix you some breakfast.'

'No time. I'll grab something on the way.'

'Let me help you, at least.' She tried to tug the suitcase from him, but he held fast.

'I *have* it, Eva.'

Cal strode down the hall to the stairs. Eva trailed behind. She didn't want to grovel, but the thought of being without

Cal right now was unbearable. She couldn't live through this week without him. She could not bear another killing loss.

Somehow, she kept her tone breezy. 'I have a great idea. How about I make you a nice, big breakfast. Cheese omelette, wheat toast. The works. You can relax, read the paper, and go out later on the mailboat.'

Cal kept walking. At the bottom of the stairs, he paused and smiled stiffly. 'It's only a week, Eva. I'll be back before you know it.'

Eva wanted to wrench the cases from his hands. She wanted to block the door and bar his exit. Desperate pleas filled her throat, jostling for release.

Cal's look was icy. Nothing she did would stop him. If she acted like a weak, begging fool, that's the image he would carry of her all week.

That alone might push him to find someone else. He might, no matter what she did. Every time Cal left the island, Eva worried herself sick. The flesh was so weak. There were so many temptations.

Churning inside, Eva envisioned a young, beautiful girl in Cal's arms. Entwined with him. Filled with him.

'You know I normally don't mind if you go, Cal. Any time but this week, I –'

He sighed. 'We've been over and over this, Eva. I don't approve of this craziness, and I won't be a party to it.'

'What do you want to do, Cal? Forget?'

'When it suits you, you forget better than anyone.'

'What then? Should I pretend it never happened? Should I act as if we never had a child?'

His face went tight. 'No, Eva. All I'm asking is that you get past it. Move on. He was my son, too. I loved him every bit as much as you did.'

'*Do*, not did. Don't say it as if –'

'No word games, Eva. I'm telling you it's as much my loss as yours. You deal with it your way. I have mine.'

'I know that.'

'No, you don't. All you think about is poor Eva, martyred

for life. This isn't about me or the baby or anyone but you. I will *not* stay and watch you wallow in it. I will *not* participate in this nutty spectacle of yours. The whole thing makes me *sick*.'

He brushed past her and slammed out of the house. Numb inside, Eva watched him cross the grassy span to the jetty. The mainland ferry was angling towards its island berth. Four mournful blasts of its whistle warned unseen boats and swimmers to make way.

As the ferry glided nearer the dock, the captain added several playful toots for good measure. On this final jaunt of the season, the mood on board the *Island Queen* was always festive.

Cal's broad back was to Eva. She imagined the satisfied smirk on his face. He was glad to be leaving her, glad to escape. She was left to mourn the tragedy, alone.

If only Cal would agree to have another baby. If only the evil force who took him would return the precious son they had lost.

7

Tom, Tom, the piper's son.
Stole a pig, and away he run;
The pig was eat, and Tom was beat,
And Tom went howling down the street.
'Tom, Tom, the Piper's Son'

A learning-disabled child is like a switchboard after some joker has scrambled the wires. Chaos prevails.

By painstaking trial and error, logical connections have to be established and reinforced. Then the links must be soldered with endless repetition. The moment when everything finally clicks is indescribable. Imagine a cool shower after a long, punishing drought. Think of a street person moving in with Delia Smith.

This morning I've had two such moments. Jason Laks has made real strides in double-digit subtraction, and Rob Cruzen has finally stopped reversing his capital N. Danny Goichman is on my schedule next. I'm hoping for a hat trick.

Danny suffers from FLK syndrome. More plainly put, he's a funny-looking kid. The condition, seen mostly in boys, involves a constellation of unfortunate features. At eight, Danny exhibits almost all of them. He's short, soft, clumsy, and near-sighted. He's prone to hard knocks and tears of exasperation. His only friend in the world is another FLK. Such children tend to bond on the bench during ball games.

Whatever can go wrong with a kid, goes wrong with the Danny Goichmans. They wet the bed, need bottle-thick glasses, and have allergies to everything that's fun. They're tone deaf and colour blind and favour outfits pitting stripes against plaid. Their body parts grow in inexplicable shifts:

42

ears one year, feet the next. Puberty for them holds the promise of cystic acne and fresh opportunities for social rejection.

Difficult though it is, being an FLK has its benefits. Like most, Danny Goichman is kind, sweet, and compassionate. He's also incredibly persistent. The tiniest victory keeps him going for months.

Entering my room, he waves a pudgy hand. 'Hi, Mith Logan.'

I find the lisp endearing. So is the duck waddle and the aw-shucks expression. 'Good morning, Mr Goichman. Ready for some script?'

'I gueth.' His round shoulders hike to his oversized ears, tugging out his shirt tail.

We've been working on his writing skills for months. Danny is years behind the other kids, and the gap is widening. I've tried most everything in my trick bag, but we haven't made much progress.

To boost his coordination, I have him use an inch-thick pencil wedged into a triangular plastic grip. I've darkened the extra-wide lines on the page and taped the paper to the desk. Cursive writing tends to be easier for kids with poor eye–hand coordination, so I'm teaching him that instead of printing.

'What should I write?' he asks. His new front teeth are coming in. Naturally, they're crooked, mottled, and nearly the size of tusks. He'll need braces, and probably one of those headgear contraptions that look horrible and hurt like hell. FLKs never escape anything painful or unsightly. Other people get results, they have side effects.

'Try your name first,' I suggest. 'Remember how to do the "D"?'

'Down first, little loop, and then – ?'

'Big belly, remember?'

He grins. 'Like Daddy's. Fat belly, then a big loop and a little hill to start the "a".'

'Right you are.'

'Back around and a tail, then two bumps for the "n".
Bump bump – '

Danny learns best what he hears. Unfortunately, writing
is almost always taught by the look-and-do method. Kids
who have trouble picking it up are offered more and more
copying experiences. They're asked to draw in shaving
cream and whipped cream. They're told to copy in glitter
and sand. It's like expecting a blind person to learn the
tango by having bigger and bigger people demonstrate
the steps.

Before coming to Hinsdale, Danny worked with the
learning disabilities teacher at the local elementary school.
He was put through all the usual hoops and offered all the
standard solutions. After six months, the teacher dismissed
him from her rolls, writing: 'Student has failed to benefit
from remedial services.'

Danny Goichman has flunked therapy. Few people can
make such a claim.

He finishes his first name and starts on the last. He
talks himself through the complex dips and turns. By the
time he struggles through the final 'n', I'm exhausted for
him. But I find the strength to whistle and cheer.

'Ith it okay?' he asks shyly.

'Nope. It's fabulous.'

'You mean it? Even the "G"?'

'Even everything. Have you been cheating on me, Danny
Goichman? Have you been going to some other teacher and
practising behind my back?'

'No, Mith Logan,' he swears. 'I didn't practith one bit.'

'Okay. But I want you to write a little bit every day over
term break. Will you do that?'

His look is grave. 'A *little* bit. I promith.'

I peel the masking tape off his paper and tack it on the
bulletin board behind my desk. 'I'm very, very proud of you,
Danny boy.'

Budding walrus teeth glimmer through the grin. 'I am
very, very proud of me, mythelf.'

Pip Stafford is next on my list. I'm riding a crest, and I

44

refuse to let that scrawny demon drag me under. Maybe there'll be a magical change in Pip's attitude. If such a miracle occurs, I'm prepared to abandon my suspicions.

Pip's appointed time comes and goes. I watch the jerky progress of the wall clock. The boy is five minutes late. Then, nearly ten. It occurs to me that he's not going to show up, but I dismiss the thought as preposterous. Pip is eight. Kids that age don't ditch classes.

More time passes. My astonishment turns to worry. I try the headmaster's home number, but there's no answer. In the main office, I look up the extension for Weldon House and dial. The distant ring sounds like mean taunting. After five repetitions, I'm bumped back to the central switchboard. 'Hinsdale School. How may I help you?'

'Sorry,' I mutter. 'Wrong number.'

I spot Pip's best friend Jonah dashing down the hall in denim shorts and a flame-red T-shirt. He's going full tilt, but I manage to catch him.

'Any idea where Pip is, Jonah?' I huff.

He shows me his palms. 'No, Ms Logan. I haven't seen him. Maybe he's b-busy or something. I d-don't know. *Honest!*'

The lie weighs so heavy on his tongue, the kid is stammering. Jonah's a nice little boy, but he has dishrag tendencies. Whatever Pip says, Jonah does. I'm hoping he'll wake up one morning with a backbone. Otherwise, he's destined to become one of those men who marries a pit bull, works for the Marquis de Sade, and sighs a lot.

I smile. 'Sure. No problem. I thought Pip and I had an appointment, but I must be mistaken. He probably told me he couldn't make it, and I forgot.'

Jonah's eyes pop with amazement. He can't imagine audacity like his friend's going unpunished. 'I gotta go now. Okay?'

'Fine. But no running in the halls.'

He jaunts stiff-legged to the door and exits. I wait a beat and follow. Stepping outside, I spot him darting across the soccer field. He aims toward the centre of the woods, where a slim path hems an ancient stand of silver birches. The leaves are beginning to turn. Gold and crimson flares light the cool green canvas.

Lagging far enough behind so I won't be seen, I cross the field. Jonah sinks deeper and deeper into the thicket. For a time, I catch random glimpses of his red shirt through the greenery. Then, he's engulfed by shadows.

At the edge of the copse, I pause to listen. I hear only bird songs, restless insects, the crinkly flutter of wind-tossed leaves.

Entering the path, I tread lightly. The way has been cleared for shorter folk. I keep my hand raised to ward off the sting of stray branches. A sweet loamy stench rises from the forest floor. My nostrils itch with allergic current. I press the base of my nose to suppress the rising sneeze. Once I get started, I tend to keep sneezing for several minutes. Quiet, it is not.

Twenty yards in, the path forks. To the left is Piney Woods Pond. The Hole, as it's affectionately called, is a favourite hideaway for Hinsdale's older students. They fish its murky depths for sunnies. They skip pebbles across its sullen face. They go there to road-test forbidden vices like smoking and leering at girlie magazines. On sultry nights they sneak there for skinny-dipping. The water has a ripe, wretched smell that clings like Krazy Glue. The boys don't seem to notice, but an hour of mischief at the Hole is obvious to the adult nose for days.

I head right. Kids Pip and Jonah's age wouldn't dare invade the bigger boys' retreat. Instead, the little ones have claimed a small clearing fifty yards north. At the centre is a rock formation that resembles a giant toad. Not surprisingly, the place is called Frog's Rock Hollow.

The Hollow is mischief-central for the young kids. Secret clubs are formed and consecrated here. Cabals plotted, rehearsed, and reviewed. The ground is peppered with torn trading cards and fossilized candy wrappers. The trees facing the toad are etched with infantile obscenities, mostly

46

involving teachers and academic pursuits. My personal favourite is 'Scroo Spelling'.

Decades back, the rock toad was painted a vivid green. Approaching, I spot its emerald glint through a tangle of branches. Soon, I hear voices.

'You stir. I'll do the words,' Pip orders. 'Abracadabra, alla-kazam. Hokus, pokus, finokus – ' he chants.

'You sure about this Pip? We could get in trouble.'

'Sssh. You'll mess up the magic if you talk.'

'What if someone gets sick or dies or something?'

'I told you, it's just a chasing-away spell. All it'll do is make her leave Hinsdale.'

'But what if – '

'Shut *up*, Jonah. I *mean* it.'

'Okay.'

'Hokus, pokus, finokus, sha-zam!'

There's a pause filled with thoughtful humming. 'Looks ready. Now hold her still.'

Her?

I hear shuffling. A menacing growl.

'Hold on, Jonah!'

'I'm trying.' There's more shuffling. Then a shrill, out-raged bark.

Furious, I stomp into the clearing. Aunt Sadie wrenches free from Jonah's grip and bounds to the edge of the copse. Her hackles are raised, teeth bared for maximum effect. Snarling, her eyes dart between her two assailants.

Spotting me, she yaps shrill accusations. She races over and presses against my leg. She's panting hard. Muddy glop streaks her plush coat, but she seems otherwise unhurt. I brush off the worst of the mess with the side of my hand.

'It's okay, girl. Easy now.'

Her breathing settles. Furious, I turn to the boys. Pip has a Snoopy beach towel draped across his shoulders. Another towel wraps his head in a makeshift turban. A large stewpot rests on the toad-shaped rock. It's filled with more of the goop that was smeared on Aunt Sadie's coat.

From what I can see, the recipe includes soil, Coca-Cola, dried leaves, and at least one fat, wriggling worm.

'What's going on here?'

Jonah unravels. 'We were just playing, Ms Logan,' he whimpers. 'Please don't put us on report.'

Pip levels a finger at Sadie. 'No dogs allowed on central campus. And she tried to bite me. I'm telling my dad.'

I work to contain my fury. 'We'll tell him together, Pip. Come on, Jonah. Let's go.'

We struggle through the woods. Jonah whimpers all the way. There are no visible dents in Pip's arrogance. The kid swaggers like a seasoned bully.

'Dogs who bite aren't allowed here,' he mutters. 'I'm telling that, too.'

After we cross the soccer field, I instruct Sadie to go home. Without hesitation, she trots off in the opposite direction toward the senior dorms. Apparently, all has not yet been forgiven.

Approaching Administration, Jonah comes to a trembling halt. Sobbing, he buries his face in his hands.

'Please, Ms Logan. *Please!*'

I comfort him until he's calm enough to continue. 'We're just going to talk, Jonah. That's all.'

I have to prompt him the rest of the way. The boy is steeling himself for a major punishment. But when we reach the headmaster's office, no one's there.

I remember seeing Stafford's packed schedule for the day. The headmaster has a luncheon and appointments off campus every hour all afternoon. As I recall, he's busy most of the evening, too. Still bent on swift justice, I march the kids to the assistant head's office down the hall. He's not in either. Neither is the lower school dean.

I dismiss the runts with a stern warning and a promise to discuss the incident with headmaster Stafford first thing tomorrow. Jonah looks mildly relieved at the stay of execution. Pip acts bored.

His image stays with me when I leave the boys behind.

Someone has to reach that kid and bring him back before he gets any further away.

My Jeep is parked in the lot adjacent to staff quarters. Beyond stands the headmaster's house, a gracious Georgian. I've always viewed the house and the man with unreserved admiration, not to mention weak knees. But now I can't help wondering if those stately façades might conceal some unthinkable secret.

Fallen leaves fleck the windshield. I brush them off and start the drive to town.

8

Doctor Foster went to Gloucester
  In a shower of rain;
He stepped in a puddle, up to his middle,
  And never went there again.
                              'Doctor Foster'

The road linking the school to Grangeville is famed for its scenic speed trap. Sheriff Wendell Huff shifts the location daily, posting his sole deputy around one of the many blind bends in the Grangeville Road.

A mile into the drive, I spot Deputy Harley Beamis in the overstuffed flesh. He's posed beside his catch of the day, a sporty red BMW convertible with New York plates.

The deputy has a squashed face, a gourd-shaped head, and the body of a bloated bowling pin. He lifts a meaty hand as I approach, ordering me to stop.

I curse under my breath. I wasn't speeding, but I can always be cited for something else. There are several hundred arcane traffic laws on Grangeville's books, many dating back to horse and buggy days. Harley's nailed me four times in a year for nameless, numbered violations. I've had a fifty-three, a twenty-eight, and two sixty-sevens.

I haven't bothered to ask what the numbers mean. Battling tickets here is a waste of time. The constable who presides in weekly traffic court is Harley's brother. The only practising lawyer in town is Sheriff Huff's son. To challenge or try to change the laws, you have to deal with Mayor Rick Beamis, Harley's father, and the town council, which is chaired by Harley's mom, Lucille.

Traffic tickets provide necessary revenue for road maintenance and repair. I try to think of them as a patriotic duty.

50

I press the button, lowering my electric window. 'What is it this time, Harley?'

'Just a friendly hello is all, Beth. How's things up at the old school?'

The swarthy man in the BMW puffs his impatience. Harley turns to glare. 'You got a problem, fella?'

The man sheepishly eyes his watch. It's a Rolex. Added to the BMW, that gives him two strikes in Harley's book. I want to warn the poor guy to tread with caution. Fortunately, his own instincts are in decent working order. 'No, officer. I'm just running late,' he says.

'Must be why you were speeding like your butt's on fire. Sorry, buddy. Late's no excuse.'

'I know, but –'

'You just hold your fancy horses.'

'Yes, officer.'

Harley hitches his belt. 'Now then, Beth. Where were we?'

'Things are fine at the old school, Harley. Finishing up.'

'Going away over the break?'

'I haven't decided.'

His smile frames a crooked fence of teeth. 'How about we get together next week, then? Have dinner maybe.'

'Chances are I'll be away, Harley.'

'Hope not. Been thinking of you lately. Bet we'd hit it off *real* good.'

I groan in silence. Once Harley sets his mind on someone, he's notoriously hard to shake. Most of last year, he stuck to Patsy Culvert like a barnacle. Patsy finally shed him by claiming she had a rare, fatal, contagious disease. Thankfully, Harley's every bit as dumb as he is annoying.

'Actually, I'm seeing someone,' I tell him.

'That so. You engaged?'

'Not exactly.'

'Good, then I still got time to change your pretty little head.'

His khaki uniform is rumpled and grease-stained. A bulging sack from Dippin' Donuts occupies the passenger seat of his Dodge. Harley is rumoured to have a dozen-a-day cruller habit. He's also quite fond of low-end beer. As a consequence, his midsection has taken on a life and personality of its own. It wriggles and strains against his shirt like a chained Houdini.

'Okay if I move on now, Harley?'

'Just hang on a sec 'til I send this fella on his way.'

Beamis ambles toward the BMW, filling out a ticket. At the rear of the car, he stops to enter the plate number. Finished, he tears the citation from the book and hands it through the driver's open window.

'Next time you pass through here, stick to the speed limit, fella. We don't take kindly to uppity rich boys thumbing their fancy noses at our laws.'

'Yes, officer.'

'Grangeville's a peaceable, God-fearing community. Not some Solomon Gomorrah like that rotten apple place you come from. You remember that, buddy.'

'Yes, officer.'

Harley strides on to the deserted road and makes a grand show of directing the BMW off the shoulder. 'That's it. Keep backing her straight up. That'll do her. Now straighten those candy ass wheels of yours, and you're clear.'

The sleek red car aims south. I'm eager to follow, but Harley and his stomach block my way. Lazily, he circles around, plants his elbows on my open window, and props his stubbly jaw on his palms. His breath is a haze of rancid fry grease.

'Now then, teach. How come you want to play so hard to get?'

'I told you, I'm seeing someone. I need to go now, Harley. Please move.'

His grin hardens. 'What you *need* is to let that starch out of your britches, babycakes. Now how 'bout a little smoocheroo to break the ice?'

He edges towards me. 'Cut it out, Harley.'

His mashed face presses further into the car. Sweat and

52

tobacco rise from his uniform. 'Come on, now. What can a friendly little kiss hurt?'

'I said, cut it *out*!'

He grabs my neck and mashes our lips together. His tongue probes, trying to part my gritting teeth. I shove my palms hard against his shoulders, but that doesn't budge him.

He's pressing my mouth so hard my teeth ache. His free hand finds my breast and clamps it like he's hitching to a tow.

A cry of outrage sticks in my throat. Groping around, I find the window button. The glass slides up, trapping Harley's tiny brain. Releasing me, he yelps in horror.

'What the hell're you doing? You trying to take my damned head off or what?'

I let the glass down just enough so he's able to wedge his cranium out at an angle. His face flames crimson. A line of spittle strains from the corner of his mouth. 'Crazy bitch . . .'

Raising the window, I meet his furious gaze.

'Try touching me again, I'll take off more than that ugly mess between your shoulders, Harley Beamis.'

'I'm an officer of the *law*, missy. You remember that.'

'The *law* is an *ass*, mister. *You* remember *that*.'

Irate curses trail me as I drive off, but Harley stays put. When he's assigned to man a speed trap, the deputy is expected to remain there for the duration of the shift. Nothing, short of an emergency donut run, could make him abandon his post.

The incident leaves me shaky. I can still feel the raw press of Harley's mouth and the painful pinch on my breast. My cheek burns. Vengeful fantasies crowd my thoughts.

I tune the radio to soft rock. Art Garfunkel volunteers to let me use him as a bridge. His honeyed tones soothe the worst of my pique. By the time I reach the head of High Street, I'm back in reasonable control.

The town's main road is lined with angled spaces. I turn into a vacant slot two blocks down. I feed a quarter to the parking meter and twist the knob. When the metal snaps back, I flash on the same thing happening to Harley Beamis's neck. That brings a smile.

I pass the Sack O'Suds and the IGA and Nancy-Lee's News and Notions. Kletter's Pharmacy is the glass-fronted store at the end of the street. The window display features bright paper leaves and back-to-school supplies. A sign proclaims a half-price sale on incontinence aids and the suggestion that I stock up. When I open the door, a bell jangles.

Emma, the Kletters' oldest daughter, stands behind the counter. Annie, next in line, kneels at the magazine rack, replacing last month's unsold stock with fresh editions. Joanna, the ten-year-old baby of the clan, sprays diluted vinegar on the counter tops and rubs them clean with wadded newsprint. 'Hey, Ms Logan,' she calls. 'You come to see Craig? He's still at summer school.'

Craig is nineteen, a longer, lankier version of his sisters. All the Kletter kids have their father's reddish hair, blue eyes, and freckled complexion.

'No, sweetheart. I need to speak to your dad. Is he here?'

'Daddy went to see a man about a horse,' Emma says coyly.

'Did not,' Joanna challenges. 'Seeing a man about a horse means you go pee, Emma. Daddy's over at the tavern, playing poker.'

'I swear, letting you in on something's like putting it on the nightly news, JoJo.' Emma rolls her eyes. 'She wasn't supposed to tell anybody.'

'I won't say a thing,' I assure her.

'Hope not. If Momma hears, watch out.' Emma aims a furious face her sister's way. 'How come you're such a damned little tattle-tale?'

'Am not a tattle-tale,' Joanna snuffles. 'And I'm telling Momma you said the D word.'

'Next time those gypsies come around, I'm selling you back to them, you dumb baby. I don't care how little you're worth,' her sister says.

54

'Go choke.'

'You first.'

The bell jingles again as I slip out the door. I can only hope it signals the end of the round.

The Dog & Pony Tavern stands at the foot of High Street between the Chevy dealership and the Lutheran church. The tavern was a barn in a former incarnation. Except for the neon pub and brew signs, the exterior remains unchanged.

Inside, the décor is classic testosterone. Stuffed animal heads line the walls, their eyes glazed from years of non-stop sports viewing on the large-screen TV. Portraits of John Wayne and men of similar nuance and sensitivity hang over the mantelpiece. There's a pool table and several arcade games. The jukebox features country & western songs and the worst of Frank Sinatra.

The bartender has a handlebar moustache and the build of a sixteen-wheeler. His name is Pete, and he doubles as the bouncer. Neither role is terribly demanding. Pete's size is sufficient to keep most everyone in line. And his mixology skills are rarely challenged. A whiskey shot with a beer chaser is the drink of choice here. Brave individualists take their beer or whisky straight. For state occasions, the beer is dyed and the whiskey shots are served in Jello cubes. Rumour has it someone once ordered a strawberry daiquiri in this town. Poor fellow hasn't been heard from since.

Will Kletter and three men I don't recognize huddle at the sole occupied table in the rear. The checkered cloth is littered with plates and glasses, playing cards, a basket of popcorn dregs, and a half-empty pitcher of generic brew. The dealer flicks two cards in Will's direction. Will eyes them balefully and folds his hand.

'That's it for me, boys.' Standing, he turns out the pockets of his jeans. 'Cleaned me out again. Same time next week?'

'Sure.'

'If any of you snag some work by then, we'll make the game next weekend.'

'Okay, Will.'

'You might want to stop in at the Roadhouse, Marty,' Kletter suggests. 'I hear Pop's hiring.'

'I'll do that. What do we owe you on the lunch check?'

'It's on me,' Kletter says. 'Losers weepers.'

'You sure you got enough left to cover it?'

'I'll manage. Jack and Gary, you might want to check down at the Exxon. I hear they're short a mechanic and a pump jockey.'

'Thanks, Will.'

The men rise. I take in their ratty clothes, unkempt hair, and blackened fingernails. It's likely Will plucked the trio from the men's shelter in Independence Center. Kletter's incurably generous. He'll do anything for anyone, except risk denting the other person's pride. Today, he's managed to pass on cleaning-up money along with his job tips. But I'd wager his card cronies have no idea they've been helped.

After they're out the door, I approach the table. Will tugs a spare roll of bills from his jacket pocket and peels a few on to the check. He wears a work shirt, worn denims, and battered boots. His hair looks home-trimmed. Stray curls spill over his collar like carrot peelings. You'd never guess the man has millions. In addition to the pharmacy, Kletter holds sizeable interests in several local businesses and a number of major corporations nationwide.

'Good to see you, Bethany. You okay?'

His gaze settles on my left cheek, which Deputy Beamis has branded with a streak of beard burn.

'I had a small collision with one of the bigger kids. It's nothing.'

'Meeting someone for lunch?'

'Actually, I came to see you.'

He stifles a smile. 'I take it my kids spilled the beans.'

'Your beans are safe with me, Will.'

'Thanks. Earleen hates gambling, even when there's no gamble involved. Have a seat. Can I get you something? A sandwich?'

'Nothing, thanks.' I take the seat opposite him. 'I just have a quick question.'

Will's been retired from the Hinsdale Board since his son Craig was a sophomore. But he was a member two years back when Stafford was hired. Trying to go about this subtly, I ask how the Board fills high-level vacancies.

Will's brow hikes, but he keeps his scepticism to himself. He tells me the process involves placing ads in major newspapers. The position may be posted with the placement offices of select universities. If all else fails, the Board hires an executive search firm specializing in the education field.

'Is that how you found Adam Stafford?'

'Mind if I ask why you're asking?'

'Call it curiosity.'

His look turns grave. 'What's the problem, Bethany? Stafford giving you trouble?'

'No. Nothing like that.'

'You sure? Because I won't let him or anyone forget what you did for our Craig. That boy would never have made it to graduation without you. Much less college.'

'How's he doing?'

'Just fine. Thanks to you.' His eyes lock on mine. 'You can trust me, Beth. If there's anything I can do to help you, it'd be my pleasure.'

I tell him the truth. I'm worried about Pip. Knowing more about his background would be useful, but Stafford isn't talking. Pip's file tells me nothing. I describe the headmaster's record as 'unavailable'.

'I don't even know where Pip went to school before Hinsdale. It's strange,' I tell him.

Kletter's frown deepens. 'To be honest, I had the same impression about Adam. That he was holding something back. Between you and me, I argued against his appointment.'

'You weren't satisfied with his credentials?'

'It wasn't that. Man looked terrific on paper. Top schools, superb recommendations. The works. It was just a feeling I had. That he wasn't altogether on the up and up.'

'Hiding something?'

'Felt that way.'

57

At my urging, Kletter recounts what he can remember of Stafford's history. I already knew that the headmaster was educated at Wesleyan and Yale. He began his teaching career at a private school. Later, he moved into administration, where he rapidly advanced. Stafford was recruited for Hinsdale from another boarding-school. But Kletter can't recall the school's name or location.

'I wish I could have a look at his record,' I muse aloud. 'Dr Stafford's contract is up, so the current Board probably has his file for review.'

Kletter shrugs. 'If that's the case, I'm afraid I'm less than no use to you. Joe Whatley is still smarting from that Savings and Loan business. The investigators couldn't get enough for an indictment, but they hounded Joe for months. Everyone imaginable was called in to testify. Including me.'

'What happened?'

'Nothing. But Joe was furious with me for cooperating. Called me a traitor. Things got so strained between us, I finally decided to quit the Board. I thought he'd cool off faster if we had fewer dealings with each other. He didn't.'

'There's no one else on the Board you could ask?'

'Wish there was,' he says. 'Joe's been chairman for ever. Rules Hinsdale's business with an iron fist. If Adam's file is under consideration, you can bet the only way to it is through Joe.'

My stubborn side hates to give up, but I know it's hopeless. 'Thanks anyway, Will.'

'Sorry, Beth. If there was any way –'

Leaving the Dog & Pony, my eye drifts to the animal heads on the wall. I wonder if they saw it coming. I wonder if some seventh sense warns you when you're stepping into a lethal trap.

9 On the drive back to Hinsdale, I'm fixated on Adam Stafford. There has to be a way to find out more about our esteemed headmaster and his steamed-up son.

Several approaches strike me as promising. But they all disintegrate like spider webs when I seek a firmer hold. So much information is retrievable at lightning speed today. Birth and hospital records. School registration rosters. Rent rolls and house titles. Motor vehicle logs. Income tax and charge account histories. But, short of hiring a private investigator, I have no idea how to gain access to such things.

I could pay a professional to spy on my boss. I could also go sky-diving without a parachute.

Someone on staff must know more about Stafford than I do, but who? The headmaster keeps his professional distance. He's cordial enough, but not particularly close with anyone at school. Any private life he has is decidedly private.

Poking around at random might get me some answers, but it's too risky. Hinsdale is the smallest of small towns. Secrets, rumours, and flu germs are equally impossible to contain. Still, somehow the headmaster has been able to avoid the contagion. Aside from occasional whispers about the reasons for his divorce, little is ever said about the man.

There has to be a way.

Heading north, I pass Old Logging Road. Twenty years ago, the unpaved trail was Hinsdale's sole link with Grangeville. Bad weather rendered the road impassable. In the dead of New Hampshire's difficult winters, the school was cut off from civilization, sometimes for months.

I can't imagine being that shut off and isolated. I can't

59

imagine anyone living that way in this era of instant communications and no privacy. Not even Adam Stafford.

It has to be an illusion. No one as public and involved as the headmaster can exist in so complete a vacuum. Somewhere, Stafford has an ex-wife. A family. There have to be former neighbours, old friends, past classmates, lost loves.

But how do I find them?

A truck draws close behind and swings around me. When it pulls ahead, I spot the bright caution sign plastered to its rear bumper. My thoughts swerve to Harley Beamis lurking behind some curve in the Grangeville Road.

I check my speedometer. Horrified, I realize that I've been whizzing along at nearly twenty miles over the legal limit.

I pound the brake. The last thing I need now is another run-in with the deputy. I can still see his furious face wedged in my window.

There's no sign of him in my rearview mirror. No sirens or flashing lights.

But as I round the bend in the road, my relief hits a roadblock.

Harley's Dodge is angled to block the lane. Beside it, Deputy Beamis stands wielding a radar gun and a smirk. Flooring the brakes, I lurch to a stop inches from his passenger door.

Harley pauses to deposit the speed gun on the driver's seat. He swaggers toward me, smoothing his stubbly hair. 'Well, well. Lookee here.'

'All right, Harley. Just give me a ticket.'

He waggles a chiding finger. 'Not so fast, ma'am. Book says I have to call this in and run a check on you first.'

I'd like to strangle him, but I'm in enough trouble. 'Cute, Harley. Let's be grown up about this, shall we?'

'Licence and registration, please.'

'I don't have time for this, Harley.'

'We gonna do it the *easy* way or the *hard* way?' he snarls.

'Is there a difference?' I mutter. Fishing through my

purse and the glove box, I find the papers and pass them along.

Harley swaggers toward his car. He squeezes into the driver's seat, wedging his gut behind the wheel. I see him talking into the hand mike of his two-way radio.

Finished with the call, he fishes a book from the rear seat of his car and flips through it. I presume it's Harley's bible: Grangeville's *Uniform Traffic Code*.

He talks into the mike again. Several minutes pass before he ambles out of the car and strides my way.

Consulting a slip of paper, he ticks his tongue. 'Bethany Logan's your name?'

'Harley Beamis, you little devil. When did you learn to read?'

'Currently residing at the Hinsdale Country Day and Preparatory School for Boys, Upper Grangeville, New Hampshire?'

'Give it a rest, Harley. This is ridiculous.'

'Step out of the car with your hands up, Ms Logan.'

'Come on, Harley. This is life. Not a Clint Eastwood movie.'

The deputy wrests a .45 from its holster. Levelling the barrel at my forehead, he rasps, 'I'm *asking* you to step out, *now*!'

Daddy always taught me not to argue with lunatics or deadly weapons. Faced with both, I open the door.

'Easy now. No sudden moves,' he barks.

I would laugh. But I'd like to be able to do so again in the future. Palms aloft, I ease myself out of the car.

'Turn around,' Harley orders.

When I do, he shoves me roughly against the car.

'Grab some metal and spread 'em, sister.'

Again, the chuckles rise in my throat. But they're stilled by the bite of the deputy's gun against my neck. I hear a click, which could be the safety on the gun or the final snap of Harley's sanity.

'Put that thing away, Harley. It could go –'

'I give the orders here, bitch!'

With his free hand, he pats me down. It takes him for ever to track down one side, armpit to ankle, then the other. His moves are rough and perfunctory. Coldly professional. It's almost worse than the crude groping I expect.

'Seems you're clean. Now turn around. Nice and slow.'

I do as I'm told. I have a vivid image of Harley at the Dog & Pony, dining out on the story of how he spattered my brains all over the Grangeville Road.

'— And then I shot the uppity bitch. Blew her fool head right off her shoulders. You shoulda seen her body dance, boys. Went on for the longest time even though she was havin' a real, real bad hair day.'

Harley stares at me. The muzzle twitches beside his cheek like a crazed third eye. 'Now, you get the hell out of my sight, you dumb cow.'

I get into my car and shut the door. Remembering my papers, I roll down the window. 'I need my licence and registration, Harley.'

Smirking, he shakes his head. 'That's six points you got today for a two-eighty-four, Ms Logan. Record shows you've got fourteen prior points for moving violations, plus these six makes twenty. Under ordinance 3479, that's an automatic six-month suspension of your driving privileges.'

'You can't do that.'

'Can and have. Now I'm going to be real nice and let you drive back to your residence today. After that, if I catch you on the road, I'll have to pursue you to the full extent of the law, which includes — '

'All right, Harley. I apologize for humiliating you, and you're sincerely sorry for manhandling me. Now can we please forget the whole thing and act like sensible adults?'

'— Which includes the use of lethal force where an officer on duty deems it necessary.' Harley leans closer. 'I catch you driving in my jurisdiction, I'll put you out of your misery, you lousy little cock-teaser. You read me?'

If I had any questions, the pistol cleared them right up. Hopefully, Harley would cool off in time and come to his limited senses.

'Loud and clear.'

Harley struts to his car and eases it on to the shoulder. I start the Jeep and slowly drive toward school.

10

Fast and steady had a race
Fast fell down and broke his face.
'Fast and Steady'

Near the close of each term, a bubble of eagerness builds among the students. Special events fuel the mania. In addition to awards night, we've had moving-up day, the dorm dramatics festival, student government elections, and closing assembly. The frenzy of activity is a welcome diversion from going home, leaving friends, losing touch. The terror of change.

Most staff members weather these transitions unscathed, if not gratefully. But I dread the parade of parents arriving to fetch their sons. Devoid of kids, this place has a phantom limb feel. Their absence is palpable; like a deep, unscratchable itch.

I know I should forget all that and focus on the mountain of end-term record-keeping. I have follow-up tests to score, detailed reports to write, budget projections, materials requisitions, and programme plans to file. It's a huge undertaking, especially for the terminally disorganized, such as myself. Paperwork inspires me to dazzling feats of death-defying procrastination.

Just yesterday, I recalled every man I'd ever fallen for and why I should have known better each time. I made a three-strand necklace of paper clips with a matching bracelet. I paired every one of my students with his perfect future career. Billy Brodsky: insurance salesman. I couldn't choose between orthodontia and a pet shop for Rob Cruzen. Pip Stafford was easy. Pro-athlete or serial killer. Maybe both.

On the final day of the summer session, I have piles of

work yet to do. But even that daunting fact fails to move me. My Adam Stafford obsession has become an almost full-time job. All my spare time is devoted to plotting revenge against Harley Beamis.

That rotund redneck has me boiling. I loathe injustice and abuse of power and poor personal hygiene, all things the deputy so splendidly represents.

Above all, I hate feeling trapped. There's no public transportation here, so the licence suspension renders me a virtual prisoner at Hinsdale. I could beg rides from my colleagues, but since I'm determined to wallow in my outrage, I prefer to keep it pure.

I try not to think about how I will fill the upcoming term break. Without a car, I can't move freely between school and the surrounding towns. I can't pass the time, as I usually do, with unnecessary errands and random roaming. I'll be forced to stay here. To face myself. To think.

I can't bear the idea of being stuck on a deserted campus. Only Adam Stafford and a skeleton staff will remain to oversee the few students who live too far away to go home or have no one at home to receive them. I don't want to be one of them: a rootless soul in need of warehousing.

Junior Olympic finals are scheduled for today. That means rivalry, revelry, and no classes. At the start of every term, the boys are divided into a grey team and a green team. From then on, points are granted to the winners of designated contests. Bonuses are given for sportsmanship, gentlemanly conduct, and acts of courage. The score to date is a tie, a situation that occurs with striking frequency.

Final track and field events will be staged this morning. The afternoon schedule includes championship matches in soccer, baseball, and lacrosse. Typically, at the end of the day, only a point or two will separate the teams. Doing the gentlemanly, sportsmanly, courageous thing, the winning squad will offer the losing squad a shared victory. Somehow, the fact that this happens almost every term does nothing to lessen the high drama of it all.

I spend two hours in the bleachers, but I fail to catch

the crowd's enthusiasm. Competition is alleged to be good for children. But I've seen these so-called games reduce even the sweetest boys to their basest components: blind ambition, raw ego, screeching frustration, sweat, and tears.

The adults are worse than the kids. Caught up in the moment, they shriek. Curse. Encourage mayhem. *'Get him, Adam! Kill! Attaboy!'*

The starter pistol gives me a headache. So does the Athletic Director's amplified bark: *'All participants in the fifty-yard dash report to the starting line. High hurdles up next. And the winner in the four-hundred relay is –'*

Pip Stafford stands perpetually in the victor's circle. So far, he's taken first place in the standing broad jump, the shot put, and three foot races. Danny Goichman brings up the rear every time, still slogging toward the finish line while the crowd barely contains its impatience.

I alone keep shouting encouragement. 'Go, Danny!'

Pip gets a medal, Danny gets a consoling pat on the back. Pip gets a trophy, Billy Brodsky gets first aid for a nasty scrape and a bruised psyche. Pip basks in celebrity; Rob Cruzen crumples his honourable mention certificate and skulks like a shrunken ferret to the water fountain.

This is Pip Stafford's day. The kid revels in the attention. He's beaming like a new flashlight. But whenever he looks my way, his expression curdles.

I've had enough. After Pip breaks the school record in the ten and under high jump, I slip away. With any luck, I can knock off a few of my delinquent reports before lunch.

Everyone is congregated at the games. The other side of Schoolhouse Lane is desolate. Away from the commotion, I notice that the day has taken a hard turn for the worse. Dark clouds mass overhead. Menacing shadows shroud Central Green.

I resist a powerful urge to turn back. *Sorry, Dr Stafford. I would have gotten my reports in, but there was this really creepy low-pressure system.*

With a sudden surge of determination, I walk faster. I'll

finish the damned paperwork. I want to get away from Hinsdale, away from vexing mysteries. I need a break.

There's a gap in the clouds. An insolent sun peeks through. With it comes a firmer conviction that I must reconnect with the world outside of Hinsdale. No wonder the smallest occurrence at this place strikes me as momentous. I've let the school swallow my life. It's all I think about. All I know.

So Pip doesn't like me. Big deal. So Adam Stafford likes his privacy. Who doesn't? I'm determined to put such trivia out of my mind. I will finish up, say goodbye, and spend a couple of weeks on more global issues. My niece doesn't have a teddy bear backpack. Nabisco is threatening to reformulate its Mallomar cookies. Things like that.

I let myself in through the Administration Building's back door. Recalling Aunt Sadie's sudden appearance the last time, I lock the door behind me. The dog is still off moping happily at the senior dorms. By report, they've gotten her hooked on pepperoni pizza and corn chips, but otherwise she's fine. I miss her and want her back, but I don't relish any unexpected intrusions at the moment.

The building is tomb still. My steps reverberate. Approaching my office, I fumble for the key.

I'm calculating how many hours it will take me to complete the six remaining reports I have to write. Figuring two to three hours for each, I'm prepared to work straight through the night if necessary. I have enough junk food stashed in my desk to sustain me. I have everything I need.

And then some.

As I open the door, my jaw drops. My office is a disaster. The desks and chairs are overturned. The floor is awash in shredded papers. Everything has been ripped off the bulletin board and knocked from the shelves. My students' prize papers are reduced to crumpled wads. My files have been opened and emptied, the contents dumped in a heap. The few reports and requisitions I've finished have been ripped to irredeemable bits.

Dried brown glop covers everything. The walls are

striped with it. It's smeared on the books. Even the pictures on my desk have been coated with the stuff. My heart aches at the sight of my smiling young mother, caked with mud. I dampen a tissue with my tongue and wipe her image clean.

I know it's Pip Stafford's handiwork, but I can't believe it. Eight-year-old kids don't behave like this. Or do they?

Recently, I've read news items about murders committed by a tiny seven-year-old in the Midwest. An angelic-looking Chicago boy of ten has been credited with a body count to rival Ted Bundy. True, these kids are not the norm, but neither is Pip Stafford. Pip has demonstrated a precocious capacity for seriously monstrous behaviour.

Anyway, the circumstantial evidence is overwhelming. Who, besides Pip, would have the mud recipe? The motive? The raw nerve?

I want to murder the little twerp. I want to haul his scrawny little butt in here and make him clean up every scrap of this revolting mess.

Fury drives me to the door. But no further. I have to wait for the lunch break when I can get Pip alone. Confronting him in the middle of the games would only give the little brat more attention.

I right my desk chair and slump on it. What a godawful mess. All my work, all the kids' work is ruined. My personal things, my best books. I feel sick. Invaded.

Seriously pissed off.

Over an hour remains until lunchtime. I consider leaving things exactly as they are to show the full magnitude of the crime. In my head, I try Pip's case, convict him, and ship him off to a miserable munchkin prison. I conjure a truly draconian place with stone mattresses, an all-gruel menu, and no video games.

But reality keeps rearing its ugly head. Adam Stafford will undoubtedly find some way to absolve his precious son. I imagine him dismissing this as a 'simple personality conflict'. With mud.

Worse, Stafford may refuse to believe Pip is involved at

68

all. With a sinking feeling, I realize I have no proof. No witnesses. I have nothing to stand on but the shaky plank of my own suspicions.

My rage isn't huge enough to suffocate my reason. I love my job and want to keep it. I don't want to leave Hinsdale, especially by force. Although it's about as likely as flying elephants, Pip Stafford *could* be innocent.

Cool off, Bethany. Think this through.

Crouching in front of my files, I replace the folders in the drawers in alphabetical order. I lift a mangled stack of papers and start sorting.

Some of Danny Goichman's early work lies atop the heap. Fondly, I straighten his crumpled pages and stack them in chronological order. I'm heartened by what I see. Laboured though it's been, the kid has made real progress.

Clearing the mess feels good. Nostalgia salves my fury as I come upon the very first project Danny did with me. As an icebreaker, I have most of my kids write an autobiography. Danny's is aptly titled 'My Little Life'.

The cover is torn, but the crude self-portrait he drew is intact. Staring at a mirror, Danny captured his essence: Dumbo ears, dense glasses, look of permanent perplexity, tentative smile. On the first inside page is the Polaroid I took of the child in all his shy, gap-toothed splendour.

Inside is the story I wrote while he dictated. Danny's tale centres on his long, valiant struggle with bedwetting, which bedwetting invariably won. He details birthdays and Christmases and the birth of his twin baby sisters. '*Julie and Jill are smart, beautiful girls, Mommy says. Not like me.*'

Danny's poignant narrative sprawls for five pages. At the end, he declares his intention to be a kindergarten teacher some day. '*That way, I can have my sisters in my class and teach them all the important stuff.*'

Even now, funny-looking Danny makes me smile. Calmer, I sift through more of the wreckage.

Soon, an entire section of the floor is clear. Moving on to the next stack of papers, I find Billy Brodsky's work. I burrow down through that to Brian Carmichael and Rich Tesler and Mark Kipness and Seth Lapine.

At the bottom of the heap is another autobiography. The name has been torn from the cover. Flipping the page, I find a picture I recall as being Pip Stafford. It's not one of my Polaroids. When I tried to take his photo, Pip refused.

I remember thinking at the time how odd it was for such a little boy to be so camera-shy. But rather than make an issue of it, I asked him to bring a picture in from home. It took days and several reminders, but he finally showed up with this poorly focused shot of himself as a toddler.

The life story Pip told is sparse and peculiar. Most kids of all ages seize any opportunity to talk about themselves. Not Pip. Instead, he described what he owned: *'I have a Sega Genesis system and five cartridges. I have an autographed ball my dad caught at a Yankee game. I used to have four fish, but now I have three because one died on the floor last Tuesday. His name was Hubert.'*

I'm struck by what he didn't seem to have. Where are the fears and feelings? Where are the memories? Doesn't the kid have dreams?

Give it up, Bethany. Besides misery, all you've ever gotten for your concern about Pip Stafford was more misery.

I cull the rest of young monster Stafford's work from the debris. When I try to transfer the tottering pile to his folder, Pip's photograph falls away and drops to the floor. Retrieving it, I notice the back of it.

Mind racing, I gape in disbelief. Finally, I've found a key to the truth. Time to track down the door and unlock it.

11

Old woman, old woman, old woman, said I,
Whither, ah whither, ah whither so high?
'To sweep the cobwebs from the sky,
And I'll be with you by and by.'
                              'There was an Old Woman'

Like most Grangeville motorists, I've taken special note of
Harley Beamis's routine. The deputy goes off duty at four
o'clock, sharp. At his dilapidated frame house on Spring
Street, he changes into civilian clothes and downs his
dinner donuts. Less than an hour later, he's out the door.

By five, Harley ambles into the Dog & Pony Tavern.
There he remains nearly every night until closing. Planted
on his favourite stool at the end of the bar, he sucks down
massive quantities of generic beer and spews bullshit like
some Rube Goldberg contraption gone dangerously awry.

At ten after five, I steal from my apartment toting a
suitcase. As I pass, noises burst from the Kolars' place next
door. There's a crash of piano keys. A jarring thud. Worried
that someone might be hurt, I pause to listen.

For a moment, the only sound from inside is rasped
breathing. I'm about to knock when I hear a moaned: 'Yes,
tiger. Yes!' And then, 'Right there. *Mmmmm*! Feels so good!'

Relieved, I keep walking. The little tykes are fine.

I've spent the past few hours setting my office back in
presentable order. The note I've slipped under the headmaster's door states that I've been called away on a personal emergency. That feels true enough. The delinquent
reports will have to wait for my return.

The entire school is assembled on the soccer field, where
Junior Olympic trophies are being distributed. Heading for
my car, I hear blasts of frenzied cheering as the winners

are announced. At such a time, no one is likely to notice my departure. But as I slip into the Jeep, my heart hurls itself against my ribs.

I hate skulking off this way. I hate sneaking around. I worry about leaving Aunt Sadie. As long as there's a single living soul on campus, my fluffy beige friend will be fed and sheltered. But she's bound to miss me, sooner or later.

I miss her now. I could use her moral support. I'm afraid of what I might find out on this trip and more fearful of what I might not. This feels wrong. Probably *is* wrong. I hit the gas and angle toward the road.

By now, Harley Beamis is certainly at the Dog & Pony, but I navigate the windy length of the Grangeville Road with my heart in my throat.

I travel south, girding for the minimum five-hour ride. Anxious to reach my destination, I pick up a burger and fries at a fast food drive-through. I munch my way toward Connecticut, lulled by the greasy food and the mesmerizing rhythms of the road. Blur of phone poles. Blink of headlights. Speed-stretched streaks of hazy cloud.

Traffic is sparse and moving briskly. Having no licence, I lag behind. It's nearly eleven when I turn off the Merritt Parkway in Stamford. Ridgemount Lane is a tiny cul-de-sac carved out of the cultivated woods two miles north. My sister's is the rambling brick house at the end of the block. Architecturally, the structure combines elements of the classical Tudor style with strong shades of neo-conspicuous consumption. The place has six bedrooms, five and a half baths, a pool with cabana and spa, and a tennis court. The security lights blaze on as I enter the chevronned brick drive.

Before I'm out of the car, Ruthann bursts from the house and rushes up to greet me. Even at this hour, she's dressed, jewelled, shod, painted, and groomed. My sister's idea of slipping into something more comfortable is trading over-the-counter stocks for mutual funds. Taking pains not to smudge, budge, or mutilate anything, she wraps me in a perfumed hug.

72

'Beth, I can't believe it! I had the strangest feeling you were going to show up tonight.'

'I've been trying to call for hours, but your line's been busy.'

She frowns. 'I know. One of the neighbours stopped by with the same complaint. Turns out Amelia's Executive Barbie was on an extended call.'

I laugh, but Ruthann fails to join me. She's staring at something over my shoulder. 'Amelia Paige Atkinson, what are you doing up at this hour?'

My niece is wearing a pink cotton nightie and bunny slippers. She drags a huge stuffed unicorn in her wake. Lights from the house cast her sturdy little form in silhouette. She hurtles toward me and leaps into my arms. 'Aunt Beffney. You're here!'

She plasters my face with sloppy kisses. 'I love you a zillion billion and three.' My head fills with the warm scent of sleep and shampoo.

'That's all?'

'That's a whole, great big bunch,' she declares.

'Even though I don't have your surprise yet?'

Her face droops a trace but recovers quickly. 'Even though anything. You're my very favourite-ist person in the whole world.'

'Except Mommy,' I prompt.

She frowns at my foolishness. 'Mommy's a mommy, not a person.'

Ruthann nods. Her hair has been bobbed short, salon-streaked, and sprayed to the point of paralysis. 'All right, young lady. Say goodnight to Aunt Bethany and get yourself back to sleep. It's way past your bedtime.'

'But I already went to bed. I'm not sleepy any more,' my niece whines.

'Well, I am.' I muster an extravagant yawn. 'Long day, long drive. How about coming up and keeping me company while I get some rest, kiddo?'

'Okay,' she says grudgingly. 'But I am *not* going to sleep.'

Ten minutes later, I'm curled up on the spare bed in my

niece's room, which could pass for a Laura Ashley museum. Thirty seconds later, Amelia is unconscious. Treading quietly, I sneak out. I pause next door to kiss my sleeping nephew on the forehead.

Greg appears to have grown about a foot since my visit six months ago. The kid is developing cheekbones and other suspicious signs of impending adolescence. On the phone last month, he proudly boasted that he's now capable of producing really bad body odour. He knew I'd be proud.

I ruffle his dense brown waves. 'Sleep tight, tiger. See you in the morning.'

Downstairs, I find my sister in the den. She has set out a bottle of expensive Chardonnay and a platter of virtuous nibbles. I scan the discouraging array of veggies, fruits, and rice cakes.

'Are you sure we're related, Roo?' I ask.

'Wouldn't hurt you to lose a couple of pounds, Beth.'

'Oh yes it would.' I lift my glass. 'At least this will provide some of my minimum daily allowance of empty, unhealthy calories. To you, sis.'

'Great seeing you, Bethie. It's been for ever.'

We clink glasses. I drink in the sight of my sister, loving her with the usual fierce ambivalence.

'Where's Lee?'

She shrugs. 'What's going on with you, Beth? You look strung out.'

Though I'd intended to put it off until morning, I spill the whole sordid tale of Pip Stafford.

'This kid's only eight?' she says.

'Eight, going on incorrigible.'

'Sounds like the bad seed.'

'The bad seed could take lessons.'

For the next two hours, we talk about almost everything. As always, I'm amazed at the vast differences between us. Ruthie's by the book, I am barely in the footnotes. She is practical, community minded, politically conservative, tidy beyond belief, and a creature of predictable habit. I am none of the above. And so much more.

It's difficult to imagine how a single set of parents could produce such divergent offspring. For years, I've cast around for a reasonable explanation. I always fall back on the age difference, though I doubt that's it. I am younger, but only by twelve minutes. Otherwise, Ruthann and I share identical genes. Growing up, we also shared rooms, clothes, friends, confidences, fear of the water, allergies to shrimp and pineapple, and the chicken pox.

I've been told we're a soul divided, split from a single fertilized egg. Still, somehow, her half emerged hard-boiled while mine got slightly cracked and loosely scrambled.

She yawns. 'My God, look at the time. I'd better turn in. Kids'll be up in a couple of hours.'

It's almost three. 'Isn't Lee coming home?'

'Lee?'

'Your *husband*, Roo. Remember?'

Her lip quivers. 'Lee's – I mean – we're separated, Beth. I didn't want to tell you over the phone.'

'I'm sorry.'

'No, you're not. You never liked him.'

'Maybe not, but you did. What happened?'

She swipes a tear. 'Not what, who. I found out he was having an affair with his bridge partner.'

'Horseface Hannah, you mean?'

I met the woman once when Roo talked me into attending one of Lee's tournaments. The evening far exceeded even my lowest expectations.

'I guess she looks good enough to him.' She bites back a sob. 'It's been going on for months.'

'That little prick. He doesn't deserve you, Roo.'

A tiny smile tugs at her mouth. 'I like the sound of that.'

'That he doesn't deserve you? He doesn't.'

'Not that. I like the sound of: Lee, the little prick.'

'Well, he is one.'

'Has one, too,' she says, giggling.

Together, we enjoy a laugh. But Ruthann soon dissolves in tears. Life's not easy, even for my solid, mature, sensible twin.

I hold her as she weeps on to my shoulder. 'Ssh, honey. Take it easy.'

'I keep thinking I must've done something wrong. I feel so lost, Bethie. If only Mom – '

The unfinished thought spreads like nerve gas. The rock vault closes in my chest. A hard shot of guilt acts like Novocaine. Deadens my tongue. Numbs the impossible feelings. Stepping away, I crumple.

'Why can't you ever talk about it, Bethie?'

I shake my head.

For two decades, an army of well-intentioned people have been playing this tug-of-war, trying to drag the feelings from me. I'm told I should let go, set the poison out to evaporate in scrutiny's glare.

My voice breaks free. 'Don't blame yourself for this Lee business, Roo. You did nothing wrong.'

Her words ride on anguished tics. 'My lawyer – says – I should – take – him – for everything – he's worth. But I can't even think – '

I want to say her lawyer's wrong. Lee's not worth much; she should take him for more. 'You don't have to deal with any of that now, honey. Go ahead. Cry it out.'

And she does. She weeps rivers of grief. Torrents challenge her custom-blended base and her everything-proof mascara. The crying will help, I think. Sorrow is easier to bear when it's diluted.

While she sobs against my chest, I chance a peek at her future. There'll be ample time for the nasty business side later. With two kids and endless things to divide, such a parting is never pleasant or simple.

In theory I've always been against alimony and property fights. But where my sister is concerned, theory flies out the window. I want Roo whole and happy again. I want her and the kids to remain as spoiled and unspeakably overprivileged as they've always been. Most of all, I want that arrogant bastard she married to pay through the nose for this crushing humiliation. Horseface Hannah, of all people. All I can say to that is: neigh.

76

I steer her from the room like an invalid. 'Come on, Roo. I'll tuck you in and tell you a night-night story.'

'Thanks – Bethie.' She's still bawling her heart out. 'I – feel so – much better – now. Thanks – to you.'

'I can see that.'

The master bedroom suite is a sea of mauve and silver silk. Everything is perfectly coordinated and criminally neat. Not a wrinkle defies the perfect contours of the quilted spread beneath the bed's silken canopy. Throw pillows clump in obedient groups.

I help my sister undress, as if she's three. Normally, Ruthann plays mother to my renegade child. The reversal feels strange, but I can't say I mind it. Doing unto others has certain clear advantages over having others doing unto you.

'It'll be okay, sweetie,' I soothe.

'For you, too, Beth,' she snuffles back.

That stops me short. For a time, Ruthann's problems have made me forget my own. Now, they come flooding back. What I learn on this trip may well make all the difference. I can only hope the change is for the good.

12

Trot, trot to Boston.
Trot, trot to Lynn.
Look out, baby,
You're going to fall in.
'Trot, trot to Boston'

By the time I drag myself out of bed, the house is deserted. A note in my sister's prim hand flaps from a magnet on the refrigerator door. I am to help myself to the waiting coffee, fresh-squeezed juice, and homemade bran muffins. After that, my mandate is to have a pleasant day.

The note goes on to explain that Marta, the Colombian housekeeper, is due to arrive at nine. I should also expect scheduled appearances by Manuel, the Portuguese gardener, and Oswaldo, the Mexican pool man. Kinga, the Swedish sitter, will pick up the children at camp and ferry them to their various post-vacation-activity activities.

Before she had kids of her own, my sister used to join me in scoffing at frantic parents who programmed their children's every waking breath. But while Greg was merely hypothetical, Roo caught the bug. From birth, my niece and nephew have been pummelled with ceaseless, relentless enrichment.

The madness isn't limited to the children. My sister's schedule would challenge an air traffic controller. During her spare nanoseconds she has her hair and nails done, takes aerobics, and studies Japanese, often all at once. Today must be an extraordinarily light one. According to her note, she'll return from work by six-fifteen. In case I need to reach her, she leaves her office number, her beeper number, and the number in the car. Dinner will be served by Hilde, the German cook, promptly at seven. If my pleasant day out isn't over by then, would I kindly call Bela, the Russian receptionist at the agency, and let her know?

I have to chuckle. Even in cataclysm, Roo is Roo. She's ever efficient. Always attendant to the most minuscule detail. Poor darling has never known the joy of irrational thinking or the release that only a first-rate tantrum can provide.

I down two cups of coffee. I try to dupe my sluggish neurons into believing the Java is not decaf, but they're not that easily fooled.

Patsy Culvert harps that I'm hopelessly addicted to caffeine, which is, as she smugly asserts, a drug. I prefer to consider coffee a neutral necessity. Sort of a foundation garment for the brain. Without it, my thoughts sag. Reasoning bounces around, unsightly. My attitude yields to the brute force of gravity.

At the back of the pantry I find some soft drinks that promise a genuine jolt. That's where Ruthie stashes the company contraband.

I try one of her bran muffins, but the taste is far too wholesome. Rummaging through the pantry again, I discover a large bag of candy corn. It's stale, probably vintage several Hallowe'ens ago. I'm certain Ruthie only bought the stuff for decoration. My sister dismisses trash foods as unfit for human consumption. She claims she has no use for sweets, but I know better. As kids, we would duel to the death over the larger share of a Twinkie. I can still see the rapturous look on little Roo's face as a Hershey's kiss melted teasingly on her tongue. My sister has experienced the sacrament of chocolate. One never really forgets.

The petrified candy requires patient chewing, but the sugar, artificial flavouring, and preservatives are precisely what my weary body craves. Two handfuls and a couple of Pepsis later, I start to come alive.

After a brisk shower, I head out. Twenty minutes later, I'm bucking the downtown Norwalk traffic. I find the place easily enough, but no parking space. On my fourth circuit

79

of the block, I spot a small sign pointing toward Town Hall. The municipal building is two blocks away. In the broad, adjacent lot are plenty of free spaces.

The shop is closed when I arrive, but an eager young man races up behind me, wielding the key. He has the small head, broad jaw, and twitchy manner of a chipmunk. He's dressed in dark slacks, a tweed sports coat, and a dotted bow-tie.

'Sorry to keep you, miss. Just be a minute.' He fiddles with the doorknob, anxiously jiggling as the lock resists. 'Had to stop at the post office. Took for ever.'

At last, the door swings open. The young man stumbles in, waving for me to follow. 'People take no pride in their work today. An hour to get stamps, would you believe?'

He's flipping on the lights as he blithers. Strutting about the shop, he turns the page on the wall calendar, adjusts the clock, and feeds stacks of freshly minted singles, fives, and tens to the cash register. Finished, he assumes his post behind the desk. 'There now. How can I help you?'

I fish Pip Stafford's picture from the pocket of my khaki shorts. On the back is the name, address, and slogan of this store: *O'Malley's Fine Photo Finishing – Memories in a flash*.

'Do you remember this little boy?'

I'm praying that the photograph will inspire a flood of helpful recollections. Hopefully, Adam Stafford bringing his film here means he and Pip lived in the area. If I can learn precisely where, I'm sure I can find a neighbour willing to fill in some of the missing pieces.

With a fleeting glance, the clerk hands the picture back. 'Nope.'

'Please take another look. This was taken at least six years ago.'

His lips purse in distaste. 'I can see that. We only use Kodak papers and a top processing plant in Atlanta. Unfortunately, the former proprietor wasn't as meticulous. Look at the quality. So grainy.'

'Where can I find the former owner?'

'You can't. Mrs O'Malley passed on a year ago.'

My heart sinks. 'But she must have left records . . .'

'Actually, she did. Boxes and boxes of them. How'd you know?'

'I just figured.'

'I've kept them in the basement. Guess I thought they might be worth something some day.'

'Great. Mind if I take a look? I need to find out where this child's family lived.'

'Oh, no. That won't be possible.'

'I'll gladly pay you. This is *very* important to me.'

'I'm afraid you misunderstand. The records Mrs O'Malley left are forty-fives. Everly Brothers, Dion and the Belmonts. Like that. I think they belonged to one of her former clerks.'

'She didn't leave *customer* records?'

'No, those she took. Right before closing, we got into a foolish wrangle over some fixtures. Mrs O'Malley got mad and walked off with the sales files.'

'No customer records?' I dumbly repeat. I can't accept that my final chance is crumbling to ash. 'Nothing on computer?'

'Nothing period. Months after the old lady died, I called her son. I was planning a big promotion for the shop. Thought I might be able to cut a deal with him for the mailing list. He told me Mrs O'Malley had moved to a senior residence. Her room there was small, so she had to toss out everything but the bare essentials.' For a moment, he's lost in reverie. 'I guess it's true what they say: you really can't take it with you.'

Heading toward Town Hall, I pass a toy shop. They carry teddy bear backpacks in assorted colours. I choose the red bear for its honest, open expression.

Next, I need a gift for my nephew. Greg is your typical ten-year-old male, delighted by anything revolting and/or violent. The boy's ideal gift would combine hordes of dead things, ugly insects, and toilet humour. Eagerly, I search

81

the shelves. But if such a perfect plaything exists, the store is understandably out of it.

I seek help from a lanky adolescent stockboy. He recommends a video game. The package features a slavering lizard. 'Kid'll love it,' he assures me. 'It's really gross.'

Though I know it's a long shot, I stop in at several shops on the way to the car. No one recognizes Pip's snapshot. None of the salespeople I question is familiar with the name Stafford or an educator of Adam Stafford's description.

But that doesn't tell me much. Norwalk is a sizeable city surrounded by a slew of small towns. Adam and Pip could have lived in any one of them and not be known to the people I've approached.

Or they might have lived somewhere else entirely. Adam could have had his film developed while he was in the area on business or simply passing through. Someone other than Adam might have taken Pip's picture here or elsewhere, had it developed, and sent it on. I see no end to the discouraging possibilities. But I do not discourage easily.

At Town Hall, I bypass the parking lot and head for the building. There, I stop at the Hall of Records, the Board of Health, the Superintendent of Schools, and the Mayor's office. At each office, I show Pip's photo around and ask if anyone is familiar with people named Stafford. One woman at the Board of Health eagerly reports that her silver pattern is Staffordshire's Victorian lace.

'Hey, if you come across anyone else who has it, let me know,' she pleads. 'The pattern's discontinued, and I'd kill for six more settings.'

I'm back at Ruthie's before eleven. Several empty hours stretch before me. I search for a nice non-productive way to fill them. A long bout of sneezing uses up several minutes. But when it subsides, I'm at a loss.

I'm out of my element in this house. Even the most devout procrastinator feels constrained in the face of alphabetized spices and CDs. Chastened by Ruthie's fastidiousness, I go to the study.

82

I force myself to tackle the overdue reports. Soon, I'm lost in recollections. Scribbling away, I finish the first one in record time. That spurs me on. Aside from two bathroom breaks and a gourmet lunch of chunky peanut butter and sliced bananas, I work without interruption. I get through three reports.

I'm so absorbed, I don't hear my sister's key in the lock. It takes Amelia's flying tackle to wrench my thoughts from Danny Goichman's motor development.

'Aunt *Beffney*! Guess *what*? I'm gonna be in Mrs *Brand-stetter's* class!'

Prying her little arms loose, I am able to breathe again. 'That's great, sweetheart. Mrs Brandstetter must be very, very nice.'

The child shrugs. 'I don't know. She's new.'

'I bet you're going to love kindergarten.'

Tiny furrows pleat her brow. 'They just *call* it that, you know. It's not really a garden.'

'Is that a fact?'

Eager nod. 'They have to do it inside because of the rain and everything.'

'Makes sense.'

She props her hands on her hypothetical hips. 'You only *call* it a kinter-garden because that's its name, Aunt Beffney.'

'Thanks for telling me, sweetie. I always wondered about that.'

Greg is slumped against the doorframe. '*Kinter-garden*,' he mocks. 'You're such a bean dip, Amelia.'

'*You* are.'

Greg snickers. 'Bean dip, shrimp dip,' he taunts. 'Dippy little dippity-do.'

Amelia is fast losing control. Five-year-old fuses are not all that long. 'Take it back, Greggie. I *mean* it.'

'Cheesy little bean dip.'

'Take it *back*!'

Amelia charges at her brother like a buffalo who's been

83

photographed by one Japanese tourist too many. Caught off guard, Greg topples.

'All right, you two. That's enough,' Ruthann says.

Recovering, Greg reddens. 'I'm gonna kill you, you little twerp.'

'Mommy, *Mom*!' Amelia screams. She's encamped behind the rock-solid fortress of Ruthie's thighs.

'Cut it out, you two,' Ruthie pleads ineffectually. My sister's harshest voice wouldn't slice warm butter.

'Come here, you little mealy bug,' Greg orders. 'Face the music.'

'*Help*!' Amelia screeches. 'Mommy, please! Don't let him give me a music face!'

'Gregory Atkinson. That's enough!' Ruthie shrills.

Greg grows ever more threatening and obnoxious, which inspires Amelia to unprecedented histrionic heights. Ruthie rails on, escalating her threats to the level of pure absurdity.

'Quit it, or you're getting your own apartment, Gregory. You too, Amelia. I swear it.'

I bite back a smile. Even at my age, watching a sibling squirm brings a certain guilty pleasure.

'I'm gonna squash you, you little mealy bug.'

'*Mommy, HELP*!'

I've had enough. I haul out the gifts, which distracts the kids at once. Amelia dashes off to fill her backpack with Barbie paraphernalia. Greg heads to the playroom to try the new game.

Ruthie draws a cleansing breath. 'How'd it go with you today, Beth?'

'It didn't. The snapshot was useless.'

Ruthie sighs. 'Can't say my day was any better. For months, I've shown the Beckmans everything in the county that's come on in their range. I've taken them out nights, weekends. Put up with their bratty little boy and their slobberhound. Finally, I thought they were ready to put a binder on the Wallach's Point place. Then, first thing this

84

morning, I hear they've bid on an exclusive with the Medavoy Agency.'

'Sorry, Roo.'

Her eyes are sad. 'Guess it's not my millennium.'

'Mine either.' Drawing Pip's picture from my pocket, I toss it toward the trash can.

The photo hits the rim and bounces out again. Before I can bend to retrieve it, Ruthie does. As her eye catches the image, her expression shifts.

'What, Roo? You *know* him?'

She stares in silence.

'Roo? Answer me, damn it.'

That breaks the spell. 'No, the baby's not familiar – '

I want to strangle her for subjecting me to a blip of false hope. *Bean dip.*

' – But I *do* know the house.'

'What house?' Grabbing the shot from Roo's hand, I peer at it hard.

'This house.'

My sister points to the amorphous blob behind the smiling tyke in the stroller. Staring, I make out vague stripes that could be white clapboard and several shiny rectangular spaces that might be windows.

'That's the Potter house in East Norwalk,' Ruthie goes on.

I try to bring the blur into better focus. 'You sure?'

'Absolutely. I sold it last month for close to the asking price. They should all be that easy.'

'You know the *address*? You can actually tell me how to *get* there? I can't *believe* it!'

'Calm yourself, Beth. No big deal.'

'Yes it is. You don't know what this means to me. How can I ever thank you, Roo? Name it.'

She frowns, considering. After a beat, her look brightens. 'I know. You can murder Lee.'

'You really think that little bastard's worth a prison term?'

She settles an arm on my shoulders and steers me

toward the kitchen. 'All right, Beth. For now, you can peel the potatoes. But think about bumping Lee off for me, will you? I honestly think it would help.'

13 When I went out for a walk one day,
My head fell off and rolled away.
And when I saw that it was gone,
I picked it up and put it on.
                    'A Walk One Day'

My sensible sister keeps me from charging out the door.
Adam Stafford's possible former neighbours aren't likely
to welcome a stranger who comes knocking after dark. This
is the New York Metro-paranoid area. Not Grangeville.

'Get some rest, Beth,' Roo says. 'You look beat.'

'I am.'

When her real estate office opens in the morning, Ruthie
promises to get me the neighbours' names and phone numbers from the reverse directory. I can call. Make appointments. Act rationally. Which would be a refreshing change.

She's right. But anticipation keeps me up and tossing.
Near dawn, when I've finally slipped down the well to
unconsciousness, I'm awakened by a violent shudder.

My first groggy thought is of an earthquake. Cracking an
eye, I see nothing unusual. Then, as I watch, the mattress
sprouts a large, straining hump. Fear grips me. But soon
the mound erupts in giggles.

'Come on, Amelia. It's too early,' I grump. Turning over,
I burrow under the pillows.

I am joined by a mass of curls and warm, eager breathing. 'Can't I stay? Please, Aunt Beffney?'

'Okay, but only if you go right to sleep. No talking.'

'*No* talking,' Amelia vows with great feeling. But an
instant later, she launches a barrage of how-comes. 'How
come you're not a mommy, Aunt Beffney?'

'Because I'm not ready. Now hush.'

'How *come* you're not ready?'

'Because I haven't met Mr Right.'

'Who's that?'

I sigh. 'I mean I haven't met the right man yet.'

'Alec Wrightman's daddy, you mean? He's *old*.'

Five-thirty a.m., and the child wants to play 'Who's on First?' 'I mean I don't have a boyfriend, Amelia. Now how about some sleep?'

'How come you don't have a boyfriend?'

'It's complicated.'

'How come?'

She's scrabbling up my back, now. Scaling Aunt Everest. 'Don't you *want* to be a mommy?'

'I'd rather be asleep.'

Amelia flops back on the bed. 'I'm gonna have lots and lots and *lots* of kids.'

'How come?'

Amazingly, we drift off. Roo allows me to languish in bed until almost seven. Camp has ended for the summer, but Amelia is enrolled in a two-week dance and nature session, while Greg has soccer and tennis and golf. Afterwards, both kids make their usual rounds of piano, karate, nature, religion, art, riding, and French. I'm sure I've left something out. Roo has not.

My sister manages to have the two of them dressed, fed, equipped for the dizzying day's agenda, and out by eight-fifteen. By nine, the phone rings. It's Roo on the line from her desk at Flanders Realty. As she reads them off, I copy the names and numbers of the ten current property owners on Norwalk's Buckingham Lane.

At the first two homes I call, there's no answer. A young Spanish-speaking woman picks up at the third number. I remember a smattering of my high school Spanish, but not nearly enough to explain the reason for my call. I blather something incoherent and hang up.

My next attempt yields a busy signal. Moving on, I reach a gruff male voice at the home of Milton and Lila LeBlang.

Before I'm able to introduce myself and explain the purpose of the call, he snarls: 'Not interested.' The line goes dead.

Moving on, I reach an answering machine followed by an answering service. The busy line stays busy.

I put down the phone. I can't afford to waste my few remaining chances. Ruthann's cautions aside, I'm convinced I'll have better luck in person.

According to the map I pilfered from Ruthie's kitchen drawer, Buckingham Lane is in the eastern part of Norwalk, near the Connecticut Turnpike. The area's centrepiece is Stew Leonard's, a mammoth market and gardening centre with a pets' zoo for the kids. The company's founder used to be hailed as a marketing pioneer. The store provided bulk goods at bargain prices. That, and the friendly family atmosphere, drew hordes of devoted shoppers from miles around.

Roo used to moon over her man, Stew Leonard, claiming he covered every detail. At his indictment it emerged that he'd even thought of short-weighting and tax evasion. The company was fined millions and the founder found himself in a cell.

Buckingham is a small, narrow street half a mile from the market. Ancient maples arch overhead in a bower of thick, welcome shade. The houses are of the modest, trim, largely style-free type Roo calls starter homes. Tidy fences frame small, well-tended lawns. Several of the yards are cramped with kiddie pools and swing sets. Sedans and minivans line the drives.

I stop at the first house on my list, property of Jane and Mitchell Algus. The bell draws a short, pretty woman with a pie-face and long black braids. She has a cordless phone pinned to her ear by a shoulder and a mewling, red-faced toddler astride her hip.

Still chatting on the line, she motions me to a small, cluttered kitchen. The counters sprawl with grocery bags, magazines, and clipped coupons. Cartoons blast from the small TV set near the double oven. Grabbing the remote, she flips it off.

'Right, Mom. 'Bye, then. Speak to you soon.' She smiles broadly at me. 'Sit down, please. Want some coffee?'

'Thanks, I'm fine. I just –'

'Tea, then?'

She puts the kettle on and settles the weeping babe in a high chair. His curly hair is rumpled. The bib of his checked overalls is drenched with mournful drool. Poor little guy appears inconsolable. But the sight of a lidded clown cup turns him right around. Grasping the handles, he flashes a toothless smile.

Bustling about, the woman sets out two cups. She lines a tray with doilies and transfers brownies from a bakery box. Astonished, I realize she hasn't asked so much as my name yet. Even in Grangeville, folks aren't this neighbourly and accommodating.

'Please, you don't have to go to all this trouble.'

Her smile is as broad as the baby's. 'No trouble at all, Nicole. Mitchell's so glad to be working for your Dan. I've been hoping you'd find time to come by and get acquainted.'

I stand. 'I'm sorry. Obviously you're expecting someone else. I'm not Nicole.'

Her jaw drops. 'Who are you, then?'

'Bethany Logan. I'm trying to track down some people who lived on this block about six years ago. Name's Stafford. Did you know them?'

The woman lifts her son and clutches him protectively. 'I'll have to ask you to leave.'

'A little boy named Pip Stafford? The father's Adam?'

'You have some nerve, lady. Some nerve.' She hustles me out the door and slams it shut.

I fare no better on the next two stops. A small child in a sundress answers the door at the home of Stan and Sally Buckstone. When I ask for her mom or dad, she informs me that her mother is in the shower.

'I'll come back in a few minutes, then.'

She frowns, annoyed at my incomprehension. Cupping her lips, she leans closer. 'She *really* went to the cleaner

90

and the vet's. That's what it *means* when you say your mommy's in the shower.'

At the Doris and Armand Vella residence, I find a sitter and four squabbling kids. Whoever was talking on the phone when I tried to get through to the Irizarry place, has gone out.

The final name on my list is a Mr H. P. Riley. His address corresponds to the sombre saltbox at the end of the road. This house stands in stark contrast to its neighbours. Painted a smoggy grey, the place huddles behind a six-foot-high link fence capped by fang-like spikes. Instead of the standard bird feeders and window-boxes, this home is festooned with BEWARE THE DOG and NO TRESPASSING signs.

The gate is locked. When I jiggle the latch, a disembodied voice growls from the lamppost.

'Who's there?'

Mute with shock, I wheel around, searching. Finally, I spot the tiny speaker embedded in the upright. A red light winks on beside it.

When I've recovered enough, I state my name. 'I'm trying to track down friends of mine who used to live here, Mr Riley. People named Stafford. Did you know them?'

The light on the post glows green and the gate creaks open. I step through warily, watching for the promised vicious dogs.

A second speaker is perched beside the door. 'How'd you know Stafford?' the phantom demands.

I offer a bent version of the truth. 'I worked with him. We lost touch.'

'Oh yeah? How do I know you're not in on it?'

'In on what?'

'Spell that name of yours.'

After I do, there's a long silence. I'm about to quit and leave when the speaker squawks to life again. 'You check out okay. Come on in.'

I check out?

With a mechanical clack, the door drifts open. Inside, I face inky darkness. Blackout shades bar the sunshine.

Grim painted walls and dour furnishings steal any stray atoms of light.

'Up here,' the voice commands. 'And step on it. I haven't got all day.'

Fear propels me in reverse. 'Thanks anyway, Mr Riley. I have to go. Sorry to bother you.'

I'm halfway down the walk when the front door flings open. A huge man storms out, gesturing wildly. 'What's the story, lady? You want to hear about Adam Stafford and the kid or not?'

I haven't mentioned the headmaster's first name. This Riley person must know him. 'I do, but —'

'But not enough to deal with the likes of Riley, that it?' the giant roars. 'Don't worry yourself, lady. Hap don't bite.'

Riley is a mountain of a man. Six-five, minimum, with a flat-top, granite features, and deep-set steely eyes. He wears hunter's pants, combat boots, and a camouflage vest. Around his waist hangs a gear belt with slots for knives, guns, spare ammo, and grenades.

I'm tempted to bolt, but this weirdo may have the information I want. 'Were you a friend of Adam Stafford's?'

'Friend?' Riley snorts. 'Be like trying to cosy up to a rattler.'

'But you knew him? Knew his family?'

'Oh, I *knew* him all right. I had his *number*, which was *up*.'

'Did the Staffords live here long?'

'Stayed ten months on a two-year lease and bolted. Stuck Pete Lindstrom for the rent and utility bills. I warned Pete not to rent to that scum. I sent Lindstrom caution vibes. Shipped them all the way to Dallas, Texas, which cost me big time. But Pete chose to *ignore* me. Hap *hates* ignorance. It is *not* bliss.'

'Bolting on a lease doesn't sound like the Adam Stafford I know.'

'Yeah? Well, maybe you don't *know* him so frigging *well*. Depends on your *lens*, you see what I'm saying? First time I laid eyes on the guy, I used my 30x corneal penetrating

92

eye beam with a pair of scopes and a brain filter. That baby can see through *any*thing, any*body*. Stafford was a maggot farm. Bad as that Bundy guy, only he was worms. Cops could have cracked the case wide open, if they'd listened to me. But they never do. Not about Hoffa. And not about Jackie boy, the quicker ripper-upper.'

'What case do you think Adam was involved in?'

'Not *think*. I *know*. You want proof, I'll show you.'

'That's okay . . .'

He puffs his contempt. 'Have it your way. Sooner or later, you'll have to face it. Everyone will. Stafford's just the *tip* of the iceberg. Vatican's involved, CIA, even those crooks who own the Loews East Theatres. Lowest of the Loews, they are. Order a large popcorn, those scumbags fill up the bottom half of the bag with air. It's frigging unAmerican.'

Riley's eyes are skittering madly. 'Plus, they promise you Sharon Stone and try to slip you a share-of-Sly-Stallone instead. It's all an elision. Sneaky bastards.'

'Very interesting, Mr Riley, but I really should be going.'

'No way to run, lady. No *place*. You can't escape this thing. Governor of Missouri's part of it and that one-eyed Israeli guy and those bozos in Vermont with the ice-cream company. Goes right up to the front office of the *New Yorker*. The goddamned *top*!'

I back slowly towards the fence. Riley raves on, frothing like a mad dog. 'It's gotten to NATO, Plato, OPEC, *Star Trek*, you name it. Spreading like kudzu, it is. Spreading fast as Maggie Thatcher's butt.'

'You'll have to excuse me, Mr Riley. I'm running late.'

He spews his contempt. 'Whole *world's* running late. Whole frigging *universe*. Every goddamned one of you's so far behind, it's *hopeless*. Trouble is you look at a man's face, crawl into his cre*den*tials. You figure a pretty Ivy boy like Stafford couldn't commit such a crime. But you're all wrong.'

Curiosity slows my retreat. Riley has crossed line from frightening to near funny. 'What crime?' I expect Riley to charge Adam with some monumental sin against humanity. The murder of Christ, perhaps. Or the invention of voice mail. I can't wait to tell Roo about this crackpot. She should keep him in mind in case a doomsday bunker comes on the market. Or a nice padded cell.

'The Haskel kidnapping.'

That stops me cold. Ethan Haskel's abduction commanded front-page headlines for months. On his second birthday, the towheaded toddler had been snatched from the nursery in his family's home right here in Norwalk. A massive international effort yielded no solid clues. There was the usual flurry of parental pleas and posted rewards. The FBI pursued countless leads, but the little boy was never recovered.

'Are you suggesting Adam Stafford took the Haskel child?'

'I'm not suggesting any such thing. I'm *saying* he did.' On his fingers, he enumerates the reasons. 'First: Stafford moves in to the Lindstrom place alone. No sign of a wife or kid. Then, two days after Ethan Haskel's snatched, I'm out for a walk. Passing the Lindstrom house, I hear a baby crying. Next day, I run into Stafford at the bank. When I ask about the kid, he tries to hand me some bull story about a stray cat. I damned well know the difference between a cat and a baby.

'Two: I call the cops, the FBI, every possible interested party. Naturally, they give me the usual runaround. The entire military-industrial complex has had me pegged as a loony since the business with that starship from Jupiter. But that's beside the point. When I can't get any of those clowns to take me seriously, I start surveilling the Stafford place on my own. I hook up my insta-cam with a motion-sensitive molar remote. I bug Stafford's place with this sweet new audio system. Thing's sensitive enough to pick up a fly fart at two hundred yards.

'There was a baby in that house all right. Woman, too. Name of Jenny. I caught plenty of talk between her and Stafford. *Real* interesting stuff. Two of them went on and on about the authorities. Kept saying how worried

94

they were about getting found out. They were careful not to mention the Haskel case in so many words, but it doesn't take a genius to add two and two.'

No, it doesn't, I think. A paranoid lunatic can handle the task nicely. I'm sorry I've stuck around to hear him out. The man is a raving wacko. 'That's very interesting, Mr Riley. See you.'

He doesn't seem to hear me. 'Things were moving right along. I almost had enough to nail the bastard. But Stafford must've gotten wind I was on to him. Probably found one of my bugs or got a look at the camera. Maybe one of my bugs got loose and bit him. Happens. Who knows? Anyway, that's when he ran.'

'Sure. Whatever you say.'

His shoulders hitch. 'Fine. No skin off my knees. Shame about that Haskel kid, though.'

I keep walking.

'Shame about his family, too. Six years now, and they don't know whether their son is dead or alive. Must be hell.'

'Sure, Mr Riley. I'm sure it is.'

'Goddamnit, I *told* you, I've got proof.'

I'm not inclined to argue with the nut. But taped innuendo isn't proof. Especially when the tapes are imaginary.

He seems to read my mind. 'I'm not talking about the tapes now. I've kept track of Stafford over the years. Followed his moves. He still got the boy with him, I suppose.'

'Of course.'

'Well, I can prove to you that boy's not Stafford's at all. He's Ethan Haskel.'

I pause. 'How can you prove it?'

'Come on inside. I'll show you.'

As I recall, that was precisely what the wolf said to Red Riding Hood. Just because Riley is paranoid, doesn't mean he can't be after me. 'Thanks anyway.'

The giant rolls his shifty eyes. 'You are one piece of work, lady. Just stay there. I'll bring it *out* to you.' He disappears inside and returns with his arms full of computer equipment. 'Pain in the butt,' he mutters as he goes inside for more.

My mind is reeling. What is this man up to? And why is he so fixated on Ethan Haskel? Could he have been involved in the kidnapping himself?

'Don't know why I bother,' he mutters. 'Nobody gives a fried banana.'

In minutes, he has a laptop computer linked to a printer and the phone line he has snaked out the door. Seated on the grass, he works the keyboard.

The screen lights with white characters on a sea of sapphire blue. Riley types some commands and waits a minute. A multicoloured display greets him by name and invites his input. He types again. Over his shoulder, I read the initials, NCMEC.

Before I can ask, he explains. 'That's the National Clearinghouse for Missing and Exploited Children.' His fingers fly again. The screen changes. A graphic image forms, starting at the top of the display and slowly scrolling down. In seconds, I see that it's the face of a small boy. The child has pale eyes and a halo of fine blond curls. My mouth goes dry. This baby bears a striking resemblance to the snapshot I have of Pip Stafford.

Under the image is the name Ethan John Haskel. The child's date of birth, height and weight, and parents' vital statistics are also listed. So is the date of his disappearance: August 29, 1988.

My stomach churns. Pip was born in August of 1986. He and Ethan Haskel are exactly the same age. But I can't accept the insane implication. 'So they look alike. So do lots of babies.'

Riley lifts a mammoth hand. 'Hang on.' He presses a rash of keys. Waits. Pecks again. Sniffs his impatience. 'There. It'll come up in two or three minutes.'

'What will?'

'Shot of how the Haskel boy would look today. Computer calculates bone and muscle growth. How the features would develop. Probable changes in teeth and skin. Differences in hair tone and texture. The works. The likenesses it puts out are uncanny. Central agency works them up on all the open cases once a year. They're sent out to police departments, plastered on milk cartons, blown up on posters. Like that. Kids have been identified, sometimes ten, fifteen years after a snatch from these updates.'

The screen goes dark. Slowly, a lighter haze lines the top. Gradually, it spreads downward. I recognize the peak of a head. A shock of light hair. The smooth span of a forehead.

My temples throb. The brows are visible now, slim and arched. I see the eyelids. Lashes. Pale staring eyes.

I can't recognize the face yet. Nor can I rule anyone out. The wait is excruciating.

By degrees, the nose forms. The ears. More of the hair is revealed. A cold fire builds in the pit of my stomach. It could be Pip.

I hold my breath. The graphic carves the upper lip. The rest of the mouth. The contours of the chin.

My mind bristles. I'm washed by dizzy heat.

Riley's mouth curls in lazy satisfaction. 'Looks like you've seen yourself a ghost, Miz Logan.'

'It can't be. It's impossible.'

'Not at all. Right now, the experts claim there are only two, three hundred stranger abductions a year. Couple of years back, the same jerks put the number at 50,000 or more. They manipulate the statistics for the techno-environmentalist cabal. That Billy Gates character from the software company is the mastermind.

'Stafford was probably one of his agents. Gates is young. Wears ugly glasses, too. But he knows how to pick a staff. He's got that llama guy from Tibet and the King of Morocco. Happens I heard it right from the horse's mouth. Dustin Hoffman himself called to tell me. Man is good. Smooth. Pretended it was a wrong number, but I knew.

'Anyhow, cases like the Haskel baby are big business. Stir the pot when the citizenry gets too complacent. It's all subliminal. Causes anarchy and immune system disorders, but they don't give a rat's ass.'

I block out his crazed rambling. Mind reeling, I mutter. 'What if Pip Stafford *is* Ethan Haskel? My God. What do I do?'

A smug grin smears Riley's face. 'Simple, Miz Logan. You find the boy and return him to his family. And you do it before that so-called daddy of his gets wind you're on to him and hits the road again.'

Riley prints out the damning picture on the screen and thrusts it at me. 'Watch your back, Miz Logan. And whatever you do, don't mention Hap Riley's name.'

14 I try Ruthann at the agency, but the receptionist tells me my sister is out with clients. Neither Roo nor the children are expected home for hours. I can't wait.

I leave a note under the refrigerator magnet explaining that I had to get back to Hinsdale. I don't say why. I'm crossing into perilous, unknown territory. I love Roo and the kids far too much to drag them with me.

On the long ride back to New Hampshire, I try to plot a sensible course of action. But I've entered a maze. I have no idea how to proceed. And I see no way out. The obvious escape routes are blocked by circumstance.

I can't go to the Grangeville police, not when half of the force is Harley Beamis. Even if I could be guaranteed a private audience with Sheriff Huff, chances are the man would not believe me. Adam Stafford is a pillar of the community. It would take far more than me, Hap Riley's raving allegations, and some newfangled computer gimmickry to bring the headmaster down.

By now, almost everyone has surely left Hinsdale for term break. I don't trust any of the few remaining staff members enough to let them in on a ticking bomb like this. If only Hal were still around. I'd give anything for my friend's generous ear and wise counsel. But he's on a trip to the Australian outback. He's not scheduled to return until two days before the fall term. By then, all this could be history. Including me.

I'm forced to consider the unimaginable. Snatching a child. Running off with him. Racing a step ahead of the law.

What if we're caught? I could wind up in jail. Worse, if Stafford finds out what I know, it could put Pip in serious peril. Who knows what desperate measures the man might take to cover his crime?

Pressing the window down, I force a few slow breaths. I'm in way over my head here. And sinking fast.

Slow down, Bethany.

Thinking rationally, I realize there is no particular rush. No one but that madman Hap Riley knows what I've learned. So many years after the kidnapping, Adam Stafford must be confident that he'll never be caught. Otherwise, he'd be hiding behind a phoney name. Keeping a much lower profile.

I have time to examine my options. I can find out who's been handling the Haskel case and contact them. That is, *if* the case is still open. But even if it's not, I'm sure I can persuade someone in authority somewhere to take this ungodly mess off my hands.

That feels much better. I have time. Breathing room. My stomach settles. My AWOL appetite makes a tentative return. At the next exit, I leave the road and find a diner. In the restroom, I splash my face and comb my hair. Feeling close to sane, I down a grilled cheese sandwich and a Coke. When the waitress returns, I order coffee and rice pudding. I keep telling myself there's no rush.

It's not quite 3 p.m. when I cross the state line to New Hampshire. What remains of the ride would put me on the Grangeville Road before the end of Harley Beamis's shift. Killing time, I stop at a roadside shop and pace among the geegaws. The store features genuine New Hampshire wood carvings made in Taiwan and ten-cent penny candy. A sign at the front promises EAR PIERCING WHILE YOU WAIT. Normally, I'm amused by such absurdity, but not today. The incredible truth about Pip Stafford rides my shoulder like a sharp-clawed bird. It whispers mockingly, ceaselessly, in my ear: *Adam is a kidnapper. Pip is not his little boy.*

Nearing four, I get back on the road. I will hit Grangeville during the twilight zone between the close of Harley Beamis's shift and his standard arrival time at the Dog &

Pony. It's a risk, but I decide to take it. I'm anxious to get to Hinsdale and see Pip/Ethan with my own eyes.

I do not run into Harley, but my relief is fleeting. Approaching the turnoff to the school, the full horror of the situation slams at me again. Pip is not Pip. Somewhere, his real family lives with the constant ache of loss. For years, they've had to bear the cruel burden of hope. Every blond little boy could be theirs. Every knock at the door could bring the child back to them. Any breath they'd drawn in a different way could have averted this hideous pain.

Once, while Roo was down with the flu, I took Amelia and Greg to Rye Playland for an afternoon of serious spoiling. Amelia fell asleep in her stroller. Greg was doing his third turn on some child-sized Waring blender, working his way into a nauseous frenzy. Dying of thirst from a luncheon of hot dogs and chips, I ducked ten yards away to the water fountain. When I returned five seconds later, Amelia was gone.

I found her two breathless minutes later, gawking at Greg's ride from beside the ticket counter. But I'll never forget the utter terror, the tearing inside that signalled my slow, excruciating inner death.

I imagine taking Ethan Haskel home, seeing his family restored.

Driving the campus road, I spot some kids playing stickball on the Primary Green. Pip Stafford is among them, hunched with a stick bat on his shoulder.

Not Pip, I sternly remind myself. *Ethan Haskel*.

I pause to watch him. Poor baby. How awful it must have been for him. Little guy was ripped from his mother's arms. Wrenched from everything warm and dear and familiar. Carried off by a monstrous stranger.

Then, he was branded with a new name. Crammed into a new world and ill-fitting identity. Saddled with bewildering rules and prohibitions.

All the vexing pieces fall into place. This is why Stafford's so secretive. This is why he taught the child to avoid talk-

ing about the past, being photographed. Their whole existence hinges on this monstrous lie.

No wonder the kid is hurt and angry and confused. No
wonder he looks for ways to unload the pain.

I ache to race over and hug him. I want to soothe him
as I would a broken bird. I'm overcome with feeling for the
child, but I have to keep every bit of it to myself.

I've been spotted. The trio of boys stops playing. They
stare my way. Leaning on the stick bat, Pip's face forms a
hateful dare.

Not Pip's face. Ethan's.

I repeat the name Ethan Haskel, trying to drill the
unthinkable fact through my resistant skull. Ethan is Pip.
Pip is Ethan.

Only two lonely cars occupy the staff lot. One is Patsy
Culvert's white Mazda Miata. The other belongs to Gus,
the handyman. I pull in beside his battered Ford.

As I step out of the Jeep, Patsy bustles up behind me.

'Beth, Beth, Beth. Where *have* you been?'

'At my sister's.'

Her face looks pained. Or maybe it's the noose-tight tank
top and suffocating jeans. 'You simply *don't* run off without
a word like that, dearie. It's not *done.*'

'Yes it is, Patsy. I did it.'

'Well, you should have heard the flying rumours. Dick
Bruce said you had some awful illness in your family, and
Denny D'Amato told everyone you were sick yourself.
Norma thought maybe you were pregnant, but I told her
you always look that way.'

'Sweet of you.'

Circling her, I grab my suitcase from the trunk. As I
head toward staff quarters, Patsy follows. She's buzzing in
my ear like a bloodthirsty mosquito. I want to slap her.

'Hinsdale's a very small place, Beth. If I were you, I'd be
more careful of my reputation.'

If you were me, I'd hang myself. 'Thanks for the hot tip,
Patsy.'

102

'All right. Be that way,' she huffs. 'I don't know what's come over you, Beth. Honestly.'

'Sounds like everyone else does, Patsy. Why don't you just ask around?'

Staff quarters have the hollow, empty feel of an abandoned cave. Upstairs, I drop my suitcase and flop wearily on the bed. There I lie for the longest time, staring at the ceiling.

Shadows mass, nature's Rorschach test for the terminally perplexed. In them, I see horrifying images. A lurking stingray. Slithering eels. Bobbling swimmers swallowed by ravenous waves.

All your fault, Bethany. My death is all your fault.

It occurs to me that I don't have to do anything. I could lie inert indefinitely, surrendering to the inexorable forces of atrophy and decay. Somewhere, I read that it takes a mere three days to die of thirst. But it's a lousy way to go, wrenching cramps, senses screaming.

I consider the sadness my passing would bring. Danny and Billy would surely miss me. My father and friends. Dear Hal. But surely Roo and the kids would be hit hardest. I conjure Amelia's plaintive little voice: *Aunt Beffney's never* ever *coming back? How can that be, Mommy? Doesn't she love us any more?*

My eyes fill.

Beth, a suicide? How sad, they'll say. First her mother, now her.

Starvation takes an incredibly long time. Weeks and weeks. After a while, the body begins to feed on itself. Excess fat is cannibalized. Then muscle tissue.

I imagine my familiar contours flattening to bone. Flesh sagging. My skeleton poking through the papery remnants of my skin.

I picture myself a gaunt, dull-eyed waif from medieval fiction. Wrapped in rags. Wailing misery.

But real starvation needs no dramatic embroidery. The wasting body struggles for survival to the last. Eventually, all but the most vital functions cease. Voluntary movement is lost. Reason crumbles. The senses misfire, spewing wild hallucinations. Finally, a thick, black curtain descends, stifling the last gasp of consciousness. Coma sets in. Then comes the slow descent to death.

My stomach rumbles in ardent protest. My thoughts swerve abruptly to dinner. Nothing fuels the appetite like imaginary starvation.

During term break, most people gather for informal meals in the kitchen. But I can't face the thought of eating with the likes of Patsy Culvert and Pip.

Ethan.

Adam Stafford rarely takes his meals with the staff, but I can't risk even the slimmest chance that he might. I couldn't possibly face him. When next I see that man, it had better be his mug shot over a headline trumpeting his arrest for the kidnapping of Ethan Haskel.

I head for the Roadhouse. The town's only 'elegant' dining establishment serves an excellent meatloaf and mashed potato special. Nothing on the plate requires chewing, which is my concept of culinary utopia. My taste buds can rest quietly throughout the meal, all the way to the tapioca dessert with whipped cream, which is included. As an added benefit, Harley Beamis has been banned from the restaurant since he tossed a chair through the plate-glass window during a drunken snit.

Marla, the host and waitperson, seats me in front of the window's replacement. There are ten other patrons, quite a crowd by Grangeville standards.

Waiting for the food, I catch snips of conversation from the Bartlesbys, who occupy the table to my rear. Usually, I feel some guilt over my penchant for eavesdropping. Tonight, I deem it a necessary diversion. Maude and Howard Bartlesby own the local hardware store. Married for decades, they have their conversational waltz down pat.

'How many times have I told you not to give that dead-beat credit, Howie?'

'Millions and millions of times, Maude.'

'So, did he stiff you? Or what?'

104

'You know he did. What can I say?'

'You can say I was right.'

Deep sigh. 'You were right, Maude. You're always right. Even when you're wrong, you're right. *Especially* then. Happy now?'

'What's that supposed to mean?'

'Don't ask me. I'm always wrong, Maude.'

My attention drifts to the men seated two booths down. Craig Cassell is the local dentist, orthodontist, and dealer in antique decoys. His younger brother, Kurt, operates a combination insurance and travel agency out of his High Street home. Between them, they have five ex-wives and a dozen children.

'What're you thinking, Craig? Coconut cream or blueberry?'

'Neither. If we're talking Thanksgiving in Cancun, I haven't got much time to shed the flubber.'

'Speaking of which, I had a better idea. What would you say we hit Europe? London? Paris? Maybe a week on some sultry Greek island.'

'I'd say it sounds too expensive.'

'You'd be amazed,' Kurt says. 'I just booked a couple of international flights today. Fares are dirt cheap.'

'So am I, little brother. What are we talking?'

'Try two to Heathrow for under a grand. And that's last minute. Client decided to take his kid over during vacation. Called today looking for the next available flight. I was able to get them out of Logan on the red eye. Not bad, eh?'

'Which client?'

My heart squirms, waiting for his response.

'You know I don't breach confidentiality, Craig. Would you tell me who has plaque? Now about that dessert. I'm leaning toward the blueberry.'

I pay the check and leave. On the frantic drive back to school, I'm terrified that Adam and Pip might be gone already. I recall Hap Riley saying that he's followed the headmaster's movements over the years. The nutcase could have called for some reason and tipped Stafford that I was on to him.

With a flood of relief, I see lights blazing in the headmaster's house. His car is in the garage. As I watch, the light comes on in an upstairs bathroom. A small figure I recognize as Pip stands at the sink. After a few minutes, the bathroom goes dark and another room lights down the hall. Must be Pip's bedroom.

Ethan's.

Soon, a large figure crosses the living room. I can tell it's Adam. The television screen glows. The headmaster slumps in an armchair and props his feet on a hassock.

Logan Airport is nearly a three-hour drive. International flights require check-in an hour or more before departure. Even if Stafford was booked on a trip as late as midnight, he would have been on the road by now.

I've let my imagination run wild. Every schoolchild in the area is on vacation. Any one of several thousand other fathers could have booked the tickets Kurt Cassell described.

Adam isn't taking the Haskel boy anywhere. At least, not for now.

15 Eva dismissed Cal from her mind. No time now for regrets or recriminations. The Silence was about to begin.

Every year on the anniversary of her loss, Eva observed an ancient family ritual and slipped into total seclusion. For seven days, no boats were permitted to dock at the pier. The island suspended phone service. Mail was held at the central depot. Rand's link to the mainland electrical cable was disconnected. The house went still.

As the whirring of machinery ceased, Eva tuned to inner tides, the spectral voices of her ancestors: *the Silence is for peaceful introspection.*

Eva's island neighbours respected the ritual. So did the local boatsmen, who were barred from Rand's shores for the duration. Owners of the ferry company set their season's closing date to correspond to the start of this hallowed time. Even the noisome outsiders who camped in the state-owned nature preserve on the island's north side complied with the temporary ban. In six years, Eva hadn't heard a single note of protest.

Except Cal's.

You must not think of Cal, Eva. You must not allow sorry thoughts to interfere.

The Silence is for rest and redemption. The Silence heals.

She busied herself with necessary preparations. Rich summer rains had the cisterns brimming. Eva filled an oaken bucket and ferried water to the catch basin beside the back door. Without electricity to fuel the pump, there would be no running water.

The Silence is simplicity. Through simplicity comes grace.

Eva never minded what Cal deplored as the 'goddamned inconvenience'. She cooked in an iron kettle over the hearth. She bathed in the metal tub she set beside the

107

stove. She laundered the clothes with a scrub board and basin. Eva's people had lived this way for countless generations. Every time she performed a chore by ancient rote, Eva felt the powerful connection.

The Silence is reaching back. Remembering.

The past returned to her in ragged bits. Closing her eyes, Eva recalled her tiny son. She pictured the downy surface of his head, the bubble toes and velvet skin. She recalled his greedy suckling at her breast. The power of his need coursed through her, tugging fiercely at her womb. Her heart swelled, then shattered.

Eva's memory served up the baby's cries. How piercing they were, how ripe with significance. Gladly, Eva had obeyed his every command, catered to his every unnamed desire. Reverently, she'd observed him as he grew and changed and absorbed the world with terrifying speed.

She smiled, remembering his toddler voice. 'Up,' he'd demand with great authority. 'Up, Mama.'

Eva pictured his shaky, splay-legged stride. She relived the breathless anxiety she'd felt as he explored his expanding universe. He'd seemed so new, so vulnerable. The child had bird bones. The substance of a cloud. Eva was always mindful that he could be lost, broken. Taken from her.

And so he was.

You should have seen it coming, Eva. You should have found a way to stop it.

Pain clawed at her throat. She peeled the vegetables and cut fish chunks for the stew. Stirring with a long-handled spoon, she inhaled the fragrant steam. Her grief eased a merciful bit.

She ate near the hearth, staring trancelike at the lapping flames. She chewed slowly, savouring each bite. Her senses were fully alive.

The Silence is for awakening. Knowing. Accepting. Healing.

Finished with her meal, Eva went to the kitchen. She filled the ancient tub with water she'd heated to near scalding on the stove. Shivering in the chill evening air, she stepped in and lowered herself by excruciating degrees. Her pulses throbbed. Her skin glared scarlet.

Eva scrubbed herself with a sea sponge and glycerine soap. When the water cooled, she settled back until her long hair spread like pond lilies on the surface. The scent of her mother's camomile shampoo returned her to her childhood. How safe the world had seemed to her then. She'd been blissfully unaware, cloaked in warm, pretty lies and empty promises.

Eva dressed in her trousseau gown, sheer white organza trimmed with lace. Noting how limply it hung, she felt a pang of loss. She'd gone to her wedding night with full breasts and a firm, girlish body. Before the baby's birth, she'd ripened to near bursting. Her belly was a giant swell, her navel popped out like a turkey timer. She recalled the taut sheen of her skin, the arrogant radiance that presages fresh life.

Now, she was squeezed dry. Shrivelled. Nothing but ice and bone on the surface. Crumbled to cold ash inside.

The Silence is rebirth.

Seated before the hearth, Eva brushed her hair in languid strokes. When it dried, she plaited it in braids. She wound them extravagantly as her mother had taught her years ago, and fastened the ends with hair pins.

The fire had dimmed to a sputtering glow. As the final embers blackened, Eva climbed the stairs. The past echoed in her mind. Nine years ago, her precious baby was born. Two years to the day later, the child disappeared.

Eva could not tell anyone, not even Cal. But in her heart she'd always known her little boy would return some day. He would come back to her during the Silence.

The Silence is for taking and giving. Every blessing requires a sacrifice. From every sacrifice comes a blessing.

Eva had made the ultimate sacrifice. Some day, somehow, she had to extract a blessing from that gaping void.

Maybe this would be the year. Maybe her little boy was already on the way.

16

Little Bo-Peep fell fast asleep,
  And dreamt she heard them bleating;
But when she awoke, she found it a joke,
  For still they all were fleeting.
                                    'Little Bo-Peep'

I spend half the morning on the phone, trying to reach someone who'd been involved in the Ethan Haskel kidnapping investigation.

From everything I know, the FBI handles all child abduction cases. But at agency headquarters in Washington DC, I'm passed from department to department like an embarrassing mistake. Finally, I'm shunted to a Special Agent Sanchez, who remembers that the Haskel inquiry was coordinated out of one of the agency's satellite offices in Connecticut.

Between calls, I head to the staff lot. From there, I keep an edgy watch on the headmaster's house. Vividly, I picture Adam taking the child and stealing away. Vanishing again, probably for ever.

Back in my room, I try the FBI field office in New Haven, Connecticut. They refer me to Bridgeport which passes me to Hartford. There, a gravel-voiced woman instructs me to try Bridgeport again. 'Ask for Travis Richardson. Rest of those clowns don't know their ass from a hole in the wall,' she says.

Richardson is out, so I leave a message. After another quick check of the Stafford house, I return to my apartment to await the agent's call. The heat outside has plastered my white T-shirt to my back and turned my denim shorts to blue accordions. Now, the clothes freeze dry in the wintry blow of the air conditioning.

Too impatient to sit idly, I dial the *New York Times*. There, I'm transferred to the research department.

'I'm looking for information about the Ethan Haskel kidnapping,' I tell the man who answers. 'Specifically, I need names of the people who headed the investigation. Can you help me?'

'Sure. Name and address please.'

I hold the line while he processes my request. I have pen and paper ready to copy the names I need. So simple. Why didn't I think of this in the first place?'

'Okay. You're all set Ms Logan. You'll be receiving these printouts in two to three weeks. You understand there'll be a charge of ten dollars for each article?'

Grasping straws, I try the Norwalk paper next. Since the Haskel baby was kidnapped there, it follows that every detail would have been covered in local print.

No doubt it was. But the *Hour* offers no clipping service. Back issues are warehoused at the local library, the voice on the phone explains. I'm welcome to go there and dig through them myself.

Nearly another hour passes without a return call from Special Agent Richardson. Fed up with waiting, I try the Bridgeport office again.

'Travis Richardson, please.'

'Sorry, he's out. Care to leave a message?'

'I already did. Any idea when he may be able to get back to me?'

'Not any time soon, I'm afraid. Richardson had a heart attack. They've got him in intensive care. Talking quadruple bypass. Can I help you?'

I give it one last shot. 'I'm trying to find out who worked on the Ethan Haskel investigation.'

'Didn't I speak to you earlier, ma'am?'

'Maybe.'

'Well, I'd still suggest you try our people in Hartford.'

Thoroughly disgusted, I slip out for yet another check of the headmaster's house. As I enter the staff lot, I hear the distant churn of an engine. Stafford's garage door drifts open and his car angles on to the circular drive. Pressed out of sight behind a tree, I watch him stride purposefully back to the house.

For the next ten minutes, nothing happens. The rising sun stabs my eyes, making it nearly impossible to see. Finally, the headmaster's front door flings open.

The boy, Ethan, appears. As he charges across the lawn, Stafford's voice booms after him. 'Get your jacket from Jonah's room, and come right back, Pip. We're leaving in half an hour.'

Easy, Bethany. Leaving may mean they're going to town for lunch.

I have to know. Circling widely, I press in the cover of the woods. Approaching the house, I'll be out in the open for a good twenty yards. There's no sign of Stafford, but he could peer out at any moment and spot me. What's the choice? Drawing a deep breath, I race across the lawn.

Leaning against the house, I wait for my breathing to settle. When it does, I edge toward the sound of a muffled voice inside. It grows louder and more distinct as I move towards the front of the building. Stafford is talking on the phone.

As I near the open window, a distant sound from behind draws my attention. There's a sharp yip. Flutter of feet. Hard panting.

Aunt Sadie, no!

The dear mutt picks this of all times to reconcile. She bounds toward me, beige fur flying, waving her tail like a white flag. When she reaches my hiding place, she barks eagerly and plasters my face with sloppy kisses.

'Down, Sadie!' I rasp. 'Not now!'

She wants to play. My reproach only fuels her frenzy. Her yapping grows more insistent.

Stafford stops talking. For a beat, there's a hard silence. I hold my breath. 'Hang on, Joe,' I hear him say. 'Something's going on.'

He's coming out to check. In desperation, I turn to Sadie. 'Please girl. You *have* to go.'

112

I hear the front door open. Footsteps strike the walk. They're aiming our way.

'Please!'

Sadie's look is harsh.

'Go now!'

At last, she wheels and trots across the lawn toward the staff lot. Breathless, I press behind a hedge.

Stafford is still approaching. Any closer, he'll be able to spot me.

Stop!

He slows. Stands still. 'Damned dog,' he mutters. He turns and walks back toward the house. As he does, my nose itches fiercely. I feel the approach of a sneeze attack. Pinching my nostrils hard, I pray for the feeling to pass. Slowly, it does. The tingling eases. Goes away. Soon, the front door slams.

Stafford's conversation resumes. Through the roaring blood in my ears, I struggle to hear what he's saying.

'No, nothing serious, Joe. My brother's a carpenter. His old truck's shot. And he's been offered a really sweet deal on a new one for cash. So I've agreed to lend it to him.

'Right. Ten thousand will do it. Should be enough in the savings account to cover that. I'll sign the transfer slip when I stop by to pick it up. Hundreds will be fine.

'Great. Thanks, Joe. I'll be there within the hour. 'Bye.'

I hear him cross the room. Heavy footsteps climb the stairs. Peering inside, I spot four suitcases in the hall. This time, there's no question he's planning to run. I can't let him take the boy.

Racing to the Jeep, I find Aunt Sadie posed to block the door.

'Move, Sadie. I'm in a hurry.'

She blinks at me, the shaggy beige mule. 'No games, girl. This is an emergency.'

She won't budge. I stalk around to the passenger door, but Aunt Sadie beats me there and continues the stand-off.

'All right. You win. You can come.'

113

Wriggling with joy, she waits for me to open the door. She leaps in, and we drive across campus. At Weldon House, I leave the motor running. The dorm is unnaturally quiet. I find no one inside except the Haskel child and his friend Jonah. The boys are sprawled on the couch in the day room, watching TV.

My throat is chalk, but I do my best to sound offhand. 'Hey, Pip. Your dad sent me to pick you up. Car's out front.'

Suspicious, he hesitates. 'Why'd he do that?'

'He had to go to town for something. He asked if I'd bring you there to meet him.'

'What if I don't want to go with you?'

I hold my face blank. 'Fine. He said he was in a hurry. But I guess he'll understand.'

Playing the odds, I turn to leave. If the boy doesn't follow soon, I'll be forced to grab him. The campus is almost deserted, but I don't relish a scene.

Come on, Ethan. Come on your own.

I step outside, propping the door open behind me. I can hear the two boys talking. Jonah, dear obedient soul, is trying to convince his obstinate pal to do as I've asked.

'Your dad's gonna be mad,' Jonah warns.

'Why'd he want me to ride with that witch? Bet her car has cooties.'

'You oughta go, Pip. Honest.'

I keep a wary eye on the campus road. Stafford had asked Pip to get his jacket and come back right away. Any minute now, he could decide to drive over and fetch the child.

I commence a silent three-count. If the boy hasn't followed by then, I'll have to grab him and run.

One – Two –

Still poised at the door to the dorm, I'm watching from the corner of my eye. Finally, the child rises from his chair. He slaps his friend's hand and slings the jacket over his shoulder.

Refusing to acknowledge my existence, he strides through the door. With a shrug, he ambles toward the Jeep.

114

He pats Sadie through the rear window and slides into the passenger seat. As he fastens his seatbelt, my stomach cramps with a force that makes me gasp. I clutch the car to keep from collapsing.

What the hell are you doing, Bethany? How in the Lord's name is this thing going to end?

Mercifully, my focus clears. I get into the car.

The boy stares sullenly at the road. He says nothing as we exit the campus road and turn toward Grangeville.

What do I tell him? How can I possibly explain?

Before I'm struck by a decent inspiration, flashing lights fill my rearview mirror. Harley's Dodge is coming up behind us. His siren howls.

I can't stop. It would be Harley's greatest pleasure to blast off my skull and leave the rest of me for roadkill. He'd return the child to Adam Stafford. The Haskels would never see their little boy again.

'Hang on!'

I floor the gas pedal. My car surges ahead. Harley's Dodge shrinks in the distance.

But the deputy soon recovers from his shock and speeds up to catch up. His siren whoops. Flaming lights fill my rearview mirror.

'You better pull over,' Ethan warns gleefully. 'He's gonna give you a ticket.'

'Not if he doesn't catch us.'

The turnoff for Old Logging Road lies ahead. Swerving hard, I veer on to the unpaved trail. After several heavy rains, the surface is a muddy soup. My Jeep can handle it, but I'm betting Harley's Dodge can't. In winter, the deputy uses the town's official four-wheel-drive vehicle, but during the summer months he rides his own bomb to trap donuts and speeders.

The going on the trail is sloppy and slow. Still, I'm out of firing range by the time the deputy's Dodge ventures on to the river of mud behind me. Soon, I hear the impotent whirring of tyres. Harley's outraged voice comes over the

115

bullhorn: 'In the name of the law, I order you to pull over. In the name of the – '

Thank you, Lord.

Harley's screams fade as we jolt over the remains of the sodden path and ease back onto the Grangeville Road.

'That was *great!*' the boy exclaims, his hostility forgotten. 'That was seriously cool.' At long last, I've found a way to impress him.

My moment in the sun soon ends, however. As we cross the Grangeville town line to Independence Center, he grows irate.

'Hey, stop. You said you were taking me to town.'

I swallow hard. 'I said I was taking you to your father, and I am. I'm taking you to your real mother and father.'

'You're nuts. I'm getting out of here.'

He grabs the door handle, but before he can open it, I flip the switch, engaging the child locks.

Furious, he pounds against the window. 'You let me out of here! Right now!'

'Ssh. Please listen to me. I know this is going to be hard for you to understand, but Adam Stafford is not your father. He took you from your real parents when you were a little baby.'

'*Let me out!*'

He lunges for the wheel. The car lurches wildly. I pry his fingers free, but he's a dervish, reaching and tugging. We're all over the road, swerving dangerously from lane to lane. Bumping on to the shoulder, the car screams into a skid. I hold on for dear life until the wheels regain their traction.

'Stop it, Pip! You're going to get us killed!'

'Let me out! I want my father!'

He's fighting like a madman. Wrenching the wheel. An oncoming car appears in the approach lane.

'Let go, Pip. *Now!*'

My words don't penetrate. The approaching car looms larger. Every time I try to twist the wheel out of harm's way, he wrenches it back. We're on a collision course with the oncoming vehicle. I gird for a crash.

116

But Aunt Sadie intervenes. Leaning over the seat, she catches the back of Pip's collar in her teeth. She growls menacingly. The boy freezes.

'Don't bite me,' he whimpers.

Leaning hard on the wheel, I avoid a collision by inches. The Jeep wavers in the hard rush of air as the car passes safely by. The irate driver blasts his horn. Several moments pass before my trembling stops.

'Sadie doesn't bite – ' I begin. Peering over, I read the gleam of fear in his eyes. Right now, that fear is my best weapon. My only weapon. 'She doesn't bite, unless you give her a good reason.'

'Get – her – off – me.'

'I will if you promise not to touch the wheel again.'

He gnaws his lip, considering. An impressive growl rumbles deep in Sadie's chest.

Ethan cringes. 'Okay, I won't. Now, make her stop.'

'Down, Sadie.'

The dog settles in the back with a smug look on her furry mug.

Ethan resumes his sullen staring. I can't help feeling for the child. 'It's hard, honey. I know. But it's true. Your real family's name is Haskel. You were taken from them when you were only two.'

'That's a total lie.'

'I can show you. Look.'

Thankfully, the printout Hap Riley gave me is still in the car. I fish it out of the glove box. At first, the boy refuses to look at it. But soon, his eyes drift to the drawing.

'This isn't me.'

'Yes, it is. It's a computer image made from the baby picture your parents gave the police. Look at the birthdate. Look at the name.'

'I am looking. It's not me. This kid's name is E – '

He can't read it. 'It says Ethan John Haskel. That's your real name, the name your parents gave you when you were born. I don't know why Dr Stafford did this, but – '

117

'No way! You're a dirty, filthy liar. Let me out of this car! *Let me out!*'

He pummels my arm and shoulder. A missed punch hits the horn. There's a wrenching blast. Sadie yaps a rebuke. Startled, the boy stiffens. He leans back and folds his arms. His face is cold and angry.

For the next couple of miles, we have the road to ourselves. Then, at a light outside of Independence Center, a long-haul truck falls in behind us. For an instant, I gaze out the side window. The child takes advantage of the lapse. He leans hard on the horn. The din he raises is dreadful.

Before I can wrench him loose, the trucker blasts his air horn and angles into the lane beside us. The light is still red, but I step on the gas and speed away.

The truck follows, barrelling behind us at breakneck speed. Riding the downgrade, he has the advantage. I spot a side street ahead to the left. It leads to a small covered bridge. No way the monster sixteen-wheeler can make it through that.

Tyres spitting rock, I make the turn. I speed down the street toward the bridge. Racing through, I don't see the haycart stranded on the far side. I spin the wheel hard to avoid it. The Jeep totters and threatens to tip. I'm bashed against the window.

I stomp the brake hard. The car limps to a halt.

My skull feels like a cracked egg. I'm struck by a spike of pain. Aunt Sadie barks her outrage. The kid whimpers like a kid.

'Are you okay?' I ask.

His eyes are huge. 'You're bleeding.'

I pull a wad of tissues from my purse and press it against the rising lump. Blood streams from a ragged gash at my temple. 'Head cuts bleed a lot. I'll live. Hush, Aunt Sadie. I already have a headache.'

'I didn't mean to hurt you,' the boy whimpers.

'I know. I understand how hard all this must be for you, Ethan. How confusing.'

118

He shakes his head stubbornly. 'No you don't. You don't get it at all. Adam Phillip Stafford, the Third. It's always been that.'

'Adam Stafford is not your real father. He took you from your parents who loved you very much. *Still* love you.'

His face sets. 'I don't care what you say. It's a lie. I don't believe it.'

'It's going to take time. I know that. Now please, it won't help anything if you get us into an accident.'

He seems calmer as we continue the drive southward. At least he's not battling me any more.

Sadie snoozes in the rear, snoring lightly. For nearly an hour, we roll along without a single crisis. I allow myself to consider it might continue that way. But then, the engine stutters.

I check the dash. The fuel gauge hovers at the base of the red zone. Up ahead is an Exxon station. I can make it.

'We need gas,' I tell Ethan. 'I'm going to pull in up there. Promise me you'll behave.'

His gaze is ice. The motor hitches again.

'Okay. Have it your way. Aunt Sadie? Guard him.'

The dog yawns.

'Watch him, Sadie,' I order.

Lazily, she rises to her feet. The child does not notice that the big beige fuzzball is semi-conscious. He shrinks down in his seat.

'Tell her not to bite,' he begs.

'Okay, Sadie. No biting – unless it's absolutely necessary.'

I make it to the station on fumes and coast to the pumps. As I feared, both islands are marked self-service.

The boy looks suitably intimidated. Keeping an eye on him, I get out and check the instructions on the pump. I have to pay inside first.

I consider taking the child with me, but what will I do if he makes a scene? 'Don't move,' I tell him.

Racing inside, I find three patrons ahead of me on line. A plump woman with a platinum chignon is perched on a stool behind the counter. She's waiting on a pale kid with stringy hair and a pitted complexion. The teenager has a pile of snacks assembled on the Formica surface. The money pile beside it is insufficient.

'How much for the Reese's Pieces?' he asks.

'Dollar forty-seven.'

'Take them off, then. But leave the Hershey's miniatures.'

'Those are one eighty-nine plus tax.'

'I'll take the small Mounds, then.'

After they negotiate the purchase down to an amount the kid can afford, a squat bald man stops up to buy five dollars' worth of high test.

I keep peering out the window. So far, there's no sign of trouble at the car.

Next up is a reedy woman with a tight red perm. She's buying lottery tickets. Two quick-picks. A play four. An exacta. Jolting with impatience, I watch her pencil in her numbers for the Super Jackpot.

'Hear it's up to twenty-two million.'

'Should go higher by drawing time,' says the clerk. 'Near thirty.'

'Boy, could I ever use thirty million.'

'Tell me about it,' the clerk agrees. 'That'll be five dollars.'

'And a pack of Kools. No, make it Carltons. And I need a Bic. Not that one. The yellow.'

Finally, I'm able to step up and toss my twenty on the counter.

'Regular or super?'

'Super.'

'Want a receipt?'

'No.'

'Sure that car of yours'll take twenty dollars' worth?'

'Please. I'm in a rush. Would you just activate the pump?'

The clerk frowns. 'Guess I can give you change if she's under.'

'Whatever. Please hurry.'

She hurries *very* slowly. At snail speed, she pivots on her stool. In slow motion, she sets a pair of glasses halfway down her nose. With great deliberation, she inputs data on

120

the electronic touch pad. Then, she removes the glasses, replaces them in the case, and rotates back to face me.

'There. You're all set.'

I race out to the pump, shove the spout into the neck of the gas tank, and squeeze the trigger to start the flow. As the numbers begin to twirl on the dial face, I check my watch.

It's nearly two. Poor kid must be starved. They have sandwiches and a case full of soft drinks inside. I'll ask what he'd like and buy it for him.

The boy's head isn't visible through the rear window. I open the door quietly, thinking he must have fallen asleep. But when I peer into the car, all I find is Aunt Sadie.

The dog is furious. And the little boy is gone.

17

A shoelace binds Aunt Sadie's collar to the door handle. The skin on her neck is rubbed raw and rimmed by fiery welts. Anxiously, I fumble with the knots.

'Hang on, sweetheart. Almost done.'

The look on her face is pure indignation. Sadie has been abused, outsmarted by a diabolical child. I know the feeling.

I take the dog with me to search the station. Neither the clerk nor any or the patrons remembers seeing a small, blond boy. No one offers help or sympathy. They seem entirely underwhelmed by the notion of a missing child.

'My Pauly runs off all the time,' the reedy woman assures me. 'Problem is, he always comes back.'

I check the restrooms and the mechanics' bays. I look inside the used cars warehoused on the unpaved lot. No sign of Ethan.

Sinking to my knees in the pebbled soil, I peer through the latticework girdling the foundation. The dry dust starts me sneezing. I go on for fifteen, twenty loud bleats. After each sneeze, I bless myself. I can use all the help I can get.

I stare down storm drains littered with paper scraps and wads of gum. Opening the lid of the garbage dumpster, I use a stick to rummage through a foot or more of slimy, smelly debris. At the base is a rotted ooze of fruit peelings, soda pop, crumpled snack bags, clotted coffee grounds, and cigarette wrappers.

I'm reminded of the gruesome gunk the boys concocted to drive me away from Hinsdale. It occurs to me that their spell worked like a charm. I have strayed so far from my life's normal course, I can't imagine how I'll ever find my way back.

Beside me, Aunt Sadie conducts her own futile search.

122

The dog lopes in tight, anxious circles. Her head droops, and her ears poise like divining rods. At intervals, she stops to paw the ground, churning a dusty haze that makes her sneeze.

We get in the car and coast half a mile in each direction. I stop at every place large enough to camouflage a child: homes, shrubbery, tree trunks, farm stands, road signs.

I fight a rising panic. What if something has happened to him? What if he's had an accident? What if he took a ride with some evil stranger? He might have stumbled into another abduction. Or worse.

My mind swirls with horrifying possibilities.

The fearsome blast of a horn pulls me back. I've drifted across the centre line. Almost hit another car.

Shaken, I drift to the shoulder. As I do, I spot a pay phone fifty yards up the road. Pale legs extend beneath the circular metal casing. It's worth a look. I kill the engine and slip out of the car with Sadie. Treading lightly, I approach the booth from its blind side. I hear a small pleading voice. 'Could you try again? He's *got* to be home.'

Circling quickly, I grab the child from behind.

He flails against me. Screams: 'Let go of me! *Let me go!*'

I cage his arms. When I lift him, he kicks back with his heel. Sharp pain blossoms on my shin.

'I can't let you go, Ethan. I have to take you home – '

'Stop calling me that. My name is *Pip!*'

He butts his head up at my chin. I bite my tongue so hard, I see stars. Aunt Sadie circles us, whining.

'Your family misses you, Ethan. They want you back.'

'I – AM – NOT – ETHAN!'

'Yes you are. That's the name your parents gave you: Ethan Haskel.'

'I'm not! *I am not!*'

I hold him fast, though he's squirming madly. I'm terrified that a passing motorist will think I'm abusing the child and report me to the police.

'Your parents love you, Ethan. They've been trying to find you for such a long time.'

123

'No. Don't say that.'

'Six years, Ethan. They'll be so happy to have you home again.'

'No!' He presses his hands over his ears and squirms wildly. 'Nonononono!'

'Ssh, baby. Take it easy.'

'I hate this. I hate *you*!'

'I have to take you home, sweetie. It's the only way.'

'You can't do that. You can't. It's a lie. It's not fair.'

He crumples, weeping. Harsh sobs rack his slender frame. I turn him round to face me.

'I know you're scared, Ethan. I understand.'

'Please don't make me go.' His voice is so tiny, terrified. 'I don't even know them.'

'It's going to be all right, honey. You'll see.'

'What if they don't like me?'

'They'll love you. They do already.'

'I don't even remember how to have a mom.'

I hug him close. 'Neither do I, sweetie,' I murmur in his ear. 'Neither do I.'

At last, his weeping stills. I help him into the car and buckle his seatbelt. His face is dirt-streaked and stained with tears.

Until we cross the Connecticut line an hour later, he sits unmoving and silent. As we pass the state's welcome sign, I feel his eyes on me.

'You okay?' I ask.

He nods. 'How much longer?'

'About an hour and a half. Hungry?'

'A little.'

'I can't stop if you're going to cause trouble.'

'I won't.'

Off the highway, I find a Burger King with a drive-up window.

'I'm counting on you,' I say sternly.

His chin dips in grudging agreement.

Without incident, I order at the rear of the shop, drive around, and pick up our food.

I'm heartened to see that the boy is in good appetite. After downing his own cheeseburger, fries, and a chocolate shake, he ogles my remaining chicken nuggets.

With a pang of regret, I pass them over. 'Only for you, pal. Believe me.'

That wins a near smile. Ethan munches the chicken and finishes my Coke. In the rear, Aunt Sadie chews the last of her quarter-pounder. Daintily, she licks her muzzle clean.

'Feel better?' I ask the boy.

With a grudging nod, he crumples the wrappers and stuffs them in the bag. I catch the look on his face, watch the questions forming.

'What do you want to know?' I ask gently.

'Where do they live? These people.'

'In a town called Norwalk, Connecticut. It's a nice place. Lots of young families. Good schools, too.'

'They have other kids?'

'I don't know. I don't think so.'

'But they're nice?'

'Sure. I'm sure they're very nice.'

Sinking inside, I realize how little I know about Ethan Haskel's family. The printout I got from Hap Riley lists nothing beyond a Norwalk address and phone number for the boy's mother, Eva Haskel, and his father, Calvin Eric Trent. I don't even know if the pair are married or why the child bears his mother's surname. I'm in the dark about what these two people do, how they live, what they're like. They could be mean, wretched people. They could have dark souls and shrivelled little hearts.

What I *do* know is that this little boy belongs to them. I've run with him because Ethan's parents are the victims here, two poor souls whose baby son vanished in the dead of night. For all these years they've suffered. For all these years, they've been forced to deal with bitter questions, empty arms, a relentless, gaping void in their lives. That's the fact, the only thing that matters here. Bringing Ethan home is the only way to set things right.

Ethan sighs. Hunched against the window, he has

resumed his mute vigil. In minutes his eyelids flutter and drift shut.

Asleep, he looks impossibly small and vulnerable. I block out the chorus of aches and bruises clamouring to remind me about his diabolical little brain, bruising fists, and raging temper. For the first time, I allow myself to believe this mess might lead to a fortunate conclusion.

He's still sleeping when we reach the turnpike exit for Norwalk, Connecticut. Off the ramp, I angle toward the kerb and pause to regroup. I've gotten this far. What now?

Weighing the options, I decide to take Ethan to the local police. They have to be better equipped than I am to handle the child's return to his parents. There must be standard procedures in a case like this. Ways to cushion the shock and ease the transition.

A fellow motorist directs me to the central precinct. In the parking lot, I prod the child awake.

'We're here, buddy. Come on.'

Rubbing his eyes, he regards the stern building. 'Those Haskel people live here?'

'No. This is the police station. They'll take you home.'

'Why can't you?'

I ignore the desperate edge in his voice. 'It's better this way.'

It's nearly 2 p.m., past the lunch-hour peak, but the lobby is jammed. A horde of impatient people jostles toward the main desk, pelting the pale, balding clerk with requests.

'They got my boy in the jail again. Where do I go to bail his sorry ass out?' one woman demands.

'Which office does the gun licences?' a man asks.

'Where do I apply for a parade permit?' asks a slim adolescent in an Eagle Scout uniform.

Ethan and I join the crowd, inching forward. I grip his shoulders, but he ducks and tries to break away. Clutching his wrist, I hold fast.

When our turn finally comes, I lean toward the clerk and tune my voice to a whisper.

126

'This child was kidnapped. I'm here to return him to his parents.'

'Kidnapped?' The clerk gawks as if I've grown a second head.

'Please,' I rasp. 'I need to speak to someone in private.' The name Ethan Haskel is sure to ignite a firestorm of attention. The situation is volatile enough as it is.

The clerk scowls. 'Soon as I have names, I'll call inside.'

'My name is Pip Stafford,' the boy shouts. 'P-I-P S-T-A-F-F-O-R-D.' He stabs an accusing finger at me. 'She *stole* me from my dad. She forced me in her car and locked me there. She made me come all the way here from New Hampshire. I want to go home right this minute! I want you to get her away from me and lock her up in jail!'

The crowd falls silent. Everyone stares at us, bug-eyed.

I rush to explain. 'He's not Adam Stafford's child. He's the child who was kidnapped from the Haskels six years ago. I can prove it.'

'Don't believe her. She's a rotten, dirty liar!' the child yells.

'It's the truth. He's Ethan Haskel.'

'Am not!'

We're both pressing to be heard, voices tangling.

'He's confused.'

'She's nuts.'

'Please call someone. Stop it, Pip. Stay still.'

'See. I told you my name was Pip.'

'Ethan, I mean.'

'Get off of me. *Let me go!*'

The crowd listens, rapt. The clerk shakes his head. 'Whoa. Just hang on.'

Ethan struggles to escape my grasp. 'I hate you!' he screeches.

As the clerk turns to the intercom, Ethan leans down and sinks his teeth into my fingers. Rockets of pain fire in my head. By the time I'm able to gather my wits again, the wretched kid has broken loose. He's dashing toward the

127

door. He ducks outside. Racing hard, I catch him halfway across the parking lot.

The boy flails and shrieks as I haul him back inside. The crowd parts for us, eager for an encore. When I approach the desk, the clerk is on the intercom. His back is to me, bald head bobbing like a buoy in a storm.

'Better get down here ASAP, Piasecki. Woman comes in babbling that her kid's Ethan Haskel. You ask me, she belongs in a rubber room. Meanwhile, the kid'll need temporary placement. Ask O'Hallaghan to get DCYS over here. I'll put out the description.'

Hearing that, I freeze. DCYS is the Division of Children and Youth Services. They'll slap Ethan into a shelter or foster home. By the time I can convince them I'm not crazy, the child will probably have run off and found some way to reconnect with Adam Stafford. That is, *if* I can convince them. I have to get out of here. And fast.

'Hey, lady! Wait up!'

The clerk has spotted us.

'Wait!' he calls again, his voice trailing me like darts.

Clutching the child in my arms, I charge outside, wishing I'd parked closer. I fling Ethan into the back seat, hop in front, and lock the doors.

Barrelling out of the lot, I ease into the flow of downtown traffic. For the next fifteen minutes, I drive through a dizzy weave of back roads.

I'm a nervous mess. Every stray sound jolts my heart. I shrink at the sight of any car that could possibly be a cop's. The child is tossing a major tantrum in the back seat.

'Take me home! I want to go home right this minute!'

Aunt Sadie tries to mollify him with licks and nuzzles, but it's useless. Ethan's shrieks persist, poking holes in my crumbling patience.

'I want my father! *I want my father now!*'

This cannot go on much longer. I'll simply have to deliver him to the Haskels myself. No matter who engineers it, the child's return is bound to be a shock.

'*Take me home!*'

I pull over. The Norwalk map I took from my sister's house is still in the glove box. The address listed on Riley's printout for Eva Haskel and Calvin Trent is 3 Rand's Lane. Checking the street legend, I find no such listing.

'You *have* to call my dad! Call him *right now!*' Ethan is red-faced, screeching wildly. 'I hate you, you ugly witch! Take me home or I'll kill you dead!'

I recheck the computer printout. Definitely Rand's. Definitely Norwalk. Again, I consult the map. No such street.

The map is highly detailed. It's hard to imagine any street small or insignificant enough to be omitted. But a third painstaking perusal of the alphabetical street listing confirms that there is no Rand's Lane. There is nothing at all named Rand's: no road, street, avenue, court, or circle.

Nothing.

'I want my father!'

Trying to tune out his screams, I scan the body of the map. I track a narrow path, leading with my finger. Once I've trailed the full distance from east to west, I go back and repeat the process an inch southward. Over and over again, I say the magic name: Rand's.

'Call my dad!'

I'm halfway down the map when something at the corner of the page catches my eye. The name I seek sits at the centre of an irregular strand of small beads of land. The print is tiny but legible: Rand's Island.

'Drop dead. Let me go!'

I return to the printout. What I thought was an initial L for 'lane' is, in fact, an I for 'island'.

The word makes me cringe. Island equals water, water equals death.

Sit here, sweetheart. Momma's going for a nice long swim.

Transported back, I feel the sandy grit on my skin. The heat of the sun's breath. I sit unblinking, staring at the empty space my mother left. Waiting for a message to pass through the grim, silent lips of the sea.

Don't come after me, Bethie. Stay right there, honey, and make a big, beautiful sandcastle.

I watch until my eyes ache. Until it's dark. Until two policemen arrive to carry me away.

My horror blunts Ethan's screams. I can barely feel his fists, clashing against my arm.

Slowly, the hideous memory eases its hold. I'm returned to the fearsome present. The child still wails his misery. I must get him home.

18

We're in the northwestern sector of Norwalk, near the Merritt Parkway. Rand's Island is part of a starfish-shaped archipelago off the city's south end, known as SoNo.

Two summers ago, I was dragged there by Roo and the kids. It was the neatest place, they assured me. I would definitely love it. They planned a big day: lunch at a dockside restaurant and a movie on sharks at the IMAX theatre.

Everyone had a wonderful time, except me. I hated being so near the vast Long Island Sound with its dark face and determined currents. The water might seem innocent to most people, but I knew better. I had witnessed the sea's seductive power, its cruel magnetic draw. The briny scent was enough to trigger strong protective instincts. My insides curled tightly, recoiling from a danger I could not bring myself to name.

The others seemed blissfully blind to the peril. My niece Amelia was so lulled by the rolling surf that she nodded off in her booster seat, blonde curls bobbling toward her junior portion of fish and chips. After lunch, my nephew Greg stood at the wooden rail for nearly an hour, pitching bread beads and oyster crackers to the swooping gulls. Even Roo relinquished her manic super-efficiency for a while. My sister sat happily idle, staring at the surf until we were nearly late for Amelia's ballet class.

'What's wrong, Beth?' she kept asking me. 'Why so quiet?' I couldn't answer her. There was no way I could ever put so vast a horror into words. It was so much easier simply to stay away. That day, I vowed never to venture so close to my darkest demons again.

But now, I have no choice. Folding the map, I start the car.

'I want my dad,' Ethan whimpers. 'Please. Please, *please* take me home.'

'I am, honey. I'm taking you home right now.'

Soon, we're in SoNo. At the district's heart is the large brick contemporary Maritime Center, which features marine life exhibits and a sea school for aspiring sailors.

According to Roo, this area was once dominated by commercial fishing operations, body shops, and boating supply houses. Now, the main streets boast galleries, boutiques, supper clubs, and trendy restaurants. In season, scores of visitors stroll, sip, sup, and shop here. Stalled in the resultant traffic, I watch them swarm the sidewalks.

'I wanna go home,' Ethan drones deliriously. 'Please.'

'Soon, sweetie.'

We pass the area's crowded core. Adjacent to the Maritime Center, I spot a large blue sign: HOPE DOCK — ISLAND FERRIES DAILY.

Circling the Center's crowded parking lot, I finally find a space. We get out and approach the fenced landing beyond the sign. Nearing the broad expanse of open water, I battle my rising dread. Aunt Sadie wedges her flanks against my leg like a bookend. Grateful, I scratch behind her ear.

Get a grip, Bethany. You have to do this.

The posted schedule lists departures every hour on the hour until four. It's not quite three.

Time moves in pained slow motion. I turn my back to the sea and try to pretend I'm somewhere else. I think of dear stodgy old Grangeville. I think of the Hinsdale School with its lofty aims and antique traditions. Boredom is a blessing I've taken far too much for granted.

I wait until ten after, but there's still no sign of an approaching ferry. Nothing passes through the inlet but a rusty trawler and a garbage scow.

At a quarter-past three, lights on the railroad bridge flash wildly. A commuter train streaks through in a flurry of noise and sparks. Ethan watches, rapt.

After the train vanishes in the distance, I take his hand

and start toward the Maritime Center. The child's feet move, but he's dragging. He doesn't protest when I lift him. Lanky legs cinch my waist. A heavy load lolls on my shoulder. Something stirs deep inside me. I tighten my grip.

At the main desk stands a teenage girl with a doughy face and hair like tumbleweed. She's chewing gum and juggling starfish. Our appearance breaks her concentration. She stumbles and drops one of the dried creatures. It lands hard on the counter, scattering stacks of membership brochures and exhibit maps.

'Whoops.' Her giggle sounds demented. 'Next tour's at four. You folks interested?'

'No thanks. We need to get to Rand's Island. Any idea when the next ferry will show up?'

'That'll be Memorial Day. They're closed for the season.'

'Then how can we get to the island?'

Ethan whimpers. He's getting heavier with each moment. I balance his bottom against the counter.

The young woman cracks her gum. 'Beats me.'

'There must be a charter company. Something.'

'Maybe. Your best bet is to ask over at Baron Brothers. Clete Baron knows everything about everything around here.'

The place she describes is two blocks east on Water Street. A sign at the entrance declares that Baron Brothers, Inc. is the world's largest distributor of first-quality bluepoints.

The company occupies a slim grey building. Beyond, several low-slung boats await unloading at the dock. Hopeful gulls swoop and settle on the pier pilings. The air is a warm salty broth.

Two men in reflective vests operate the long-necked rigs that haul metal cages full of oysters from the belly of the boats to the open shed at the building's rear. Inside, a row of grim-faced, swarthy men in heavy aprons separate the day's catch by size and quality.

Ethan stalls outside to gawk. Masses of shellfish cram the metal bins. At the back of the cavernous room are bulging bushel sacks. A ripe, fishy stench assails me. The air billowing out is arctic. Aunt Sadie shivers hard and trots ahead.

'Come on, kiddo.'

Reluctantly, the boy follows. He's run out of protests. He looks dazed.

The main office walls are lined with nautical charts. Ledgers and order books cram the shelves. At the scarred roll-top desk sits a burly man in a plaid shirt and faded denims. Startling blue eyes beam from his lined, leathery face. His hair is the black of coal dust.

'Hey there.' Leaning down, he holds his weathered hand out to Aunt Sadie. 'Aren't you a beauty.'

Sadie preens at the compliment and strikes a haughty pose. Passing a hand beside her muzzle, the man pulls a dog biscuit from thin air. Ethan chuckles. Best sound I've heard in days.

Smiling, the big man turns to me. 'Name's Clete Baron. How can I help you, ma'am?'

'I'm Bethany Logan. We need to get to Rand's Island. Apparently, the ferry's closed for the season. The young woman at the Maritime Center said you could help us find a way across.'

His smile fades. 'Sorry. No can do.'

'Why not?'

'Nothing's allowed to dock at Rand's 'til next Monday. Been that way the last week of every August long as I can remember. Haskels spend the week in seclusion. Meditating and the like. Some sort of family thing, very private. Guess it's good for them though, especially Eva. Poor girl's had the dickens of a time since her boy was taken.'

I glance at Ethan. He's hanging on every word.

'Terrible, terrible thing,' I say. 'I can imagine how she must be suffering.'

'Hard to believe how it's changed her. I bought this business from Captain Haskel, Eva's daddy. Started working for him way back when Eva was just a snip.' He shook his head. 'She was something else, that one. Smart as a whip

134

and so pretty it took your breath away. Never even went through an awkward stage like most. Future looked bright as they come. But since this damned thing happened . . . Don't think she'll ever get past losing that baby.'

'What if Eva got her child back?'

'After all this time? Wish it could happen. But I don't suppose there's much chance. Do you?'

I set my hand on the child's slim shoulders. 'Yes I do, Mr Baron. This boy is Eva Haskel's son. All it'll take to get him home again is a boat.'

19 Robin-a-Bobbin
Bent his bow,
Shot at a pigeon,
And killed a crow.
'Robin-a-Bobbin'

I scramble to explain how I discovered the Haskel child's
true identity. Clete Baron sits expressionless, rubbing
rhythmically between Aunt Sadie's ears.

I keep searching his blue eyes for a verdict. I desperately
need him to believe me. Considering how things went at
the police station, I'm afraid he won't. Mercifully, this
time the child keeps still.

'The printout was the capper,' I say finally. 'One of the
neighbours had a computerized update made from Ethan
Haskel's baby picture. Let me show it to you.'

Ethan still stands calmly. Leaving him with the oysterman, I duck out and retrieve the rumpled page from the
Jeep. Baron glances at it. His gaze swerves from the paper
to the child. 'Amazing how they do that.'

'You see? It proves this is Ethan.'

'Proof's standing right there.' He nods in the boy's direction. 'Soon as you said he was the Haskel child, I could see
it clear as day. You look just like your daddy, son. Spitting
image of Cal.'

'My father is Adam Stafford,' Ethan sighs. 'Why won't
anybody listen to me?'

'*You* listen to *me*, young fellow,' Baron chides gently. 'You
can't remember way back to when you were just a little
baby. No one can.'

'Why can't I just go home?' Ethan wails.

'Don't you worry, son. You're going to love Cal and Eva.

136

And they're going to be thankful to the bone to have you back. By and by, you'll get used to things being how the good Lord intended. Now, I'm gonna call over to the island to let them know to expect you.'

He tries several numbers, then, frowning, hangs up. 'Thought only Eva cut service, but your aunt's phone's down. And so's your grandpa's. Think all the other Rand's folk have come ashore for the week.'

The boy brightens. 'There's a grandfather?'

'And a grandma and aunts and uncles and more cousins than you'll ever need,' Baron tells him. 'The island bunch stick pretty much to themselves, but half this town's related to the Haskels one way or the other.'

'Grandparents,' Ethan echoes reverently. 'Jonah's grandma and grandpa came to school last month. They brought candy and baseball cards and tons of Pogs. They even got some for me. It was awesome.'

Baron grins. 'Had a grandson of my own two weeks ago. Can't wait 'til he's big enough to spoil silly. Figure it's my job.'

'But they're *not* my grandparents,' the boy sighs. 'I'm not who she says. Honest. My name's Pip Stafford. It's always been that. Adam Phillip Stafford, the Third. My father is the headmaster at the Hinsdale School in Grangeville, New Hampshire. Call there and ask. They'll tell you.'

'It's gonna take getting used to, son.' Baron pats Sadie's flanks and pulls another biscuit from the air behind her tail. 'First thing we need to do is get you and your folks reacquainted. Let you get to know the place. Rand's is a beautiful spot. Prettiest of all the islands, if you ask me. But you don't want to ride there on one of my smelly old rigs. Let's see what I can arrange.'

The oysterman dials Moon's Marina up the street.

'Gloria, it's Clete. Let me speak to Bobby. What about Mike, then? Damn, I forgot. Be the same at Och's and Vista, you think? Right. Thanks anyway.'

Baron looks grim as he explains to us: 'Got a big boat

137

show coming up at the end of the week down in Stamford. Everyone's out setting up or making deliveries.'

'Please,' Ethan begs. 'I've got to get back to New Hampshire. My dad's waiting for me.'

'Don't worry about a thing, son.'

'But he doesn't know where I am. He'll be worried.'

The child's agitation is rising. I sense a fresh tantrum brewing.

'At least let me call him,' Ethan begs.

'The oyster boat will be fine, Mr Baron,' I say. 'The important thing is to get going soon.'

'Problem is, it'd take at least a couple of hours to get one unloaded and refuelled for you.' He frowns in thought. 'Got an idea.' He dials again. 'Hey, Tillie. It's Clete Baron. Jackson still delivering? Great. Patch me through to the boat, will you?'

The child whimpers. 'You have to let me talk to my dad if I want. It's a free country.'

I pat his back. Forsaking the remains of her biscuit, Aunt Sadie nuzzles against his calves. Neither of us wants another of his tirades. 'Ssh,' I urge. 'Easy, tiger.'

Baron is on the phone again. I can't hear over Ethan's mewling, but the oysterman hangs up smiling. 'All set,' he tells us. 'Let's go on out back. Jackson'll be here in a couple of minutes.'

The big man takes Ethan's hand and walks him toward the dock. I force myself to follow.

Passing the shed, the child slows to watch the sorting operation again. Clete Baron feeds the boy's fascination.

'We farm 24,000 acres of beds off the Connecticut shore. Got twenty-two boats out harvesting most every day of the year. Three are metal-hulled to break the ice come winter. Typical week, we bring in upwards of 3,000 bushels. Sometimes more.'

'You must have a lot of fishermen,' Ethan says.

Baron shakes his head. 'You don't fish for oysters, son. Oysters are farmed. Pulled up from the bottom by dredges. Half of what we bring in is empty shell. Come July, we lay

138

out a half-million bushels of empties in our beds. Baby oysters move in and start growing. Takes four or five years for them to reach market size.'

The child is awed. 'So many oysters.'

'And lots of demand, thank the Lord. We ship across the country and worldwide.'

Ethan's nose wrinkles. 'But oysters are gross.'

Baron's jowels shimmy with the laugh. 'Do me a favour and don't let that out. Will you, son?'

'Okay.'

'I'd be much obliged.'

We continue toward the dock. The sun's glare obliterates the space beyond the point. I hear the churning motor before the boat chugs into view. It's a two-tiered rig, painted gaily. I'm reminded of a tugboat from a child's book, something sweet and charming and terrifyingly inadequate.

'We're going on that?'

Baron chuckles. 'Don't worry. She's sound as a dollar.'

'Since when is the dollar sound?'

'That's our mailboat,' Baron says. 'Hasn't missed a scheduled run come hell or high water for as long as I can remember. Jackson Quint's top notch. Man's done it all. Major races. Solo ocean crossings. Finest seaman you'll ever come across. Mark my words.'

I mark certain ones: *hell, high water, ocean crossings.* My skin erupts in a hot, electric rash.

The mailboat glides in between two oyster rigs. A man in his twenties mans the helm. His face is tanned a lovely melanoma brown. He flings a line on shore, follows with a graceful leap, and ties up.

The young skipper wears a cropped shirt, cut-off jeans, and boat mocs. A baseball cap rides his sun-scorched curls.

'Okay, Clete,' he calls. 'What's your big emergency?'

'Jackson Quint. Meet Ms Bethany Logan. Ms Logan found the Haskel boy and brought him back to us. They need a ride over to Rand's. Thought you'd be willing to oblige them.'

'Ethan Haskel?' Quint's mouth falls open. 'You sure?'

'You heard it from me, Jackson,' Baron says gravely.

That appears to be good enough. Quint smiles. He makes a dramatic bow. 'Jackson Quint at your service. Be my pleasure to take you to Rand's.'

I start toward the dock, but my knees fail. Panic surges through me. Clete Baron's worried face wavers at my side. 'You okay?'

'I'm fine.' My voice sounds hollow. I'm grateful when the oysterman grips my arm.

Aunt Sadie barks, urging me to shape up. Then she trots on to the narrow pier, setting a brave example. Her beige fluff swings jauntily. Her muzzle has the arrogant heft of a hood ornament. Ethan trails the dog in a listless shuffle. Quint hops on deck and helps the boy and the dog aboard. Then he turns an expectant gaze my way.

'Any time, Ms Logan.'

'I'm coming,' I say, but I'm stuck. The dock is so narrow. Mere splinters of wood shield me from the monstrous surf.

Baron tightens his grip on my elbow and strides ahead. I want to cooperate, but my feet have their own agenda. 'Just give me a second,' I plead.

Quint steps ashore and approaches. 'Boy wants to say goodbye to you, Clete.'

The two men exchange a pointed look. With a shrug, the oysterman ambles toward the mailboat.

As Baron climbs on deck, Jackson Quint leans closer. His whisper is warm on my neck. I catch the minty scent of his breath.

'You got a thing about the water, Ms Logan?'

'Just a touch.'

'But you don't want to spook the little boy, is that the idea?'

'That's it.'

'Good thought. I'm going to help you through this, understand?'

I try to nod, but my neck feels rusted.

'Just do as I say.'

Turning his cap backward, Quint points to the Yankee

symbol on the bill. 'Okay, Ms Logan. Keep your eyes right here and follow me.'

'I'll try.'

'Not try, *do*,' he orders. 'Ready?'

'Not quite.'

'Yes you are. Come on.'

I focus hard on the bill of his cap. As the blue insignia pulls ahead, I shift my weight and edge my free foot forward. I manage one step. Another.

Suddenly, there's a gurgling beneath the dock. Sounds like the sputtering choke of someone drowning. The vacuum suck of air-starved lungs. I freeze.

'Don't stop, and don't look down,' Quint commands. 'Walk.'

The cap edges forward. Somehow, I follow, though my joints have seized up like a bad engine. I strain to keep my thoughts centred on the insignia, but horrifying sensations seep through the cracks in my resolve. My head fills with the sea's briny stench. Whoop of gulls. Angry currents pummelling the boat. I am blinded by sparkles of fear.

'I – can – not – do – this.'

'Yes, you can. Now move. Keep moving. Another few steps. Here we are.'

His cap jolts to the right. I can't find the insignia. A rising scream sticks in my throat.

Hands grab me. I pass through a void. When I emerge, I'm seated in a cushioned chair that's bolted reassuringly to the deck. Clete Baron stands at the bow with Ethan and Aunt Sadie. I watch the eager sweep of Clete's arms, but his words are gobbled up by the gusting wind.

Jackson Quint studies me with a searching frown. 'That wasn't so bad. Now was it?'

'Compared to what?'

'What happened, Ms Logan? You have a run-in with Old Man River? Get sick at Sea World? What?'

I shrug. 'Forget it, okay?' I hear the edge in my voice and regret it. The guy is trying to help.

Quint fetches a towel from the helm and dabs the sweat from my forehead. 'Try to relax. We've got clear skies. Fine weather. Should be smooth sailing all the way to Rand's.'

'How long?'

'Under an hour. You'll be all right?'

'I'll be fine.' I speak with more conviction than I feel. Quint removes his baseball cap and hands it over.

'I said, I'll be okay, Mr Quint. I don't need anything to stare at.'

His lip twitches. 'That's not for staring, Ms Logan. That's in case you should chance to lose your lunch.' Cupping his hands, he bellows: 'All ashore that's going ashore.'

Clete Baron leads Ethan and Sadie around the engine house to the port side. Ethan sits on the bench beneath the rail. The dog perches protectively beside him.

Crossing toward the dock, the oysterman pauses to shake my hand. 'This is a good thing you've done, Ms Logan. Took guts.'

I notice he does not mention brains. 'Thanks.'

He turns to Ethan. 'You take care, son. I'll drop by to say hello real soon.' Aunt Sadie gives him a long, meaningful lick goodbye. She's clearly smitten.

Clete Baron clambers back on shore. Jackson Quint starts the boat. We glide into the channel. Oily engine fumes ride the strident breeze. Straightening the wheel, Quint sounds a warning blast and churns full speed ahead.

20

At the siege of Belleisle
I was there all the while,
All the while, all the while,
At the siege of Belleisle.

'Belleisle'

I'm crouched in a thimble, tossed in a vat of molten lava. Horrific heat sears my lungs. My eyes burn. My flesh curls at the edges.

'Want a Coke?'

Jackson Quint keeps smiling at me. He fails to grasp that I am no longer here. The real Bethany Logan has been swept off into a raging river of fear.

'How about a beer, then?' he persists. 'Or I can mix you the speciality of the house: Long Island iced tea with a shot of thorazine.'

Armageddon with a wet bar? I don't think so. I glower at him, hoping he'll catch my drift and drift away.

'At least the kid seems to be enjoying the trip,' he says.

Following the meaningful tilt of Quint's head, I chance a glimpse. Ethan is kneeling on his seat, chest on the railing, trawling his fingers through the tides. I bite my tongue to keep from screaming out to him. There could be eels in the water, poison jellyfish. Worse, he might catch the salt-bleached bones of some tormented soul drowned at sea.

How long ago did she go for that swim, Bethany? You sure she didn't come out?

Aunt Sadie is glued to Ethan's side. The faint breeze ruffles her fine, beige fluff. Her eyes flutter shut. I've never seen the pooch look more blissful.

'What a day,' Quint exalts, breathing deeply. 'Seems I

143

love the sea every bit as much as you despise her, Ms Logan. Guess I must've been a fish in a former life and you were something dry and solid, like a tree.'

'Who knows? Maybe I was a fish, but it didn't work out.' His laugh is contagious.

'That's better,' he says, smiling his approval. 'Sure I can't get you something?'

'Actually, some dry, solid ground would be wonderful.'

'Ask and ye shall be given.' He points to a small, green mass in the distance. 'That's Peach Island. Start of the Norwalk Archipelago. The group has sixteen major islands and lots of smaller ones, called hammocks. The whole chain was formed by glacial deposits 22,000 years ago. A Dutch explorer named Adrian Block discovered and named it in the 1600s.'

'The sea is too damned big,' I shiver.

'Technically, the Sound is an estuary. That's a mix of salt and fresh water. She's only a hundred and ten miles long, twenty-one miles wide at her broadest point. That's tiny compared to most of the seas and oceans. Think of her as a big bathtub, only the rubber duckies are real.'

So is my terror, buddy. I hug my knees.

Quint points out another blip of land. 'That's Tavern Island. Used to be called Pilot's, back when the skippers of tall ships favoured it as a place to stop and regroup. Bigshot producer named Billy Rose bought it in the 1950s. Rose built a huge mansion and fitted it out like the Taj Mahal. He shipped in priceless art works, exotic birds and animals. You name it.

'For a while, Tavern was a popular summer playground for the rich and famous. Lillian Hellman wrote *The Little Foxes* there. Place was hopping until Mr Rose died. Family who took it over are plain people. Filthy rich, I'd wager, but plain.'

I cling to Quint's running commentary. Better to dwell on that than the fearsome chop that's suddenly risen around the boat. The Sound is shaking its watery fists at

144

us, bashing the hull. The deck dips and sways. My stomach lurches in its own capricious rhythm.

Quint points to the large block of land ahead. 'That's Sheffield's Island. History books say the Algonquin Indians gave it to a minister named Thomas Hanford as a gift. But I'd bet it wasn't that simple. The early settlers had a convenient way of misreading the natives' friendly gestures. A smile meant they wanted you to have their daughters. A handshake said their *casa* was your *casa* – for keeps.'

Like most of the islands, Quint says, Sheffield's passed through several owners and incarnations. At various times, the place was a cattle farm, a hotel, and a flourishing community, large enough to support its own offshore school. Quint draws my attention to the broad stone building on the island's leeward side.

'Way back, the government bought a piece of Sheffield's to build that lighthouse. It's part of a whole system of lighthouses threaded through the Sound. There's a dangerous ledge running off the coast here, part of the continental shelf. At low tide, it's so shallow, you can actually walk between some of the islands. Plenty of unsuspecting sailors have run aground.'

I imagine ramming the rock ledge, the boat cracking apart like brittle bones.

Quint reads my fright. 'Don't worry, Ms Logan. I've been sailing these waters since I was old enough to reach the helm. Know them like the back of my hand. Maybe better.'

We pass Shea's Island, recently renamed to honour a local soldier killed in the Vietnam War. Chimon, the largest of the chain, is famous with birders for its heron rookery. Wood, Dog and Ram Isles have been privately owned for generations. Stormy, true to its name, has lost buildings and much of its shoreline to violent nor'easters.

Ethan and Sadie haven't moved from their lazy perches at the side of the boat. They're totally absorbed by the breeze, the motion, the engine's buzz. I feel every bit as stiff as those two look liquid.

145

Quint loves these islands. He regales me with the archipelago's colourful history. Pirates sailed these waters, sometimes burying their ill-gotten booty on the shores. During the Revolutionary War, the area was rife with privateers, armed colonial raiders bent on commandeering valuable cargo from British supply ships.

On his way to establishing the centre of the Mormon church in Utah, Brigham Young stopped here and baptized a small colony of converts. German spy subs patrolled the inky depths during World War I, their movements guided by signal stations perched on the islands' lofty bluffs. And throughout Prohibition, the archipelago's hidden coves were favoured by rum-runners, who would set anchor under cover of darkness and row stealthily ashore with their bounty of liquid gold.

More recently, some of the islands have spurred pitched battles between environmentalists bent on preserving the fragile tidal plains and power companies equally determined to milk the land for every drop of profit potential.

'The biggest flap was over Cockenoe Island,' Quint says. 'Back in the sixties, a local realtor sold the place to a dummy corporation. Buyers claimed they were planning to build a yacht club. Turned out the real new owner was a power company called United Illuminating. They intended to use the site for a nuclear plant. Figured they'd have it up and running before any of the locals noticed. They figured wrong.'

Legends surrounding the archipelago abound. Eagerly, Quint recounts ancient rumours of arson, unsolved murders, illicit affairs, and family closets crammed with unseemly skeletons. One island is said to have been the site of unknown scientific experimentation sixty years ago. He doesn't know exactly which island or the specific nature of the tests, but according to local lore, they had some dark, dangerous purpose.

'Islands have a way of fuelling the imagination,' he explains. 'Which isn't to say that some or all of the rumours aren't true. Island folk are a separate breed. I suppose living apart the way they do brings out the best and the worst in people.'

I look anxiously over at Ethan. He's still staring dreamily out over the hull. I feel a pang of guilt. I've torn this little boy's world apart. Left him scared, confused, drifting. What have I done?

I keep reminding myself I had no choice. Ethan belongs here, with these people. This is right. No question. Except I still have a few.

'What about Ethan's parents?'

'Cal's great,' Quint assures me. 'Solid as they come. Eva's been on the skids since the kidnapping, but who can blame her? Craziest damn thing.'

I cannot disagree. Cruising the island chain, it's doubly hard to fathom the eerie circumstances surrounding Ethan Haskel's abduction. The case had gripped national attention, holding centre ring in the media circus for months.

The Haskel infant was taken from his island home, stolen from his crib some time between midnight, when his mother last looked in on him, and seven in the morning, when she checked on him again.

All that time, his parents slept across the hall. Neither of them heard a thing, though the mother described herself as a light sleeper. Not a peep from the family dog, who slept at the base of the stairs and normally barked at the slightest disturbance. A summer drought had left the ground around the house too parched to hold footprints. But no strange fingerprints were found. No evidence of forced entry.

At first, the child's parents were prime suspects. But both of their stories held up under intensive questioning. Lie detector tests confirmed their proclaimed innocence.

The scope of the investigation was unprecedented. Not since the Lindbergh baby had a kidnapping so captured and incensed the public. The staggering number of missing child cases today have numbed us to all but the most incomprehensible and horrifying, and the Haskel case was both of those. But a massive manhunt unearthed no significant clues or witnesses. There were no reports of suspicious activity that night at the island's docks or in the surrounding waters. A check of boat registries and marina activity along the entire Atlantic seaboard yielded no positive leads. The promise of enormous rewards generated a flood of crank calls, but no hard information. The authorities were stymied.

Speculation abounded that the Haskel child must have been targeted for some particular reason. Otherwise, why would a kidnapper choose to operate in so remote and difficult a location? The logistics of the crime were mind-boggling.

The perpetrator had to find a way to arrive by boat unseen. He had to secure a safe, secret mooring. Somehow, he had to slip into the Haskel home in the still of night, take the baby, and get out again undetected. Opportunities to case the premises first or observe the family to determine its routines were severely limited.

Fleeing, the abductor would be visible in open waters. The archipelago was monitored by the Coast Guard and marine police. Local fishermen and oystermen were on the lookout for poachers and polluters, especially during the night hours when such activities generally took place. The odds of a strange boat being observed and noted were overwhelming.

Yet somehow, the man who took Ethan Haskel had disappeared without a trace.

How? And why? None of it makes sense, especially when I factor in what I know about the perpetrator. Why would Adam Stafford, of all people, steal someone else's baby and try to raise the boy as his own? The man is bright, successful, and incredibly attractive. Any number of women would have been glad to help him to have all the babies he might want the conventional way.

Even if he had some crazy motive for the crime, why choose this boy? This place? I cannot begin to penetrate the insanity.

Quint points to another island off the bow. 'That's Crow

Island,' he says. 'It's mostly submerged at high tide, so it's not generally listed on the charts. That's Grassy. Used to be a sheep pasture. Now, the town owns it.'

We pass Goose Isle and the Peck's Ledge lighthouse. A small island named Manresa seems to sag under the sprawl of a mammoth electrical plant that's been painted the tacky blue of bad eyeshadow.

Quint shifts course. Shading my eyes, I spot a small green spur in the distance. Soon, the mass broadens and takes on definition. The island resembles a verdant pie, sliced in wedges. On the side we approach, wooded clumps flank three grassy clearings. Each holds a quaint stone-and-clapboard house.

'That's Rand's dead ahead,' Quint tells me. 'Have to take the long way in to avoid the shallows.'

A sand beach dotted with scrub pines frames the land. Weathered docks protrude at intervals. Leeward stands another of the archipelago's many antiquated lighthouses. Bright boards sheath the tower like a patch on a wounded eye. Windward, a slim jetty juts like a beckoning finger into the surf.

'Nice,' I have to admit.

'Rand's is a beauty,' Quint agrees. 'State owns a nature preserve on the far side. The rest is private and peaceful beyond belief. Place is almost paradise.'

'Except for what?'

Before Quint can answer, there's a monstrous blast. A giant plume of water spouts beside the boat. I duck, but I'm soaked by the backsplash.

Quint waves his arms. 'Easy, you old coot!'

'What was that?' Ethan cries. Aunt Sadie barks her indignation, incensed as she often is by the depths to which some humans are prone to sink.

'Just a wet welcome, son. Don't you worry,' Quint says.

The next blast hits even closer. With a thunderous slap, displaced water swamps the hull.

Puddles slosh around my feet. Horror chills my blood. What if the boat sinks? No way I could make it to shore.

149

I'm no match for the crushing might of the currents. I imagine the fearsome pressure holding me under, forcing my lungs to swell, then burst.

'Come here, Ms Logan,' Quint calls. 'Take the wheel.'

I can't find the words to argue, and I can't muster the muscle to go along. Rolling his eyes, the seaman yanks me bodily from the chair and walks me like the condemned to the control console. He moulds my rigid fingers to the wheel.

'Just hold her steady as she goes,' he orders.

'Okay.'

'I said "steady", Ms Logan. What you're doing's the hula.'

'I'm doing my best,' I snap.

'Do better.'

I clutch the wheel. But the thing has a mind of its own. It wriggles defiantly in my grip, makes unexpected dips and turns in its struggle to break free. I want to insist that Quint take it over, but he's bounded in a breath to the forward rail. He pulls off his sodden shirt and waves it fervently toward our assailant.

Please, Lord, make the madman stop shooting. Please keep the boat afloat.

I know what it is to drown. In guilty imaginings I have drowned a thousand times. I've lived every inch of the gruesome struggle. Racing thoughts, muscles shrieking.

Put me down! I can't go. I have to wait for my mommy.

Mommy's gone, Bethany.

'That's enough, Duck,' Quint calls. 'I surrender.'

Mommy's never coming back.

A white-haired man in madras shorts and a Rolling Stones T-shirt rises on shore. His arms drop. Sun glints off the long barrel of his weapon.

Quint reclaims the wheel.

'That's your Uncle Duck, Ethan. Real name's Gresham Weems, but everyone just calls him Duck. Some kidder, huh?'

'My uncle has an actual *gun*? Think he'll teach me to shoot?' Ethan is intrigued.

150

'You just ask, son. Man's got a heart of gold.'

Heart of gold, mind of bedbugs. I'm drenched. Trembling. Ankle-deep in sloshing bilgewater.

'If he's so nice, why was he shooting at us?' My voice has shot up an octave.

'That was only meant to turn us around,' Quint replies evenly. 'Old Duck probably thinks I forgot about the boat ban. Wants to remind me. He's harmless, really.'

My temper flares. 'Harmless, my foot. What if he hit the boat with that thing? What if he hit one of us?'

'He did, Ms Logan. That's why we're wet.'

At that, the shape of the weapon registers. Clear plastic barrel, bright red-and-yellow moulded stock. My nephew Greg has one exactly like it. 'A Monster Blaster?'

'Exactly. Great big water gun. Between you and me, Duck is nothing but a big, old kid. Loves toys. Practical jokes, too.'

We're fifty yards from the jetty and closing fast. Quint stalls the engine. In the ensuing silence, he calls to the cotton-haired man. 'Hey, Duck. Where's Eva?'

The old man scowls. 'You know better than to come around this week, Jackson. Eva sees you, there'll be hell to pay.'

'Don't think so. Not when she finds out what I brought her.'

'Oh yeah? And what's that?'

Blocked by the wheelhouse, the old man cannot see Sadie or the boy.

'Go get Eva,' Quint insists. 'It's only right that she hears first.'

With a sceptical frown, Duck Weems shoulders his toy rifle and ambles across the lawn. Jackson Quint starts the engine and manoeuvres the boat to shore. Expertly, he edges into a narrow slip lined with bumpers.

Facing land, I feel the fear knots loosening. I try to ignore the raging menace behind me.

Aunt Sadie bounds on shore and edges toward the anchor. She snarls at the unfamiliar hulk, barking her fierce distrust. But I think it's wonderful. Rooted and substantial.

Rand's *is* a glorious place. Wild geese and snowy egrets strut the beach. Beyond, the lawns are peppered with Joe-Pye-weed and starbursts of goldenrod. The woods are dark and lush. Clutching Quint's outstretched hand, I step ashore and draw a ragged breath of relief.

Moments later, Uncle Duck emerges from the stone house ahead of us. He's accompanied by a slim young woman. She's oddly dressed in a cream satin gown inset with tattered lace. Several sizes too large, the dress droops to her bare feet. Inky wisps of hair frame skin that's pale to the point of translucence. Her expression is grave, her eyes downcast. Her gait is a spectral glide.

Ethan pulls a breath. 'Is that her?'

'I think so.'

'She looks weird.'

'This is a special week on the island,' Quint says. 'Sort of a holiday. That's why Eva's dressed like that.'

His explanation seems to satisfy the child. I set aside my own reservations. Better to think ahead.

Soon, I'll be back in Norwalk. My sister's house is only twenty minutes from the downtown dock. I'll see Roo and the kids again. Indulge in more family spoiling. I can curl up with Amelia and sleep until this well of unease and tension runs dry.

Even the worst nightmare has a waking end. Even this.

21

When I went out for a walk one day,
My head fell off and rolled away.
And when I saw that it was gone,
I picked it up and put it on.
                              'A Walk One Day'

Duck Weems and the woman stand facing us. Jackson
Quint cracks the silence. Setting a hand on the boy's head,
he says, 'This is your son, Eva. This is Ethan.'

Eva accepts the news unflinchingly, as if she expected it.
'My son.'

Duck's green eyes pop. 'What in the world is this, Jackson? Some kind of joke?'

'Of course not. This is Bethany Logan. She's a teacher.
Had Ethan in her class. She figured out who he really was
and brought him home.'

'How'd she do that?' Duck sputters. 'FBI, cops, half the
world's been working on the case for six long years. Whole
lot of them haven't been able to find so much as a hint of
what became of Eva's boy.'

'Tell them how you figured it out, Ms Logan,' Quint urges.

I keep the story brief. 'Ethan's been living at a boarding-
school in New Hampshire, Ms Haskel. The man who took
him is headmaster there. But at the time of the kidnapping,
he lived in Norwalk. A former neighbour always suspected
this man might be involved in your son's abduction, but
the police wouldn't listen. The neighbour followed the case
anyway. He gave me this.'

I fish the printout from the pocket of my wet shorts. It's
a sodden, gluey mass. The print is muddied. But the image
is clear enough.

Uncle Duck takes the page and studies it gravely. When

153

he offers it to Eva, she pushes his hand aside, dismissing the need for confirmation.

'My darling.' Eva Haskel's eyes have been fixed on the child since she emerged from the house. Her hand edges toward him. 'My boy.'

Recoiling, the boy whispers urgently: 'Get her off me.'

His mother drifts closer. The boy shrinks beside me. He turtles his head, trying to burrow between my ribs. I've been promoted in his affections from pure evil to the lesser of two.

'My sweet baby,' Eva coos. 'I always knew you'd come home to me.'

'I'm *not* a baby,' the child rails.

Smiling, she says, 'Of course you're not. You're a strong, big, beautiful eight-year-old boy.'

She strokes Ethan's pale hair with the back of her finger. I feel the anxious shudder that runs through him.

'But I remember exactly how you *were* as a little baby. So sweet-tempered. So bright. You were only nine months old when you took your first steps. Only ten months when you started talking.' Her tone is reverent.

Curiosity draws Ethan's face out of my ribs. 'What'd I say?'

'You said, "gah-kah", which was your word for cracker. And "buh" was the way you said ball,' she answers solemnly.

The child snickers. 'Gah-kah? Buh? How'd you figure out what I meant?'

'A mother knows, darling. Even without words, I could tell when you were lonely or sleepy or coming down with a cold. I knew what displeased you and the things you enjoyed.'

Ethan eyes her with open scepticism.

'You liked me to read you stories,' Eva continues, 'especially pirate stories. You loved making mudpies in the wet sand and paddling in the water with your grandfather. You enjoyed watching your grandmother bake and having your daddy draw you pictures. But your very favourite

154

thing of all was standing on the jetty, watching the boats go by.'

'It was?'

Eva smiles. 'You were such a curious little one. "What's that boat called, Momma?" you'd ask. And you remembered every single thing I told you. Not even two, and you could tell a sloop from a cutter and a ketch from a yawl. You knew the difference between a jib and a mainsail. You recognized Alvin Darley's Highlander and the Berensons' Merit 25 and the Nonesuch Bill Case won from Larry Gardner in a game of five-card stud.' Her laugh is musical. 'You used to tell me you were going to have your own Hobie cat one day and sail it all the way to the moon.'

The boy scowls. 'How come I don't remember now?'

'Because six years is a very, very long time for a child. Even the strongest memories fade eventually,' his mother says. 'The mind has to make room for all the fresh things a boy has to learn later on. But this is still your home, Ethan. And very soon, everything will feel familiar to you again.'

Ethan eases his hold on me. I pass Quint a silent signal. Time to go.

'Think Ms Logan and I will shove off and let you people get reacquainted,' he says.

'Good idea,' I second quickly.

'Unh-uh. You can't leave.' The child clutches my hand.

'You'll be here with your mom, sweetie. With your family. You'll be fine.'

'No way. Not without you.'

'It'd be our pleasure to have you stay on as our guest, Ms Logan,' the old man says.

'It's what Ethan wants,' Eva Haskel states simply, as if she cannot imagine denying the will or whim of a child.

'Probably would be easier for him to adjust if there's someone around he knows,' Quint concedes.

I'm hopelessly outnumbered. Plus, they're right. It does seem unusually cruel to sever the boy's normal ties and set him adrift in a sea of strangers.

155

'I guess I can stay for a little while . . .'

Quint hands me a soggy card. 'When you're ready for the return trip, give me a call. 'Bye, Eva. Duck. You take care, son.'

Eva walks him to the boat. Quint unhitches his rig and takes the helm. The motor roars to life, and the mailboat putters noisily away.

Part of me wants to scream for Quint to turn around and get me out of this place. But I have to do what I can to make this easier on Ethan. Selfishly, I want to be sure he's in good, loving hands. At first glance, Eva Haskel does seem more than a little strange.

The rest of my immediate needs can be managed by remote. I can call to report Adam Stafford to the authorities. I want that man locked up, and fast. I shudder at the thought of him roving freely among innocent children.

I also have to touch base with my sister. Roo has severe mother hen tendencies. Even the briefest unexplained absence makes her edgy. Her nerves, pecking and squawking, get on mine. 'Worried sick' is a favourite phrase of hers. Making cold calls to morgues and hospitals is a favourite activity. I'd rather let her in on my planned itinerary than be sent off on one of her extended guilt trips.

Eva Haskel has turned her attention to me. 'Let's have a look in the attic and find you some dry things to wear. Uncle Duck, go tell the others the wonderful news.' Striding rapidly toward the house, she motions for us to follow.

'I need to use the phone, Ms Haskell,' I call after her.

She does not break stride. 'Sorry. Service to the island is disconnected for the week.'

'But I thought – ' Wouldn't she cancel the observation now that her son was home?

'Sorry,' she repeats.

She's halfway across the lawn. I hurry to catch up with her. 'You don't understand, Ms Haskel. Wait – '

There has to be some way to reconnect the phones. Or maybe someone else on the island has a working line.

'Ms Haskel?'

156

My foot slides on something squishy. Peering down, I'm repulsed to find the lawn peppered with goose droppings. On skittish tiptoes, I continue toward the house. Maybe this is what Quint meant when he said Rand's was *almost* paradise.

I'm able to resume a normal stride on the stone walk. The door is open. I wipe my soles on the hemp mat and trail Aunt Sadie inside.

The shades are drawn. The air hangs like musty curtains. After the door closes behind me, I'm overwhelmed by the weight of the silence. The slightest sound reverberates in contrast. Eva Haskel's husky whisper fills the gloom.

'Welcome, Ms Logan. And you, my darling Ethan. Welcome *welcome* home.'

She shows us around her house. A galley kitchen spans the rear. At the far end sits an iron stove crowned by a ring of copper pots. An ancient refrigerator fills the dim alcove beside it. There's a broad sink flanked by glass-faced cabinets. A galvanized tub crowds the centre of the room.

'As you can see, we have everything you could possibly want right here,' says Eva.

Through a slender passageway, we enter a pantry crammed with provisions. Aunt Sadie's tail wags approval. There are sackfuls of beans and grains. Bulging bags of flour and powdered milk. Two shelves hold Ball jars packed with homemade preserves and pickled vegetables. Meats and cheeses in mesh bags hang to cure from exposed pipes in the ceiling. Tins are full of teas, crackers, spices, herbs, and coffee beans. One broad shelf boasts enough bottled water, candles, and first-aid supplies to satisfy the most demanding doomsday survivalist. Some of my personal essentials are conspicuously absent, however. Not a single box of Oreos. No Cheezits or Devil Dogs or Yankee Doodles. But maybe the Haskels keep such treasures as I do: on open display like fine art.

The dining-room furnishings are spartan. Ladderback chairs rim the long table. A dozen framed photos of Ethan

157

as a tiny child line the buffet. All have the grainy quality of the picture I found at school.

A rag rug fronts the broad stone living-room hearth. The furniture here is plump and sombre. The sofa sports a funereal coat of maroon velvet. Heavy lamps squat on ponderous wood tables. Stiff rows of leatherbound books pack the shelves. Images of the baby Ethan fill every spare surface.

Trailing Eva to the second floor, I have to squint to see where I'm going. Everything is swaddled in gloom. I'm wondering why she doesn't flip on a light. Then, the horrifying fact sets in.

There's no electricity in this house. The intensity of the quiet means no refrigerator hum, no swirling fans or air conditioning, no electrons darting neurotically through the wires.

'No lights?'

'Light? Of course,' Eva says.

I flush with gratitude. Silly me. Of course there is electricity. This is the twentieth century.

But instead of throwing a switch, Eva Haskel strikes a safety match. In the ensuing burst, she tips the glass crown of a kerosene lamp and lights the wick.

Aunt Sadie recoils. I pat her fuzzy flanks for our mutual comfort. Eva Haskel's skin glows in the lamplight.

'Normally, we draw power off the mainland cable,' she explains. 'But no links to shore are permitted during the Silence.'

'What's that?' Ethan asks.

'You will come to understand,' his mother tells him.

The child persists. 'Is it like Hallowe'en?'

Eva's eyes devour her son. 'The Silence is unique, unlike anything. It's an annual observance that dates back many, many generations in our family.

'We live in simplicity for the week. At the end, there's a wonderful celebration. We have a feast and a special ceremony. One of us is singled out to be honoured. Something tells me this year it will be you.'

158

'That's so cool. Wait'll I tell Jonah!'

The boy is entranced. I'm closer to horrified. I can't be stranded on this glorified pool float for a week, especially without electricity.

In rural New Hampshire, power failures are commonplace. But even the shortest outage makes me restless. Aside from whining and overeating, I don't know how to do much of anything the old-fashioned way.

A horrifying list of deprivations loops through my mind. No heat or instant hot water. No nuked popcorn or mindless TV. No instant coffee in the morning or cocoa at night. No quick fix of raisin toast to fall back on in an emergency.

This can't be happening. 'You must have something, Ms Haskel. Some way to contact the shore. How about a cellular phone? A two-way radio?'

'All outside communications are forbidden during the Silence.' She brushes a blond wave from Ethan's forehead. 'This year we must serve the fates in true gratitude.'

'That's fine for you. But I can't stay here. Certainly not for a week.'

She doesn't hear me. Doesn't see me. Aside from the child, nothing exists for her. 'The trouble is behind us, my darling,' Eva croons. 'Momma's going to see that no harm ever comes to you again.'

22

Over the water,
And Under the water,
And always with its head down.
'A Ship's Nail'

At the tug of a rope, rickety stairs disgorge from the second-storey ceiling. Clutching the rails, I follow Ethan and Eva Haskel to the attic. Aunt Sadie lurches behind.

The air here is stifling. I'm forced to stoop beneath the severe downslope of the roof.

Scraps of light pierce the gable vents. Vaguely, they illuminate the stacked paintings, ancient tools, and abandoned toys crowding the space to the right of the stairs. The area to the left is packed to the rafters with storage boxes. There are steamer trunks, shipping crates, and wooden chests festooned with brass studs and metal cinches.

Aunt Sadie heads right to check things out. Her nails clack a rakish time-step.

Kneeling, Eva Haskel rummages through the trunks. From time to time she pulls out a garment and holds it up for mental measure against me or the boy. Some of the things are discoloured or stiff with age. Some are soiled or pocked with moth holes. But Eva is blind to the defects.

Nor does she suffer from an excess of taste. One blouse she favours is a flouncy white concoction, guaranteed to make me look like a substandard poodle. Another would be perfect for some enchanted evening in a Siberian gulag. But fashion is far from my immediate concern.

'When will phone service be restored?' I'm trying to sound reasonable. No mean feat from the wrong side of the rabbit hole.

160

'First thing Monday. Don't worry, Ms Logan. I'm sure you'll be perfectly comfortable with us until then. Ah, here. This should do nicely.'

The skirt she displays is a voluminous black drape. Just the thing for those casual nights at the coven.

'You don't understand. I can't be out of touch that long. I have to call my family. People at work.' I don't mention the police, but that necessary contact weighs heavily on my mind. What if Adam Stafford somehow finds out where we are? The man is a kidnapper. Who knows what else he is capable of doing?

I keep hoping that someone from the Norwalk PD will come looking for us. The scene Ethan and I staged there should have made someone curious enough to follow up.

Smiling, Eva shows Ethan a hand-sewn shirt and an Alpine-looking set of shorts with embroidered suspenders.

'These will fit you, I think.'

He makes a sour face. 'They're nerdy.'

'You're looking at family history, my darling. All this is a piece of who you are.'

'I'm not a nerd.'

'Of course not. But you're a part of us, of this.' The sweep of her lace-draped arm encompasses the sum of the island. This is Eva Haskel's universe. All she needs.

'Seriously, Ms Haskel. You don't need to bother finding me so many clothes. I really can't stay. There simply has to be some way to make contact with the mainland.'

'I'm afraid not.'

'What about a boat, then? It'll only take an hour for someone to get me to shore. I'd gladly pay.'

'All craft are banned from our shores for the duration, Ms Logan. Neighbours who choose to spend this week ashore tow the remaining boats when they go. The last of them sailed yesterday morning.'

'But there must be something? A rowboat? A rubber raft? All someone would need to do is get to one of the nearby islands and call from there.'

'*All* boats are included in the ban. There is simply no way off this island during the observation.'

'Then I'll flag down a passing boat.'

She smiles sadly. 'Unfortunately, Rand's is surrounded by dangerous shallows. Charts warn craft in the area to keep their distance. Boats with Rand's as their destination can only approach through the narrow safe channels. Others rarely venture near enough to see what's happening on shore.'

'Don't you have some way to signal passing boats?'

'I'm afraid not.'

She's found a frock for me. It's a striped canvas creation with covered buttons. Wearing that, I could pass for a nice set of lawn furniture.

'But you must have some way to communicate. What about emergencies? What if someone got sick?'

'The Haskels have lived on this island for six generations, Ms Logan. We've survived all manner of emergencies on our own. I can assure you we can cope perfectly well for a few days without help from the mainland.'

She doesn't assure me in the least. I feel trapped, suffocating. Spending another day or two on this glorified water-bed for Ethan's sake is one thing. No way I'll be able to take it for a week.

The dust and the situation start me sneezing. Eva blesses me twenty, thirty times.

Aunt Sadie jaunts back, huffing, and flops in a fluffy heap at my side.

'Almost done,' Eva declares. Finished sifting through a large wardrobe, she unlocks a splintery crate. 'These belonged to my Great-Great-Aunt Euphemia's son Luther. He was about your age when he – '

'When he what?' Ethan says.

His mother blinks as if she can't comprehend the question. 'Luther was built like you. Strong but slim.'

'Did the kid croak or what?' Ethan persists.

'You mustn't say such terrible things, my dear,' Eva chides. 'You mustn't even think them.'

162

For the next few minutes, she rifles through more ancient castoffs. I pass the time racking my brain for some way off the island. I consider signal flares. Notes in bottles. Carrier pigeons. Placing a giant 'Help' sign on the beach to snag the attention of a passing plane.

I'm trolling the depths. But I refuse to declare this hopeless. Maybe Jackson Quint will decide to come back for me without my calling. Maybe some passing boat will venture ashore, despite what Eva says. Likely, no one beyond the local area knows about this cockamamie ritual. What's to stop some out-of-towner from sailing through one of the safe passages and docking at Rand's?

The question leaps to my tongue, but I don't ask it. I'm down to a few nuggets of hope. I can't afford to have them examined and declared bogus.

Eva Haskel hands me a stack of stale-smelling garments. Cradling a larger pile in her arms, she crosses to the stairs. Her gown is soiled. Her skin is soot-streaked. Coils of hair droop like broken springs from her intricate coiffure.

At the base of the stairs, she stoops to retrieve the kerosene lamp. She leads us down the hall, pausing at the first door on the left.

'This is your room, darling. For tonight, you can sleep on the daybed. First thing tomorrow, I'll see about getting you a proper bed from storage.'

Over the child's shoulder, I view the dreary space. The wallpaper, a stodgy nautical print, has aged to the tepid brown of weak tea. Matching print curtains hang limp and grimy. The wood on the crib and rocker beg for polish and a dust rag. The only toys are a few wretched dolls and some whittled boats heaped in a broken basket. Replica lighthouses with broken crowns are the sole decorations.

Ethan saunters in and shuts the door.

Eva Haskel shows me to a room at the end of the hallway. There's a single bed with a bilious corduroy cover. A broad drafting table dominates the facing wall. Beside the window is a shelf crammed with volumes on construction and design. Diplomas and professional certificates hang in

163

a neat quartet beside the shelf. By the stingy lamplight, I read the recipient's name: Calvin Trent.

'Ethan's dad is an architect?'

She nods. 'My husband is in Ridgefield this week, supervising a project.'

'Too bad there's no way to tell him the good news.'

As if she hasn't heard, Eva crosses to the drafting table. Resting a hand on the polished surface, she stares at the gathering dusk.

'Too bad,' I say again, but my words don't penetrate. 'Ms Haskel?'

'Call me Eva, dear.'

'Fine, it's Bethany.'

'I'll leave you to rest and change then, Bethany. Whenever you're ready, I'll see you downstairs.'

The salty wash has glued my shorts and shirt to my skin. Peeling them off, I wince at the scent of seawater. In the pile of ratty hand-me-downs is a faded robe of patchwork silk. Wrapped in that, I pad down the hall to the bathroom.

Dropping the robe, I step into the narrow shower stall. But a twist of the taps yields a vapoury sigh. All I'm sprayed with is a harsh reminder of my predicament. No running water.

No running.

Foraging through the heap of clothing, I settle on a long floral dress. Looking at it, all I feel is foolish. But when I slip it on, I'm seized by an odd dislocating sense. Traces of lilac cologne cling to the fabric. The stays retain the shape of a long-dead stranger's body. Fastening the buttons, I'm moulded to the pinch of that woman's waist, the spread of her hips, the swell of her bosom. My flesh fills the silent void she's left behind. I've slipped on someone's past. And it fits with eerie certainty.

I'm tempted to change back into my own soggy clothes, but I dismiss the urge as ridiculous. This is a dress. A length of cloth. Buttons and hooks. Nothing more.

164

As I reach the base of the stairs, Eva calls from the living room. 'There you are, Bethany. Come join us.'

The gloom has been vanquished by a trio of lamps. A warm blaze crackles in the fireplace. Cooking smells waft from the squat iron kettle suspended above the flames. Aunt Sadie sprawls beside the hearthstone.

'Look how well the dress fits,' Eva says. 'As if it were made for you.'

Entering the room, I face a circle of strangers.

Eva says, 'I've invited some of the family to dinner, Bethany. Everyone's so anxious to see you and Ethan.'

Eva introduces the couple on the couch as her parents: Laurel and Captain Anthony Haskel. Ethan's grandmother has pewter hair heaped on her head and fastened at the crown with shell combs. Pale powder cakes her crêpey skin. She has owlish eyes, thin lips, and a stern expression. She sits so stiffly, there's barely a crease in the prim sapphire dress. Her greeting is a curt nod.

Captain Haskel rises and pumps my hand. He cuts a commanding figure in grey slacks, a striped tie, and a nautical blue blazer. He has a craggy face and eyes of untempered steel. His chin is an axe-head.

'Welcome aboard, Miss Logan. You cannot imagine what it means to us to have that boy of ours home again.'

'I'm glad.'

Eva turns to the pair seated on plump armchairs beside the hearth. 'You met Uncle Duck earlier, Bethany. This is Great-Great-Aunt Rowena.'

The old man looks supremely ill at ease in his dark sports coat, starched white skirt, fawn trousers, and brown wing-tipped shoes.

The doubly great Aunt Rowena is a wizened creature with a hunched back and skin that's fallen in lazy pleats. Cruel arthritic knots bind her fingers. She's swaddled, neck to toes, in wintry black.

She appraises me boldly. 'I don't know why you call her big, Eva. Looks to me like she's built just right. Sturdy aft section, solid hull, nice set of bow ornaments.'

'Aunt Rowena!' Eva flushes.

'Well it's true. Just because you've starved yourself down to the struts doesn't make it a good thing. Back when a woman was a woman, we knew how to accentuate the positive. Never forget your great-grandmother Landis. That woman had a pair of jibs on her, I'll tell you. On a hot day, you could stretch out and rest in their shade.'

'Mind your mouth, Rowena,' Duck says.

'No I don't, Duck. I don't mind my mouth at all.'

'Old bat just loves flapping her lips,' Laurel grumbles.

'Woman's supposed to have a few peaks and valleys, is all I'm saying,' Rowena persists. 'I don't care how popular that anorexia thing of Eva's is, I happen to find it very unattractive. Unnatural, too. Haskel women have always tended toward the beefy side. Take Laurel, for instance.'

'I haven't seen you on the cover of a swimsuit issue, Rowena,' Laurel says.

'Well, I saw you,' retorts Rowena. 'Think it was last June's *Whalewatcher's Gazette.*'

'Never mind,' the captain chides. His words have an instant effect. All carping stops and the conversation evacuates to higher ground.

Eva turns to the figure huddled in a shadowy space beside the couch. 'Bethany, meet my brother, Caleb. Caleb Haskel; Bethany Logan.'

Caleb is a hulking young man with dark, dangerous good looks. Dense hair. Strong bones. The kind of eyes you'd find staring back from the black of a cave. A flock of jitters flutters through my chest.

'Is this your first time on these islands, Bethany?' Laurel asks.

I tug my eyes off Caleb. But they keep drifting back.

'First time. Yes.'

'I'm sure you'll find it most pleasant.'

'Why, Laurel? You planning to leave?' Rowena chuckles, pleased with her own nasty wit. The captain silences her with a look.

'When's dinner, Eva honey? Your Uncle Duck's starved.'

166

'What else is new?' Rowena sniffs. 'Wouldn't hurt you to wait a while, Duck. You've got plenty of blubber stored.'

'When were you planning to serve, Eva dear?' the captain asks mildly.

'Soon as Ethan comes down,' Eva says.

'Wonder what the boy could be doing up there so long?' Duck muses.

Walking down the hall, I noticed that the nursery was empty. So was the bathroom. All this time, I've pictured Ethan down here, playing in another room to escape dull adult chat. Now cold fear grips me.

'Ethan's not upstairs,' I say.

'But he has to be,' Eva says. 'Oh my God. Not again.'

'Keep calm,' the captain insists. 'We'll find him. Eva, check the house. Help her, Caleb. Don't forget closets and cupboards. Boy could be playing hide and seek.

'Laurel, go check the neighbours'. They're all ashore this week, but he may have wandered over to have a look around. Aunt Rowena, you stay here and keep our guest company. Duck and I'll see to the beach and the woods.'

'I'm going with you,' I tell him. The child is not in this house. I can feel it.

The captain hesitates, then nods agreement. Aunt Sadie perks up and bounds to join us.

Outside, Captain Haskel stands staring at the broad, blackened vista. The sky is grim. No moon or stars.

Eva's father remains firmly in command. 'Search the woods, Duck. I'll take the east beach to the lighthouse. Bethany, you walk that way, toward the rocks.'

Aunt Sadie stands at the edge of the lawn. 'Come on, girl.'

Starting beyond the jetty, the dog and I make a slow sweep of the darkened sand. I peer behind every tree trunk. I stare at the branches, hoping to spot a small figure folded behind the leaves. No sign of him.

'Ethan?' I call.

The tide is tumbling in. Greedy monster, gobbling the

167

beach. Watery limbs strain toward me, teasing. Sadie jaunts ahead, setting a brave example.

Dense woods divide Eva Haskel's property from her neighbours'. I'm forced to tread an ever-shrinking band between the shoreline and the trees. Encroaching water soaks the sand beneath my feet.

'Ethan? Sadie!'

The dog has trotted well ahead. She waits impatiently for me to catch up. Grasping her collar, I continue on to the southern tip of the island, where the beach abruptly ends in a rocky outcropping.

Scrabbling on all fours, I scale the rock hill and peer beyond.

No Ethan.

Turning back, I quicken my pace. The tide is still advancing, shrinking the beach to a suffocating tube.

I force myself to peer out over the boiling surf. Beyond the breakwater, the sound billows like a black satin sheet. No boats, no swimmers. Far away, a world away, I spy the seductive haze of shore lights.

'Ethan!'

Behind me, Eva Haskel's house looms invitingly. Maybe Duck Weems or the captain has found the boy by now. I picture the little beast huddled in front of the fire, revelling in his relatives' attentions.

Aunt Sadie sloshes through the rising tidewater to my right. She's my mooring. My barrier reef. As vines of panic coil around my legs, I jabber nervously at the dog.

'Kid's probably in the house right now, don't you think, girl? Here we're soaked and miserable and Ethan's probably roasting cosily by the fire.'

Nearing the jetty, I turn toward the house. But I'm quickly stalled by uncertainty. The captain asked me to search the beach to the island's eastern extremity. Did he expect me to examine the jetty as well?

With a shudder, I face the long plank walk. Perched on squat pilings, it juts out over the dizzying surf.

168

'The captain must've looked here, right? I'm sure he did. Let's go, girl.'

But the dog stands pat, aiming a loaded look my way.

'I can't go out there, pal. No way.'

Aunt Sadie sniffs her contempt and trots toward the pier. She struts across the skinny wooden span, showing me how easily it can be done. I'm terrified for her. Terrified period.

At the end of the walk, Aunt Sadie comes to a sudden halt. Her tail drops and her ears twitch like seeking antennae. Bowing her forelegs, she leans out over the edge.

Suddenly, the water ten yards out whips in a frantic froth. There's a sharp sound. Another furious splatter. Then a small, strangled cry: 'Help!'

'Oh my God. Ethan?'

Racing toward the voice, I spot the boy splashing wildly in the dark currents.

'Over here!' I shout. 'Swim this way.'

The child's arms churn. He's gulping for air. 'Help,' he sputters. 'Can't move. Something's got me.'

'Kick your feet. Arm over arm. You know how. You can do it.'

'Can't. I'm stuck.'

The noose of fear tightens so hard, I can barely speak. 'Swim, kiddo. Push.'

'Let me *go*!' He shrieks. 'Stop it!'

A bout of furious coughing leaves him limp. Bristling with horror, I watch him sink beneath the waves.

Swallowed by the currents. Taken. Lost.

The mighty Sound sucks him in. Burps a ragged line of bubbles.

All your fault, Bethany. All your fault.

Before I can move, the child bursts to the surface five feet from the jetty. 'Quick,' he gasps. 'Get me out of here.'

Desperately, I search for help. There's no one. I drop prone on the plank walk. The surf is mere inches from my face. Rabid frothing.

169

Aunt Sadie barks encouragement as I strain to reach the boy. 'Here. Give me your hand.'

But he's still too far away. Breath held, I edge out further. I'm perched precariously over the seething surf. Numb with fright. 'Now!'

Our fingers touch. Stretching hard, I catch his slippery wrist.

'That's it. Easy.' Slowly, evenly, I drag him closer.

'Help!'

The child resists. Pulls with superhuman force. I'm losing purchase, sliding over the slick planks towards the water.

'Help!' he screams. 'Help me!'

Aunt Sadie clamps my skirt in her jaws. As she pulls, my foot hits a wooden upright. I splay my legs and coil my feet around the rails.

That halts my forward skid. 'Easy, now, Buddy. I'm going to pull you in. Don't fight me.'

'Hurry! Quick! I gotta get out of here before the monster comes back.'

'There's no monster.'

'Yes there is,' the child splutters. 'I could've made it except for him. I could have gone home.'

'Take it easy. I've got you.'

'Get me *out* of here!'

Slowly, cautiously, I scrabble backward. Sadie howls like a crazed coyote as at last I haul the sopping child out of the water. She barks at us, then dashes off to bay at the anchor.

The dog's commotion draws Eva and Rowena Haskel from the house. I hear them calling out to us as I draw the trembling little boy on to my lap.

23

She gave them some broth without any bread. She whipped them all soundly and put them to bed.

'There was an old woman'

The women offer Ethan hot soaks, warm towels, dry clothes, and frantic sympathies.

'Here's a nice pair of pyjamas for you, sweetheart,' Laurel chirps.

'The boy's not sick, Laurel,' says Rowena. 'He still has to eat his dinner.'

'Why must you always criticize?'

'Why must you always screw things up?' Retracting her fangs, the old crone turns to me. 'We Haskels always dress for dinner. Always have. In my day, we'd set a formal table in the parlour. Good silver, china. The works. Every night a special occasion.'

Eva towels the boy's hair. 'You gave us such a fright, my darling. You can't go off swimming in the dead of night like that. It's terribly dangerous.'

Ethan submits miserably to the overwrought attentions. He's limp with exhaustion. 'But I have to go home. Want my daddy. Stupid monster.'

'I know what would be nice!' Laurel claps her hands. 'A little tea.'

'A little *brandy* would be nicer,' Rowena adds drily. 'And a *lot* would be nicer still.'

'Hold up your arms, darling. That's the way.' Eva pulls on the pyjama top and slips the bottoms beneath the towel cinching Ethan's waist. Thick vertical stripes give him the look of a miniature convict.

Duck Weems barrels through the back door. His face is

171

florid. Leafy debris cakes his clothes. 'Heard you call, Laurel. Where'd you go, son? We searched all over.'

'Dumb monster got me,' Ethan whines. 'He held my feet so hard, I couldn't swim away.'

'Monster? What's he talking about?'

'Boy got it in his head to try to swim in the water. Says it had *tentacles*.' Rowena reports with exaggerated solemnity.

Catching her pointed look, Duck nods. 'Sounds like that thing's come back again. Don't you think, Rowena?'

'Thing?'

'Yes. The *thing*, you know.'

'Oh. You mean the *demon*,' the old lady intones.

Duck bobbles his head. 'Right, the *demon* thing.' He eyes the child severely. 'Best stay out of the water unless you've got one of the grownups along, son. We island folk know how to handle the demon thing. Takes years of experience. Special techniques. You go swimming alone, you're plain asking for trouble.'

The front door slams, and the captain appears. He's sweat-soaked and huffing. Wet sand cakes his slacks and blazer.

'Boy's here? Thank goodness. Where'd you find him?'

'He was trying to swim ashore,' Eva replies. 'Got caught on something. If not for Bethany – '

Ethan has collapsed in a shrimplike curl on the couch. He's sobbing feverishly. 'I want to go home. I want my dad.'

The captain perches beside the boy and pats the slim, heaving back. 'You were stuck out there? Must've been scary.'

'It was the demon thing,' Ethan snuffles. 'It was *huge*.'

'I was telling the boy he mustn't ever go swimming without one of us.' Uncle Duck winks. 'Said we know how to handle that mean old demon thing from all the other times he's come around.'

The captain scowls. 'There's no need to frighten the boy, Duck. You listen to me, son. There's no demon thing or any such nonsense out there.'

172

'But something grabbed me. I could feel it. It wouldn't let go.'

'Thoughtless folk dump all manner of junk in the Sound. Things you wouldn't imagine. Chances are you caught a piece of old tyre or plastic tubing or Lord knows. Happened to me more than once, and I can tell you it felt for all the world like a nasty old monster had taken hold. Mighty hard not to panic at a time like that. And it's tough to work yourself loose when you're upset. Good thing Bethany came along to help you out. I trust you thanked her properly.'

The child sneers his heartfelt gratitude.

'The rest of what Duck said goes, young man. Children don't swim alone on Rand's. Never, under any circumstances. That's our rule.' The captain's tone bars further discussion.

'You *sure* it wasn't the demon thing?' Ethan asks meekly.

'You've got my word. And I want yours that you won't go trying any more foolish stunts like that. You have to start accepting that we're your family, son. You belong here with us, and here you'll stay. You're going to love it on the island. Now, dry your tears. We've had enough sorrow around this household to last a lifetime.'

Ethan mops his face with the captain's hankie.

'That's better. Now, it so happens your mother's made a special dinner in honour of having you home. Everyone brought a favourite dish to go along. And your grandma Laurel made her best dessert. Don't suppose you're hungry?'

The child sits up. Shrugs. His resilience is astounding. 'If you're all eating, I guess . . .'

The captain's stern look doesn't waver. 'Not at all. You feel like skipping supper, that's fine.'

'The boy has to eat, Poppa,' Eva says.

'No need to fuss at him, Eva,' her father chides. 'Child knows his own appetite.'

'I guess I'm a *little* hungry . . .'

'Well, then. You can try a bite or two. See how they go down.'

A tall, hefty young woman in tattered jeans and a paint-spattered shirt joins us. She flings her plump arms around Duck's neck and busses him loudly. 'Hey, sweetheart. Hope I'm not too late.'

'Just in time, Jeannie girl.' Patting her square-fingered hands, Duck's colour rises. I note the matching wedding bands.

Butterscotch wisps droop from her high-pitched ponytail. Approaching me, she blows the overgrown bangs from her forehead. Her bronze-flecked hazel eyes are wide and warm. 'I'm Jeanette. Just came by to say hello.'

'Bethany Logan.'

'Good to meet you.'

She goes to Ethan, hands propped on knees. '*Hey* there, cutie. I'm sure you don't remember, but *I'm* your Aunt Jeanette.'

'Yeah,' Ethan says. 'So are we eating now?'

'You're welcome to join us, Jeanette.' Eva's icy tone belies the invitation.

The smile freezes on the young woman's face. 'Thanks anyway. Have to get back to the kids. You people go on. Don't let me disturb you.'

The captain says, 'Shall we?' Everyone stands and mills toward the dining room. Caleb strides in last. My heart does a drum roll.

Before I get to the table, Jeanette slips up behind me and whispers in my ear: 'Heard you're a teacher. That so?'

'Yes.'

'Something I'd like to discuss with you, Ms Logan, if you don't mind.'

'Sure. What?'

'Any chance you could stop by my place tomorrow? I'm in the cottage near the lighthouse.'

'Sure. Is the morning good?'

'Great. See you then.'

The captain directs me to a chair. Heaping platters crowd the sideboard. Eva serves.

When the last dish has been distributed, the captain

174

claims the head seat and bows his head. 'Thank you, Lord, for the bounty you have bestowed upon us this day. Thank you for the blessings of peace, hope, and health. And above all, thanks for reuniting us with our dear boy Ethan.'

There's a chorus of 'Amens'. Before the sound dies, the child tackles his food like a ravenous sow. Aunt Sadie daintily attacks the bowl Eva has set out for her under the sideboard. I'm starving too, but I try to exhibit a tad more restraint. *Slobber slowly, Bethany. Gobble with your mouth shut.*

The food is insufferably mature and wholesome, but I'm too hungry to care. Even Caleb's musky presence fails to derail my freight-train appetite. Fortunately, he's seated three places to my left where I can't see him unless I lean forward. I can almost put the sexy stranger out of my mind. Almost.

Eva Haskel has prepared a vegetarian stew and fresh biscuits. Rowena has smoked the trout and baked a sweet potato pie. There's a salad and fruit plate courtesy of Uncle Duck. Laurel's contribution is a strawberry cheesecake so rich I consider eliminating the middleman and spackling it on to my thighs.

Talk at the table is bland. The captain moderates the discussion, passing his attentions around the table like a shaker of salt.

I learn that Rowena is halfway through her reread of the complete works of William Shakespeare. *Hamlet* remains her favourite play.

'Suppose I relate to the family lunacy,' the old woman chortles. 'If Old Will were still around, he could write a real family nut story. Call it *Haskel*.'

The captain frowns. 'I think you're giving our guest the wrong impression, Rowena. Every family has its little quirks.'

'True, Captain. And some have their *big* quirks and their even bigger kooks.' Satisfied, she sets her rumpled jaw.

Laurel offers a gardening report. 'I've upped the nitrogen and used the black plastic to keep down the weeds and you

175

wouldn't believe the change. I'm talking double the size tomatoes. Squash big as baseball bats. Next year, you'll have to try it, Eva dear.'

'I will, Momma. You can help in the garden if you like, Ethan,' Eva offers. 'Cousin Caleb can even clear you a vegetable patch of your own.'

The captain's look darkens. Chastened, Eva bites her lip. She has clearly spoken out of turn.

'Caleb? What are you up to?' asks the captain.

My pulse pounds. Breathless, I await the sound of his voice. The first tempting peek under his tantalizing surface.

The handsome stranger takes his time.

'Caleb?'

I lean for a better look. Soon, a slow smile warps his perfect mouth. The sensuous lips part, revealing cracked crooked teeth. 'Kale cut tree. Split log,' he drones.

Everyone praises the young man's contribution. Even Rowena displays genuine delight. She may be a nasty old witch, but she shows true affection to her retarded grand-nephew.

I inwardly groan at my miscalculation. My talent for misjudging men has risen to dizzying new heights.

'That's the attitude, Caleb,' the captain says. 'Keep up the good work.'

'Kale work.' The young man beams.

His crooked smile is engaging. 'Cutting wood sounds hard,' I say.

'Hod,' he concedes.

'You, Duck? How'd Jeanette like the new paint job?'

'Everything's fine but the living room,' Duck says. 'Jeannie finds the beige depressing. Maybe when Caleb's free, he can slap on a coat of white.'

'Kale paint.'

'Seems foolish seeing the place is just a vacation home. Jeanette's *awfully* particular,' Laurel says.

'If she's so particular, what's she doing with Duck?' Rowena snickers.

'Everyone *knows* that,' Laurel mutters.

Duck reddens. 'You leave Jeannie alone. All of you. So happens she's a very special girl.'

Grinning smugly, Rowena says, 'Right, Duck. If she wasn't so special, I'm sure you wouldn't have awarded her the Duck Weems Scholarship.'

The captain frowns, slamming the subject closed. 'Eva tells me you're a teacher, Bethany. What's your subject?'

'Learning disabilities. I work with the boys who need extra help.'

Ethan slips me a wordless warning. I'm not to mention that he's one of them.

'Nothing better than working one on one. Always believed in it myself,' the captain says. 'You'll have your lessons here with me, Ethan. Just the two of us.'

'You mean, I don't have to go to *school*?'

'Not a formal school, no.'

His eyes are huge. 'Wait 'til Jonah hears *that*!'

'Anyone for more cake?' Laurel asks.

The captain says, 'What have I been thinking? I've forgotten to make the toast.' Crossing to the sideboard, he pops the cork on a bottle of Dom Perignon and pours a round.

I eye my crystal flute, warily watching the manic fizz. I like champagne, but I don't trust it. I've come to associate the drink with clumsy seductions, forced merriment, and the maiden voyage of the good ship *Titanic*.

Lofting his glass, the captain says, 'To you, Miss Logan. And to our Ethan. Home again.'

I take just a sip to be polite. But the wine vaults directly to my head.

The captain excuses himself from the room. After he leaves, the calm collapses. Everyone talks at once. The lamplight flickers in the eager rush of breath.

Rowena's rumpled lips purse over sharp, yellow teeth. Laurel croons, Eva flutters. Caleb echoes a long beat behind. Duck tells a joke. Everyone laughs while I'm still waiting for the punchline. Ethan and I are the only quiet ones. The child looks glazed. His face droops.

The captain returns and the raucous group snaps back to order.

My wooziness is worsening. 'If you'll excuse me, I think I'd better go lie down.'

'Certainly, dear,' Laurel says.

'You okay?' Uncle Duck's kindly face sways like a storm-tossed tree.

'Fine. Just a little tired.'

'Understandable. You've had a long day,' Duck says.

'Best lie down before she falls down,' Rowena mutters.

'Let me help you, Bethany,' Eva says.

'No really. I'm fine.' My words stretch like heated wax. Forcefully, I clip them short. 'If you'll excuse me –'

'Go on and see our guest to her room, daughter,' the captain commands. 'Make sure she has everything she needs.'

I don't argue. I'm too focused on the daunting task of traversing the room.

''Night, everyone.'

'This way, Bethany.'

I follow Eva with the grave concentration of the seriously impaired. How could this be? I've had almost nothing to drink.

By the time I reach the second floor, Eva has crossed to the end of the corridor. A cloud of whispers wafts up from below me. I can't tell who's speaking, but I catch intriguing scraps.

Think she'll do it again? one voice says.

Christ, I hope not.

Have to keep her away from him. Hope for the best.

I don't know what they're talking about, and I'm in no shape to make an intelligent guess. Stiffly, I trail the slender wraith to her husband's study. Eva strips the covers, helps me out of my sandals, and hands me a nightgown.

Too weary for words, I slip it on and flop down on the bed.

'Shall I bring a basin so you can wash?' Eva asks.

She floats from the room. I know I'm supposed to be

178

waiting for something, but the thought darts beyond my reach. The room spins like a crazed carousel. I close my eyes to block the queasy image.

Seriously, Bethany. How could you be this blotto on a couple of sips of champagne?

I hear a flurry of footsteps. There's a distant cry. Then, an electric silence.

My pulse pounds. Sharp questions pelt my muddled mind. What happened down there? Who screamed? Was it something to do with those whispers?

Before I can gather my thoughts, a furious tide of exhaustion rolls in and sweeps them away.

Them and me.

24

See, see what shall I see?
A horse's head where his tail should be.
                                    'See, see'

I snap awake, heart racing. This is not my room. Not my bed. Panicked, I search the darkness.

My head pounds. My tongue feels furry. A sour swell rises at the back of my throat.

Where the hell am I?

Slowly, I gather the rags of memory. Was it only yesterday I left Hinsdale? Seems a world away. Another lifetime.

I remember snatching the little boy. The hideous ride with him down from Hinsdale. The terrifying trip across the Sound on Jackson Quint's mailboat.

The rest comes flooding back. The Silence. This ritual week. All mainland ties severed. No means to reconnect with my normal life.

The room is bleak and cold. Groping around the unfamiliar space, I search the closet for a robe.

The floral dress I wore last night dangles from a padded hanger. My sandals have been wiped clean and meticulously aligned on the floor. The attic castoffs hang with military precision. Fresh underwear is folded on a side shelf. Another holds wrapped toiletries. I've been installed.

Padding down the hall, I catch a muffled noise from the nursery. The door is open a crack. A tepid glow seeps out.

Treading nearer, I hear Eva Haskel murmuring. 'There, there, darling. That's my sweet baby boy.'

I expect the child to protest. But he says nothing.

'Such a *good* little sweetheart,' Eva croons. 'Want Momma to sing to you?'

I gird for the boy's response. Any second now, he's bound

180

to erupt with angry objections. Go for it, kiddo. Tell her you're no baby. Tell her what she can do with her stupid song.

Not a peep.

Come on, big guy. Toss one of your famous tantrums. Say something fresh. Anything would be better than this stolid silence. I never wanted to see the kid broken like a headstrong horse bound for field work.

But he stays mute.

I suffer a twinge of doubt. Maybe I haven't done the child any favours. Maybe he was better off living the lie. Pip Stafford was a monster, true. But a live beast is preferable to a doormat.

Eva sings in a high, flimsy voice. 'Hush, little baby, don't say a word. Momma's gonna buy you a mockingbird – '

Okay, buddy. Give the lady what for. Tell her you'll say all the words you damned well please. Tell her what she can do with her stupid mockingbird.

Maybe he's asleep. That's the only reasonable explanation for this passivity. I edge closer. The floorboards screech.

'Bethany? Is that you?'

'Yes.'

'Come in.'

Dressed in a man's terry robe, Eva sits in the dusty rocker. She's swaying gently, clutching a tube of blankets to her chest.

The cover on the daybed is undisturbed. No sign that anyone has slept here.

'Where's Ethan?'

Her smile looks forced. 'At my parents' house. The captain thought he might be more comfortable staying with them.'

'But why?'

'My son has been with that awful man Stafford for years. He's not accustomed to the company of a woman, the captain says.'

Would have been good of the captain to have his say

before I was sentenced to a week of hard time here on East Alcatraz.

'I heard you singing.'

Rising, she sets the blankets down in the crib.

'I was just sitting here, thinking. I suppose I'll have to redo this room. Ethan's not a baby any more.'

Not a baby and not a Dickens character. 'Not a bad idea.'

'Does he have a favourite colour?'

'I honestly don't know.'

'What about interests? Is there anything he particularly likes to do?'

'Sports, definitely. All kinds. He's a terrific athlete.'

'Would you know – ? Is he still fond of boats?'

I shrug. 'He enjoyed the trip over from the mainland.'

'But he's not fascinated the way he used to be.' Pain pinches her pale face.

'New Hampshire is landlocked, Eva. Other than the occasional lake, there's not much opportunity for boating.'

Her eyes fill. 'Of course, he was bound to change. But it's so hard to accept. My own son, and I barely know him.'

'You will.'

She shifts the blankets to the centre of the crib. The surrounding sheet is dust-caked. Eva is fastidious about the rest of the house, but this room is grimy and bleak. Maybe she's maintained the nursery as a shrine to her kidnapped child, unwilling to disturb even the dust mites.

'Tell me about him will you, Bethany? What sort of boy has my baby become?'

I choose the words carefully, discarding the loaded ones. 'Spirited. Popular with the kids. Active.' Sounds so much better than the honest alternatives: wild, manipulative, uncontrollable. Pain in the butt.

'Is he a good student?'

'He's very smart. But he needs special help in reading.'

'Then he'll have it.'

Returning to the chair, she starts to sway again. The rockers have been worn dull. Pale ruts mark the space beneath them. I wonder how many times during these past

182

six years Eva has sat here in the dead of a sleepless night, cradling frail memories of her lost little boy.

'I hope you're feeling better,' she says.

'Much. I can't imagine how I got so tipsy.'

Her look darkens. 'You need to understand, Bethany. The past has left an indelible imprint on this place. On us. Our family history touches everything here. Directs everything.'

I don't see what that has to do with my strikingly low tolerance for alcohol. But I leave it alone.

'Have you always lived on Rand's?' I ask instead.

'Of course. It's my home.'

'All year round?'

'Always.'

Impossible thought. To me, this is a space station. The lost kingdom of Atlantis. Front of the class in aerobics. An unthinkably alien world.

'What about school?'

'The captain taught me. And I learned from nature. We're much more finely tuned to her forces here. Storms and tides. Phases of the moon. Island dwellers celebrate all the crucial cycles that people of the land tend to ignore. I couldn't have asked for a better education.'

'But it must have been lonely.'

She looks surprised. 'Not at all. I had my family. My home. What more could a little girl want?'

Where do I begin? What would growing up have been without revolving pals? Rotating boyfriends. Outlandish joys. Excruciating humiliations. The wonderful, grand, high, ridiculous drama of it all.

'Sounds – different.' I shiver with the chill and the very idea.

'You're cold, Bethany. Would you care for some tea? Coffee?'

'Coffee would be wonderful.'

The kitchen woodstove is cold. Aunt Sadie sprawls beside it. Eva plucks wood from the brass holder, feeds it into the belly of the stove, and relights the blaze.

From a basin beside the door, she ladles water into an

183

ancient percolator. She fetches fresh beans from the pantry, grinds them in a handmill, and sets the pot on the stove to heat. I watch the whole process in awe. Nothing plugged in or switched on. Nothing up the woman's sleeve.

'The captain says Ethan will be much happier here once Cal comes home. Happier having a man around, the way he's used to.'

'When is your husband due back?'

'No boats are permitted until midnight Sunday. I'm sure he'll be here first thing Monday.' She speaks with the ardent conviction of the terminally insecure.

'How did you two meet?'

'Aunt Rowena hired Cal to design some alterations to her place. I was taken with him immediately. Made quite a pest of myself, I'm afraid. Mooning around while he was trying to get his work done.' She smiles at the memory.

'Must be hard for him. Hard for any outsider to get used to living here.'

'My husband is *not* an outsider,' she snaps. 'The island's every bit as much Cal's home as it is mine. He only goes ashore when it's absolutely necessary for his work.'

'Of course. I only meant – '

'Cal'll be back Monday morning. First thing.'

Ferreting through the cabinets, she sets out sugar, cream, and a quickbread studded with nuts and raisins.

We sip in silence. Soon, a faint pink blush tinges the sky. The first of dawn drizzles through the window. A sword of light forms and strikes the polished floor.

Eva springs to her feet. 'You'll have to excuse me, Bethany. There's something I have to do. Please make yourself at home. I won't be long.'

Barefoot, she hurries out. Peering through the window, I watch her traverse the lawn toward the woods. She reaches the thicket in seconds. Then, she disappears between two towering oaks.

'Wonder where she's going.'

Aunt Sadie yawns and log-rolls on her side.

'What can she have to do at this ungodly hour in the woods? Think she's meeting someone? A lover?'

The dog's response is a gritty snore. Sadie's a smalltown pooch. She's heard it all.

'I doubt that's it. She's obviously nuts about her husband. Besides, who is there to fool around with in this godforsaken place?'

The dog sighs. She hates it when I let my imagination fly without a net.

'What could possibly make her run off like that?'

Aunt Sadie cracks a rheumy eye.

'Come on, pal. Get up and help me figure this one out. Why did the weird lady go to the woods?'

Sadie slowly unfolds and lumbers toward me. We share a few slices of nut bread. I rack my mind for plausible explanations, but I can't think of any. Aunt Sadie has nothing to contribute but enthusiastic chewing and an occasional yawn.

Out of ideas, I set the question aside. Ethan Haskel is home where he belongs. The rest is none of my business. Idle curiosity got me into this mess. Stuck on an island, surrounded by the liquid enemy.

I pour myself more coffee. The pot is getting cold.

25

Eva hastened toward the woods, spurred by a quick pulse of urgency.

She dared not be late.

At the thicket's edge, she paused and searched the sombre sky. The twin oaks towered twenty yards ahead. Their massive crowns lowered like storm-clouds, deepening the gloom.

Slipping between their trunks, Eva tracked a narrow path through the huddled stands of sycamore and beech. The way was utterly familiar. A carpet of pine needles cushioned her steps.

The slender tunnel amplified sound. Eva heard the wind sough. Flutter of birds' wings. Unseen creatures skittering through the brush.

A silver birch marked the turnoff. Spotting its papery glow, Eva slowed.

The entrance was masked by brambled vines. She found the spot where the briars had been stripped away. The smooth green tendrils overhung the bough of an elm. Pulling firmly, she parted the drape of greenery.

The clearing was a near-perfect circle. At its centre stretched a shimmering lagoon. Eva's image wavered seductively on the surface. Carefully, she reached back and drew the curtain of vines.

Eva slipped the pins from her hair and shook it loose. She slid the cotton shift from her shoulders and let it fall in a sighing heap around her feet. Naked, she mounted the mossy bank. She wavered in the wind's caress. The playful nip of the night's chill. Breezy fingers ruffled her hair.

Filling her lungs, she dived in, shattering the pool's mirrored surface. With languid strokes, she swam its length and breadth. Scissoring her legs, she burrowed toward the

186

murky bottom. There she rested in the playful swirl of an eddy until her lungs ached.

Bursting up, she drank the air. Slowly releasing the stream, she willed her darting thoughts to settle. Eva drew another breath, trapping her worries in the vortex. Forcefully she exhaled, driving them off like an acrid fog.

Trancelike, she slipped out of the pond and poised on the spongy bank. She bowed her head and pressed her palms together.

Staring at the woods, Eva waited for the voice that could only be heard in a perfect silence. She stood in full surrender of her will. Tranquil flesh. Senses hushed. Mind a tide of warm serenity.

She'd last heard the voice six years ago. It had come to her at this time, in this place.

Since childhood, Eva had prized the bracing sting of an early morning swim. Unless the pond was frozen, she'd come here every day at sunrise. This place was Eva's best friend and closest confidante. She called it the Genesis Pool: source of all beginnings.

It was here as a timid six-year-old that she'd first found the courage to swim underwater, surrendering faith to the liquid depths. Here at ten, she'd discovered the sensitive bumps sprouting on her chest. At twelve, her first period started here with a quickening in her womb and a sticky rush between her legs. She'd lost her virginity here, taking her young lover inside her while they drifted in the whorling melt. He was a summer visitor on the island, one of the transient thieves who stopped on Rand's only long enough to grab what they could.

Growing up, Eva had come here to ponder her most important questions.

Largest of all was the matter of island living, deciding whether to remain on Rand's for life or move away.

The captain had insisted that Eva make the choice herself. He'd arranged to remove all impediments, so it was a choice of heart, not practicality. Eva recalled him telling her so in grave ceremony on the day she turned fourteen.

Mainland cousins had agreed to take her in, to raise her from now to maturity, the captain said. She could go to a mainland high school. Then on to college if she liked. She could have her fill of strangers. Fresh experiences. She could have all the noise and odd beliefs and uncertainty she'd been deprived of in the past.

Eva had come to the Genesis Pool to consider the choice fully. She'd searched the pond for hints of what life would be like on shore. But all she'd seen was the crystal clarity of this place, this way. The only way she'd really ever known.

Eva realized then that everything she needed, everything she might ever need, was on this island. She didn't have to go off in search of the future. It would find her here.

And so it had.

She'd found love. Made a home. Embarked on what had seemed a shining future. And she'd done it all without having to relinquish what was familiar to her. She still lived in her treasured place, still enjoyed the familiar pleasures. She still began each day at the Genesis Pool.

After the baby's birth, she arrived at the lagoon well before dawn so she'd be home before the child awoke for his morning feeding.

That long ago day, as she stood dripping on the bank after her swim, she'd heard the disembodied voice: *Beware the gold*, it warned. *Every tarnished lamb must be sacrificed.*

Eva had tried to dismiss the peculiar words as a waking dream or some cruel hoax perpetrated by the wind. She'd struggled to set aside her mounting unease, but the warning echoed stubbornly in her thoughts.

Beware the gold? Tarnished lambs?

What did it mean? Why did those odd phrases sound so familiar?

Dressing quickly, Eva had anxiously started home. She ached to hold her baby son. She longed for the comfort of

188

his warmth, the sweetness of his scent. Current spiked through her breasts. A rush of milk soaked her bodice.

Eva kept racing until she emerged from the forest at the twin oaks. Then, facing the house, she was stalled by a chill foreboding.

She'd forced herself to keep going, to walk inside. Behind her, the rear door slammed with dark finality.

Sick with dread, Eva climbed the stairs and went to the nursery. Her heart squirmed. Her shadow shrivelled beneath her as she approached the crib.

She didn't have to look. Eva knew her baby was gone. His absence was a crushing blow to her chest.

Facing the pond now, Eva set that unbearable memory aside. The nightmare was over. At last, her darling boy had been returned. After these six long years, she was whole again.

Eva waited at the pond until the sun climbed well over the horizon. She held herself open to the disembodied voice. But the silence held firm.

Tomorrow, she would return again. As many tomorrows as it took, she would stand listening. This time, she would not miss the warning. This time, any sacrifice to be made would not be hers.

26 I wait for the coffee jolt. But soon I realize the beans must have been decaffeinated. Most often, I can tell by the taste, but this brew had me fooled. Shamelessly, I search the pantry for the real stuff.

I find nothing of use. No real coffee. No chocolate or cola drinks. No sugary junk. Not even a small defibrillator.

If only I was back at Hinsdale. I could stroll across campus to draw a cup off the giant urn in the teachers' lounge. I could drive into town for a Mega-mug with unlimited free refills at Dippin' Donuts.

It's too early to drop in on perky young Aunt Jeanette. Way too late to forget I ever met Pip and Adam Stafford.

I can't do anything on this oversized raft. I have no choices, no freedom. I can barely breathe.

I want my life back. I want out.

I'm struck by a sudden inspiration. No doubt my sister knows dozens of boat owners in the area. She may even have a yacht or two of her own tucked away somewhere. Roo has always been full of expensive surprises.

Snatching the receiver from the wall phone, I start to dial. But the delusion shatters in a breath. Furious, I curse the dead air. Stab the tuneless buttons. Jiggle the lifeless hook.

This has to stop. There has to be some way off this island. And I'm damned well going to find it.

My clothes have been washed and folded tidily beside the sink. Shedding the robe and nightgown, I pull on my denim shorts and white T-shirt. They're tinged with a faint smell of woodsmoke.

Nothing on this floating rock feels normal, but it helps a bit to be wearing my own things. The musty garments

190

from the attic feel like ghost skins. Haunted remnants of an unrelenting past.

I want no more of them. Of this. I'm gripped by the old aching rootlessness. I need to get away.

Maybe there's a boat Eva doesn't know about or some means of communication both of us have overlooked. Aunt Sadie's rheumy eyes open a crack.

'Come on, girl. Let's look around.'

As soon as I open the door, Sadie streaks across the lawn, scattering the geese and egrets.

I hang back, keeping my distance from the water. 'Come on, girl. Let's go.'

We bypass the house and cross the rear yard. Lush shadows blanket the lawn. The grass here is high and mercifully clear of bird droppings.

A lacy stand of evergreens frames the yard. Beyond lies an overgrown meadow studded with tree stumps. I trudge through the knee-high scrub. Sadie forges ahead, hopping like a huge beige bunny.

At the centre of the stretch, we come upon the shell of a burnt-out building. Blackened beams fence the charred foundation. A broken wall stands heat-warped and smeared with soot. The ground is littered with twisted metal, blistered glass, and blackened wood chunks.

Eyeing the sorry remains, I feel a chill. Who owned this place? I wonder if anyone was injured or killed in the blaze. The intensity of the fire must have been enormous.

Aunt Sadie passes through the ruin at a skittish trot. Poised beyond, she yips at me to keep moving.

The rising sun is sharp. The sea breeze sputters its last, and the air goes limp. Heat fuses the shirt to my skin. Aunt Sadie bravely bears the burden of her fur suit.

Through a second windbreak I find a small brick building. The windows are boarded. A serious chain and padlock bind the door. I peer in through a crack in the mortar, but the blackness inside is a wall.

Further along, the land inclines sharply toward a towering bluff. I scrabble halfway up to a broad spur overlooking

191

the island's northern beach. Two outsized homes roost at the crest.

The house on the right is a stately building in the Queen Anne style. The first floor has a dark brick face and a wraparound veranda. The second floor sports decorative shingles and a line of casement windows. Turrets rise from the broad tiled roof. A profusion of bright petunias spills from the window-boxes. Trim privet frames the cut-stone walk.

A length of fishnet hangs beside the door. From that and the nautical flag, I cleverly reason that the house must belong to the captain.

The sprawling place to the left looks perfect for feisty old Aunt Rowena. The architecture is stick style, bold and brusque. Steep asymmetrical gables form the roof. Bright boards set at unexpected angles adorn the façade. The gardens abound with weeds and wild flowers.

I don't want to be spotted snooping. Leaving the spur, Sadie and I tread the precipitous downslope. Rocks spit beneath her scrabbling paws. I grope in the crumbling soil for solid purchase.

A small orchard nestles near the base of the hill. Beneath the bower of trees, a quartet of redwood tables circles a blackened grill. One of the tables has been toppled on its side. A dull white object rests on the ground beside it. From this distance, I can't tell what it is.

The path steepens. I'm forced to brace my hands against jutting rocks. Nearing the bottom of the slope, I glance again at the white object.

My stomach heaves. I blink hard, trying to dispel the revolting image. There's a human foot protruding from that table. The hideous thing is dead white. Still and bloodless.

Horror sweeps over me. Undaunted, Aunt Sadie ambles onward. She lopes behind the overturned table for a better look.

My pulse is pounding. If there's a corpse back there, I do not want to see it. If there's only the foot, I definitely do *not* want to know.

192

I will simply turn back. I'll get the hell away from here. Whoever, whatever that is behind that table has nothing to do with me. Let the islanders deal with it.

Aunt Sadie continues to nose around behind the table. Cringing, I picture her lapping the blood. Sniffing the rotted flesh.

My gorge rises. 'Stop that, Sadie!' I rasp. 'Come here.'

Peering out, she regards me with contempt. Then she resumes her morbid investigation.

'No, Sadie. I mean it!'

The dog chuffs and stays put. She's entranced with the dead stranger. Bewitched by the empty eyes. The chill, rigid limbs.

'Okay, fine. Stay if you want. I'm leaving.' Shakily, I start away, treading up the slope.

'Get away!' a voice shrills.

For an instant, I have the surreal sense that the dog has spoken. Then I spot the young woman rising from behind the table. Dark eyes dominate a small-featured face. Her hair is cropped so close, a fog of scalp shows through.

'Sorry if my dog disturbed you. We were just – '

'Who sent you?' she demands. 'What do you want?'

'Nobody sent me. I was just taking a walk.'

She backs away, pointing an accusatory finger. A canvas tote bag dangles from her wrist. 'You're the one who brought the boy home.'

'Yes.'

'Why him? Why now? Damn you. You've ruined everything.'

She wears a voluminous yellow sundress. The fabric strains over the pregnant swell of her middle.

'I don't understand.'

Clutching the belly bulge, she backs away.

'Don't move.'

She fishes in the bag and whips out an army knife. Retreating, she makes harsh slashing moves at the air.

'Stay right there,' she commands. 'Keep away from me.'

'Okay. Take it easy.'

At the edge of the grove, she turns and bolts. I'm left stunned in a sea of questions. I'm dying to know who she is. She has the trademark Haskel pallor and raven hair. But so do a lot of people.

If she's family, why would she be sleeping out here in the grove? If she's not, what is she doing on the island? According to Eva, only Haskels stay for the week-long observance. No visitors are allowed during the Silence.

From the look of her, she's not far from her due date. At such a time, I can't imagine choosing to hide out on this isolated rock. Wouldn't a sane woman stick close to home and hospital?

Her strange ramblings come back to me. *Why him? Why now?* And what could having Ethan home possibly ruin for her?

Maybe she's suffering from the pregnant crazies. When Ruthie's hormones were raging on behalf of Greg and Amelia, my level-headed sister turned into something out of a fright flick. She was especially monstrous to her monstrous husband Lee, who called me several times in utter desperation. According to him, Roo was whining, demanding, and impossible to please. Once, the pompous little dork came close to actual tears. It was lovely.

Curiosity nudges me to follow the young woman. But at the edge of the trees, I'm stumped.

Several paths extend from the orchard. One trail snakes back toward the north beach bluffs. Another weaves toward the densely wooded nature preserve. Straight ahead, a small brook tracks the narrow clearing between two rock walls.

Aunt Sadie makes the decision for me, charging toward the watercourse. She sprints over the slippery stones and patches of spongy earth.

I trail with caution. I don't want to risk a nasty spill. And I don't relish an unexpected run-in with a knife-wielding stranger and her persecution complex.

That's the third time in a week someone has come at me with a weapon. Second if you don't count Uncle Duck's

Monster Blaster, though that was every bit as terrifying as the young woman's blade or Harley Beamis's pistol. Until now, the worst I've ever been held up for is a donation to the Hinsdale PTO sunshine fund on behalf of Patsy Culvert's nose job.

The stones are slick as ice. Rushing water makes the footing unpredictable. I'm so intent, the sound doesn't register at first. But soon, the insistent hacking penetrates.

There's a boat.

A way out.

All thoughts of the pregnant woman vanish. Eagerly, I track the noise. Quickening my pace, I follow the burbling stream as it dips and curves. The engine sound intensifies. I'm getting close.

Trying to hop from one rock to another, I slip. I come down sharply on a turned ankle. A spike of pain pierces my leg. Gritting my teeth, I hobble ahead. I have to reach that boat.

The water rounds an abrupt bend. The brook widens. It feeds a finger-shaped inlet camouflaged by a stand of willows. A fishing boat glides slowly toward the far end, setting a wing-shaped wake.

A lanky redheaded man stands at the helm.

'Wait! Stop!' I call to him.

He shoots me a furtive glance, then turns away. Limping closer, I yell, 'Wait! Please wait! I need a ride to the mainland!'

The putting noise intensifies as he kicks the motor in high gear. The boat bursts from the neck of the inlet like a popped cork. Streaks into open waters. Spews a tail of foam.

'No! You can't leave. Please!'

The motor's roar drowns me out. The driver does not look back.

'Stop, please! At least call someone! Tell them I'm stuck here! Tell them – ' But he doesn't hear me. The chance is lost.

As the craft barrels into the centre of the Sound, the

195

pregnant girl appears on deck. Her bright sundress billows sail-like in the speed-churned breeze. She loops her slender arms around the young man's neck as they race toward the distant shore.

27

This little piggy went to market.
This little piggy stayed at home.
'This Little Piggy'

Nearing Eva's place, I shift course and hobble toward the lightkeeper's cottage. Maybe young Aunt Jeanette has some escape ideas. Failing that, maybe I can beg a cup of genuine coffee with cream and gossip.

The lighthouse roosts on a needle of land laced through a nest-shaped tide pool. The keeper's cottage huddles fifty yards inland, linked to the tower by a ragged trail of stones.

The white brick cottage glints in the light of a low-slung sun. Toys and beachballs litter the small fenced yard. Fish-shaped windsocks droop from an ancient boxwood. Uncle Duck's Monster Blaster lies angled against a rock.

As I open the gate, Jeanette peers out through a first-floor window. 'Bethany, hi. Come on in. Door's open.'

'Hope it's not too early.'

'Not a bit. Duck's off for his morning constitutional. He left me here hopelessly outnumbered by small people.'

'Stay, Sadie.'

'No, please. Bring the dog. Grownups of all species are welcome.'

I limp into the kitchen. The airy room is flooded with light. Pleasant change from Eva Haskel's house of perpetual gloom.

All the cabinet doors are agape. Jeanette whirls among them like a size sixteen tornado, flinging things out. Spice jars, boxed cereals, plates, vitamins, a squashed bug. I have to admire her flair for messy clutter. Woman is my kind of slob.

She works with one ham-sized hand. Her other arm

197

cradles a suckling infant. The baby is wrapped in a blue knit blanket. All that shows is a fuzzy head and the veiny dough of Jeanette's left breast.

Smiling, she strokes the babe's pink cheek. 'Zach Haskel, meet Bethany Logan. Bethany, this little piggy is my son Zachary.'

He's such a tiny thing, I'm instantly smitten. 'How old?'

'Two months today. Isn't that right, sweetums?' Her voice drops an octave when she turns to me. 'Coffee? I was just about to make a fresh pot.'

'Is it decaf?'

'No, sorry. Give me jittery or give me death.'

'My sentiments exactly. Can I help?'

'No need. Sit. Be ready in a jiff.'

She watches me hobble to the table. 'What's with the gimpy foot?'

'Twisted my ankle. It'll be fine.'

'How'd it happen?'

'I was taking a walk. Ran into this pregnant woman sleeping in the grove. She spooked when she saw me. I tried to follow her. Slipped on a rock.'

Jeanette clicks her tongue. 'Was she near bald? Loony?'

'You know her?'

'That'd be the Captain and Laurel's baby girl, Madeleine. Always was a little off. Make that more than a little. But since the pregnancy, watch out. Where's she now?'

'A young man came for her. The whole thing was so strange. She said I shouldn't have brought Ethan home. That I ruined everything.'

Jeanette snickers. 'Did she tell you about the alien? How he raped her and made her pregnant?'

'No.'

'Well, I got the whole story. Listened politely, if I do say so myself. Still, mad Maddy got all bent out of shape when I asked if he was a two-headed guy with a big green dick.' She shrugs. 'Seemed to me like a reasonable question.'

Crouching, she pokes and prods my ankle with her free hand. 'That hurt?'

'A little,' I admit.

'That?'

I nod yes as a pain pod blossoms on my calf.

Frowning, Jeanette plucks a box of popsicles from her styrofoam cooler. 'Put that tootsie up and ice it.'

'I'm sure it's nothing. Really.'

'Actually, it's a moderate contusion with palpable oedema.'

'That bad?'

She laughs when I blanch. 'Translated, that's a bump and a boo-boo. I learned how to manage such dire medical emergencies in nursing school. Now sit and put your foot up.' She flips a second chair around to face mine.

The ice feels good. The coffee better. Two cups later, my flaccid faculties are all perked up. For the first time since landing on this outsized raft, I relax a little. This house is my kind of place, wonderfully chaotic. Plus, I like Jeanette. She has heart. Cheek. A sense of humour.

She tugs the baby off her nipple and props him at her shoulder for a burp.

Edging back, she eyes him slyly. 'Sleeping on the job, are we? I'm afraid that calls for immediate suspension, mister.' Her chair groans as she shoves out from the table. 'I'm just going to run up and put this lazy good-for-nothing down for a nap, Bethany. Don't go away.'

After she leaves, I sense I'm being watched. Wheeling quickly, I spot a grotesque face mashed against the window. Squashed nose, pale skin, tongue spread like a slab of luncheon meat against the glass. Plump fingers splay beside the ears like bulldozed starfish.

Sadie snarls at the gargoyle. I gasp. 'What is that?'

'*That* is why I asked you to stop by,' comes Jeanette's beleaguered voice from behind me. 'Gideon Haskel, you cut that out this minute and haul your little butt in here.' She turns to me. 'Duck said you work with problem kids. Thought you might have some suggestions about this one. Hope you don't mind.'

The face vanishes, leaving spit and grease smears on the

199

pane. A plump little boy careens into the kitchen and circles the table tooting like a manic train. He's pie-faced with black button eyes and a scrub brush of mud-brown hair.

He tips a plastic pitcher toward a little cup. Most of the purple liquid slops on the counter and his shirt. He lifts the cup and glugs the remains.

Kid looks a little shop-worn. His front teeth are chipped, and his knees are scabbed in patchwork. I count three faint suture scars on his face before he hurtles back into breathless action.

He bear-hugs my dog, bubbles his lips, and gathers speed with outstretched arms like a jet on a runway. He aborts the takeoff half a millimetre from my face. He's so close, I can taste his warm grapey words. 'Who you?'

'I'm Bethany. What's – '

Before I can get out the thought, the child has knocked off the next three items on his agenda. He butts down the clean diapers stacked on the counter, drapes one of them on his head, and stuffs his mouth with cookies. Sugared crumbs rain on the floor. Aunt Sadie does not rush in to claim them. The wise dog hangs back, sizing up the pudgy little situation.

Jeanette sighs. 'My paediatrician said he'd grow out of it. He just didn't happen to mention what or when.'

The boy splats on the floor like a cracked egg and crawls next to Sadie. He barks in imitation and waggles his portly little rear. Barking, he scrabbles across the floor and squats on his haunches.

Aunt Sadie observes in bug-eyed amazement. After a while, she edges closer and nudges the manic child in the ribs. I suppose she's trying to locate his off-button.

Before she can, Gideon pops up like a toast slice.

'I'm a bump-bump,' he chants. 'I'm a bump-bump-bump-ity-bump-bump.'

Jeanette wears a long-suffering look. 'Okay, Giddy. That's enough.'

'Not Giddy. Bumpity-bump.'

200

'*Enough*, I said. Now go bump into the den and watch something.'

The dervish crams more cookies in his mouth and dashes down the hall. Jeanette slumps in her chair and drinks deeply of the quiet.

Nice to know I'm not the only forgetful one. I'm about to remind her that the cable is out when I hear the raucous rise of a laugh track. Electricity?

'You have power?' I ask.

'No one does this week. That set runs on batteries. With a kid like Gideon, I view it as a medical necessity. Sometimes he'll sit for ten whole seconds in front of the TV.'

'Must be hard.'

'No. It's impossible.' Her face goes grim. 'I know he's only five, but I can't help worrying.'

'Nothing wrong with that. The earlier kids get help with problems, the better chance they'll be resolved.'

A tear rolls down her cheek. 'I've tried to help him, really I have. But you see how he is – he's off the wall. Always has been. As a baby he rocked the crib so hard, I'd find it clear across the room. The only time he's not running crazy is when he sleeps. And even then, he kicks the wall and tears the bed apart.'

I pluck a tissue from the box on the table and hand it to her.

'What scares me most is he's supposed to start school this fall. It's only kindergarten, but still . . . How can anyone get him to pay attention long enough to teach him anything?'

'There are ways.'

She snuffles. 'You really think so? You don't think he's hopeless?'

I wince at the word. 'Definitely *not* hopeless.'

She blows her nose. 'You don't know what it means to hear you say that.'

Gideon is back. Hurtling into the room, he snags his foot on a chair leg. He falls hard. Sprawls out, screaming.

Jeanette scoops him on to her lap and soothes him. When he quiets down, I seize the opportunity.

201

At the centre of the table sits a candle in a squat brass holder. 'You like games, Gideon?'

'Yup.'

'Birthdays?'

'Birthdays. Oh yeah!'

'Great. Let's play the birthday candle game.' I light the wick. The flame fixes the child's darting gaze.

'Here's how you play. You and Mommy have to watch the candle very hard. When I put it out, you call "Happy birthday". First one who says it, wins.'

Jeanette nods understanding. So does her son. By long habit, I quickly size the kid up. No evidence of gross visual or hearing disability, though both should be tested. No obvious neurological damage. He can follow complicated directions, which means good language skills. Good sign.

His eyes fix on the flame. I count the seconds. At twenty, he starts squirming. By thirty, he's wriggling like an earthworm with piles. I push to thirty-five, then puff out the flame.

'Happy birthday!' he calls. Jeanette, playing along, chimes in a long beat later.

'You won, Giddy. Fantastic. Double or nothing?'

His chin dips. 'Go.'

This time, I'm able to stretch him to forty-five seconds before the geyser in his spine erupts. That makes nearly four minutes of uninterrupted sitting. Probably a new personal best.

'You beat me again, Giddy boy,' his mother exults.

'That's two in a row,' I tell him. 'What do you say?'

'One more.'

This time, he holds out for an entire minute. Jeanette and I cheer mightily. I hoist Gideon's plump little arm. 'The winner and new world champion – is – '

'*Me!*'

With that, he charges outside to celebrate with a nice explosion.

Says Jeanette, 'That settles it, Bethany Logan. I like

202

you. Gideon *works* with you. How about I dump Duck and we get married?'

'I'm flattered, really. But it's not that big a deal. Try to think of Gideon as having a very tight attention span. You just stretch it out, gradually. Go for five, maybe ten seconds more each time. There are other games you can play. I'll show you.'

'Oh, Bethany. You don't know. What can I do to thank you? Name it.'

'The only thing I want at the moment is a ride to the mainland. You wouldn't happen to have a boat? Or a cellular phone?'

She frowns. 'Not this week. No boats, no nothing. I'm afraid you're stuck for the duration.'

'There has to be some way off this place.'

The frown deepens. 'Let me think on it.'

'Thanks. I'd really appreciate that.'

'Not nearly as much as I appreciate your helping with Giddy. I'm so relieved to know there's something we can do.'

I eye the collection of candy and snack boxes on the counter. 'You should probably cut out the cookies, too. All sugary stuff. It's what I live on myself, but sweets wind some kids up.'

'Consider it done. Anything to calm that kid down.'

'I have to warn you, it's not going to be easy. My guess, no matter what you do, Gideon's going to need special help in school and plenty of patience.'

'That's what I keep telling Duck. But he's convinced there's some magical solution. Thinks maybe Giddy would settle down if there weren't so many distractions. That's why he dragged us here this week, when it's even quieter than usual.'

'You don't live on Rand's?'

'Live? Here? Isn't that a contradiction in terms?'

'To me, yes. But – '

She shakes off the impossible notion. 'I've served my time. That's how I met Duck. I was hired to take care of his wife years back when she was terminal with non-Hodgkins lymphoma. Miriam was born and raised on Rand's. Loved this island so much she insisted on coming back for the end. I spent two months. Felt like much, much more.'

'Where did Duck and Miriam live?'

'Small town outside of Boston. Same house we live in now. Miriam wanted to be on the island full time, but Duck insisted it was no place to raise a family. He won. They kept this place for vacations. Duck's only having second thoughts now because of Giddy. Thinks he might do better here without so many distractions. You ask me, spending a week once in a blue moon is *more* than plenty.'

'The Haskels all seem to love it.'

She frowns. 'Different strokes for different folks. And that bunch is real, *real* different.'

'Different how?'

'Where do I begin? The captain thinks he's Captain Ahab. Laurel thinks she's Betty Crocker. And Rowena thinks she's Don Rickles, only not so sweet.'

'And Eva?'

'I don't know what Eva thinks. *I* always thought she was Lady Macbeth. But that's a whole other story.'

'I'd love to hear it.'

'Well – '

A prickly knob thumps against the window.

'Gideon Haskel. Cut that out!'

Thump. Thwack.

'Cut it *out*! Giddy. I mean it. You'll break the glass and cut yourself.'

THUMP.

'Excuse me.' Jeanette bounds up and charges out. She's back in a tick, hauling the boy under her arm like a rolled newspaper. This little tabloid has quite an attitude. Bold-faced. Screeching.

'Sorry,' she says.

'Not at all. I really should get back, though. Eva's probably wondering.'

204

'See you later?'

'I'd like that.'

'You'll be at Eva's?'

'Unless I'm snatched by that alien.'

She grins. 'Great. I'll leave the kids with Duck and drop by. We can dish more dirt.'

'Any time.'

Heading out, I step more surely. The ice – and making a friend – has soothed my aching bruise.

28

Eva hurries from the house to meet me as I slowly cross from the beach to the lawn. Her eyes are wild, her moves sharp and electric.

'Bethany. Thank *God*. Where *were* you?'

'Why? What's wrong?'

'Nothing. It's just – You're unfamiliar with the island. There's a quicksand bog. Other dangers. I was so frightened –' She's breathless. Next, I expect her to tell me about a *demon thing*.

'I'm fine.'

'Yes, but I don't want anything to happen to you. You really shouldn't be wandering off alone.'

'I'm a *big* girl, Eva. Like you said.'

She stiffens. 'Please don't be offended, Bethany. All I'm trying to do is ensure your comfort and welfare.'

'Then find me a ride to shore.'

She shows her palms. Empty.

'Come inside, Bethany. It's so much cooler.'

And quieter.

Sadie and I follow her into the dreary house. As we enter the kitchen, there's a bold knock at the back door. Despite the heat, the captain looks crisp in beige slacks and a soft blue shirt. He sports a jaunty cap with nautical insignia. He has Ethan in tow.

'Thought I'd bring the boy by to say good morning before we start his lessons.'

Eva's thin face glows at the sight of her son. He's dressed all in white, like a little busboy. 'You look wonderful, my darling. Sleep well?'

'There's nothing else to *do* here.' His tone is a grating whine. 'No TV or *nothing*.'

'I expect you'll survive the week without it. Happens

206

television wasn't even invented when I was a boy,' says the captain.

'You're kidding me.' Ethan gawps.

'Dead serious. No TV, no computers. No video games. No VCRs.'

The child shakes his head in disbelief. 'What'd you do?'

'Talked. Read books. Listened to the wireless.' The captain catches Ethan's puzzled look. 'The radio, I mean. They had wonderful shows.'

'How do you watch a radio?'

The captain chuckles. 'Not watch, listen. I know it must sound strange to you, but we had a grand time.'

'Without TV?'

'We didn't have microwave ovens either,' I put in. 'And no calculators.'

The child ruminates on that for a minute. 'Did you have cars?'

'I did back when I used to live on the mainland,' his grandfather says. 'Clunky black ones at first. And later, long ones with fins.'

'Fish cars?' His face is wide with wonderment.

'Not that kind of fin.' The captain glances at his watch. 'Time to begin your lessons, son.'

They head for the door. Eva shadows them.

'Must you leave so soon? Maybe we can visit a while. Get acquainted . . .'

'The boy must learn, Eva,' the captain says. 'And you have work to do.'

'Couldn't it wait for a little bit? He just got here.'

His eyes flash fury. 'Stay with Bethany, son. I need a moment alone with your mother.'

Eva steps back. Her face blanches. 'No need, Captain. Go start your lessons. I understand.'

'Step outside, Eva. *Now.*'

'It's fine, Poppa. You're right. Ethan has work. We all do.'

He wrenches her toward the door. Eva looks petrified. Captain Haskel's expression holds a chilling trace of glee.

Through the living-room window, I watch them cross the

207

beach and walk to the end of the jetty. The tide is out, exposing a desolate field of dried kelp, crushed shell, and debris.

Eva stands with her head bowed as her father laces into her. His face warps in an ugly grimace. His finger slashes the sullen air. Eva slumps lower. Hangs her head. Takes his words like blows.

Finally, the captain bends, scoops a palmful of water, and flings the salty wash in his daughter's face.

Eva's mouth falls open. She blinks away the sting.

Shaken by the scene, I turn away. How could the captain be so hateful?

Munching a leftover biscuit, Ethan leans against the sink. Sadie stands poised at his feet to catch the crumbs. 'Know what the first law of the sea is?' asks the child.

'No idea.'

'Listening. When you don't, it's called mute something.'

'Mutiny, you mean?'

'Right. You get to die for that, the captain says.'

'He's talking about history. Way back when explorers and traders were out on the oceans for months or years at a time.'

'Nope. He meant now. Right here. An island is sort of a boat, the captain says. Someone gets to be boss. The rest of the people have to listen to him or else.'

He finishes the biscuit and brushes the crumbs from his shirt. Sadie sucks them down like a fuzzy Dustbuster. 'The captain is the boss now. But after I learn all the lessons and pass all the tests and grow up, I get to take over.'

'Sounds as if you're starting to like it here.'

'It's okay.'

'You like the captain?'

His face is dreamy with reverence. 'Once his boat's back, he's gonna take me to catch these great big fish that fight like crazy.'

'Pretty exciting.' Seems the old man has kept his cruel temper from the child. At least, so far.

'And Uncle Duck's going to teach me to dive. He knows

208

the jackknife and the swan and how to go off backwards with a flip and everything.'

'Should be fun.'

Ethan's fizzing like a fresh-tapped keg. 'And the captain says it's almost for sure I'll be picked for special honours at the ceremony Sunday.'

'Good for you.' I sip my lemonade. His breathless enthusiasm has me parched.

'You know what? The Captain was almost swallowed by a whale once. Just like the Jonah from the Bible.'

'I bet Jonah will be really impressed when he hears that.'

He breaks another biscuit. 'He won't. I'm never speaking to him again.'

'Sure you will. You can give him a call after the phones are turned on.'

'Nope. The captain says all that stuff is fake. So I have to forget it.'

'The only fake thing was Adam Stafford. You don't have to forget your friends, Ethan.'

'Whatever the captain says, I have to listen. Everyone on the island does. Even you.'

I'm about to argue further when I hear the squeak of the door.

Eva's narrow face is tear-stained. She forces a smile. 'Go now, my darling. The captain is waiting for you.'

The child strides from the room. The door smacks closed behind him. His fading footsteps slap against the stones.

29 I watch as Eva pulls a straw tote from the cupboard. She slips in a recipe book, pie tins, spice jars, and a whisk.

'The captain's right,' she tells herself firmly. 'Ethan's lessons are terribly important.'

I say, 'So is settling in. Getting acquainted.'

'There's plenty of time for that. The child has to learn. That's the main thing.'

She kneels to peer in a cabinet. She plucks out oven mitts and several aprons and sets them neatly in the bag.

'He's right about my getting to work, too. Mother must be waiting.' She straightens. 'There. All set. Ready to go, Bethany?'

'Thanks anyway. I'd just as soon stay here.'

'No. Please. You must come along. Gathering to prepare for Sunday's feast is part of our tradition. You'll enjoy it. I know you will.'

'Hard to resist, really. But I'm way behind on my paperwork for school. This'll give me a chance to catch up.'

'But I'd hate to think of you here alone.'

I smile with clenched teeth. 'Don't, then.'

'What will you do for lunch?'

'I'll manage.'

'But – '

'Your mother's waiting, Eva. You'd better go.'

She leaves me with a legal pad and a bouquet of sharp pencils. As soon as she's out the door, I settle in at the kitchen table. I'm ready to knock off these damned reports once and for all.

At the top of a fresh, blank sheet, I write the words: *End Term Summary*. I print the name *Goichman, Daniel R. Introduction*, I write. I underline it once. And again. Firmly.

210

Daniel Goichman is, I begin. Then, what comes is: nothing.

My thoughts run in circles, chasing moths. Sadie sits beside the sink. I know what she's thinking.

'Don't bug me, girl. I just need a minute to get organized.'

I begin again. *Daniel Goichman is a probable future orthodontist or professional walrus impersonator.*

Scratch that.

Flipping the page, I doodle a dozen eggs. One serves as the outline for a masterfully inept self-portrait. Egg-shaped skull. Question-mark nose. Lips like a fallen bundt cake.

I tear off the page and fold it into a hat. I try it on. Small.

Aunt Sadie yaps at me. Get to it.

'Okay. I'm doing. I'm working.'

I force my mind back on to Goichman, Daniel R. I think of his lisp which makes me think of drum brushes which reminds me of the time Dad took Roo and me to the New York Philharmonic and then to Rumpelmayer's on Central Park South for the most amazing sundae. Vanilla fudge ice-cream with wet nuts and chocolate sauce. Mountains of whipped cream. Cookies on the side. Ever since, I've been crazy about classical music.

Raising two pencil batons, I conduct a rousing rendition of the unfinished symphony. My song.

Aunt Sadie sniffs her disdain.

Think of Danny Goichman, Bethany.

Thinking of Danny's teeth, I slip the eraser side of two pencils under my top lip. I wonder how it must feel to be a walrus. I try to remember when I last went to the dentist. I imagine a magic eraser that removes plaque. I imagine one that eradicates dentists.

Focus, Bethany.

I lecture myself at great length on the evils of procrastination. Chastened, I repent in all sincerity and vow to reform.

Another sixty minutes down the drain.

Sadie snorts her disgust and nods off.

211

I am seriously ready to start Danny's report when I notice that Eva's pots and pans are hung in no particular order. I arrange them by size. Then, I rearrange them in size order by type: saucepans, frying pans, Dutch ovens, double boilers. I finish by dangling the colander from the front hook. Having a brain like mine, I'm understandably inclined to offer the sieve a place of special honour.

Which gives me an idea.

I ball a page and toss it across the room at the punctured bowl. I pretend I'm hurling Harley Beamis's severed head. Playing that great new game sensation: Bastard ball.

Right in!

I clump more papers. I'm on a roll. Lay-ups. Line shots. Dribble and fake. Snag the rebound. Take that, Deputy Dog Face, you big, ugly lard. Go, Logan! I sink a major long shot from behind the tub. Then one from beside the refrigerator.

Three points! Six!

Enough!

No more nonsense. I am absolutely ready to begin some actual work now. I make it through almost the entire first sentence when I hear a harsh concussion from outside.

Caleb stands over a felled hickory in the rear yard, wielding a saw. Despite the heat, he wears dark corduroys and a grey sweatshirt.

I peer outside. 'Morning, Caleb.'

He grunts in response. From a sackful of tools, he pulls an axe. He hefts the blade overhead and brings it down with a simian grunt. A slice of the tree falls away.

He hacks the trunk into even segments. Then, with a pie-shaped wedge and a sledgehammer, he splits the chunks into eighths.

He's spilling rivers of sweat. Soon, his shirt is soaked to a muddy charcoal. His hair is plastered to his skull. Crimson blotches mottle his neck.

Noting how industrious he is, I'm ashamed of myself. Why can't I be like that? Focused. Productive.

212

Obviously, what I ought to do is offer the guy a nice cold drink.

I dip a glassful of water from the cistern and plop in a couple of cubes from the ice chest. I approach between whacks.

'Want some water, Caleb?'

'Dink.'

He takes the glass and gulps the water down. A lick slops over. Dribbles down his chin.

'Want some more?'

'Maw,' he agrees.

I bring another cup. He downs it in a few greedy swallows. His face is flaming red. I can picture his organs simmering. Lava coursing through his veins.

'It's really hot out, Caleb. Maybe too hot for you to be working so hard.'

'Kale cut wood,' he tells me.

'Maybe you should wait and cut the wood when it cools off a little.'

'Cut wood,' he insists. 'Work.'

'Caleb, my friend. You put me to shame, being such a good worker. But it really is sweltering out today. Why don't you take off that heavy shirt at least? You'll be more comfortable.'

He raises a protective hand to his chest. 'Kale shirt,' he insists.

'I know, pal. And a fine shirt it is. But it's too hot for today.'

'Hot,' he concedes.

'Right. So why don't you take off the sweatshirt?'

'Sweat off.'

'You'll feel better without it. Believe me.'

He stands limp, staring.

'You need help? Is that it?'

'Hep.'

Strange that he can manage difficult tools and not be able to undress himself. But I've seen stranger. 'Okay. Let's get you out of that heavy thing.'

He offers neither a hand nor resistance. I tug off the sleeves and wrestle the sodden shirt over his head.

A grateful sigh escapes him. Turning, he stoops to retrieve the sledgehammer. That's when I spot the weave of angry welts across his back.

My breath catches. 'My God! What happened, Caleb? How did you hurt your back?'

He flinches, girding for a blow.

I force the rage from my tone. Squeeze it gentle. 'Caleb, did someone hit you?'

His eyes dip. 'Hit net.'

'Someone hit you with a *net*?'

'Kale bad. Net.' Rearing back, he whips the air in pantomime. 'Hit!'

'You're not bad, Caleb. No one should hurt you that way.'

'Good boy work.'

Turning his back on me, he centres the wedge on a log slice. The hammer strikes with a clang. The wood splinters.

I think of the fishnet hung at the captain's door. 'Was it your dad, Caleb? Did the captain do that to you?'

His bottom lip slides out like a drawer. Quivers. He looks like a petulant three-year-old. Innocent. Beautiful.

'Wood,' he says with a firm, brave nod. 'Kale cut.'

'Tell me who hurt you, Caleb. Let me help.'

'Work.'

He picks up his shirt and ties it like a cape around his neck. In ragged rhythm, he hammers at the wedge.

'You can trust me, Caleb.'

More pieces fly. The torpid air thrums with sawdust.

'Cut,' he chants. 'Cut – cut – cut.'

Fervently, he works, shutting me out. Closing out the questions. The answers. The pain.

30

Cry, baby, cry.
Put your finger in your eye,
And go tell your mother it wasn't I.

'Cry, Baby'

Jeanette stands at the water's edge, watching Gideon wrestle the surf.

Her wild child head-butts a flagging breaker. He throws a body block at a rolling wave. Drops a hammerlock on the burbling sand.

Jeanette motions for me to join them, but I keep my distance from the rabid tides. I try to ignore my terror, but I can't. It tightens like a noose, choking off my air.

Aunt Sadie doesn't try to spur on my nonexistent courage. Pooch has problems of her own. Stalking catlike, she circles the rusty anchor. Dog can't seem to let that big old sleeping dog lie.

Jeanette beckons at me again, but I can't bring myself to step any nearer the crashing surf.

Finally, she plucks Gideon from the water and hauls him on to the beach. She sets him down, aims him towards the cottage, and taps the soggy rear of his trunks.

The child takes off like a pinball. He traces a jagged line to the keeper's cottage. Jeanette watches, squinting, until Duck appears to spirit Giddy inside. Then she crosses to where I'm standing.

Her broad grin embraces me. 'You must be psychic, girlfriend. I was just getting set to come by and see you.' At second glance, her smile evaporates. 'What's up? You look all strung out.'

'That's only because I am.'

On the way to Eva's house, I tell Jeanette about Caleb. I describe the angry welts on his back. His quavering fear.

Cringing, she murmurs, 'Hard to imagine.'

'Beating the poor guy with a net, for chrissakes. What kind of a monster – ?'

She frowns. 'Strange, though. I've seen the captain deliver some mighty wicked tongue-lashings, especially to Eva. And his angry face could stop a train. But beating Caleb? I don't know.'

'Well, I do. I hardly think Caleb's capable of making up a thing like that.'

'He actually told you the captain *beat* him with a net? Caleb *said* that in so many *words*?'

I catch her point. 'Not exactly.'

'Sounded like quite a mouthful for that boy. Never have heard him string more than three words together, and even then, they're not strung all that tight. What did he say, *exactly*?'

'I think it was "net hit" or "hit net". Something like that.'

Firm nod. 'That fits. Couple of days ago, Duck mentioned that Caleb had a little accident. Seems he was splitting logs over at the captain's place. He upset a hornets' nest. When the swarm lit after him, Caleb high-tailed it home. Had his eye on the bugs, not where he was going. House came up sooner than he expected, and Caleb bashed into the wall. Guess he must have hit the spot where the captain has his old ship's net hung.'

'His back looks so raw,' I say lamely.

'Hey. Don't feel bad. It's only human to want to stand up for a simple soul like Caleb. But truth is, that one can stand up just fine for himself. Sweet as he is most of the time, Caleb's *big* trouble when he's riled. Strong as an ox, too. You want my opinion, Captain Haskel wouldn't dare lift a hand to Caleb. The old man's way too fond of his own leathery hide.'

'I feel like such an idiot.'

'Not at all. Listen, I've made more than my share of mistakes about people. When I think about Eva – '

216

'What about her?'

'Don't ask.' We enter the tomb-still stone house. 'You have lunch?'

'Not yet.'

'I'm starved. You?'

'Not really.' My stomach has yet to recover from last night.

'Maybe you'll change your mind,' she says cheerfully. 'Let's see what Eva's got for us to nibble on.'

In the kitchen, Jeanette roots around in the ice chest. She emerges with a half-filled tub of chocolate ice-cream. Grabs two spoons. She holds one out to me and starts excavating her side.

I'm drawn to the satiny scent like a flame-bound moth. 'Thanks, but I really shouldn't – '

'Sure you should, if only for my sake. Sinning alone is no fun at all.'

'Well, if you put it that way. I'll take a little taste.'

I peel off a fat chocolate curl and set it to melt on my tongue. The ice-cream is homemade. And so delicious it makes my eyes water. Thunder thighs seem a bargain price to pay for the moment's bliss.

'You were saying you misjudged Eva?'

Jeanette hesitates. Scoops another bite. 'Promise you won't say anything to the others?'

'Of course not.'

'They have enough trouble with me as it is. They'd drum me out of their tight little clan for good if they knew I'd suspected Eva of harming her child. But until you brought Ethan home again, I was pretty damned sure she had.'

'Hurt Ethan? Why?'

She slowly licks her spoon clean before replying. 'Duck thinks I'm hypersensitive because of my work. My first job out of nursing school was at Devon Hills, a private psychiatric hospital near Boston. I was assigned to the women's unit. We had a patient there the staff called Lady Black Fin. Terrible thing. Guess it stuck with me.'

'Lady Black Fin?'

'Everyone called her that. Real name was Hannah something, I think. She was young. Early twenties. But she'd already had six kids. Had them and killed them.'

'My God.'

'First few, the doctors chalked up to SIDS. Took them a while to catch on that she was suffocating her babies with one of those little crib pillows. They called her Black Fin because she was like one of those nasty fish you have to put in a separate tank as soon as their babies are born. Otherwise, they'll eat their young.'

I set down my spoon. 'What made you suspect Eva?'

'You have to know her. She's always been a little off, but it got much worse during her pregnancy.'

'Like her sister, you mean?' I remember the young pregnant girl I happened upon on my walk.

'Not as far out as Maddy and her alien, no. But strange enough. She became extremely withdrawn. Almost seemed to be sleepwalking. Then, for no apparent reason, she'd flare up.'

'Sounds like Eva.'

'Yes, only much more so. The Haskels are masters at denial, but when we were here that summer before Ethan was born, you could see how Eva's behaviour worried Cal. I heard him talking to Duck about it once. Asking whether it was normal for pregnant women to undergo personality changes.'

'My sister certainly did.'

'There are changes and changes,' says Jeanette. 'Eva was seriously off during the pregnancy. And she got worse.'

She works at the ice-cream. 'Duck and I were here the week the baby disappeared. It was really weird. Everyone covered up for Eva. Said she was in shock. Fact was, she acted as if nothing had happened at all. Spooky – it reminded me of Lady Black Fin. Eva *expected* that baby to vanish. To me, that meant she must have had some hand in the disappearance.'

'Didn't she pass a lie detector test?'

'She passed two,' Jeanette says, licking the spoon. 'But,

218

from what I've read, polygraphs can be beaten, especially by someone who believes her own lies. Still, I shouldn't have jumped to conclusions.'

'So you made a mistake about her. So what?'

She averts her eyes. 'I didn't leave it at that. I was so convinced Eva was the culprit, I did a little poking around. More than a little. One day, when I knew Eva was at her mother's, I snuck into her house and went through her things. Acted like a common thief. Worse.'

'And you found what?'

'It was so long ago. Six years.' She's being evasive.

'Tell me, Jeanette.'

The ice-cream is collapsing in a soupy slush. Jeanette eats faster, trying to outpace the meltdown.

'So what did you find?' I urge her.

'Ethan's back now. What difference can it make?'

'Maybe none. But I brought that little boy home. Be nice to know he's in good hands.'

Her voice dips in chocolate-scented conspiracy. 'Eva was on several heavy psychiatric meds, the kind we gave our in-patients. I figured if she was that wacko, she had no business caring for a baby in the first place.'

She runs her spoon along the container's side, rounding up strays. 'One day, I managed to get Eva alone. Started her talking about Ethan. She rambled on about an old family curse. Said it affected the children, especially the boys.'

'Sounds like a great spooky campfire story. The kids at my school would eat it up.'

She stares longingly into the empty container and sighs. 'Ghost stories. I guess that's all it is. But at the time, it really gave me a major case of the creeps. I thought we might be looking at a genetic thing. You know – multiple generations of Lady Black Fins. Especially after Ethan's kidnapping and what happened to Duck's boys.'

'Which was?'

Her face falls. 'They all died as young kids. So tragic.'

'What happened?'

'I honestly don't know. Duck won't talk about it. None of them will. If I try to bring it up, they change the subject.'

'That's so sad.'

'The worst. But that's not all. Not the end of it. Come, I'll show you.'

We trudge out into the scorching heat. Caleb has gone. He's left behind a tidy stack of wood.

31

Down where the woodbines creep;
Be always like the lamb so mild,
A kind and sweet and gentle child.
Sleep, baby, sleep.

'Sleep, baby, sleep'

Jeanette has a giant's stride. I have to scurry to keep up with her. Now I know how my niece feels when she mewls for me to slow down.

'Stop it, Aunt Beffney,' she has been known to say. 'You're walking too *loud.*'

As we cross the island, I quiz Jeanette about some of Rand's more intriguing features. Approaching the charred remains, she tells me that the burnt-out building was once a laboratory. The facility was constructed during the Depression and operated in total secrecy for almost a decade.

Now, Aunt Sadie skirts the blackened ruin, training a wary eye. The dog has always been cautious. But since we arrived on Rand's she's acted suspicious, verging on paranoid.

'From what Duck says, the doctor who ran the place was quite a character,' Jeanette continues. 'He built the lab here hoping to keep his experiments private. Designed the place to look like a regular house. Kept the door locked, shutters drawn. But no one thought anything of it.

'For a long time, the neighbours believed the doc was just another summer resident. He had plenty of company, but so do most of the islanders in season. Mainlanders love to vacation here. It's like falling off the end of the world. Only much more convenient.'

'Not to me.'

'It took years before word finally got out the doc was bringing hardened criminals to Rand's. Murderers, rapists. Charming folk like that. Doctor Frankenstein, or whatever his name was, bailed them out and paid them to participate in his studies. After he finished with them, the doc turned his convicts loose. Gave them a ride to shore. Pocket money. Bye-bye, bad guys.

'Scheme could have gone on indefinitely. But one of the doc's lovely graduates went ashore and had himself a killing spree. When the cops nabbed him, he confessed to everything, including his little working vacation on Rand's.' She shook her head. 'After that, the islanders were desperate to close the lab down. But the doc refused to go gently. Pulled all kinds of legal manoeuvres. Made threats. Islanders finally decided to give him a traditional send-off. Bonfire included.'

Through the stand of pines, we come to the boarded shack. 'What's that?' I ask.

'Schoolhouse. At least, that's what it is when the captain has a kid around to teach. He'll be in his glory again, now that Ethan's here. Nothing he likes more than a little mind to bend.'

A few of the boards over the window have been stripped away. The door lock droops open.

'What qualifies him to teach anyone?'

'You know the old saying: He thinks, therefore he is.'

'Takes more than that, especially with a kid like Ethan.'

'Maybe so. But logic has nothing to do with how things work here. To the Haskels, everything is dictated by tradition. Always have; always will. Ethan will be prepared for life on Rand's, one way or the other,' she says sourly.

'What if he decides to live somewhere else when he grows up?'

'He won't.'

'How do you know?'

'Same way I know the sun will come up tomorrow.'

Approaching the bluff, Jeanette veers right. We plod

across a wide sandy stretch and scale the dunes beyond. The sun is searing. Aunt Sadie huffs like a stream train.

I'm fading fast. 'Are we almost there?' I sound like a cranky five-year-old.

'Almost.'

The beach shrinks back to reasonable size. The bordering land blazes green again. Shade trees temper the blistering heat. Aunt Sadie flops beneath one and stages a sit-in.

I'm tempted to join her, but curiosity binds me to Jeanette. We pass a strip of weathered bungalows. Each is bounded by a patchy square of lawn. Each leads to a shabby dock, bobbling in the currents. The bungalows remind me of Monopoly houses. Faceless in their uniformity. Not worth much.

'Summer people,' Jeanette sniffs. 'They don't give a damn about Rand's. Couldn't care less what happens here when they're not. Not much better than the campers who come to squat over at the state preserve, if you ask me. No wonder the Haskels are so opposed to outsiders.'

'I didn't think you cared that much yourself.'

She nods sheepishly. 'Maybe not about the island, but I do care for Duck. Family means the world to him, Miriam's included. He's so anxious for me to fit in here. But it's impossible.'

I'm forced to play Amelia's game. 'How come?'

'Wish I knew. I've tried for years to get the Haskels to accept me. But they won't. Guess I'm looking for excuses. Can't be me personally, right? After all, what's not to love?'

'Nothing I can see. Maybe they're just a hard bunch to crack.'

I'm tweaked by guilt, thinking how distant I've remained from Dad's new wife Lillian. The woman can't help it if she's vapid and shallow. It's not her fault that she's dumb as a rock and has no values to speak of. For my father's sake, I really ought to call my stepmom once in a while. Have a talk with her. All it would take on her end is a few strings and a ventriloquist.

Jeanette continues, 'They're convinced I'm after Duck's

money. That I brainwashed him with some sort of evil sex spell after Miriam died.'

'And did you?'

She shoots me a swift glance to see if I'm serious, then giggles. 'Yes, but he's not complaining.'

'They probably find it hard to get past the age difference.' I think of Hal Kreidman. And I feel homesick and hug-deprived. 'Duck's such a kid compared to you.'

'That happens to be true.'

We've come to an iron fence twined with ivy. The low gate lolls on broken hinges. The latch sounds like a mewling cat when Jeanette pulls it open. Inside is a curved cement walkway. Weeds poke skyward through the cracks. The footing is treacherous.

The place has all the charm of an abandoned city lot. All the amenities, too. Crushed cigarette packs. Busted beer cans. Roach butts. Used condoms.

'What is this?' I ask, gesturing at the ruins.

'Depends who you ask,' Jeanette tells me. 'Campers from the state preserve come here for merrymaking and vice. The Haskels come here when their time for such things is over. This way.'

Two granite benches mark the end of the solid path. We slog beyond, high-stepping through the undergrowth until we come to a cluster of gravestones.

The cemetery lies in a broad pool of shade. The oldest stones at the rear have been thinned by age and blackened to char by the elements. Some are tipped or toppled. Miriam Haskel's shiny granite memorial centres the first row. Space remains for several more dead Haskels to lie beside her. There's ample room in front for future moribund generations.

The newer graves are neatly tended, planted with annuals and spreading yew. I see nothing peculiar. Then Jeanette steps between the back rows and clears a mound of thatch with the toe of her sandal.

She exposes a small granite plaque, sunk level with the

224

ground. The surface is engraved. *Benjamin*, it reads. *May 15, 1912 – September 12, 1917.*

Jeanette proceeds down the row, exposing more and more flat markers. *Dear Departed Mortimer. Born: October 5, 1922. Gone home: October 16, 1929.* And, *Solomon Joseph. Age three. Taken for an angel: July 5, 1940.*

She moves on to the space between the two front rows.

'Duck's boys,' she says, her voice catching.

My own throat clamps at the sight of the three adjoining stones. Nathaniel, Marcus, and Randall, aged seven, five and three. All died within a five-year period.

Jeanette uncovers two more lost souls named Alexander and Jared. So many stones. So many children.

'Dear Lord,' I say softly, 'what happened to them?'

'Don't ask me,' says Jeanette. 'The Haskels refuse to deal with it. Won't even tend the kids' graves.'

I shiver. 'Maybe it's one of those oddball genetic faults. You wouldn't believe how many things can go wrong with a kid . . .'

Jeanette stares at the wrenching memorial to Duck's lost sons. 'Maybe,' she says. 'But – '

Her unspoken words fill the air. What if it isn't a cruel, inherited fluke?

And what if it is?

Either way, could there be future victims? More stunted lives to bury and hide beneath the earth?

32

Multiplication is vexation,
Division is as bad;
The Rule of Three doth puzzle me,
And practice drives me mad.
'Multiplication is Vexation'

Gideon and I are faced off at the kitchen table over a hot game of 'Concentration'.

The contest is fierce. We're playing for high stakes: glory and Fruit Loops. True, the cereal is loaded with sugar. But it's the rare child, indeed, who'll jump hoops for wheat germ.

Jeanette cages the little boy on her lap. He struggles to escape as I turn up two of the eight index cards on the table. Kid grunts with the effort. Sounds like someone trying to stuff an elephant's butt into stretch pants.

The artwork is mine, and I use the term loosely. There's a rough approximation of a bell on one card, a crude star on the other. I offer him a two-second peek, then flip the cards face down.

'Okay, Gideon. What were the pictures?'

'I don't 'member.'

'What do you *think* you saw? I'll give you a prize just for trying.'

'I'm *trying* to go play.'

'That doesn't count. How about a bonus peek?'

I turn the cards up again. Give him four long seconds to look. Flip them.

'What did you see, Gideon?'

'Nothing,' he squeals. 'I gotta go now. Bye-bye.'

'Let's try two different ones.' I turn over pictures of a ball and a cat.

226

'What did you see?'

'Fruit Loops. Yummy.'

He lunges like a striking cobra. But I beat him to the prize, sweeping the cereal into my hand.

'Gimme!' he demands. '*My* Fruit Loops.'

'You gotta be in it to win it, buddy. Let's try something else.'

Setting aside the index cards, I offer my makeshift shell game. I place a penny under one of two identical bottle caps Jeanette has fished out of the recycling bin.

'Here's how it works. You watch the caps. Try to follow the one with the penny. When I stop moving them around, you tell me where the penny is.'

'I don't want a dumb penny. I want my Fruit Loops. I wanna go play!'

Gideon stiffens, bashing Jeanette on the chin. I hear the crack of her teeth. She lifts a hand to her rattled mouth. The kid seizes the chance to stage a jailbreak.

As he bangs out the door, Jeanette spews a weary breath. Her face is bleak.

'Give him time,' I assure her. 'He'll get there.'

'Where?'

'Patience, Mommy. We'll try again when he's calmer.'

'Sure. Shouldn't take more than twenty, thirty years.'

I rise to leave.

'Do you have to go, Bethany? Having you around makes this place almost bearable.'

'Same to you. But I'm way behind on my end term reports. As long as I'm stuck here, I'm determined to get them done.'

I chant that mantra all the way to Eva's house. Entering the tomblike space, I keep my focus. No detours or distractions. I've already wasted an entire day here. I will do those reports. I stride directly to the kitchen and take a seat.

The pad is ready. Pen – ready. Brain? Thready.

No matter. I will get to work. As long as I'm stuck here,

227

I'm going to make the time count. Call me single-minded. Call me a con with a mission.

I'll show those dirty rats who framed me. I'll learn the law. File an appeal. Get out and run for Congress. Find a cause. Fix it. Become a professional inspiration. Go on the lecture circuit. Cut an infomercial. Sell my story to Spielberg. Attend the Oscars in a chic but elegant black strapless number.

Okay. I've slipped a *teensy* bit off the track.

I write two coherent introductory paragraphs about Danny Goichman. I read them over. Good start.

Moving on to the programme summary, I think of trying Danny on a computer, which reminds me of my nephew Greg, which reminds me of Roo's pregnancies, from which I make the dazzling leap to psychiatric medications.

Forget it, Bethany.

I know where this train of thought is heading. To a serious derailment. Nothing will be gained by snooping around in Eva Haskel's things. The children whose hidden gravestones I saw died long ago. Those tragic deaths have nothing to do with now. Or with me.

I return to the report. I complete the programme summary and move on to the goals for the coming term. I work in a fury. I knock off Danny's report and Robb Tretter's. I'm halfway through Alan McGillis, writing the term goals and objectives, when I collide head-on with a wall of truth.

What's the point? After all this, do I really believe I can return to my job at Hinsdale?

Forget me. Can the school survive? I can just picture the screaming headlines: HASKEL KIDNAPPING SOLVED – HINSDALE HEADMASTER SUSPECT.

I imagine the parents stampeding to transfer their kids from the school. The well of applications drying up.

And it won't end there.

The state is sure to investigate. The headmaster a kidnapper? How could such a man be brought in to run a school, they'll ask? Where was the hiring process? Where was the judgement of the Board?

228

Sooner or later, some reporter mole will dig up something that should have tipped the directors about Adam Stafford. Surely, the man once hedged on his golf score, plumped his tax deductions, fibbed to his priest.

The school Board will meet in shamefaced secrecy. They'll vote to suspend operations.

Sick inside, I think of life without Hinsdale. No more dorms and rolling greens and secret gathering places. No more songs, banners, blazers, wide-eyed kids. No more cafeteria food. No more Hal.

A hundred and thirty year tradition down the drain. And I'm left holding the plug.

And for what?

So Ethan Haskel can live on a giant raft with strangers? Friendless. Isolated. Stuck with a nasty, dictatorial grandfather. A sabre-tongued old woman. A nervous, neurotic wreck of a mother. Some family band this is: Eva and the Wackos.

I need to know exactly how wacko Eva is. What if she still suffers from a serious emotional imbalance? I owe it to Ethan to find out.

I climb the shadowy stairs and head for the bathroom. No prescription bottles in the medicine chest. No medicines of any kind.

I pause at the door to Eva's bedroom. Going through Pip and Adam's files at Hinsdale was bad enough. This is a serious invasion of a couple's privacy, a raid on their personal space. I feel like a prurient teenage babysitter, rifling the drawers.

But what's my choice? I can't leave this place until I'm satisfied Ethan will be safe. I could never forgive myself if that child suffered some deliberate harm here.

Venturing inside, I scan the room. There's a double bed with a brass head and footboard. A maple dresser and armoire. Twin nightstands and a blanket chest.

Opening a night table drawer, I'm staggered by the variety of birth control devices. An economy pack of condoms. A diaphragm case. Spermicidal jelly. Vaginal foam.

The sponge. Ovulation chart. Everything short of a chastity belt and a bedside cold shower.

The other nightstand tells the flip side of the story. A bustier. An abbreviated teddy with bikini pants in sheer black lace. I find it hard to imagine Eva wearing such things. Or taking them off.

No medications.

Quickly, I run through the dresser drawers. I try to shut my mind and eyes to everything but medicines.

Nothing.

Nothing unexpected in Cal's armoire. Nothing in the blanket chest but blankets.

I open the closet door. Eva's clothes, mostly long cotton shifts, hang in a regimental row on one side. Cal's jeans, khakis, work shirts, and a single navy suit line the other. A high shelf holds several storage boxes. One by one, I haul them down. I try to convince myself someone *could* keep medicines in such a place. I do not succeed.

But I don't stop, either. I want to know more about Eva. I need to get some handle on this family before I leave.

Only sweaters in the first box. The second is packed with scarves and gloves. In the third, under a pile of yellowed blueprints, I find a baby book. The design fundamentals detailed inside are Ethan Haskel's.

Seated on the floor, I page through the book. The initial entries are standard. Birthdate, height, time, and weight. A stunted family tree. Godparents: Caleb and Madeleine Haskel, Eva's slow brother and surreal sister. Two pages are devoted to a detailed growth chart. There's the typical list of firsts: tooth, word, step, slept-through night, solid food. This is followed by a comprehensive account of the infant's favourite things in every conceivable category. Favourite food: oatmeal. Favourite song: 'Eensy, Beensy Spider'. Favourite body part in a supporting role: thumb.

I turn to an exhaustive account of Ethan's first birthday party followed by a page of notations on his ever-expanding vocabulary. From all this scrupulous attention, future generations might conclude that Ethan Haskel was a major world figure. A deity, perhaps. And they'd be right.

After the initial section, there are several pages of photographs and baby memorabilia. Halfway through, I discover an odd notation.

Echoes of the Genesis Pool
Screams of clear blue silence
Ringing cold.
Spikes of warning from the glacial depths
Splinter away.

Reading on, I find more strange snips of verse. Paranoid ramblings. Several times, Eva repeats one set of phrases: *Beware the gold. Every tarnished lamb must be sacrificed.*

Turning the final page, I shake my head. What does it mean? And what, if anything, does it mean for Ethan?

A spark of light strikes a crystal box atop the dresser. Catches my eye. Rising, I notice a blue object inside the box. When I lift the lid, I find a plastic vial full of pills that could pass for blue M&Ms.

The label has been removed. I slip one pill into the pocket of my shorts and replace the tube in the crystal container.

Aunt Sadie bounds up the stairs. Poised in the doorway, she squirms in agitation. I'm thinking she needs to go outside. Then I hear the pad of footfalls mounting the stairs.

I shove the book in the box and the box in the closet. My heart hammers as I dash into the hall. I wrench to a halt as Eva's head clears the landing.

'There you are, Bethany. Everything all right?'

'Fine.'

Approaching, she peers past me into her room. Her brow arches. My heart sinks. I've left the closet door ajar.

A sly smile wavers on her lips. Her penetrating stare shifts my way. 'Is there something I can get for you, dear?'

'No.'

'Nothing you need? Are you sure?'

I feel like a guilty child. 'Nothing.'

'Did you have a pleasant day, I hope? Not too lonely?'

'It was fine. I got some work done.'

'Perhaps you'd like to rest a while before dinner, then. Rowena has invited us all to a barbecue at her house.'

'Good idea.' Anything to get away from her piercing gaze.

Retreating to my room, I collapse in a grateful heap on the bed. Thank the Lord for Aunt Sadie. If not for my guardian canine, Eva would have caught me rummaging through her things.

I think of Lady Black Fin, consuming her young. Hard to imagine what some people are capable of doing. Impossible to predict.

33 Far below, the dark sea dances, tossing its lacy hem. It's a coy, seductive display. But I'm not fooled.

Misty shadow blankets Rowena Haskel's yard. Citronella lamps, spitting puffs of flame, and soot tails, light a circle of Adirondack chairs and a long redwood table.

Near the house is a blazing barbecue pit. Caleb stands beside it, turning four plump birds and a rack of ribs on a heavy skewer.

The long rod rests in the crook of two Y-shaped branches. Their tips are impaled in the ground, but the apparatus would collapse without the young man's steady support. Caleb looks enraptured by the solemn responsibility.

I wave to him. 'Hi, Caleb. How's it going?'

'Cook,' he grunts in dismissal. 'Chicken.'

'After all that wood you chopped today, you must be exhausted.'

'Watch ribs.'

'Caleb's always been a hard worker,' Eva explains. 'Nothing the captain hates worse than laziness.' To punctuate the point, she hurries inside to help in the kitchen.

'Work,' Caleb reiterates.

'That you do, pal. Harder than anyone.'

Laurel steps out, mopping her hands on a linen apron. Her long emerald dress has muttonchop sleeves and a suffocating collar. All the Haskels seem oblivious to the heat. And other things.

Laurel holds the screen door open for Duck, who steps out toting a large silver tray full of hors-d'oeuvres.

'Jeannie spent hours on these, folks. Look good enough to eat, don't they now?'

He passes among us, pressing everyone to sample his

233

wife's concoctions. Razor-thin smoked salmon with *crème fraîche* and dill. Shrimp on cucumber slices. Endive boats filled with egg and caviare. Tiny chicken satays with a peanut dipping sauce.

Rowena, clad in a stifling charcoal suit, hunches on a split-log porch swing. 'Why didn't that baby bride of yours bring them along herself, Duck? She turning shy all of a sudden?'

'The kids and all,' he mutters. 'Jeannie's busy.'

The old woman huffs, 'Bet she is. Can't be easy keeping a doting old fool wrapped around your little finger like she does.'

'Shut your trap, Rowena. What do you know?'

The old woman smirks. 'I know that one about fools and their money, Duck. Bet poor Miriam is spinning in her grave watching you moon over that overgrown child you married.'

Duck's colour rises. 'Miriam would want my happiness.'

'No doubt. Question is, what does your precious Jeannie want?'

'So happens she loves me, Rowena.'

'Oh, sure. Maybe we should just go ahead and change your name to Goose.'

I rise to my new friend's defence. 'Jeanette's delightful, Duck. I really enjoy her company.' I wish she were here now for several reasons. The pill I took from Eva's room sits heavily in the pocket of my skirt.

Duck nods. 'She thinks the world of you, too, Bethany. Couldn't get over how you got Giddy to settle down. Sounds like some kind of miracle.'

'Not at all. Gideon wants to learn. All kids do. He just needs help figuring out how to succeed.'

Duck muses, 'Doubt the captain would agree with you there. He's old school. Thinks a firm hand and a big voice are the ticket for any child. Swears a few good licks would settle Giddy right down. Can't bring myself to do it. Just isn't my way.'

234

'Hitting kids only teaches them to lash out when they're angry.'

Duck tips his head toward Caleb. 'Firm hand sure has worked with that one, though. You should've seen the tantrums he threw when he was younger. Carried on something awful. Now, he does what he's told. No fuss. No questions.'

I watch Caleb rotate the heavy skewer. He's dripping sweat from the fire's heat.

'Training and teaching are two different things,' I say angrily.

Rowena snickers. Her eyes glint with malice. 'You want to argue that with the captain, here's your chance.'

Captain Haskel struts into the yard. Ethan trails a deferential step behind, trying to mimic the man's imperious gait. Every few steps, he casts an anxious eye at the captain. Then he waits like a starving gull for any stray crumb of approval.

The captain makes a slow round of greetings. He ducks inside to say hello to Eva and Laurel. Mounting the crest, he takes in the last gasp of sunset. A scarlet burst flares at the horizon. The colour leaches slowly from the sky, then fades to ash.

Returning, the captain sets a proprietary hand on his grandson's shoulder. 'Something tells me this young man is going to be my best pupil yet – ' he announces.

The child beams.

' – As soon as he learns to apply himself fully.'

'I tried my *best*, Captain. Honest.'

'Nonsense.'

'Tell him about the reading, would you, Bethany? He won't believe me.'

I say, 'Ethan is dyslexic, Captain Haskel. That means – '

'I know *exactly* what it means. It's a fancy Latin way of saying he's been allowed to get away with sloppy work. Half-hearted effort. I'm well aware of how they coddle children on the mainland. Boy doesn't want to read, he's dyslexic. Girl doesn't care for math, the numbers are to blame. If youngsters prefer fooling around to schoolwork, they're retarded. If they prefer acting up, they're emotionally disturbed. Bunch of malarkey.'

'Dyslexia is real, Captain,' I argue. 'Ethan doesn't see letters the way you and I do. He has trouble connecting symbols to sounds. If you want him to learn, you need to understand that.'

'Miss Logan, I've been teaching longer than you've been on this Earth. And without a single failure. Even Caleb learned his lessons. Took him longer, but he stuck with it. Gave it his all. Didn't you, son?'

Caleb keeps his eyes on the skewer. 'Good boy.'

'That you are. Fine young man. Credit to us all,' the captain declares.

'Cook,' Caleb intones.

The captain scowls my way. 'Caleb learned despite his so-called disadvantages, Miss Logan. So will Ethan. Isn't that so, son?'

Ethan shrugs. 'I guess.'

'Not guess. Will. Say it, son.'

'Okay. I will.'

'Like you mean it.'

'I *will*!'

'That's the ticket. Now let's show everyone what you can do when you put your mind to it.'

Captain Haskel slips inside. He returns a moment later wielding a bible. Rattling the pages like a sabre, he approaches the child.

Ethan squints at the text.

'It's too dark. And the print's little.'

'Read, son. No excuses.'

'Buhl – ' The child's voice quavers. 'Ball something?'

'The word is "blessed". Now go on.'

'Blessed – are – the – poor – in – ' He struggles with the word. 'S-something. I don't know that one. I can't.'

'Sound it out,' the captain roars. 'No negativity, young man. You can do it.'

The child struggles to name and blend the sounds. Tears well in his eyes.

'The Bible is way too hard for him, Captain. Ethan learns best with a multisensory approach. I can send you materials – '

'Nonsense!' His voice slashes through mine. 'Every student of mine reads the Holy Book. Then we move on to the great works and the history of the family. That's the foundation. No exceptions.'

He struts toward his son. Holding the volume to the young man's chin, he orders, 'Read, Caleb.'

Caleb's dark eyes cling to the swivelling skewer. They are lit by a spark of panic.

'I *told* you to *read*,' the captain booms.

The young man's gaze darts to the bible. He swallows hard. 'Bless it meek. 'Herit earth.' A line of spittle sidles down his chin.

'That's it.' The captain nods smugly. 'Go on, son.'

The young man's body heaves with effort. 'Bless it missy full. 'Tain missy.'

'Blessed are the merciful. They shall obtain mercy. That's ob-*tain*. Pronounce clearly, Caleb. Enunciate.'

'Tain.'

'Better. Continue.'

Caleb spins the skewer faster. Gulps a breath. He's not looking at the text; he has it memorized. 'Bless it poor hot – '

'That's pure *in* heart, Caleb. Read carefully.'

'Purine hot,' says Caleb. 'See God.'

'Exactly.' The captain sniffs. 'Blessed are the pure in heart, for they shall see God.' Closing the book, he claps his son's sweaty back. 'A fine job, Caleb. See how it's done, Ethan? Hard work and determination. I expect no less from you.'

'Yes, sir.' Fear pinches his voice to a squeak. 'I'll do it. You'll see.'

That fear is what the old man wants. 'Good,' he says.

'Remember that, son. Blessed are the pure in heart, for they shall see God.'

I think what I cannot say. Don't forget the persecuted, you old sonofabitch. They get the keys to the kingdom.

34 I pick at my food and break away early. I have no appetite for anything here but escape.

Descending from the bluffs, I pause to stare at the water. Hazy lights glide in the distance. Passing boats give the island wide berth as if they sense that Rand's suffers from some dread infectious illness.

Which it does.

A person can be marooned on this place. Stripped of normal ties and identity. Left to sink in a mire of misguided ideas. I can't let that happen to Ethan.

I take the long route around to the island's other side. Shedding my shoes, I walk the beach. I pass the dark line of bungalows. Nearing the cemetery, I think of the tiny grave markers. So many young lives have been lost here. This island must not be allowed to claim any part of another child.

I round the island's eastern spur, where the beach yields to a narrow gravelly strip. Birds flap overhead in ragged V formation, pacing the sombre clouds.

Soon, I spot the lighthouse looming ahead. A sandy rise blocks my view of the keeper's cottage. Scaling the hill, I'm dismayed to see that the house is dark. Jeanette must be sleeping. And I'm in serious need of a sympathetic ear.

As if on cue, a whipcrack sounds from the nearby shrubbery. Aunt Sadie hurtles through, snapping branches, and falls into step beside me.

I haven't seen the dog since this afternoon on the way to the cemetery. She smells like pickled sweatsocks. She sports a beard of matted sand.

'What have you been up to, girl?'

She sneezes, shedding most of the fake whiskers.

'You okay?'

Jaunting ahead, she shows me that she is. Then she

doubles back to check whether the same can be said for me.

'You missed the dinner show, Sadie old girl. And it was true theatre of the grotesque. I think Captain Haskel learned his teaching methods from the Marquis de Sade.'

The dog lopes at my side.

'Much more of that, and reading will be the least of Ethan's problems. Poor kid could suffer serious ego damage.'

Sadie nudges her muzzle in my palm. She's offering herself for my petting pleasure. It's one of the many services the beast performs on my behalf.

'I guess what I should do is discuss the problem with Eva. After all, it's her son and her father.'

Sadie's tail wags. She approves of my logic.

'Eva certainly adores that kid. I'm sure she wants what's best for him.'

We cross the beach and pick our way through the bird droppings.

'The big trick will be convincing her that the captain's way off base. You can't teach by intimidation, especially a kid like Ethan.'

The first floor of the stone house is dark. A pale glow seeps from a high rear window.

'Let's go talk to her, buddy. Help her see the light.'

I let myself in through the unlocked front door. Sadie peels away and lopes toward the kitchen.

'Come on, girl. I need you.'

She keeps going.

'Some best friend,' I grouse.

Alone, I mount the murky staircase. The only light I see is a wavering glow from the baby's room.

My heart aches at the thought of Eva sitting there night after night. Pining for her lost, little boy. Pining still, since Ethan has yet to come home to this house.

Maybe that will help me make my case. If Eva wants her son back, she must reclaim him. She has to start making wise, considered decisions on the boy's behalf. She

240

can no longer afford to play the sorry victim, clinging to a vanished dream. Her child has been recovered. He's a real flesh and blood little guy with his own quirks and issues. And he desperately needs his mother's protection.

I rap at the nursery door. No answer. I knock harder, calling Eva's name.

Still nothing.

Pausing, I train an ear. Not a sound.

Eva must have left the lamp burning by mistake. She's probably asleep. I'll have to wait to speak to her in the morning.

Disheartened, I head toward the study. Halfway there, I hear hard breathing from the nursery. Then an anguished grunt.

Turning back, I pad to the door and press it open.

My stomach lurches. My mind rejects the unthinkable thing it sees.

35

Then up Jack got and off did trot,
  As fast as he could caper,
To old Dame Dob, who patched his nob
  With vinegar and brown paper.

'Jack and Jill'

Demon dreams invade my sleep. A dozen times I wrench awake, tossed from an imagined nightmare back to the real thing.

Before dawn, I hear Eva padding down the steps. The rear door closes with a thud. Aunt Sadie issues an unconvincing growl, then falls silent.

I span the hall and peer out the bathroom window. Eva dashes across the darkened lawn. Passing between the tall oak trees, she vanishes into the woods.

Somehow, I drift off to sleep again. When my eyes snap open some time later, the sky has paled. I dress and sneak out of the house on tiptoe. If Eva has returned, I do not want to see her. Not until I've sorted out what I saw of her last night.

Heading toward Jeanette's house, I plod through pockets of heavy fog. Emerging from one, I spot Gideon and Duck on the pier.

The child stands at the jetty's end, pudgy arms furled overhead like a sail. He's shirtless, clad in baggy dotted trunks. I take in the soft pink skin and the porcupine hair. The bow legs and marshmallow belly. All the essential features are there. Gideon Haskel is well on his way to becoming a funny-looking kid.

Duck hovers behind his son, coaching. He presses the boy's ball-shaped head to his chest and edges him nearer the edge of the narrow span.

242

'Ready, set –' Duck calls.

Gideon flops into the water like a felled tree. He pops up spluttering, paddles back in a splashing froth, and scrabbles on to the dock.

'Here I go again! Ready – seddy –'

'Wait a minute, Giddy. Watch me first,' Duck advises.

But the child is a body in motion. 'One – two – set – go!'

There's a giant splat. The gasping kid flutters back to the pier and clambers out.

Duck grabs a chubby hand and plants his son firmly on the beach. 'Now, watch,' he orders.

Before Gideon can muster a fresh head of steam, his father strides to the centre of the jetty. The years melt away as he stands, tanned and muscled, in the sun.

Duck poises for an instant, then takes off racing. In a few dizzy bounds he's at the end of the narrow pier. Springing skyward, he tucks in a roll. Then he snaps straight and pierces the water like an oiled spear.

He surfaces a startling distance away. But in a few nimble strokes, he's back at the jetty. Patiently, he stands with the child. Encouraging. Instructing. Captain Ahab could take lessons.

Jeanette opens the door with a finger to her lips.

'Zach just fell asleep,' she mouths. 'Make yourself comfy. Be right down.'

She carries the bundled infant upstairs. I'm drawn to the kitchen, where the scent of perking coffee acts like smelling salts.

Jeanette is back in a breath. She fills two giant mugs. Handing mine over, she clacks her tongue. 'What's up, girlfriend? Bad night?'

'You wouldn't believe.'

'Try me.'

The picture etched in my mind defies description. Haltingly, I describe the horrifying scene I came on last night in the nursery.

Eva was lying on her back, skirts bunched, naked below

the waist. Her legs were splayed. Her face was crimson and contorted. She was bathed in sweat. Writhing.

I'd witnessed something similar once before, and I won't soon forget it. Roo recruited me that night to fill in for Lee in her natural childbirth group. Happened to be the class when they showed the living colour film of an actual birth. Perfect cure for the odd maternal twinge.

I try to convey the power of last night's scene to Jeanette. 'Eva seemed to be in some sort of a trance. She didn't hear me when I knocked at the door. Didn't answer when I called her name. I'm sure she had no idea I was there. The woman was *gone.*'

Jeanette sighs and pours another round of coffee. 'Sounds like pseudocyesis. Hysterical pregnancy. We had a couple of cases at Devon Hills. Both women swelled up as if they were really nine months along. Went through the whole birthing process, exactly the way you're describing.'

'You think Eva honestly believed she was giving birth?'

'I'm no shrink, Bethany, but if you want my amateur opinion, I don't doubt it. That woman is seriously woo-woo. Nothing she did, no matter how weird, would surprise me. Can't see any way she's going to improve either, unless she's forced into treatment.'

'She's on some kind of medication now. I found this.'

I show her the blue pill. Jeanette nods. 'That fits. We used this a lot at the hospital. It's stelazine. One of those the docs at Devon Hills used to call *big* medicines. They're for serious psychotics. People with delusions. Stelazine, or something like it, is used on a maintenance basis. In crisis, they get a shot of something stronger. *Great* big medicine that knocks them out.'

'So Eva must be under a doctor's care.'

The young woman frowns. 'I wouldn't bank on that. One of the cousins in town owns a pharmacy. Sends over whatever the captain asks for. The Haskels believe in self-help. And they're not inclined to trust outsiders.'

'I'm worried about Ethan, Jeanette. With the captain for

244

a teacher and that nut-case for a mother, what chance does he have?'

She sips at her mug. 'What's the alternative?'

'The Division of Children and Youth Services should be involved. They can sort things out. Decide who can take proper care of Ethan until Eva gets her head straight.'

'I don't know, Bethany. This bunch will go ballistic if you go to the authorities.'

'What choice do I have?'

'I'd be glad to take Ethan. Look after him until things get sorted out.'

'That's sweet, Jeanette. But he has a father. Other close relatives. Anyway, you've got your hands full with Gideon and Zach.'

'Must be something I can do.'

'Only if you've figured out a way for me to get to shore. The sooner I get the wheels turning, the faster this mess can get sorted out.' I try not to dwell on the fact that my interference created this mess in the first place.

Her finger pops up. 'Actually, I had a possibly brilliant idea in the middle of the night. Occurred to me when I was nursing Zach. We can signal from the lighthouse.'

I think of that bright beacon blazing across the Sound. I picture a rescue boat speeding us back to the mainland. 'Would that work?'

She shrugs. 'Can't see why not. Light hasn't been used for decades, but we can get Caleb to rip down the boards over the tower windows. Shouldn't be too hard to fire up the signal lamp. They must've used oil or kerosene back in those days, and we've got plenty of both. Some passing boat is bound to spot the flash and motor over here to find out what's going on.'

'You're a genius, Jeanette.'

'We'll see. First thing we have to do is get Caleb.'

I volunteer to track the young man down.

'Great. Could take a while to get everything spiffed up in working order. Probably best to wait until after sundown in any case. Signal isn't worth much during daylight.'

'Whatever you say.'

I leave to look for Caleb. The fog has cleared. The sky is polished clean.

36 Caleb, flushed and grim, clears the remains of last night's festivities in Rowena's yard.

He sets the Adirondack chairs in a pristine line. Gathers the citronella lamps and deposits them in a storage bin. He rakes cold ash from the barbecue pit. Finally, he scrapes the skewer clean and scrubs it shiny.

'That looks wonderful, Caleb. Now, will you please go see Jeanette? There's something she needs you to do.'

'Yard job,' he insists. 'Clean yard.'

'The yard *is* clean, Caleb. It's *immaculate*. Now please.'

I touch his arm, and without warning ignite a rocket of rage. Rearing back, he roars like a stuck beast. Then he staggers forward, clubbing me with a massive forearm. I'm tossed like a rag doll into the boxwood hedge. Sharp sticks poke my spine. I'm scared breathless.

I struggle to my feet, tracking Caleb's every move. The overgrown boy may be sweet and slow, but his temper is a firestorm.

Caleb wavers on his feet. Blinking hard, he works his tongue over chapped lips. He's unsteady, dazed. Emerging from the fog of fury.

'Kale mad. Bad boy.'

'It's okay.' I back off, hands hiked in surrender.

'Hit net. Bad. Ow!'

'No problem, buddy.'

'Bad sorry. Make nice.'

He edges toward me, petting the air.

I back away. 'That's all right. Just forget it, Caleb.'

'Clean yard. Go 'Net house,' he chants gently. 'Clean – go. Cleango-cleango.'

Once again, he's a large, gentle lamb. My fear subsides and I push back the burning urge to flee. We need Caleb's help to get the signal light running. My bruises quiet from a scream to a noisome buzz. I take a seat at the redwood table.

Caleb examines the lawn with excruciating care, searching for debris. He finds a broken toothpick. He shrieks with joy as if he's hit oil.

I do not try to hurry him along. Live grenades take cautious handling.

He keeps up his quest. Plucks out a sliver of glass and a petrified bit of smoked salmon. A balled cocktail napkin. Another sliver of glass.

'Clean,' he says, after an eternity. 'Good clean.'

'That's great. Ready for us to go see Jeanette?'

He faces me sternly. 'Kale go job.'

'Right. Jeanette needs you to do a job.'

'Sit,' he orders.

I do as he says. Whatever he says. Sit. Stay. Roll over. Play dead.

'Fine,' I say. 'You go alone.'

He keeps an eye on me, even as he lopes out of the yard. I don't move until he's safely out of sight. As I'm about to leave, I hear my name.

'Bethany, hey,' Rowena calls. 'Come on in and join me for breakfast.'

'Thanks anyway, Ms Haskel. I've got work to do.'

'It'll keep.'

'I'm way behind in my reports. Really.'

'Think *sweets*, Bethany girl. Think *hot, rich* Java and a great big plate of sweets.'

Her dining room is set with formal silver service. Scones and cookies mass on a china plate. Dainty porcelain cups rest on tatted placemats. Antimacassars drape the tapestried chairs. I feel as if I've slipped into a Victorian novel. With a snake.

Rowena leans towards me, dewlaps propped on twiglike hands. A nasty grin spreads across her pleated lips. 'So what's the deal with you, girlie? You come here looking for a cash reward? Or what?'

'I didn't come looking for anything,' I bristle.

Dry chuckle. 'We're not exactly what you expected. Admit it.'

'All I *expected* was to bring Ethan home to his family.'

The wicked eyes narrow. 'Maybe so. But I'd wager this isn't the *kind* of home you had in mind. Bet you're having second thoughts. Am I right?'

I munch a cookie. My thoughts are none of the old crone's business.

She continues, 'Tell you the truth, I'm not so sure you did that boy any favours bringing him here.'

'Why is that?'

She bites at the scone and scowls. Fishing in her mouth, she plucks out a partial denture. 'Damned thing.' She prises mashed raisin off the plastic bridge. 'Don't get old, girlie. That's my advice. All that's left of me is spare parts and out of order.'

'Don't you think it's best for Ethan to be with his family?'

'Might be if his family wasn't *this* family.' Rowena slips the denture in her mouth and locks it in place with her tongue. 'Cal's the only one near normal. Naturally, he high-tails it off the island every chance he gets.'

'What's wrong with the others?'

She dissects a scone, flicking out the raisins with a rutted nail. 'What's wrong is they're Haskels. Captain likes to call his ancestors colourful. Cuckoo says it way better.'

'*His* ancestors?'

'I'm no Haskel, proud to say. I married in. My late husband Franklin was crazy, too. But he was fun crazy. Thought he was filthy rich. Lived that way no matter what he had. Sort of like Donald Trump. Minus the bimbo.'

'Every family has its share of unstable people.' I think of my mother. I think of me.

'This one's got *way* more than its share. Trouble is, they refuse to come to grips with it. Only one who tried was the captain's mother, Edith. Great lady. A little nuts herself, but sharp. Years back, she even invited a scientist to come to Rand's and study the family, try to figure out what made them tick.

'Dr Houck was his name. Brilliant man. Spent almost a year here, observing, taking histories, doing tests. Unfortunately, the Haskels didn't care for his conclusions. Burnt the poor man out: lock, stock and laboratory. Threatened to ruin him and his family if he ever tried to make his findings public. Houck was lucky to get off this rock wearing his skin.'

The coffee has cooled to bitter sludge. 'I thought the burnt-out lab belonged to someone doing secret research with criminals?'

She slurps, scowling. 'Plenty of stories have been floated to cover what really happened. That's one of them. Truth is, Edith hoped Dr Houck would find a comforting explanation for all the lunacy. Maybe a magic pill.'

'What *did* he find?'

Rowena sighs gustily, reaches for another sweet. 'Nothing good. Never forget the day Houck gathered us together to make his report. We were all up Edith's place. Whole family. Old lady had set out a big spread. Champagne punch, too. Guess she expected some reason to celebrate.

'We're all having a grand time, talking and drinking. Then Houck drops the bombshell. He stands up and tells us the Haskels have a strong predisposition to mental illness. *Predisposition*. That was his word. Seems the lot of them are slated for the trash bin, even before they're born.

'Houck tells us he'd gone back ten generations in his research. Story was the same way back then.' She twirls a knobby finger at her temple. 'Majority of the clan had always been nutso. Especially the women. Houck says there's no sign of things improving. In fact the loony gene seems to be getting stronger. The people sicker. And there is no cure.'

I try to imagine the proud Haskel clan, hearing that

250

sentence of perpetual doom. 'You must have been devastated.'

'Guess some were. Me? I'm the practical type. Franklin and I talked it over. Decided to do what Houck said and just forget about having kids. Tell you the truth, I never was all that keen on the idea. Kids are selfish, picky, and they soil their pants. I want all that, I've got me.'

'Seems pretty drastic to advise the family not to have children. Mental illnesses can be treated. There's therapy. Medication.'

'Guess if you want to take your chances, that's the way to look at it. But not me. Haskels have a real nasty kind of wacky disease. "Mass and persistent delusion", Dr Houck called it. The nutty ones believe the family's cursed. They're always looking over their shoulders for some enemy. Afraid they'll be destroyed if they don't see the trouble coming and hit back first.'

'Did Dr Houck say the crazy ones murdered their children?'

'Lord, no.' The dull eyes spark with shock. 'Nothing like that.'

'I saw the family cemetery. So many of the Haskels died in childhood. Especially the boys.'

'Who told you such nonsense?' She chortles, at ease again. 'Bet it was Duck's girl Jeannie. Am I right? That one's got some head full of nonsense, I'll tell you.'

'I saw the graves, Rowena.'

Her face lights with a devilish smirk. 'Was one of the *boys* named Solly Joe?'

'Solomon Joseph, yes. I think so.'

'One named Morty?'

'There was a Mortimer, yes. And Duck had three.'

'Right. Let me remember, now. Natty, Marky, and Randy?'

'Nathaniel, Marcus, and Randall. That's right.'

She snickers. 'Those *boys* happened to be Yorkshire terriers, Bethany girl. Except for Morty. He was half Yorkie, half who-knows. Haskels have bred those little ankle-biters

251

for generations. Eva had the last of the line. Gave it away to a cousin after the baby went missing. She blamed that dog for not raising a ruckus when Ethan was snatched. Guess she had to blame someone.'

'Dogs,' I mutter. A wave of dizziness hits me as I envision the row of tiny gravestones.

Rowena pats my hand. 'Do yourself a favour, dearie. Don't listen to anything Jeannie says. Duck treats that girl like she's made of glass. Fills her head full of fluff and stories. Probably thinks the truth will shatter that heifer of his. Or scare her off.'

'Wouldn't she be more frightened thinking those graves belonged to dead children?'

A mocking smile lights the old woman's eyes. 'Don't go looking for things to make sense, dearie. Not here on Rand's.'

37 The greedy man is he who sits
And bites bits out of plates,
Or else takes up an almanac
And gobbles all the dates.
                    'The Greedy Man'

The door to the small shack stands open. The captain's voice thunders through.

'And *again*, young man. Start here.'

Ethan reads in a halting monotone. 'At the – '

'That's *turn*. Simple word. Try it once more.'

'At the *turn* of the – keh – '

'That says *century*.' The voice drips disgust. 'Listen to me, son. At the turn of the nineteenth *century*, the Haskels moved from Dingle Bay to the rich farming area of Ireland known as the Burren.'

' – known as the Burren.'

'Correct. Try it *again*.'

I barge in, battling rage over the man's cruelty. 'Thought I heard voices. What are you two up to on this fine sunny day?'

'Lessons,' the old creep spits. 'If you'll *excuse* us, Miss Logan.'

You, I *won't* excuse, dickhead. 'Go right ahead,' I say pleasantly, standing my ground.

The captain and Ethan sit in stiff-spined chairs at a pocket wooden table. The old man's look is of spite. His grandson hunches in defeat, cringing. 'Ethan needs to give this his full attention, Miss Logan. Nothing is more important than productive labour. I'm sure you understand.'

'Oh, I do.' Folding my arms, I perch against a bookcase crammed with texts. 'Just pretend I'm not here.'

253

With a dismissive swat, the captain complies. 'Where were we?'

'In some Dingle place,' the child says miserably.

Whence came this nasty old dingle.

'Start again at the beginning.'

The boy squirms in his seat. 'At – the – turn – of – the – nineteenth – keh –'

'That's *century*,' the captain howls, bashing the tabletop. 'Say it.'

'Century.' The small voice wavers. Brims with tears.

'Again!'

'Century.'

'*Again* – like you *mean* it,' the old man roars. The bastard is in his glory. This misery loves the company of an intimidated child.

'*Century*. I'm trying, Captain, honest. I'm doing my –'

'No excuses!'

A tear slides down Ethan's cheek. The captain swipes at it savagely.

'None of that. Now sit up like a man and do it correctly.'

Ethan's eyes dart my way. They're full of pleading. I wink in sympathy. Hang on, kiddo. Help is on the way.

'At the turn of the nineteenth century, the Haskels came –'

I want to tear the stupid book apart. I'd like to ball up the pages and force them down his crêpey old throat. But I may need the evidence.

'Your family history sounds fascinating, Captain. I'd love to read it.'

'*Please*, Miss Logan. The boy is doing his work.'

And *I'm* doing *mine*. 'So can I borrow the book?'

'I'm afraid not. The work was compiled for family members only. I can't let any of the copies out.'

Copies. Where are the other ones? While he hammers at the child, I scan the bookshelves.

The volumes are ancient. Their pages are yellowed, the covers frazzled pale. They range from pre-primers to col-

254

lege texts. I spot a first edition of Samuels on Economics. Sienko and Plane on Chemistry, vintage 1962.

On the bottom shelf are two threadbare St James bibles. They're squeezed into a row of identical volumes, all with faded red buckram covers and black-taped spines. Those match the torture device the captain continues to fling in his grandson's face.

'That's Burrrrrren, son. *Roll* those Rs.'

Ethan screws up his face and chugs like a constipated engine.

'And *again*.'

The boy does as told, sprinkling spit. He's pale and sweaty, a shadow of his former rotten self. I suddenly want the old kid back, the spunky beast who gave better than he got.

'I mean read the *passage* again,' the old geek howls.

Tormenting the child claims his full attention. Kneeling, I pull out a basic biology text and flip through. Replacing that, I page through *Astronomy I*.

Ethan repeats the same few lines, again and again.

'And *again*.'

The captain does not glance my way. The complete works of Jane Austen are dressed in a mouldy jacket. I slip it off and wrap it around the Haskel history I'm cradling in my lap. Perfect fit.

Standing, I fake a yawn. 'You planning to work all day? It's really gorgeous out.'

The captain reddens. 'We're *trying* to focus here, Miss Logan. Now, *please*.'

'I only said – '

'The disruption is intolerable. I'm afraid I'll have to ask you to leave.'

I force a smile. 'Actually, I should go work on my reports. Mind if I borrow this to read later?'

'Fine. Be my guest.'

I clutch the purloined book and exit quickly. I won't be your guest for long, you old prick. After tonight, I'm out of here.

38

One flew east; one flew west.
One flew over the cuckoo's nest.
                    'One Flew East'

Nearing the windbreak, I hear noise. Crack of branches. Eager muttering. Eva is having a lively conversation with herself. I cast around for a hiding place. I've had my daily fill of crazy Haskels.

Nothing around but open field. She's just beyond the pines. I'll have to face her. I steel myself as she passes through the trees. This is as good a time as any to confront her about the captain.

'Morning, Eva. Got a minute?'

She glides by as if I don't exist. Or she doesn't. Her eyes are fogged. Her long pink shift trails across the scrub grass. She cradles her imaginary infant in her arms.

'I'm concerned about Ethan, Eva. The way your dad is with him may be – '

She chants: ' "Ladybird, ladybird. Fly away home. Your house is on fire, and your children will" – shhh, darling. Momma will protect you.'

'Eva?'

'Momma will always protect you.'

I wave in her face, but she doesn't flinch. Her bare feet move with animal fleetness.

'Mommas keep their babies safe and happy and clean,' she croons.

'Eva, *please*! This is *important*!'

As she crosses the field, her murmurs grow angry and incoherent. She gestures wildly with her free hand. A cry escapes her. Suddenly, she grips a fistful of her hair and pulls.

Long black strands flutter to the ground. I rub my scalp, feeling a sympathetic ache.

'No! You can't take him!' she keens. 'He's mine. *My* baby.'

Limbs flailing, she races across the scraggly field. She passes the burnt-out building. Nearing the shack-turned-schoolhouse, she slows to a gentle glide. Quiets.

Her lips mould into a careful smile as she peers inside the shack. 'There you are, my darling,' she says. 'Morning, Captain. Working hard?'

I erupt in a rash of gooseflesh. I must get Ethan away from this. Away from these people. I don't dare leave that defenceless little boy here until the authorities sort things out. I'll have to take him with me.

39 I find Aunt Sadie in Eva's foyer. She's in a fretful mood, circling on the rug. Her chuffing breaks the brittle silence. I light two kerosene lamps in the living room and perch between them on the couch.

The dog trots in and stands sentry at the entrance arch. Her edginess is worsening. The dark eyes dart in her head. Her hackles stand at attention.

A musty scent assails me as I open the book on my lap. The Haskel history is a hodgepodge.

Recollections contributed by various relatives are interspersed with family documents. I leaf through birth, marriage, and death certificates. Professional licences. Business records. Diplomas and awards.

The stories are mostly mundane. I skim through rambling accounts of Haskels living in late eighteenth-century London. Haskels emigrating a hundred years later to America. Haskels drifting from New York to the Midwest then back to Connecticut, where they finally took root.

Halfway through the book, I spot the first mention of a family curse. The chapter was penned by Euphemia Haskel in May of 1932:

> In the middle of the last century, the potato crop failed, and Ireland suffered a terrible famine. Many people fled, migrating across Europe and to the United States. Many of those who remained grew increasingly weak and desperate. Thousands succumbed to starvation and disease.
>
> Grandfather was a modest farmer named Donat O'Dowd. As the famine worsened, he decided his family should leave the country. Before the arrangements were completed, the youngest,

Catherine Mary, took gravely ill. The O'Dowds considered sending some of the healthy ones ahead to America. But in the end, they elected to stay together.

Miraculously, Donat's family suffered no mortal losses. The season after the famine passed, Donat harvested a record crop. With the profits, he acquired parcels of land that had been forfeited for taxes or abandoned in the mass exodus.

Local leaders were threatened by the O'Dowds' newfound prosperity. The remaining neighbours who had not fared as well were poisoned by envy.

When the Connolly girl, a fair, gentle creature from neighbouring Ballyvaughan, was murdered, everyone was quick to blame Donat O'Dowd.

Christine Connolly was betrothed to Donat's oldest son, Sean. But someone planted the ugly rumour that Donat himself was enamoured of the girl.

The tale grew more outlandish with every telling. Before long, local people had the dead girl pregnant with Donat's child. They claimed Donat had murdered her in a rage after she'd threatened to reveal that he had sired the child by force.

One night, a drunken horde stormed the O'Dowd house. The mob dragged Donat in the yard and there they hanged him. His wife, Bridget, was forced to watch. Then, the men carried her back inside, barred the doors, and set the house on fire.

Everyone perished but the O'Dowd's oldest girl, Maureen, who was in Limerick at the time, helping her aunt tend a new infant.

When Maureen learned what had happened to all her kin, she fell in a swoon. For many weeks, she lay unconscious, at the murky fringe of death. The doctors despaired of saving her. Her aunt made ready for the funeral of the final surviving O'Dowd.

Then, one night, Donat came to his surviving daughter in a dream. He told her of a curse against the family. He urged her to rise and battle those forces that would sooner see her dead.

Maureen recovered. Fearing for her life, she took the surname of her aunt's husband and went by that name, Haskel, for the rest of her days. But the curse was passed to her by blood. And to her issue. And to theirs for all eternity.

Maureen Haskel lived to the age of ninety-six. For all those days, she kept the hex a secret. Only on her deathbed did her children learn of the family curse. Then Maureen told them what dark sword hung over them. She revealed the sacrifice they must make to appease the angry fates. These were her words:

I turn the page to read Maureen Haskel's dying message to her children. But an ink slash hides the words.

40

Caleb prises free the last of the window boards. Dusty glare floods the tower. My nose fills with the sweet stench of baked bat droppings. I sneeze two dozen times, churning the long-dead air.

Jeanette flaps her hand to clear a breath hole. 'I don't know, Bethany . . . This is a way bigger mess than I had in mind.'

Everything in the narrow space is caked with filth, most critically, the bowl-shaped reflectors at the centre of the tower. These are used to magnify and project the lamplight into the Sound, Jeanette explains.

'I don't know,' she says again.

I scrape at the crud on one of the reflectors. It sticks like burnt oatmeal.

'Maybe if the three of us work on it – ' I speak warily, gauging Caleb's reaction.

'Sounds okay to me,' Jeanette jumps in. 'You game, Caleb?'

Wrinkling his nose at the wretched smell, he echoes. 'Game.'

Jeanette claps his back. 'Good deal. I'll go to the house and get supplies.'

We work for hours in the heat. Using spoons, we scrape through fifty-odd years of neglect. Anything sharper could damage the reflectors. My forearm aches. My fingers cramp in claws.

'Anyone for a lemonade break?' asks Jeanette.

'I could be convinced.'

Caleb eagerly seconds the motion. 'Kale dink.'

We navigate the winding stairway to the ground floor. Outside, the air seems so fresh my head spins.

Caleb and I wait in the yard while Jeanette ducks into

the keeper's cottage for refreshments. I hear the blast of the battery-operated television, then a series of thuds. Probably the giddy child, bouncing off walls.

The three of us drain a pitcher of iced lemonade and a bowlful of corn chips. I suck in the cool briny air.

I don't want to go back to that tower in the worst way. But once again I'm shamed by Caleb. The big guy wipes his mouth on his sleeve, sets his jaw, and forsakes the shady comfort of Jeanette's yard for more hot, smelly work in the lighthouse.

A stifling eternity passes before Jeanette pronounces the job complete.

'That should do it.'

'And me,' I add.

'All set, Caleb. Why don't you go clean up and have a rest before dinner?'

'Wash,' he agrees enthusiastically. 'Eat.'

We follow him down and out the door.

'Terrific job,' I tell him. 'Thanks so much.'

He flashes a brilliant smile and waves goodbye. For a blink, his good looks dazzle. Then the smile goes vacant and strange. With a heavy heart, I watch him lumber away.

'What happened to Caleb?' I ask Jeanette. 'Do you know?'

'One of those things. Real pity.' She clicks her tongue. 'Duck told me he wandered off as a little guy. Fell in the water and nearly drowned. Suffered brain damage.'

Drowned. I feel a rush of heat. The air melts. Jeanette stands beyond the soup, staring. 'Bethany? You okay?'

Slowly, I struggle back. Rise to the surface. Shudder off the clinging drops of dread.

Jeanette says, 'What's wrong? You look green.'

'Nothing.'

'What kind of nothing?'

'I can't talk about it.'

'Sure you can. Spill.'

'I can't, Jeanette. Believe me.'

'I don't believe you. Talk.'

I open my mouth to protest.

'*Talk*,' she says. 'Talk to me.'

Something in her tone, her look, the moment, breaks the ancient jam. My chest boulder shifts a notch. I part my lips and let my heart spill through.

41

Whistle, daughter, whistle;
Whistle for a pound.
I cannot whistle, mammy.
I cannot make a sound.

'Whistle'

Jeanette sits cross-legged in a dapple of leafy shade. Sinking beside her, I let the story flow.

I was my mother's favourite. It was a simple fact of our family. I was Mom's favourite; Roo was Daddy's girl. Worked out fine.

Secretly, I knew I was better off than Ruthie on this score. Mom was funny and beautiful. Mom could sing like an angel and raise one eyebrow at a time. She could wiggle her nostrils and make three-leaf clovers with her tongue. She had pool-blue eyes and hair the red of sweet potato skin. Her scent was the frozen silver of the moon.

I never considered it then, but I suppose Roo had the same smug preference for our father. She probably favoured his slim moustache and the wavy crest of his hair and the way he blew fat smoke rings at the sky. The best approach is to prize what you have. To love the ones who love you. If only I could remember that when it comes to men. If I'm attracted to a guy, you can bet he's a loser. Or I am. It's uncanny.

Jeanette, frowning harshly, tells me not to change the subject.

I go on. When Roo and I were nine, something happened to our mother. She lost her smile. Her colour. Over the next few months, she got slower and slower like a toy with old batteries.

Then, she stopped.

264

For a very long child's time, maybe weeks in the trim hourglass of adults, she stayed in bed. Grandma, my mother's mom, came to stay and take care of us. She told Roo and me that our mother was sick. It wasn't a cold, she said. Not catching. But we were to stay away and let Mom get some rest.

When Grandma wasn't looking, I'd peer through the keyhole of my mother's bedroom. I can still picture my mother like that, framed by a metal exclamation point. She looked like a low range of hills capped by snowy blankets. Never moving. Always turned like a shameful picture toward the wall.

I'd whisper to her, psst. But she never heard me. I was certain that she'd died, that the lump I saw was nothing but her dried-out shell.

Every day, the doctor came. One morning, he stood frowning outside the door, flanked by Dad and Grandma. They were listening hard, too intent to notice me crouching in the shadows.

My mother wasn't getting better, the doctor said. Actually, she was worse. Suicidal. He said they had to put her in a hospital. I'd never seen my father cry before.

They took my mother away on a stretcher, wrapped in sheets. You could barely tell her pale, scrawny form from the linens.

My father told us she was going to a hospital. But it wasn't like any hospital I'd ever seen. Clarion Knolls was a beautiful place with spreading trees and broad green clearings. Large sunny rooms. Quiet halls lined with paintings of flowers and boats and happy families hanging out on lawns. The patients didn't look sick. Only tired.

Dad took us to visit on Sundays. Roo and I went dressed up, dressed alike, bearing a pile of gifts.

Every week, Mom said she was much better. *Much.* And she looked it. Her skin was pinker. Her eyes sparkled like little suns. She started laughing again, though not always in predictable places. Like the time Dad told her Uncle

Paul had a bad heart attack and needed bypass surgery. I'd never seen her laugh so hard.

'Was she on drugs?' Jeanette asks me.

'Never occurred to me then, but probably. Yes, I think so. She certainly wasn't herself. Uncle Paul was always a favourite of hers.'

One Sunday, when we pulled up the driveway, she was waiting in the lot. Her hair was in a new style, one side tucked behind an ear, the other hanging in a vamplike dip. Her blouse was open so you could see the cleft between her boobs. She had on a short skirt. High heels. Bright red lipstick.

Dad was delighted. He told her she looked stylish. Sexy, he whispered loud enough for me to hear. Like a *Cosmo* girl, he said, chortling. Like the cover of *Vogue*.

Mom told us she had a surprise. She took us behind the building where she stayed. There was a table waiting, set with a linen cloth and our favourite dishes: fried chicken, potato salad, coleslaw, rolls. Soda, too. And cake.

I remember her exact words: 'I have taken care of everything for today. It's all set.'

She was so proud. Happy. I imagined she'd just returned from a long trip. I pretended we were picking her up at the airport like we did the time she went to visit her brother Joey after his hernia operation in Duluth.

My mother was back. I was elated.

After we finished eating, Mom said there was a craft show in the visitors' lounge. She'd made some jewellery. Beaded stuff, she said. And she wanted us to see it.

'You two go,' she told Dad and Ruthie. 'Beth and I will be in after we clean up.'

The minute they were out of sight, Mom clutched my hand. She told me the really big secret she'd saved for best and last. She was getting out today. She'd been discharged.

She'd reserved rooms for a family vacation on the beach. She and I were going first to check things out and get settled. Roo and Dad would join us after a while.

She had a duplicate set of car keys in her purse. Money

and a credit card. She said she didn't need to pack any clothes. She told me she'd sent all the essentials on ahead.

I didn't think twice about getting in the car. Leaving Roo and Dad at the nut hospital. Good.

I didn't think about how far we drove. Hours and hours. Stopping only to pee and grab a bite. I was helium happy. Floating with it. Over the moon.

Looking back, I see that she was over some moon of her own. But at the time, it felt wonderful. Perfect.

She kept driving and driving. Slowing to read town signs. Hotel signs. Shaking her head: no. Not here. Driving more.

I kept asking what she was looking for. But she wouldn't say. 'It's a surprise, sweetheart. Be patient.'

Finally, she exclaimed: 'There!'

The motel was on the water in a town called Misquami-cutt. My mother loved the name. Rolled it on her tongue like rich chocolate.

'Miss Kwammy Cut, meet my daughter Bethany Anne.'

The town was small. Boisterous. Crammed with low-end motels and the kind of bars that feature wet T-shirt contests. Souvenir shops. Hot dog stands. Grizzled men in plaid shorts, undershirts, and black socks. Women with rollers in their hair and matching fat rolls. There were nuns in habit, too, pale as bread dough, dead serious, hands hidden in the black flow of their sleeves.

Mom was thrilled. 'Isn't it perfect, Bethie?'

I told her yes. Anywhere she was felt perfect to me.

She checked us into a seedy place called the Heaven's View Motor Inn and Beach Club. I remember how she laughed at the name. 'Heaven's View. Isn't that the living end?'

I agreed, though I didn't understand.

She laughed harder. 'Living end. You get it?'

Again, I told her yes.

Our room was on the third floor, overlooking a scrawny strip of littered sand. There was no elevator. No one to carry our bags, said the lady at the desk. Didn't matter. We had none.

Mom said it also didn't matter that I had no bathing suit. I could swim in my underwear. She stripped to her own bra and panties to show me. Said no one could tell it from a two-piece. I pretended that was so.

Whatever she said was fine with me. Ice-cream before dinner – fine. Going to the beach before we called Dad and Ruthie. Double fine. I loved being alone with my favourite parent, having her to myself. She cared about me most of all, that was the main thing.

It was almost sundown when we got to the beach. Everyone else had left. The sand underfoot was cool. The surf hammered the shore, desolate and angry.

My mother gave me a paper cup and a wooden stick to work with. She told me to build her a beautiful castle.

'Sit here, sweetheart. Momma's going for a nice, long swim.'

Twice she returned to tell me things. 'You know how much I love you. You and your sister. How much I've missed you. You know all that?'

I packed the base of the castle, squared the edges. Busy moulding the tower, I told her, 'Yup.'

She took off again. Walked a while on the sand. But she kept turning back to me. 'Hasn't your daddy taken good care of you? Him and Grandma?'

'Sure.'

'Grandma adores you. Both of you.'

I carved a window in the tower. Otherwise, the princess couldn't lean out and let down her hair. 'I know, Mom.'

'You girls are the most important thing in the world to me, sweetheart. You know that, too?'

'Uh-huh.'

'You'll never forget?'

'Nope.'

'Okay then. You sit right where you are and keep working on that castle. I've been thinking about this swim for months, Bethie. Nice long swim is exactly what I need.'

'Fine.'

'Don't you move. Don't come after me.'

'Okay.'

'You understand, sweetheart?'

I tell her yes.

I decide it's Rapunzel in the tower. Rapunzel herself. I need to give her long, long hair. Major hair streaks wavering down the wall. Lots of small wriggly lines is what it'll take. Mom's walking away. Not looking. I sneak into her purse and snitch the comb.

She hates it when we go into her purse. But this is important. Anyway, she's said she's not coming back for a long, long time.

Remembering the rest, I fall silent.

Jeanette asks gently, 'She drowned?'

I can only nod.

'It wasn't your fault, Bethany. You were a little kid. There was nothing you could do.'

The words pierce. I'm stung by the sharp-edged truth. I was the favoured. The chosen one. My mother chose me to bear this awful pain.

42

With her nurse's eye, Jeanette examines me for emotional bruises.

'You okay, Bethany?'

'Fine. And I'll be even better after we signal for a boat.'

'Can't blame you. But we'll have to wait to light the lamps until it's dark out. How about we meet back here after dinner?'

'Sounds good to me.'

'Have your stuff ready. Soon as Eva or the others see a boat approaching, they'll do everything they can to scare it off.'

So I recall. 'You'll tell Duck to keep away with his Monster Blaster?'

'Sure, but I can't do anything about the captain. Or Eva. Or Caleb, for that matter. If someone orders him to, that guy could pull a ship apart, board by board.'

I shudder at the image. 'Hopefully, I'll be gone before any of them notices.'

'Exactly. Which is why you should be packed and ready.'

'All I have to take with me is Ethan.'

'You're *taking* him?'

'I have to, Jeanette. The captain's a monster. And Eva's *gone.*'

She frowns. 'I can't disagree. But from what Duck says, the captain's keeping that boy on a very short lead. How do you plan to get your hands on him?'

'I don't know. I'll think of something.'

Exhausted, I slog toward Eva's house. It's been an incredibly long day. The sun has burnt out. The surf laps like a playful pup against the breakwater.

Getting back to my life means another sail across those monstrous waters. Roiling swells, danger lurking.

But I can't think of that now. I have to focus on some way to get Ethan away from the captain.

43

Old Mother Twitchett had but one eye,
And a long tail which she let fly;
And every time she went through a gap,
A bit of her tail she left in a trap
                    'A Needle and Thread'

Captain Haskel, propped kinglike on his Barcalounger, barks orders at the drones.

'Get Bethany a drink, Eva. Laurel, check the roast. You, Ethan, fill the ice bucket. Put another log on, Caleb. Fire's getting low.'

Rowena chuckles. 'Pour me a spot more bourbon, will you, Ducky bird?'

'Haven't you had enough?'

'Of you, yes. Of Jimmy Beam? Not hardly.'

'You're tough enough to take sober, Rowena.'

'So are you, Duck man. Now *pour.*'

Laurel chimes from the back door, 'Dinner's ready when you are, folks.'

A roast suckling pig stares up at me from the table. The limbs are wedged at peculiar angles. The mouth gapes around a mushy apple. Poor thing looks dazed.

The captain cuts around the centre of the hapless creature and lops meat slabs from the plump, pink middle. Repulsed, I watch three piglet slices settle on my plate.

'There you are, Miss Logan. Plenty more, if you like.'

I decline. For simplicity's sake, I tell them I don't eat pork. In fact, I don't eat babies. Or cooked pink things. Or anything served in a state that tempts me to give it a name and a home.

Ethan gazes miserably at his plate. He cuts the meat into tiny cubes and hides them beneath a lettuce leaf.

272

While Laurel and Eva clear the plates, the sky darkens. There's a rumble of thunder. The air has grown edgy and thick.

I push out my chair. 'Think I left the window open in my room. I'd better go close it.'

'That's all right,' Eva says. 'We often get the odd thunderhead this time of year. Probably just blow over.'

'Better not risk it. Your husband's papers could get wet. Please excuse me. I'll be right back.'

'Caleb can see to the window,' the captain says.

'Actually, there's something I need in my room anyway.' I bite back a smile. This is much better than the sudden attack of indigestion I've had planned.

I find Aunt Sadie in Eva's kitchen, circling in a snit. She's raked the rear door with claw marks and left a puddle of protest on the floor.

The dog has a talent for escape. The average lock won't stop her. But tonight I lagged behind after Eva left and wedged lawn chairs beneath the doorknobs. Sadie has not been able to dislodge them.

She snarls at me as I blot the floor with wadded paper towels. The urine pool is large and rank. 'Was this really necessary?'

She answers with a haughty yap. *Was this?*

When the floor is clean, I lead Sadie to the yard. The bucket lies where I hid it behind a hedge.

Sensing I'm up to no good, the dog balks.

'It's the only way, honey. Believe me.'

She does not.

I'm limp from cleaning the lighthouse. Struggling with Sadie, I lose half the contents of the bucket. But the effect is more than satisfactory.

'That's great, pal. You look really disgusting.'

She is not amused. I have to coax her back to the captain's house. I walk hunched to grip her collar. The hem of my circus-tent dress keeps snagging in the scrub. By the time I need to act distressed for the family, I'm not acting.

Laurel gasps at the sight of us. 'Bethany, my Lord! What happened?'

'I heard Sadie barking. She got stuck in some bushes. Must've tried to dig herself out.'

Sadie plays her part to the hilt, complaining bitterly.

Eva shakes her head. 'Such a sight. Poor thing.'

'That glop. Isn't that the – ?' Ethan catches my look of warning and bites his lip.

'She needs a bath, which she hates. I'd like Ethan to help,' I say.

'Take Caleb,' says the captain. His eyes are on Sadie, bristling distaste.

'I would, but Sadie loves kids. And she knows Ethan. It'll go smoother with him.'

The captain shakes his head. 'The boy is wearing good clothes.'

'He can change first,' I persist. 'Of course, if you think it's too *much* for him –'

That stings the old coot. His jaw twitches. 'Haskels are not afraid of hard work. Go on, son. Help Miss Logan with her dog.'

Eva grips the child's shoulders. 'He hasn't finished his dessert.'

'Yeah, I have. I'm full. Let's go.'

The mud has dried on Sadie's coat. I brush it off as we hurry across the scrub field.

'That was my chasing-away spell, wasn't it?' Ethan asks.

'Close. I had to do without the worm and substitute coffee for the Coca-Cola.'

'Who's supposed to get chased off?'

I fill my lungs. 'Actually, we are. I thought it might be best if I took you back to the mainland for a while. Maybe find someone who can help your relatives learn how to take the very best care of you. What do you think?'

'You said I had to come live with my real family.'

'I know, kiddo. And you should. But it may take a little while for everyone to get adjusted.'

274

'I hate it here.' His voice breaks. 'The captain seemed so nice at first. But he's really mean.'

'He's old-fashioned, hon. Old school.'

'Well, his old school stinks. I like Hinsdale better.'

'Me too,' I say with feeling.

'He's a *terrible* teacher. Even *you're* good compared to him.'

I grin. 'High praise indeed.'

He sighs. 'But we can't go. There aren't any boats.'

'Jeanette's going to help us signal a ship from the lighthouse.'

'But no one can leave the island without the captain's permission.'

'*I'm* giving you permission. It's okay.'

'But *he's* the *boss*. That's the first law.'

'Don't worry.'

'But it's mutiny. You can *die* for mutiny.'

'Stick with me, kiddo. You'll be fine.'

'But – '

The lighthouse looms like a black-robed witch against the night sky. Closer, I realize we're the first to arrive. In the dark entryway, I grope around until I find a candle and matches. We climb the stairs by its fluttery light. Ethan plods up behind me, jabbering nervously. Sadie brings up the rear.

'What if they find out?' Ethan asks.

'They won't.'

'What if Caleb tells?'

'He won't. Jeanette told him it was a surprise.'

'But what if he forgets?'

'Stop, Ethan. I told you. This is all going to work out fine.'

'But what if – '

'You don't need to worry,' I assure him. Besides, I'm worried enough for two.

At the top of the stairs, I blow out the flame. If anyone happens to look this way, the candlelight could give us away. We huddle in the stifling darkness, waiting for

Jeanette. Sadie's percussive breathing beats a time-step. Her tail thumps in nagging refrain. What's happening here? Where's Jeanette?

My image echoes on the polished reflectors. A line of fretful Bethanys snakes toward a dark infinity.

'Maybe she's not coming,' Ethan murmurs beside me.

'She is. Soon.'

The silence closes in like a healing wound. The darkness thickens, takes on weight. 'Maybe she forgot.'

Prickles of doubt assail me. The child's nerves are getting on mine. 'She'll be here.'

Ethan whispers, 'She better get here soon. Dog baths don't take that long.'

I'm thinking the same thing. *Come on, Jeanette. Don't blow this.*

Finally, a door slams downstairs. The risers squeal as she trudges up to the tower.

'Bethany?'

'Up here.'

Jeanette appears in a bubble of lamp glow. 'Hey, you guys. Sorry to keep you waiting. Giddy was in rare form.'

'That's okay, but we should get started.'

'Not tonight, I'm afraid. National Weather Service has posted small craft warnings. Heard it on the evening news.'

'What about large craft?'

'Not many pass through the channel. Besides, there's no place on Rand's for a big boat to dock. We'll have to wait for tomorrow.'

The change of plans triggers a fresh round of anxieties. 'But what if the captain finds out?' Ethan asks in a panicked shrill.

'Sssh. It'll be fine.'

'But he'd get mad. He could – '

'Nothing will happen. Trust me,' I tell him with unfelt conviction.

One more day. Sounds so easy and innocent. Twenty-four little hours. No big deal.

44

I can't sleep. My mind reels with Ethan's parting look, strained and pleading.

The child had begged for permission to spend the night here at Eva's house. But the captain flatly refused.

They had to get an early start on their lessons, the old man said. The nursery still lacked a proper bed and furnishings. Later on, after everything was arranged, the child could stay with his mother. Old creep made it seem as if Ethan had requested permission to shoot illicit drugs.

I imagine Ethan now, tossing in the dark. But there's nothing I can do for him. Nothing anyone can do but wait for clearer sailing. And a boat.

In the middle of the night, the wind picks up. Hard-beaked rain pecks the window. Waves clash cymbal-like against the breakwater. The sound batters my frazzled nerves.

I'm nowhere close to asleep. Not even in the neighbourhood. I light the kerosene lamp on my bedside table and search for something to read. Nothing but architecture books on Cal Trent's shelves. I fish under the bed for the history of the Haskels. If that won't put me to sleep, nothing will.

Again, I slog through the mundane life stories of countless ancestors. I reread the sorry tale of the unfortunately fortunate Donat O'Dowd and his lynching by envious neighbours. Cringing, I picture his family trapped in their burning home. I imagine those desperate souls pounding their fists against the barred exits. Screaming.

My throat aches in sympathy. Thinking of the filled ewer in the bathroom, I steal down the hall. I drink two tepid cups of water, trying to quell the bitter lump of regret.

I ferry another cup of water back to Cal's study. As I

settle back in bed, a few drips slosh on to the family history. Hastily, I blot them with a tissue. It comes away black.

The water has spilled on the ink-slashed page. A few printed letters now poke through the spots I've rubbed dry. I see a capital B. The word 'old'.

Dipping into the water cup, I sprinkle the page again. I pat gently, lifting off more of the ink. Fragments of the text are visible: 'Be – he – old'.

Slowly, gradually, the black slash fades. The rest of Maureen's final warning to her children is revealed.

Beware the children of the curse, by their golden eyes betrayed. Every tarnished one bears the blood of the lambs. They must for their evil minds be sacrificed.

I ponder the words. What do they mean? Golden eyes? Tarnished ones? Sounds to me like vintage hokum.

Also sounds familiar. I recall that Eva scrawled similar words in Ethan's baby book. So they were phrases she got from Maureen in the family history.

So what?

Yawning, I leaf through the rest of the family book. Near the end, I come to another ink-slashed page.

Dabbing with a moistened tissue, I uncover the printed logo of a psychiatric hospital. The page is a copy of a discharge form. The line beside 'diagnosis' has been stamped DSM£ 295.30. Under 'discharge date' is typed: *'Patient terminates treatment against physician's advice.'*

The date, written in ink, washes off in a swampy mess. I can't read it. Same story with the name. All I can make out is an A in the first name and the letter S in the last.

Disgusted, I close the book. I'm no psychiatrist. I lack the means to solve the riddle of this crazy clan. All I can do is get Ethan away from them and let the experts tackle the job. There are doctors to handle the mentally imbalanced. Counselling services, social workers, hospitals. Blue pills shaped like M&Ms. Other big medicines. Padded rooms.

Counting the possibilities, I drift away to sleep.

45

In the dream, my mother pops to the surface of the sea. Her hair has grown to a startling length. It's black as squid's ink, thick as kelp.

Her skin has the sensuous sheen of molten glass. A knowing smile plays around the corners of her mouth.

I shout, but she will not answer. The stone I toss to catch her attention skips a ragged trail and falls short.

Mother? Mom?

As I watch, the sea around her darkens and churns. Black-finned fish, a flickering mass of them, surround my mother's unsuspecting form.

In horror, I watch as a bold fish skitters from the pack and nips her liquid arm. Other black fins follow, gobbling greedily. Ripping her flesh. Feeding in a rapacious frenzy.

Mommy, NO!

The water whips in a furious froth. Desperate, I try to rush in and save her. But I'm bound by a rusted anchor to the beach.

Help me. Someone HELP!

By agonizing inches, I struggle forward. Finally, I'm drawn into the sea's cold embrace.

Muscles screaming, I swim toward the frenzied fish. Urgently, I search for my mother. But she's gone. Nothing left of her but ribbons of scritching foam.

'No!'

I rake through the murky depths, battling the slick-finned fish. Then something sharp rends my skin. Clutches my arm. Tears.

NO!

'Wake *up*, Bethany. *Please*, wake up! God *help* me!'

Jeanette looms above me, heaving sobs.

'Zach's *gone*,' she shrieks. 'My *baby*!'

I'm drawn up from the fog. 'What do you mean gone? What happened?'

Her eyes skitter wildly. Her voice quavers. 'Eva took him. I *knew* she was dangerous. I *told* Duck we shouldn't come here.'

'Eva's not in the house? Are you sure?'

'Yes, I'm sure. She's gone and she's taken Zach.' She collapses against me, wailing: 'I want my baby. Please!'

'Where's Duck?'

'He went out to look for them. But she could hide anywhere. She could hurt my baby. Oh God!'

Jeanette clings as if she's drowning. Labouring under her unwieldy weight, I check Eva's room and the nursery. I look in the bathroom and walk through the room downstairs. No sign of her.

Jeanette is rambling hysterically, soaking my shoulder with feverish sobs.

'Easy, Jeanette.'

' – But it's time for his feeding. And he needs to be changed. Poor lovey will get a rash.' A hand flies to her mouth. 'Oh Lord! I forgot about Giddy. What if he wakes up? All alone like that. He'll be so scared.'

Gently, I prise her away. 'Go home, Jeanette. I'll look for Zach.'

'But I can't just sit around. I have to *do* something.'

'You will be. You'll be taking care of Gideon.'

She's torn in half. Tugged by uncertainty. 'I can't leave Giddy alone,' she says finally.

'That's right. Go.'

She grabs my arm. 'Don't let her hurt Zach. Promise me.'

'Go home, hon. I'll find Eva. I think I know where she is.'

'You do?'

'I have an idea.'

'If anything happens to that baby – '

'Ssh. Go now. I'll be there soon.'

Dense clouds cast blots of eerie shadow. Peering at the woods, I spy the towering oaks.

46

Aunt Sadie blocks the door. She arches her head and bays at the ceiling.

'I've got no time for games, girl. Now move.'

She howls again. Long and mournful. She's got the mistress-will-not-listen-to-me blues.

'Out of my way, Sadie. I *mean* it.'

She bares her teeth, snarling. She means it, too.

'That's *enough*!' I muscle my way around her and slip outside. The sun is rising. A lemon haze blunts the horizon.

'You can come with me,' I offer. But she bumps past me angrily and streaks like a load of buckshot toward the beach.

I hear her venting her pique at the anchor. Rusty growls. High yips. Fury filling the air like hot shrapnel.

The sharp chill pierces my thin cotton gown. Stabs my lungs. The grass, brittle with frost, nips my bare feet.

I race toward the woods. Passing between the oak trunks, I enter a slim cleared path. Dappled shade plays over me. The footing is sharp and uneven. I'm stabbed by pine needles. Burrs. Broken branches.

Soon, I come to a fork in the trail. Instinct urges me right, where the silver bark of a birch tree shimmers ghostlike through the gloom.

Soon, the path dissolves. The trees encroach, closing in like a posturing gang of bullies. Scrawny branches rake my arms. Claw my cheeks. Scratch hot fury.

Passing through the woods, I hear a splash. Then low singing, barely audible over the bloody thunder in my ears.

Thorns stud the leafy tangle. Pinching at a smooth spot, I pull. The greenery parts with striking ease.

Eva stands with her back to me. She is naked. Her wet hair cascades down her back and over her buttocks. Her pale form is mirrored shimmering on the face of a ring-

282

shaped lagoon. At the sight of her, my breath catches. The woman is emaciated. Wasted flesh over pointy struts of bone. Skin that's thinned to the point of translucence. She's wavering, trancelike.

'Where's the baby, Eva?' I demand.

She keeps singing. '*Hush, little baby. Don't say a word –*'

'Where is Zach?'

No response.

I grip her bony arms and shake her. Her skin is clammy and cold. 'What have you done with him, Eva? Where is he?'

'*Momma's gonna buy you a mockingbird.*'

'Stop that. Tell me!'

She's staring glassy-eyed at the pool.

Suddenly, I remember the splash I'd heard. 'You didn't. Dear Lord –'

She doesn't move, doesn't blink.

I'm filled with terror. Frozen in place. But I force myself to think of Jeanette's tiny son.

Gasping hard, I dive in and kick to the murky bottom. My body tenses from the shocking chill. Frantically, I search the length and breadth of the pool. No sight of the baby.

Bursting up, I gulp a breath. Quickly, I submerge again. I track the bottom, raking the silt.

Slowly, pressure squeezing my lungs, I cross the bowl-shaped base of the lagoon. Toward the far side is a churning eddy. Through the funnelling haze, I spot a blue bundle. The infant is swaddled inside out of sight.

Gripping the edge of the blanket, I pull with all my might. But it's caught. I can't undo the tangle of cloth. The child is trapped.

I claw through the roiling muck. Find the sharp place that's snagged the blanket. My lungs are screaming. Razor claws tear at my chest. Raking madly, I work the bundle free.

My mind bristles with horror. Gripping the baby, I struggle to the surface of the pool.

Please let him be all right. Please!

The infant lies too still in my arms. Limp and weightless.

Lord, no!

Trembling, I set the bundle on the bank. Quickly, I pull myself on to the spongy grass.

'Hang on, little guy. Almost got you.'

Finally, I'm able to peel the sodden blankets open. I steel myself for what I might find. The baby could be dead. Blue.

But he's not. It's not. The little form in the blanket isn't a baby at all. It's a drenched sack of unbleached flour.

47 I wheel around to confront Eva. But she's gone. No sign of her on the bank. Nothing but crushed ovals in the grass mark the place where she stood. That, and the trampled tracks beyond, left when she fled.

'Goddamn you, Eva!'

I have to find her. Lunatic must have Zachary stashed somewhere.

But where?

So many places to hide a tiny baby on this island. There's the schoolhouse. The camping grounds. The endless clumps of woods. The line of empty bungalows along the northern beach. Which would that crazy woman choose?

I'm not going to find out standing here. Time is the enemy. I have to get to that child before Eva has a chance to harm him.

If only she hasn't already. Fear nudges me hard. I rush toward the open drape of vines.

There I stall, uncertain. Where do I start? It will take me hours to check the entire island by myself. Better to go tell Jeanette. We can gather the others. Organize a methodical search.

Or maybe I should go see the captain instead. Bastard certainly knows how to step right in and take charge.

But he's also Eva's father. Not hard to imagine where his sympathies would lie.

While I stand pondering, my next move is revealed to me the hard way. There's a crushing blow to the back of my head. And the ground comes up to meet me in a rush.

48

Birds of a feather flock together,
And so do pigs and swine;
Rats and mice will have their choice,
And so will I have mine.

'Birds of a Feather'

My pulse thunders as I come round. I'm gripped by a keen sense of urgency. Then I remember: Eva has taken Jeanette's baby. I have to find them.

Straining to focus, I scan the clearing. Eva must have sneaked back to hit me earlier. But she's not here now.

I rise on rubber legs. I draw slow, deliberate breaths. Better.

The sun thumps hot. A warm wind rushes, pasting the sodden gown to my skin.

I retrace my winding path through the woods. Emerging, I run across the lawn to Eva's house. I pass quickly through both floors but the house is empty. There's no hint she's been here. No sign of Zach.

Hurrying toward the lightkeeper's cottage, I spot Aunt Sadie on the beach. She's still railing at the anchor. Scratching madly at its base. Kicking up sand spires and puffs of silt.

'Come, girl,' I call harshly.

Her head dips in answer. I'm busy, lady. Go yourself. Intent, she rakes the sand.

I trudge on, pressing a hand to my skull to ease the ache. Soon, the lighthouse looms into view. The reflectors in the tower flash, tossing sunbolts.

Breathless, I enter Jeanette's yard. I race toward the door. As I'm about to knock, I'm stalled by the furious hiss of her voice.

286

'I have *had* it with you, you rotten little creep.'

A shrill cry: 'No!'

'You shut your goddamned *mouth*!'

I cringe. Dear Lord, what has happened to Jeanette? Has she snapped under the strain of finding her baby gone? I understand that, but poor Gideon shouldn't be asked to pay this price.

Determined to defuse the ticking bomb, I make a noisy entrance. I cross the hall with a stomping stride, calling ahead.

'It's me, Jeanette. I found Eva but she – '

But she's here, in Jeanette's kitchen, bound to a chair. She's unconscious, head lolling on her chest, dark hair flowing.

Ethan, in pyjamas, cowers beside her on the floor.

'What's going on here? Where did you find the baby?'

Jeanette is cradling Zach. She props her free hand on her hip and scowls. 'Everything's under control here, Bethany. You can go.'

'What happened to Eva?'

'Bitch took my baby. I gave her some of what she had coming.'

'Let the police handle her, Jeanette. This is not – '

'I *said*, you can go.'

The boy whimpers.

'This has nothing to do with him. Come on, kiddo. Come with me.'

Ethan stands. Jeanette grabs him roughly by an arm and shoves him down again.

'Ow,' he cries. 'You *hurt* me!'

I move to comfort the boy, but she blocks me. 'Leave him alone, Jeanette.'

'This is *none* of your business, Bethany. Now get the *hell* out of my house!'

'Ethan *is* my business. I understand you're upset. But I will not let you take it out – '

'You won't *let* me? You won't *LET ME*!' She comes at me like a tidal wave. Spitting rage. 'You stupid bitch. Who do

287

you think you are?' She's still clutching the infant. But she's gesturing wildly, as if he doesn't exist.

She could drop him. Nearly does. I step back. 'Take it easy, Jeanette. Careful with the baby.'

'I'll do what I damned well please with him. He's mine.'

'Please, Jeanette. This is crazy.'

'Don't you *dare* call me that! *Don't you dare!*'

She keeps coming at me, swinging the swaddled infant like a club. Suddenly, she kicks out. Pain explodes in my knee. I crumple to the floor.

'*No!*' Ethan screams. 'Leave her alone!'

Jeanette feints towards me, kicking with horrifying speed and force. 'I'll knock your goddamned heart out, bitch. Crush your stupid skull. That's what you get for sticking your nose in where it doesn't belong. *Hey-ah!*' Her foot springs out. A fireball rages in my chest.

'*Stop that!*' Ethan shrieks. He rushes at her. Jeanette catches him with a foot. Sends him sprawling.

I find a scrap of voice. 'Stay away,' I tell him. On my butt, I inch toward the kitchen door, drawing Jeanette with me. I catch Ethan's eye. Motion for him to run.

Jeanette edges closer. I retreat slowly. One eye is on the boy. He's creeping toward the door. He's caught my message.

Run away. Fly!

My back hits the wall. Jeanette has me cornered. She kicks the air an inch from my skull.

'Don't, Jeanette!' I say.

Wheeling, she kicks again. Swoops towards my head. I grab for the foot and catch it. Clutching hard, I pull her off balance.

A cry escapes me as she staggers. She could fall on the baby. Crush him. But she regains her footing. Charges me, screeching.

'*No, Jeannie!*' booms from behind her.

The voice stops her cold. Duck stands in the doorway, sleep-mussed, clad in a rumpled paisley robe. He motions

Ethan toward him and loops a protective arm across the boy's chest.

Jeanette smooths her hair and smiles sweetly. In a honeyed tone, she says, 'Did we wake you, Duck honey? You go on back up to sleep now. Everything's just fine.'

'No, it's not, Jeannie. This isn't fine at all.' Sorrow weights his tone. ''Fraid I'll have to give you your medicine, sweetheart. The real *big* medicine.' He pulls a hypodermic and a medicine vial from his pocket. Ethan squirms loose. He sidles close and cowers beside me.

Jeanette shakes her head. 'No, Duck. Not the *real* big.'

Squinting, he loads a measured dose. Half the liquid from the vial seeps into the plastic syringe.

'Please, no,' begs Jeanette. 'Not that. I'll be good.'

Duck nudges the plunger, expelling trapped air. 'Come here, Jeannie. You know it's necessary.'

'No, Poppa. Don't.'

The word takes a while to penetrate. Then, it hits me. 'Poppa?'

Jeanette shifts the baby in front of her like a shield. 'I'll hurt Zach if you come any closer, Poppa. I swear I will.'

'No, Jeannie. You won't do that.'

'I will,' she says. 'Now stop.' Duck keeps moving forward. She rears the baby back. Poises to throw him.

'Don't!' I scream.

Duck takes another step in her direction. 'Easy, sweetheart.'

Jeanette, redfaced, flings with a shriek. I lunge to catch the child, but I miss. The bundle smashes into the wall with terrifying force. The blankets fly open. A rain of shattered porcelain shards fall out.

The rubber body lies on the floor. Sharp scraps of the smashed head poke from the neck. 'A doll,' I mutter in shocked disbelief.

Duck slips the hypodermic out of sight up his sleeve and holds out his arms towards Jeanette. He catches his big baby girl in a loving embrace.

'That's my sweetheart.'

'I'm a good girl, aren't I, Poppa?' Her eyes glint with fear. Her voice is tiny.

'Sure you are, honey.'

Holding fast, he thrusts the needle into her hip and jams the plunger home.

49 The old man catches Jeanette as she crumples. Gently, he lowers her to the floor.

'Thank God,' I say, spewing air. Stepping toward the unconscious Eva, I kneel to untie the rope binding her hands.

'Not so fast,' Duck says sharply. 'Leave her. Be easier that way.'

'Easier for what?'

'For this.' Reaching into a cutlery drawer, he pulls out a pistol. It's the real thing this time. Not a toy.

'No one has to get hurt, Duck. Just let us go.'

He shakes his head. 'Sorry. That's impossible. I let you go, you'll tell the police. They'll take my Jeannie away again. Probably put her in jail this time. Can't let that happen.'

'Jeanette needs help, Duck. A hospital.'

'All she needs is me to protect her. That's what daddies are for. Now tie up the boy, Bethany.' From another drawer, he pulls a tangle of rope.

'This isn't the answer, Duck. Not to anything.'

'Do it!' he snarls.

The medicine vial and hypodermic lie on the table. Slowly, I unravel a length of rope and loosely tie one of Ethan's ankles to the leg of the chair.

'Duck – why did you pretend Jeanette was your wife?'

'We didn't plan to. The others just figured it was that way. So we went along.'

'But why?'

'To save her from the stigma, that's why. If anyone knew she was a Haskel girl, they'd be watching her all the time to see if she had the sickness. That'd only make it harder on Jeannie. Bad enough she had to live with the damned

291

Haskel curse in the first place. It's all my fault, you know. Every damned bit of it.'

'How is that?'

His eyes fog with memory. 'Miriam and I never planned to have children, didn't want to take the chance. Soon as we got married, we moved away from here. We wanted out of this family. Wanted nothing to do with the Haskels and their curse.

'Things were fine for a while. Near perfect. We were happy. Bought a nice house for ourselves. Made ourselves a life.

'Then Miriam got pregnant. One of those things. She was scared. Wanted to get rid of it. But I convinced her to go ahead and have the baby. Guess I wanted a child so bad, I fooled myself into believing it had to work out some way. We agreed never to tell anyone in the family.'

He's absorbed in the memory. It's a distraction I can use.

'Why'd you bring her to the island?' I ask.

'When Miriam learned she was dying, she got it in her head to spend her last days at the family home. Jeannie insisted on coming along, so we passed her off as Miriam's nurse. I saw then that Rand's was good for my girl. Helped her relax. So I've brought her back every so often for a nice quiet rest. She keeps her distance from the relatives. Doesn't like them any more than they like her. No one's ever suspected she's my little girl. So they never look at her thinking of the sickness.'

'But Jeanette does have the family sickness,' I say.

The man looks at his unconscious daughter. His eyes pool. 'Isn't Jeannie's fault. She was such a sweet girl. And smart. Fact is, Miriam and I didn't realize she was ill for a long, long time.

'Didn't occur to us 'til way after she was grown. And we weren't the only ones. Everyone thought her first two kids died of SIDS. Even the doctor said so.'

Loosely, I tie Ethan's other ankle.

'We might never have known. But Miriam caught her

with the next one. Jeannie couldn't bear the baby's crying. Thought it meant she was a bad mother.

'Jeannie didn't mean to hurt that little one. She just held a hand over his mouth to quiet him down. Before Miriam could stop her, that baby was gone.' Turning to me, he rails, 'Hurry it up, there. Do his hands.'

I remember the story Jeanette told me about her so-called patient, Lady Black Fin. She had been talking about herself. Six babies. Six dead babies . . .

'You put Jeanette in a mental hospital?'

'Courts did, not me. Nasty place. First chance we got, we signed our Jeannie out. Had a new person at the desk that day. Didn't know any better.

'Point is, we took care of her just fine by ourselves. Didn't we, sweetheart?' He addresses his unconscious daughter. 'All we had to do was make sure you wouldn't have any more babies to worry about. Took you for that little operation and that was that.'

Duck stoops to stroke Jeanette's limp arm. 'Worked like a charm, didn't it, honey?'

I take another length of rope. Sliding it off the table, I grab the needle and the vial.

I crouch behind Ethan's chair. Pretending to fumble with the bonds, I fill the syringe with the remaining liquid.

Duck pats Jeanette's cheek. 'You were so much better after the surgery, Jeannie. Isn't that so? After a while, I even got you a little boy of your own to care for, like I promised. Remember how glad the foster care lady was to find someone to take Giddy on? We don't mind a bit that the boy's got spirit.'

He smiles my way. 'Jeannie's been a little lamb to that boy. Wouldn't hurt a hair on his head. You should see him up in his room this minute, sleeping like an angel. Not a care in the world. You're a perfect mommy to that boy, Jeannie honey,' he croons. 'Don't know why you got it in your head to pretend you had another baby.'

Roughly, he looks my way. 'What's taking so long?'

I wrench at a knot. 'I'm finished.'

'Good. Sit there.'

I cup the syringe in my palm. The needle scratches the skin of my forearm. Beside me, Ethan is snivelling scared. I'm terrified too, but I will not give in to it.

I focus on the man. The syringe. The gun. There will be no second chance.

50

Duck grabs a length of rope and comes towards me. He's thinking his chilling thoughts out loud.

' – I tie you up. Finish you and the boy. And that's that. No need to bother about Eva. Everyone knows she's nuts anyway with her false babies and her hysteria fits. Never believe a damned thing she says no matter what.'

The old man cinches my right leg to the chair.

'We won't say a word, Duck. Let us go, and the whole thing's forgotten.'

'No way. Can't risk it. I have to think of my Jeannie first. Bury her mistakes, if need be. That's how it's always been.'

Duck knots the rope around my other leg. Silently, invisibly, I shift the syringe in my hand. I clutch the barrel in my palm. The needle is wedged between my fingers, pointing out.

The old man rises. Now or never.

I look over his shoulders. 'Watch out!' I shriek.

His head whips around. I jam the needle through his robe. I feel the flesh yield, the spongy resistance beneath.

Duck roars fury and rears back. I'm losing my grip on the syringe.

Bellowing, he grabs my hand and wrenches it away. The needle dangles from his hip. I drive a fist into his solar plexus.

He crumples, coughing. Before he can recover, I grab the syringe and squeeze the plunger home.

Duck gapes in astonishment. An instant later, he sinks to the hardwood floor.

51

Ethan sits dazed as I untie him. He's bound by shock. My mind is churning. I think of crazy Jeanette. Of Duck. Of Gideon.

Can I just leave that little guy sleeping upstairs? Maybe I should run up and wake him. Take him along. But every minute is crucial here. I have to get Ethan away from these crazy people. Anyway, I've had my fill of child-snatching. As soon as we get to the mainland, I'll tell the authorities about this nuthouse. Let them sort it all out.

'Come on, kiddo. Let's get out of here.'

The child is stunned. I wrench him up and tug him after me. Eva stirs. She's coming to.

'Hurry up!' I urge him. 'We have to get *out* of here. They could wake up any time.'

He sighs. 'But how can we go?'

'We'll find a way. Come on.'

Insistently, I lead him away from the cottage. Past the lighthouse. Toward the water.

I have no idea how we're going to get off this rock. But we're going. This kid and I are *gone*.

We're crossing toward the beach, when a sharp sound reminds me. We're a trio. There's Aunt Sadie.

And my furry friend has sighted a solution.

52

Aunt Sadie stands at the water's edge, barking ferociously. Squinting past the sun's glare, I see what she's trying to say. There's a boat.

The craft hovers half a mile from shore. 'Hey!' I call. But there's no response. Whoever is on the boat can't hear me.

'HEY!' Ethan chimes in. We wait, breathless. No use.

The boat, white with a blue striped hull, bobbles in place. They seem to be anchored. Maybe fishing.

'We'll have to –' My throat jams. I can't finish the sentence. Can't possibly go with the thought.

'We can make it,' says Ethan.

'No,' I croak. 'It's too far.' Too deep, cold, dangerous, deadly. Unthinkable.

'Come on, Bethany,' he urges, pulling my hand. 'Come.'

Sadie yelps. Right. Let's get out of here.

'I can't.'

'You *have* to. What if they wake up? What if they come after us with that gun?'

I know he's right. The medicine does not last long. Eva was already coming out of it.

Growling disgust, the dog lopes to the anchor. Fur shimmying, she rounds the rusty hulk. She barks shrilly. I'm to come look.

'What, Sadie?' I sound annoyed, but I'm not. I'll grab at any excuse to delay.

Rounding the anchor, I enjoy the moment's reprieve. But what I find there sends the whole world lurching out of focus.

Sadie has dug a trench at the anchor's base. The skeleton that lies there is a small one. The finger bones are twined, the eye sockets gape. Over the arch of rib lies a hand-

297

carved plaque encrusted with sand: *Ethan Haskel, age two,* it reads. *Golden child. Given in sacrifice. Rest in peace.*

53

Three wise men of Gotham
Went to sea in a bowl:
If the bowl had been stronger,
My song had been longer.
'Three Wise Men of Gotham'

I am pummelled by the tides. Bashed by currents. Lost.

Can't keep on. No more. I'm too, too tired.

A nice, long swim is what I need now, Bethany. Don't come after me. Let Mommy go.

The child yells: 'Come *on*, Bethany! Swim.'

'I can't. Go without me.'

'Come *on!*'

Sadie struggles at my side, wet fur dragging. She yips at me. Do it!

'Go, Sadie. Go with Ethan.'

Pip.

She stays beside me. Whining encouragement.

'Kick, Bethany,' the child urges. 'Hand over hand.'

I try. One stroke. And another. But the dread is a monstrous wave, dragging me down.

How could you just sit there, Bethany? How could you let your mother drown?

Because drowning's *easy*, that's why. You simply give up and let the damned sea take you. You say to hell with everything and everyone. To hell with life. To hell with your little daughters.

'Bethany, *swim.*'

Too easy. Not goddamned fair.

My blood heats. Liquid fire surges through my limbs. I reach with an arm and pull.

'That's the *way*, Bethany. *Go* for it.'

My legs flutter. I kick furiously.

Sadie sniffs. What's this? Scaredy cat to Superwoman in one easy lesson?

'Come *on*, girl,' I shout at her. 'Let's go! Get the *lead* out!'

I glide ahead, exultant. Free of fear. The distance to the boat shrinks, then evaporates.

I'm treading beside the hull. Grabbing hold, I call, 'Hello on board! Anybody home?'

A strapping young man appears. Grey eyes glint from a square-jawed face. He's dressed in cut-off jeans and a white camp shirt. He hauls Pip on board, then me, then Aunt Sadie.

'Everyone okay?' he asks. His brow furrows; his mouth goes grim.

'Much better now.'

'What happened? Your boat go down?'

'No.'

He passes us towels. 'You swim over from Rand's Island then?'

'We had to get away. You wouldn't believe what's going on there.'

'That so?'

'I have to call the police. Can I use your radio?'

'That won't be necessary, ma'am.' An odd smirk settles on his lips. 'Would your name happen to be Bethany Logan?'

'Yes, how did you –'

'And you, son. You're Pip Stafford?'

At the sound of his name, the boy grins. 'That's me. Yes, sir. I'm Pip.'

'You're all right, pal? Not hurt?'

'Nope.'

'No one did anything bad to you? You sure?'

'I'm fine.'

'Good to hear.'

The young man turns to me and shackles my wrists in cuffs. 'Bethany Logan, you're under arrest for the kidnapping of Adam Phillip Stafford, the Third. You have the right to remain silent . . .'

300

54

Roo slams the car door and struts toward her house, heels clacking. Not so much as a backward glance at me: the family disgrace.

My niece, at least, is happy to see me. Racing out, Amelia catapults into my arms.

'Aunt *Beffney*. You're here.'

'Almost, tootsie. I'll be all the way here after a nap and a shower.'

Hand in hand, we stroll. 'Mommy said you went to the *big* house. Did you get to see the President?'

'Nope. I'm afraid I missed him.'

I don't mention the host of charmers I *did* meet during my day-long stint in central booking. There was Bertie the barfer. Dolores Detox. And Raving Ramona. To name but a few.

Amelia wriggles loose to dart ahead. 'It's time for my reruns, Aunt Beffney. Wanna watch?'

'Maybe later.'

My niece skips off to the playroom. I aim for the kitchen, where my sister sits drowning her troubles in camomile tea.

'Come on, Roo. Don't be mad.'

'Of all the harebrained stunts you've ever pulled, Bethany. This was the corker.'

'You're right. What can I say?'

'There's nothing to say. What if you get *convicted*, for godsakes? What will the future be? How will I be able to hold my head up at the club?'

'It's all I think about, Roo. Honestly.' I don't mention my other tiny concerns. Like the possible fifteen-year to life sentence I face for felony child abduction.

'I don't appreciate the sarcasm, Bethie. This whole business is very upsetting.'

The doorbell rings. Roo clacks out to answer. She returns a minute later, looking pale and distracted.

'Someone's here to see you,' she says.

The visitor is Adam Stafford. He nods at Roo. 'If you'd excuse us a moment, I need to speak to Bethany alone.'

My sister frowns. 'I don't know,' she says. 'I'd better check with her lawyer . . .'

'Not necessary,' Stafford says grimly. 'I've just come from the courthouse. All charges against your sister have been dismissed.'

55

Friday night's dream, on Saturday told,
Is sure to come true, be it never so old.
'Dreams'

Pip is waiting outside in the car. Adam does not want his son to hear this. The headmaster paces my sister's gleaming kitchen, casting around for words.

Finally, in an anguished tone, he tells me that Pip was adopted. The baby had been found through private sources, one of those grey market arrangements made at the ragged fringe of the law.

After they brought the baby home, but before the adoption was formalized, Adam's wife, Jenny, was diagnosed with a very nasty, highly aggressive form of leukaemia.

More than anything, Jenny feared losing their baby son. More than anything, she wanted Adam to keep this child and raise him. Worried that the courts might rule against the adoption in the circumstances, they kept Jenny's illness a secret. Two days after the final papers were signed, she died.

Adam remained concerned that the fraud might be uncovered some day. At any time, he feared, his son could be taken from him. So he chose to work at boarding-schools in remote areas, and he taught Pip to avoid discussing personal family business. To shy from pictures. To be constantly on guard.

Almost all of the puzzle is solved. 'But I saw a computer update of Ethan Haskel's picture from the kidnapping files. It looked exactly like Pip.'

'I'm not surprised,' he says. 'When the Haskel case hit the papers, I couldn't believe how much the picture they

303

ran of the stolen baby looked like Pip.' He shakes his head. 'They say everyone has a double somewhere. Who knows?'

'So you ran because you thought the police might accuse you of kidnapping the Haskel baby?'

Eyeing me strangely, he says, 'Pip and I were living in the Midwest at the time. We'd been there for months when the Haskel child was kidnapped.'

'But Hap Riley said – '

'Don't tell me you've been talking to that lunatic. Hap Riley made our lives miserable. Peering in windows. Always lurking around. Jenny was so terrified of him we had to break our lease and move.'

My eyes fill. 'I don't know what to say, Adam. I'm so sorry.'

'Sorry doesn't pay my son back for what you put him through, Ms Logan. You told that little boy he wasn't mine. You told him he'd been stolen!'

'What can I do?'

'You've done quite enough,' he rasps. 'Running off with him like that. Taking him to that place with those crazy, dangerous people. Pip could have been injured. He could have been – '

'Please, please let me try to make it up to him, Adam. And to you – '

He shakes his head firmly. 'Stay away from us, Ms Logan. Stay far, far away. That's all I want from you.'

56

Hard to believe only three weeks have passed. So much has happened.

Duck and Jeanette Weems now reside in the Norwalk jail, awaiting trial. Eva, I've heard, has been committed to a private psychiatric hospital. The Captain, Laurel, and Rowena have put their Rand's holdings up for sale. I suppose they view it as a way to escape the bad memories. Roo approves wholeheartedly. Her agency has an exclusive on the deal.

Hal Kreidman tells me much has changed at Hinsdale, too. Patsy Culvert has left to head the drama department at a junior college in Vermont. Richard Bruce has a new wife. Grace Amundsen has a brand new organ.

Hal has not told me everything. He says he'll fill me in on the rest over dinner tonight.

That will be nice. I try to relax, to focus on the pleasant prospect of seeing Hal. But as I cross the Grangeville town line, I'm petrified. I still have no driver's licence. What if I run into Harley Beamis? What if Adam Stafford spots me and calls the cops? I can vividly imagine the whole school gathered to cheer as I'm carted away in cuffs.

I've made the five-hour trip without a break. Now, I wonder, what was my great big hurry? I slow down to well under the speed limit.

Don't let me see Harley. Don't let Adam Stafford see me.

The nearer I come to the Grangeville Road, the larger my panic grows. *No Harley today. Please no Harley.* I repeat those words again and again, hoping they'll somehow keep the deputy at bay.

No Harley.

I need the bathroom. I need a cup of coffee. For a lethal instant, I let my thoughts roam. Next thing I know, Harley

305

Beamis is right beside me. I shudder at the ugly sight of him.

Easy, Bethany. Keep cool.

'What the hell are you doing here?' he snarls.

'I might ask the same of you, Harley.'

'Don't be a wiseass, lady,' he snaps. A figure steps up behind him. Harley stiffens. Drops the scowl. 'So what'll it be?'

'Make it a mega-mug, black. And a chocolate cream-filled with sprinkles. Oh, and a cruller for the dog. I hear big dumb dogs just *love* crullers.'

'You can just –'

His boss hovers behind, 'Thank the lady for her order, Beamis!'

Harley's jaw twitches. 'Thank you for your order, Ma'am. Coming right up.'

The boss says, 'Smile, Beamis. Dippin' Donuts prides itself on friendly atmosphere.'

Harley's lips freeze in a truly amiable rictus. He hands me a bag. I pay and go. I stifle the laugh until I hit the road.

I laugh so hard tears stream from my eyes and my belly aches. I'm so hysterical, Sadie keeps nudging me to stop. Dog thinks I've lost it. Which I have. Harley Beamis is a window man at the Dippin' Donuts. Priceless.

I can't stop giggling until I spot the turnoff for the Hinsdale School. Then the ache in my stomach returns. And my tears turn real.

I drive the campus road toward staff housing. I try not to look at the kids playing on the green. I turn up the radio to block their noise.

I park in the lot behind Grantham Hall. Sadie trots beside me, sniffing. The Garden Suite is as I left it. Quickly, I toss my things in a suitcase. I'm in deep pain. Inconsolable. Even the tinkling of the chandelier fails to bring a smile.

'Ooooh, baby!'

'Right there, tiger. *Yes!*'

Sadie sneezes her contempt. 'You're wrong, girl,' I tell her. 'I'm going to miss having amorous neighbours. I'm going to miss it all.' Angrily, I dab a tear and heft my suitcase. 'Let's go.'

I haven't given much thought to the future. I've spent these past three weeks at Roo's house, moping around and writing my reports. After I drop them off, my last official duty here, I'll be finished with Hinsdale. Ready to move on. But where?

Driving towards Central Campus, I ponder my options. I run them by Aunt Sadie. 'Maybe I'll open a coffee house, girl. What do you think of that?'

She has no opinion.

'Problem is, I'd probably drink up the profits. How about I become an independent consultant, whatever that is?'

Sadie stares blankly.

'I know. I can go to work for Amelia. I bet her Executive Barbie could use an assistant.'

We steal in through the rear of the Administration building. My office has been cleaned, the mess collected in tidy piles. I set down my finished reports and pull out the resignation letter I've prepared. It's only a formality, I know. I can't really resign a job I no longer have. But clinging to every last formality postpones the inevitable.

While I'm signing my name, there's a knock. Only Hal knows I'm coming here today. His office was to be my next stop.

'Come in, sweetheart.'

The door opens. It's Adam Stafford. 'Excuse me, Ms Logan.'

I flush hot. 'Dr Stafford. Don't worry. I was just leaving. I just stopped by to drop off these reports and collect my things. And to give you this.'

He takes the page and reads. For a moment, he is silent. Then he says gruffly, 'This won't do, Ms Logan. I'm sorry.'

'Sure. I understand. You tell me what to say and I'll write it.'

'Say you'll stay.'

My ears are playing tricks. 'I don't understand.'

'Frankly, I have no personal objections to your moving on,' Stafford says. 'But some very influential friends of Hinsdale see it differently. They sent me this petition.'

With misgivings, I take the paper. I want to stay. But I don't relish being a political pawn, shoved down the headmaster's throat.

'This is sweet of Joe Whatley, but I certainly won't hold you to it.'

'It didn't come from Joe, Bethany. I'm talking about seriously influential friends, the kind I cannot and will not ignore. Look.'

I do. The writing on the petition is Danny Goichman's. I imagine him speaking the words as he labours over them. 'We want Mith Logan back. She'th a real good teacher.' All the important players have signed: Rob Cruzen, Jason Laks, John Bueker, Billy Brodsky, and on and on.

I notice that Pip Stafford has signed his name twice. That does bring a smile. Kid's still pushing the boundaries. Still questioning limits. Still the same boy.